WILDFLOWER

BECKY
JENKINSON

Becky Jenkinson is a writer, illustrator, and teacher from Manchester, England. She graduated with a degree in animation from Norwich University of the Arts, and in 2019, moved to Tokyo, Japan, where she currently teaches English. When she isn't frequenting Tokyo Disneyland, she spends her free time hooked on video games, watching musicals, and requesting more photos of her cat back in England. *Wildflower* is her debut novel.

 @bybeckyjenkinson

BECKY
JENKINSON

ZAFFRE

First published in the UK in 2026 by
ZAFFRE
An imprint of Bonnier Books UK
5th Floor, HYLO, 105 Bunhill Row,
London, EC1Y 8LZ

A CIP catalogue record for this book is available from the British Library.

Hardback ISBN: 978-1-78512-614-7
Trade paperback ISBN: 978-1-78512-615-4

Also available as an ebook and an audiobook

1 3 5 7 9 10 8 6 4 2

Typeset by IDSUK (Data Connection) Ltd
Printed and bound in Great Britain by CPI (UK) Ltd, Croydon CR0 4YY

At Bonnier Books UK, we are committed to publishing sustainably.
Find out more here: bonnierbooks.co.uk/sustainability

The authorised representative in the EEA is
Bonnier Books UK (Ireland) Limited.
Registered office address: Block B, The Crescent Building
Northwood, Santry, Dublin 9
D09 C6X8, Ireland
compliance@bonnierbooks.ie
www.bonnierbooks.co.uk

To all the past versions of myself,
I see you, I love you.

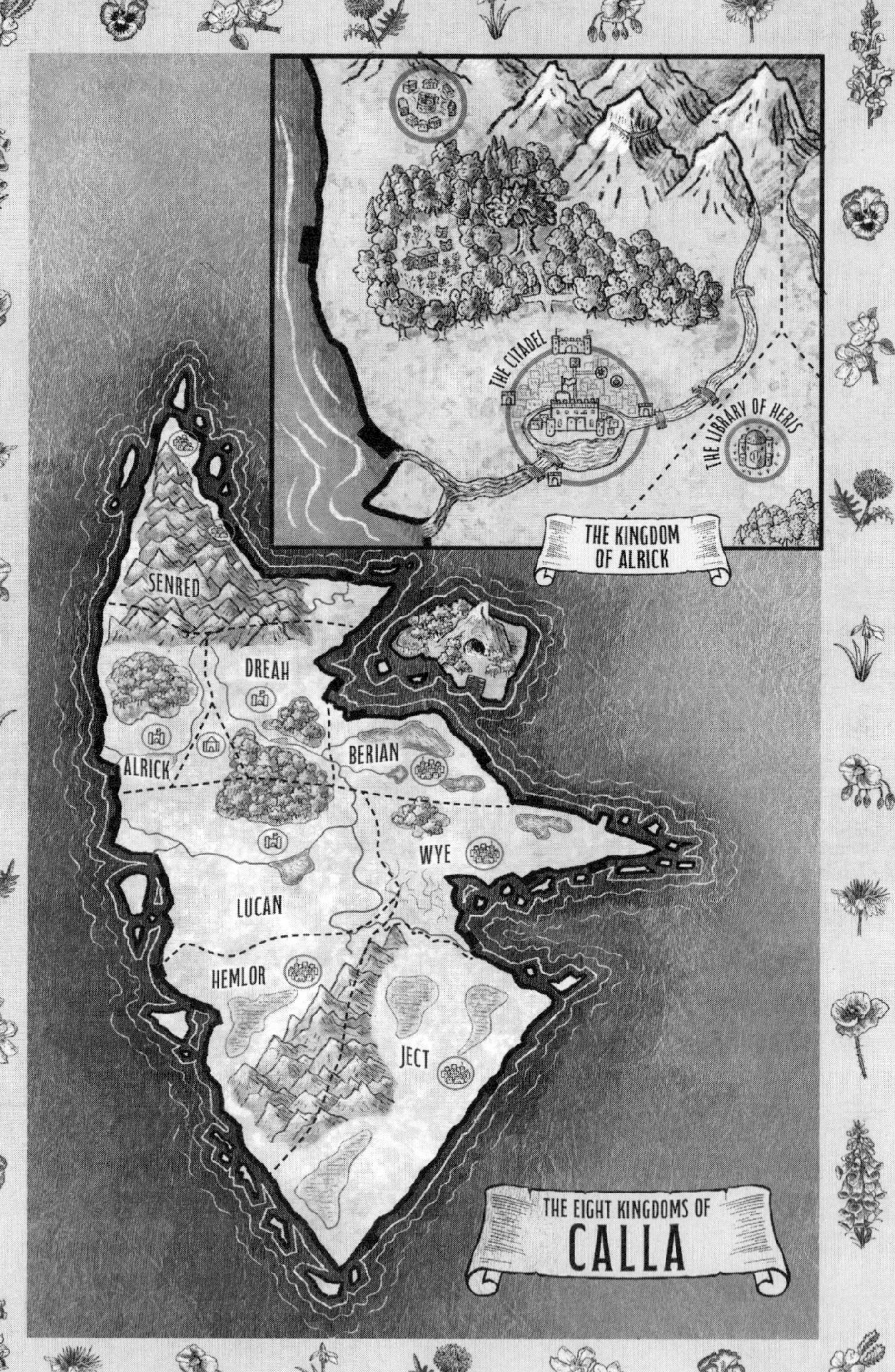
THE CITADEL
THE LIBRARY OF HERIS
THE KINGDOM OF ALRICK
SENRED
DREAH
ALRICK
BERIAN
WYE
LUCAN
HEMLOR
JECT
THE EIGHT KINGDOMS OF
CALLA

CHAPTER ONE

I saw a woman crying today, the bouquet of mourning flowers cradled in her arms like the son she lost. I'd made the bouquet myself – a cluster of fiery-orange marigolds nestled alongside dahlias in orbs of peaches and pinks, each pleated petal simmering with grief. The whole lower square is an overwhelming explosion of colour and sorrow, as expected when a Guard of Alrick loses their life. Even more so when the guard was so young. Queen Fern had commissioned me last week after the rebel attack in the forest and I'd spent hours poring over the marigolds I'd had in stock, enticing the magic within them to the surface. The same flowers Simon's mother now weeps over, tears streaming like the fountain at her back.

My bouquets are more than a message. I enchant them so the receiver *feels* the message within, as each flower has its own emotion that I can amplify. I dive into the depths of the petals, search the stems, consider each leaf and thorn and stamen, until the magic is coaxed out and confessing the deepest of sentiments. The marigolds and dahlias in Simon's mother's hands, the ones that cover the fountain and decorate the square, they understand her. They sing of sadness and eternal love, and, if I've done my job right, they will help her heal.

It also means that my shop has run out of funeral flowers, which is why I've dragged Cardamine out this morning to stock up. Tall dahlias grow just outside the citadel walls, not far past the lake to the south, so with the clear spring sky stretched above and the smell of fresh grass in the breeze, I kneel on the skirt of my pastel dress, clipping away at the flowers in the meadow and collecting them into my basket.

Cardamine lounges on his back a few feet away, his tousled ash-blond hair fallen to one side and an open book lifted to block the light, that familiar focus on his heart-shaped face. His rolled-up sleeves in the sun reveal the freckles on his skin as he scans the pages with sharp cerulean eyes. It's a peace I think he needs. His wedding planning has been taking up every spare minute recently, and as he keeps reminding me, it's not just any wedding. It's a *royal* wedding. In six weeks' time, he's marrying the crown prince of the Kingdom of Alrick, and soon my best friend will have the queen as his mother-in-law. If I could be sarcastic, I'd say that I was *thrilled* for him.

But I can't.

Because I can't lie.

I'm cursed to tell the truth.

'I think I've got enough,' I say, and place the last dahlia in my basket.

Card snaps his book closed. 'Let's make a move, then!'

He leaps up, changing pace like the rolling waves at sea. As I try to do the same, my basket catches my long skirt and, unsurprisingly, I stumble.

'Fliss, my dearest, I'm not having my maid of honour covered in even more bruises,' Card says, steadying me. 'Perhaps we need to put you in armour until the wedding. Could you do that for the next month and a half?'

If I could, I'd make a joke back. I'd protest. I'd say I'm not *that* clumsy, that he's exaggerating and I haven't fallen over in ages. Instead, I carefully choose each word and say, 'I don't think armour is my style. And I'm shorter than the average guard.'

'I'll get a cute suit commissioned for you. Perks of being a prince's husband.'

'Husband-to-be,' I correct him, and my throat relaxes in relief, like it does every time I manage to speak without aggravating the magic that binds my voice.

'Not for much longer!' Card takes my hands to help me onto the path like I'm a fragile toddler. 'Come on, you. One step at a time, there you are, good job.'

'*Card.*'

'All right, all right,' he says, freckles scrunched up by his grin. 'Anyway, did I tell you I have a meeting later today with the fashion designer? He said he'd sourced a few different laces from the Kingdom of Lucan, so you *absolutely* have to take a look. Maybe later this week? I need you to tell me which one I should choose. We can use it on the trim of your dress too, then we'll match.'

'That sounds wonderful.'

I smile up at my best friend, noting the confidence in his tone, the poised line of his shoulders. You'd think he was the royal one in this relationship – that he'd been born to rule. He fits right in at the castle without much effort. Then again, he fits in anywhere. Cardamine makes friends like a flower attracting bees. In fact, he can make conversation in no less than eight languages and doesn't show signs of slowing down. He has skills that are so foreign to me, I doubt I'll ever stop being in awe.

While we walk, Card plunges into a lengthy explanation of how they could incorporate a Dreyan poetry book he's reading into the wedding ceremony, and I'm happy to listen. This dynamic is one of the reasons Card and I get along so well. He loves to talk, which frees me from the obligation. Around him, I get to relax. Card is my best friend for a reason – he's my *only* friend.

When we first met at seven years old, I'd already learned the hard way that being cursed to tell the truth doesn't help you make friends easily. I'd spent most of my school life hiding away in the tiny library, tucked under the window among the bookshelves and dust. Then entered Card, fresh to the citadel from a small village, who'd plonked himself cross-legged before me without even introducing himself.

'What are you reading?' had been his first words to me. He'd glanced at the book about butterflies in my hands and barrelled on without waiting for an answer. 'I think I've read that one. Anyway, look what I found. Have you seen this? It has some ancient Alrickan language in it.' He'd held up an atlas of the eight kingdoms of Calla and pointed at an illustration of our own Kingdom of Alrick. 'See here. This is the citadel, but they've labelled it *carhfel.* And this is where I just moved from – Valeth. Do you know it? Probably not; it's inland and really small and boring. But not as inland as the Library of Heris. They have hundreds – no, *thousands* – of books there, and I'm going to read them *all*.'

On he'd spoken, telling me about his family, his home, his interest in languages and libraries, until the sound of the handbell signalled the start of class. I'd been wide-eyed and curious as he approached our classmates in a similarly open manner, but when it came time to take seats, he'd chosen the empty one beside mine. Either he didn't notice or didn't care that everyone else excluded me. The next day he'd brought me a book on woodland insects, and he hasn't left my side since.

Even now, as we head back to the castle in step, there's barely a break in his non-stop chatter. The only diversion is when I'm drawn off the path towards the daisies in the grass. If there are flowers nearby, I can sense them. It's a flutter of intuition rather than studied sorcery, a warm greeting in my chest. Some people in Alrick are born with a natural sense for magic, like my connection with flowers, whereas some have to use books to learn spells. Others, like Card, couldn't care less about magic – something I think his fiancé is grateful for. Prince Bastion's lack of magic has always been a sore point.

I pluck some of the daisies and braid them as we wander through the guardhouse at the edge of the lake – one of the only breaks in the tall stone walls that surround the citadel – then around the side of Alrick castle. If the kingdom were a flower head, our circular-shaped citadel would be the seeds in the centre, with the castle inside, watching over the town from its southern viewpoint. When Card finally takes a breath, I hold up the finished flower crown.

'Here,' I say.

He smiles. 'Cute. I'll give it to Bash. He's been so stressed about the rebels and his father's illness. His mother has been piling on the pressure, as usual. Ugh, not to mention that Willoh Vane keeps showing his face lately, and he *always* knows how to make matters worse.'

The scandals surrounding the sorcerer Willoh Vane are not something I ever intentionally stick my nose into. He used to be Prince Bastion's best friend, and now he's the citadel pariah because of an incident involving black magic about five years ago. It's a tangled mess, and because of my curse, it's best not to get involved, so I smile and say nothing.

In the castle courtyard, with courtiers already flocking for his attention, Card waves goodbye and I'm alone once more. How I always am without him. I head up the citadel's muddy cobbled streets, past cream-stone houses fortified with dark wood panels and plumes of smoke from slate roofs; past clattering carts carrying wheat, fruit, vegetables, and valuables we've traded with the bordering kingdoms; past people I've known all my life, some laden with fresh laundry or carrying children.

My stomach tugs with discomfort as eyes turn aside and voices hush, lest I overhear even the most mundane of conversations and then be compelled to report them to the queen. I should be used to it by now. Being avoided, I mean. But I'm not. Each time is a fresh hornet sting of hurt.

All the while, the mourning flowers around the fountain at the end of the street call to me like an orange-and-pink stain of blood on our stone citadel.

I wonder if Simon's mother is still sitting there, frozen in her grief. I hope not. I hope she's found some comfort. I hope I made a difference. But what can flowers do when you've lost so much?

I turn right towards the shop my mum and I call home. It's clear that our house is a florist's before you're close enough to read the wooden FARROW'S FLOWERS sign. I always keep an ever-growing number of seasonal flowers in pots lining the walls and windowsills, and right now, there are freesias that bloom in early spring, their petals bending backward in a variety of bold shades that welcome me home with a burst of colour. They're usually what I give Card on his birthday. Freesias are a symbol of friendship and trust, and there's no one I trust more than him.

I know my neighbours are aware of my curse. Mum has never tried to hide it. She says it's because she never wants me to feel ashamed, but I imagine the strange way I spoke as a child needed to be explained somehow – and what better way than the truth. I learned quickly how much sway my words can have. Everything I say is meticulously thought through. The truth *must* be carefully handled. Too much restraint, and it'll suffocate, kill chances, deceive. But if you let it free without care, the consequences can cause irreparable damage, so I spend my days with a tightly wound headache and forced smile, thinking through every sentence that leaves my mouth and trying to ignore my mother's guilt-ridden eyes.

Before opening the front door, I pause at the noticeboard and the wooden boxes nailed beside it. They were an idea Mum had years ago when she ran the shop full time. Her friend had mentioned that her daughter wanted to buy a bouquet for her crush but was too shy to ask for it directly, so shortly after, the anonymous request box had been born. In a lucky coincidence, it's also what retains the customers who don't want to speak with me directly now that I'm mostly in charge.

Today, when I unlock the cedar box, I find a sheet of parchment sitting inside and excitement sparks in my chest. Gods, I love getting these requests. Not knowing what kind of bouquet I'm about to create is *such* a delight. It's the silently held breath before the creative cogs in my brain leap to life, before I get to rummage through my collection and journals and do something useful that isn't related to my curse.

I slide the request form out and study it. The penmanship is interesting, like they've purposefully altered their letters in a strange and stilted way – but it's nothing I haven't seen before. Some people want to stay truly anonymous, especially with the queen squeezing every drop of information from me. However, instead of a string of sentences answering the standard questions on the form, there are only three words: *Feiyan. Collection. ASAP.*

What the gods is a Feiyan?

I flick the page over expecting to find some sort of budget or payment plan, only to find a crudely drawn map of the Kingdom of Alrick on the back. I can make out the citadel walls in the centre, the crossroads within the northern forest leading up to the mountains, and to the far northwest, there's a highlighted field with a bold arrow pointing to it. My chest tightens. *No.*

The northern forest is where the rebels have been attacking and robbing the trading wagons after being corrupted by dark magic. It's where the rumours say Willoh Vane killed an oak tree and poisoned the land. It's where Simon— Well, it's not somewhere the king and queen like anyone going. Why would someone ask me to go up *there*?

And why haven't I heard of a Feiyan? The fact I haven't bothers me. A lot. More than it should. I'm supposed to be good at this.

Inside, as the door chime fades, I'm still turning the request over in my hand as if it'll suddenly reveal a hidden clue. I place the basket of dahlias on the wrapping table in the middle of the room, puzzled.

'How was the meadow, dear?' Mum asks from the corner of our wide downstairs room. She sits at our teacup-cluttered kitchen table, long black hair loose down her back, and her typical tight-lipped smile on rose-tinted lips.

I used to grow my hair down to my waist too.

Then Lark happened and I'd wanted to burn anything he'd touched.

Months ago, in a moment of madness – with Card on hand for moral (and physical) support – I'd used some gardening shears to chop my black hair in a jagged line above my shoulders. It hadn't been enough, so I'd grabbed some blush-pink roses and barrelled my magic into their petals, bleeding the colours into my hair until the ends were dyed pink. It had worked. I'd felt lighter. Cleaner. Different. And when I'd next met Card and his fiancé at the castle, when we'd walked past a group of guards, I'd refused to return Lark's stare.

'I got some more dahlias,' I say. 'Have you heard of a Feiyan flower? I just found this anonymous request.'

I wave the paper, and Mum pulls her straight eyebrows together.

'No, I haven't. Are you sure it's spelled correctly? Did you read it wrong?'

I resist the urge to roll my eyes. Even though I'm cursed to only tell the truth, she still finds ways to doubt me.

'Yes. There's a map too.'

'Well,' Mum says, and picks up her cup of tea. She's been working a few shifts at the local tearoom since I took over most of the workload of the shop, and since then, she's hardly ever without a cup. I sometimes wonder what ingredients they're putting in those blends, because she's thoroughly addicted. 'You could always ask Creon. He might know.'

'Yeah, I might pop to the apothecary tomorrow. I have some orders to complete here first though. Did anyone come in while I was out?'

'Only the painter from down the road. He wanted some carnations for his mother's birthday coming up.'

I nod and start to transfer my freshly picked dahlias into vases I filled with slightly warm sugar water. With my eyes on my work, I try to keep my tone light.

'I saw Simon's mother earlier. She was by the fountain again.'

Mum sighs and rests a pale hand on her chin. 'Poor thing. And poor Simon. Such a horrible way to go. Although I suppose an explosion would make it quick . . . Anyway, I'm sure *that woman* will be doing everything to make the forest safe from now on so Prince Merit can come back for the wedding.'

'That woman' is what Mum calls Queen Fern. She's always held a deep resentment towards the queen, but never told me why. Mum was like this before I was first summoned to snitch for Queen Fern, so it can't only be that. It's one of Mum's many secrets – one of the topics that darkens her eyes and brings out the snap in her tone, like it does whenever I ask about my father. I don't even know his name.

I nibble the inside of my cheek. The thing about telling the truth is that there's a time and a place, and when it comes to my mother, no time ever seems suitable. I keep my head bowed so the pink ends of my hair swing over my cheeks as I busy my hands.

'Card showed me the wedding invitation list earlier. They're being sent out later this week,' I say, slowly.

'Oh?' Mum takes a sip of tea. 'Are the king and queen from Dreah coming too? Gods, I hope so. King Cyrus is a hunk and a half.'

'*Mum*.'

'What? I'm allowed to look,' she says, unrepentant. Mum always enjoys it when the Dreyan royals visit. I thought it was because they export most of the fruit teas she's so into, but apparently not.

Prince Merit, Bash's younger brother, lives in the next kingdom over – the Kingdom of Dreah – for a few months of the year because of his peace-making betrothal to their youngest princess.

It's hard to believe that Queen Fern allows him out of her sight, seeing how she's so overprotective of Bash.

I pause, my fingers resting on the stem of a particularly vivid dahlia, and fight a flicker of fear. I tried not to react when I'd read the name earlier. I tried to push it down. But the truth always comes out one way or another.

'Um,' I say, then clear my throat. 'No. Not them. It's . . . Morgana. Morgana is invited.'

Mum's back snaps straight. 'She's coming *here*?' A flash of hysteria has her pitch rising, her hands turning to claws around her teacup.

I nod, my jaw as tight as her fingers. Morgana is the sorcerer responsible for my curse. To me, she's a mystery, an invisible face. To Mum . . .

'But she never comes to Alrick these days!' Mum squeaks. 'She's supposed to be at the Library. *Here? Soon?* Gods—'

She meets my russet-brown eyes and quickly flattens her expression.

'I'm sure she won't come,' she says briskly. 'It's far too beneath her. She hasn't been back in years. I wouldn't worry about it, baby. She won't come here. No, of course, she won't.'

Mum can repeat lies to herself until she believes them.

A luxury I don't have.

I turn back to the anonymous request for the Feiyan flower. The map on the back leads into the northern forest, past the site of the explosion that killed Simon and farther than I've been before. Regardless, I'll go. I have to. I'll get the flower and deliver it, for whatever purpose the person needs. Because despite my curse, it's what I do best. I tell the truth. On behalf of others, for things they can't say themselves. Not through words or letters, but through flowers. Petals instead of carefully crafted sentences. A bouquet instead of a sonnet.

Mourning flowers for a mother's arms.

White wedding flowers for my best friend.

Feiyan for an anonymous stranger.

CHAPTER TWO

I deliver cheerful pink chrysanthemums once every four weeks to Creon at the apothecary, so when I enter his store, I'm glad to see the flowers still thriving and well in a glass vase on his desk. As they should be – one of the enchantments I put on my flowers keeps them fresh for far longer than their natural lifespan, and if they're well taken care of by their recipients too, then it could be a month before they start to wither. I've taken my mum's advice and decided to check if the old man knows anything about the Feiyan before I blindly risk heading north. Mum always looks after the shop if I need to go out for the day, and this anonymous request will certainly take up all my time. It already had me up all night. I scoured old journals and botanical textbooks but found no mention of the flower. Nothing. How is that possible? How is there a flower I don't know about?

Unless the request is a joke. A waste of effort. A prank meant to have me lost and wandering in the forest. Revenge for a time my curse got someone in trouble, or for any of the bouquets I was requested to send with less than positive intentions. But who would bother to do such a thing?

Anyone in the citadel could have their reasons.

If a customer wants to remain anonymous, they can take one of the forms pinned to the noticeboard outside the shop and fill out their choices. They can tell me which flowers they want or which emotions they want shared, their budget, their deadline, if they wish it delivered or collected, and any other information required. The bouquet will be prepared, all without revealing their identity. *And* there's a locked payment box that only Mum and I can access. It's worked flawlessly so far. So much so that I can hardly believe it was my own mother who came up with it.

These days, most of the anonymous requests I get are declarations of love, usually unrequited. Occasionally, someone wants to send a warning or ask for forgiveness, and once or twice I've been asked to create a bouquet to deliver someone's bitterness or jealousy. Granted, those times made me hesitate about following through, but I figured it wasn't up to me to control someone's message. It's *their* truth. And I know all too well what it feels like to have your words regulated. However, this is the first time that a request has me thoroughly stumped. It seems even Creon, with years that make him wiser than me, doesn't have much to add.

'Sorry, Felicity, I can't say I've heard of this flower,' the old man says, holding the request sheet close to his glasses. He's halfway up a ladder and hangs on to a rung with one hand while he examines the paper with the other. 'But this map will take you to an area of the forest with some rare fauna. I've found a few unique species of insect around there, so I wouldn't be surprised to encounter unusual plant life as well. Aside from that, however, I'm afraid my memory gets a little foggy. I haven't been up there in a while. It's too close to the cursed tree and recent rebel attacks.'

He's right. The path to this flower isn't far from the tree that started the conflict between the north and the citadel. That led to Simon's death. It's been half a decade since the original incident, and in all that time, I've never dared to see the tree for myself. It's the source of a poisonous festering disease that blighted the northern forest beyond recognition, people say, a vile and warped stain of evil that will surely corrupt anyone who goes near it, just as it turned ordinary northern citizens into hostile rebels. The king and queen sent them food and supplies to build new shelters when their villages and crops were first affected, but nothing could be done to slow the spreading rot. Or so I've heard.

Creon eyes me warily when I keep my mouth shut, as most do. 'Are you sure about this?' he asks. 'Passion is one thing, Felicity, but I've warned you before about treading too close to obsession. It's reasonable to deny a request if it's too outlandish or dangerous.'

I take the paper back. He doesn't understand. Being able to complete orders reliably is all I have. It's the *only* thing people have faith in me to do.

'I'll try to be careful,' I say.

I thank him for his time and leave the apothecary with a growing curiosity. The morning sky is painted with threads of cotton-like clouds, and it holds all the hope of a delightful day. A successful day. I stroll towards the northern gate and swing my basket, scrambling to put the pieces together. This Feiyan *has* to be incredibly rare, but I'll find it; there's no lie there.

On my way, I pass a blacksmith hammering away in his forge, each clang an accompanying note to the distant hails from the marketplace and shouts from the builders fixing a roof at the end of the street. Carpenters' sawdust floats in the air, earthy and woody, mixing with the sweetness of the freshly baked bread and clean linen hanging on lines strung between buildings. A hurried messenger, arms stuffed with scrolls of parchment, dodges the two women walking ahead of me, both carrying empty wooden buckets, probably heading to the nearest well for water.

I don't mean to eavesdrop. They wouldn't talk so freely if they knew I was right behind them.

'I would be outraged if I was Simon's family,' one of the women says. 'I know King Garland is a man of few words, but to not even bother making an appearance at the memorial – well!'

'I heard from one of the maids that his sickness has him bedbound for days at a time. His condition is *much* worse than they've let on.'

'Really? The last announcement from the castle only mentioned that the king would occasionally be absent from holding court, not that he's at death's door! Imagine if he's not able to attend the prince's wedding either!'

'I wonder if it's the northern sickness. It's no wonder the queen is so—'

One of the women catches sight of me and grabs her friend's arm. Their faces pale as mine reddens, and I quicken my pace to pass them in silence. When I'm far enough away, their whispers will surely be wondering if I'll be repeating their words when I next see the queen. It wouldn't be the first time I've unwillingly snitched on my fellow citizens.

Before I can worry too much, the familiar voice of my best friend's fiancé shakes me out of my thoughts. The crown prince is riled up and ranting, which means one thing. There's only one person that can shatter Bastion's trained composure.

Willoh Vane must be in town again.

At the gate, the road out of the citadel is to my right, but to my left, with the castle looming in the distance, townsfolk cluster cautiously at the edges of the street with guards stationed at intervals for protection. Cardamine's fiancé, Prince Bastion, stands in the centre of it all, slicked-back black hair and leather armour aglow under the sun. A brown hand clenches the handle of the sword sheathed around his waist as he faces the person he likes least in this world.

I've lost count of how many times I've encountered a similar scene – Bash flushed red, face screwed up, voice raised, and Willoh, hands in pockets, casual and collected. Despite being of a similar height and age – nineteen, one year older than Card and me – they could not be more different, and their encounters vex the prince like nothing else. They used to be inseparable, but five years ago, after the incident in the northern forest, rumours started circulating that Willoh Vane's magic was the reason for the corruption, and any shred of friendship between them was destroyed. I wasn't there to witness the details, thank the gods. Their fallout was just before the queen's paranoia reached such a degree that she started summoning me to the castle to tell her the truth, and before Card met his fiancé, so neither Card nor I were there to see what actually happened.

From what I've gathered, I suspect it's Willoh's gift for magic and Bash's complete inability to summon even the smallest of spells that really agitates the prince. I'd call it jealousy, but I know better than to open my mouth. Magic is supposed to run strong in the royal line and Bash is the only exception, much to his mother's distress.

'How many times do I have to tell you to get lost?' Bastion says through gritted teeth. 'No one wants you here.'

Willoh's expression doesn't budge from its fixed smirk. He's in a maroon leather jacket, with a brown satchel slung over a shoulder. Underneath chestnut waves of hair, coloured earrings on warm golden skin wink in the sunlight.

'My almighty princeling, you know it pains me to go too long without seeing your grouchy face,' he drawls.

'Shut up and get out,' Bash growls. His tone is not very effective at intimidating the sorcerer.

'How polite,' Willoh says. 'Anyway, I literally need to buy *one thing* from the tailor's, so if you don't mind—'

'Buy it somewhere else,' Bash snaps back.

'Somewhere else?' Willoh says, a sharpness to his voice. 'Where do you suggest? Or have you forgotten—?'

'*Get lost.*'

There are usually two ways the conflict goes from here. Sometimes Willoh grins, delighting in Bash's agitation. Sometimes he's irritable, which usually results in it escalating until something in the citadel gets destroyed by a blast of Willoh's magic. Hence why the guards are quick to sprint towards the sound of Bash's shouts.

During one particularly bad fight a few months back, the prince had to be hauled away by Howell, one of the most experienced Guards of Alrick. Bash had screamed and sworn the whole way back to the castle, blood raining down his cheek from a shard of glass that had cut him when Willoh had exploded a nearby window with a powerful gust of wind. After which Card and I spent a sleepless night in Bash's chambers comforting him as he sat, head in his hands, trying to gather himself. He was more embarrassed than angry by that point, especially because the king had reprimanded him for brawling in public like a commoner.

'You gave him a chance to withdraw,' Card had said, hand on Bash's shoulder. 'You're not to blame.'

'So everyone keeps telling me,' Bash mumbled into his hands. 'How are the people supposed to trust me to protect them? Against sorcery – against Will – I'm *useless.*'

Card paused. He always knows how to crack Bash's sorrow, how to get him to laugh when he's weighed down. So he said, 'It was kind of funny, though. Did you see how the wind blew Howell's cape over his head? He turned on the spot about five times before he could untangle himself! Is that really the best your guards have to offer, my love?'

Bastion tackled him.

Willoh hadn't come back for months after that, which, luckily for us, gave the prince some time to cool off.

Personally, I prefer to imagine that the sorcerer doesn't exist. Just another reason to turn my feet round to avoid witnessing something that puts my curse at risk of being exploited. Not because I don't support Bash, but because the queen will squeeze every detail from me. I'd rather not know. If I don't know, then I can't give her the truth she desires. If I don't see it happening, then I don't have anything to tell her. It's a small defiance to walk away and turn a blind eye, but it's my choice, something I have control over, which is the most freedom my curse allows me.

Before I can find out if the conversation before me will dissolve into conflict, I turn right and march away, passing Godfrey at his post by the citadel gates. He's the first defence of Alrick, the retired captain of the guard who loves to have a good natter with anyone who passes.

'At it again, are they?' he asks, his wrinkled skin gathered in concern. It's no surprise he can hear Bash's voice from here.

'Yeah . . .'

'Lad said he needed some supplies,' Godfrey explains, casting a worried glance into the citadel. 'I thought Prince Bastion had duties at the castle today, so I told him to be quick.'

Godfrey watched Bastion and Willoh grow from infants to best friends to whatever this is, and he seems to be the only person who has some pity for the sorcerer. When he stepped down as captain, I overheard him telling Howell that Willoh had sent him a gift basket filled with all his favourite sweets in appreciation for his service.

Something I then had to tell the queen.

I resist the temptation to look back.

'Good luck,' I tell Godfrey, then quickly hightail it out of there. I need to focus. I have a flower to find, and I can't get caught up in Bastion's feud.

Striding into the northern forest, I pass the crocuses that line the path and head up towards the crossroads. The trees at my sides are thin quills with feathery leaves that filter the sunlight in narrowing strips. As the forest thickens, humid wafts of dry moss and pine fill the air. According to the roughly drawn map, I need to take the north path, then curve northwest. I don't usually stray too far past the crossroads, so I'll be in unknown territory soon.

Which is fine.

I'll be fine.

After all, there's plenty of daylight left, and as long as the tweets and squeaks from the wildlife still follow me, I should be safe. It'll be interesting to see how the flora changes the farther I go too. I wonder if there will be any other flowers I can take home with me – perhaps some more cinquefoils, like the one I'm wearing in my hair today. Mum likes them because they can be used in healing teas, but more so because they represent a beloved daughter. I've been tucking fresh flowers in my hair almost every day of my life, but she likes it most when I choose a cinquefoil, the five perfectly circular yellow petals showing the world that I'm loved. By one person at least.

Feet starting to ache, I'm keeping an eye out for a safe place to sit and take a break from all my walking – a pleasant clearing or a fallen tree log, perhaps – when I come across an unusual scene and halt.

Partway down a deserted path, shrivelled brown ribbons of grass attempt to grow in a vast circle that seems unnaturally perfect in shape. In the centre stands a gnarled white tree, its branches twisted and barren, its trunk cracked and hollow, the very life of it purged. Around the bark, someone has tied a braided rope. I recognise it as an old custom – a traditional offering to the gods that live in the earth. Perhaps an apology or memorial of some kind, some kind of ceremonial rite. I've never seen a tree so discoloured, or so surrounded by death. It's somewhat ethereal, almost dreamlike. Like it fell out of a legend. Extinct but existing.

Horror worms up my throat. It's *the* tree. It must be. The one the king and queen tell us to avoid. The poisoned one that infected the surrounding wildlife and destroyed houses and corrupted villagers until they turned vicious.

I remember the night it happened. I'd *felt* it happen. Anyone with the slightest flicker of magic had been woken from their sleep by a weight of dread. Then the rumours came. The north had been attacked; it was an invasion by the Kingdom of Senred wanting to push their borders south. It was a secret underground group who wanted revenge for a past slight. It was an ancient god displeased with how humans were treating the land.

The story that stuck was that it had been Willoh Vane, the prince's best friend, who had found a dark magic spell and tried it out on an oak tree as a foolish prank, to show off, to prove to the prince he had more powerful magic at his command.

But I know how the truth works. I can't be certain that any rumours are true unless I see it with my own eyes or hear it from the source. However it came to be this twisted and shrivelled, this tree has caused a lot of damage since then, and it's not something I should linger by. I hurry on, my chest tight. A reminder that I'm not safe here. I'm in the rebels' territory, and if the stories are true, they're just as corrupt as the land. And what about Willoh Vane, who also lives somewhere outside the citadel? Was Creon right about my obsession becoming a risk?

No, surely not. Maybe I overcompensate a little, but helping people, completing orders, it shows that I'm more than my curse. I'm more than the queen's telltale. If I'm consistent in my work, then people will see me as reliable. Nice. Likeable. Maybe there's a future where I have more than one friend. I just want to be *trusted*. Is that so wrong? But . . . perhaps I'll walk a little faster anyway.

Besides, I already know where Willoh Vane is. In the citadel, fighting with Bash.

Soon the trees huddle closer together and above, the canopy is a woven lace of leaves. It's denser here, darker. But weirdly, when

I push on, something small starts to knock at the corner of my mind. It nudges at my senses like an invisible force that thickens the air.

It feels like magic. The flower must be nearby.

I pause, basket in hand. A slight breeze whisks around my dress, but nothing seems amiss. The birds are twittering and the path ahead of me is clear. No sign of rebels or corruption.

I take a step.

My gut tells me to run. It tells me to leave. To get out of here. I'm not welcome.

I take a step back. The feeling softens, retreats.

Huh.

I try again, and the urge to flee flashes in my mind once more. The feeling must stem from some kind of protective ward, but leaving empty-handed is not an option. I *have* to get this flower, and this seems to be the only way forward.

Testing the boundaries of the ward, I pace left and right to the edges of the path and a few steps into the trees on either side. I think the magical barrier spreads out like a bubble, but I can't work out how much of the forest it covers. Maybe this is why no one has heard of the Feiyan flower – because it's blocked by a spell. Well, if there's magic involving flowers, then it's something I'm good at. I can do this.

I lower my internal defences and march down the path with my shoulders set, feeling for the flower with my magic like grazing my hands through grass, searching for the intuitive pull in my chest. With each step, the pressure to run weighs on me. Dizzy, coloured spots flicker in the corners of my vision, woozily clawing at my balance. No, *no*, I have to continue. I have to—

A fluffy white cat pads out of the line of trees and turns its head. It's the last thing I see before I pass out.

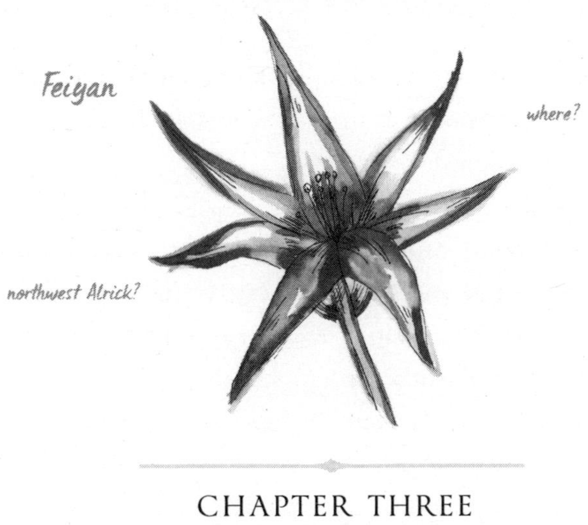

CHAPTER THREE

I squint my eyes open to find someone crouched before me. My back is against a tree, my basket at my side. And from the stinging sensation on my elbows, I can tell I've managed to scrape the skin off both. Great.

'What are you doing?' the person asks nonchalantly, as if it's normal to stumble across an unconscious girl in the middle of the forest.

I can't answer quite yet. The dizziness is clinging to me like morning dew, sticky and heavy, and it takes another minute for me to blink away the spots in my vision. To see exactly who spoke. My blood sharpens at the same time my eyes do, and the drowsiness flees in panic.

Oh *no*. Anyone but him.

Willoh Vane rocks back on his heels and tilts his head, his brown hair tickling the colourful jewels pinned down the sides of his ears.

'You awake, Princess?' he asks.

Don't speak. Don't risk it. If he learns about my curse, he could—Gods, I can't even imagine what chaos he'd wreak.

How long was I out? It must have been some time if he could get here from the citadel . . .

He reaches out a hand.

I jolt. 'Don't—'

We freeze in place – him with his eyebrows raised, that tanned hand outstretched, and me with my body pressed solidly against the tree at my back. Not that it will do me any good.

To my surprise, the sorcerer laughs and stands, tucking both hands in the pockets of his maroon leather jacket.

'Ah, of course.' Willoh grins down at me. 'Wouldn't want me cursing you.'

His eyes widen in mock fear, but his smirk is stuck tight. He's taunting me. Just like he taunts Bash. Bristling, I clamber to my feet using the trunk of the tree for support and Willoh leans on one hip, watching my every move. I can't give him any chances. I don't want to get involved – if only selfishly, so I don't have to think hard about my words next time I talk with the queen. Or Bastion. Or Cardamine. Oh gods, I need to get out of here. With wood chips on my fingers, I pick up my basket to leave.

'You haven't answered my question,' Willoh says, an edge to his voice this time.

He takes a slow step forward, which stops me from making it back to the path. More than a whole head taller than me, he has to tilt his narrow chin down to look me in the eye. This close, I can't help but notice trace scents of warm earth on him – almost sweet, like balsam in summer evenings – and strangely, chamomile. A healing herb.

'I don't have to answer,' I reply.

He gives me wide doe eyes, halfway to a pout. 'But I want to know.'

'Do you always get what you want?' I ask, glancing round his shoulder. Which route would take me to the flower I seek? Which one would take me to safety – away from him?

There's that tinkling laugh again. I scowl.

'Worried about me, Princess?'

'I'm not a princess.'

'What are you, then?'

I don't answer – my usual choice when faced with a question I can't answer with a lie. In my silence, Willoh runs his eyes over my face. Maybe he's looking for a weakness, a break in my defences.

'Do I know you?' he asks.

'Maybe. I know who you are.'

Damn. It slipped out.

'How delightful. I have *such* a reputation, I'm sure.' He grins again. With a sweeping bow, he steps to the side and holds out his arms to allow me to pass. 'My lady.'

I march down the forest path in the same direction I tried before. Perhaps I can check the circumference, walk around the border of the barrier spell. There's no way I'm returning empty-handed, even if Willoh Vane is on my heels. I look back to see the sorcerer strolling a few paces behind me, hands still in his pockets and an amused smile on his face.

'Stop following me,' I say.

'I don't know what you mean. I'm simply walking.'

I pick up the pace, gripping my basket. I should check my map again, but—

'Feeling faint yet?' Willoh asks cheerfully.

I ignore him. The dizziness *is* creeping in again, whispering at the edges of my vision, persuading me to turn back like a peony shying away from strong sunlight. I shake my head. Come on, *think*. There's got to be a way.

'If you keep going, you're going to pass out again,' Willoh says. Not as a threat, just as a fact. 'Although . . .' He catches up to my side and leans forward. I throw him the smallest of glances. 'Look at you, in your cute dress, with flowers in your hair. On second thought, by all means, keep going. When you faint, maybe you'll fall into my arms.'

I stop in my tracks so fast, I almost slip on the twigs under my shoes. Willoh tuts as if disappointed.

'What *are* you so eager to find around here?' he asks.

'I don't want to talk to you.'

'Wow, that's hurtful.'

'Do you delight in stalking women in forests?'

'You're the one heading in my direction.'

'Then be on your way.'

Willoh grins. 'Nice try.'

I consider the surroundings. The trees grow densely here, so unless I want to climb one of them, I suppose . . . *perhaps* . . . I could ask for some help.

I shoot him my harshest warning glare. 'I'm looking for a flower.'

His eyebrows raise in disbelief. He doesn't believe me. Wait – *he doesn't believe me.* Gods, that's refreshing.

'A flower.'

'Yes. Now, if you'll excuse me—'

'Describe it to me.'

I knit my eyebrows together. 'And then what?'

'Then I'll go get it for you.'

I hesitate, scanning the forest path. It's not in his nature to give help so freely. At least, that's not how Bastion describes him, and I don't want to owe a debt to one of the most powerful sorcerers in the kingdom. One rumoured to have once used dark magic.

'Why can't I get it myself?' I ask.

'Because in case it's escaped your attention, you can't make it ten steps that way without losing consciousness.'

'And you can?'

'No, I just come here to pass out for fun.'

Gods—

'You might not know how to pick it correctly,' I counter.

'I'm sure I'll manage.'

'Or you can tell me how to get around this barrier spell.'

'Or not.' He grins again, completely at ease.

Fine. I dig my hand into my flower basket and thrust the request sheet at him.

'Here.'

He unfolds the paper carefully and takes a moment to read it. I use the time to study him – his narrow jaw and straight nose, his sun-kissed skin, the way his gold-flecked hazel eyes scan the page seriously, like I've given him a complicated textbook to study. I've never seen him this close up before, so it's fascinating to put details to the name. It's like finding a flower in real life that I've previously only seen illustrated in books. I'm aware that a lot of my Willoh Vane-related information comes from some incredibly biased sources: the queen who despises him; the rumours that blame him for the corruption of the forest; and Bash, who would be screaming in my ear to run if he were here. But he's not here, and so far, Willoh hasn't hurt me or even hinted that he'd hurt me – even if his humour is grating. I'm definitely *not* envious of how easily his sarcasm comes.

Willoh raises his eyes to mine and taps the page. 'Huh.'

'Do you know where it is or not?'

He angles the page. '"Farrow's Flowers". Did you choose that name? Very creative.'

I say nothing.

'Fair enough. Well, this flower grows in a field not too far from here that you might be able to stay conscious for.'

'And?'

Willoh Vane throws me his most dashing smile. 'You'll be requiring my presence a little longer.' With a wink, he strides off the path. 'Come along, Farrow.'

I watch the back of his dark red jacket slip between two trees and waver. Am I really going to follow Bash's arch-enemy off the path into a dark, extremely difficult to find part of the forest for a flower?

No doubt about it.

Willoh doesn't murder me. In fact, he keeps to his word and leads me through the trees, holding back branches with magical gusts of wind. He even checks regularly to see if I'm keeping up. A quarter of an hour or so later, I'm no longer able to contain my curiosity.

'How do you know where this flower is?' I ask. 'I'd never heard of it before yesterday.'

Willoh glances back and I make sure I'm glaring his way. 'I'm incredibly talented,' he says.

'At knowing where rare flowers are?'

'At everything,' he says, and shoots me another smirk. Then he relents, adding, 'No, I just took a few botanical classes at the Library of Heris.'

'You studied at the Library?' I ask, surprised.

Card has talked about visiting the Library of Heris for years, but he's never found the time to go, especially once he got engaged. It sits in its own triangle of territory right between the borders of Alrick, Dreah, and Lucan. No monarchy, no title of 'kingdom' – a simply neutral ground for anyone who wishes to study. It houses the most detailed library of knowledge in the whole eight kingdoms of Calla. In fact, I bet Card would drag Bash there for their honeymoon if he could. I've never wanted to go myself. It's where Mum says Morgana resides, posing as a respectable researcher, and bumping into the sorcerer who cursed me doesn't sound like fun.

'I did,' Willoh says. Lighter than the breeze pushing the leaves aside, he continues, 'And then I didn't.'

Before I can consider what he means, we reach a vast wall of tangled thorns.

'It's up there,' he says, pointing his chin at the thorny barrier.

'*Up?* What do you mean?'

'Up,' he says, and points a finger towards the sky. 'As in not down.'

I narrow my eyes.

'Okay . . .' I say, unsure what he wants me to do. Does he want me to start climbing? I'm wearing a cotton dress and flat slip-on shoes, not to mention carrying a flower basket. Not exactly climbing gear.

Willoh angles his head to one side, smiling at my hesitation. 'How do you feel about heights, Princess?'

'I don't know. I don't think I've ever been extremely high up.'

He lifts his elbow as if he were offering his arm at a ball, and I blink.

'This is the part where you'll be requiring my assistance,' he says, and with his other hand, twirls a thin spiral of magical wind around his fingers.

'Oh.'

I realise he can fly us up to the top in seconds, or I can try to climb.

It's an easy decision to make. I've come this far, and despite Bastion's voice yelling in the back of my mind, I am *getting* the Feiyan. I am taking it home and delivering it; there's no other outcome I can accept. It's more than a flower. It's my path to a good reputation, to reliability. And, above all, being trusted. If that means letting Willoh Vane use magic around me, on me, *for* me, then so be it.

I stare at him, determined.

'Go for it,' I say, and swallow away the nerves. 'Get us up there.'

Willoh surveys me for a second. He runs his eyes over my face, over the cinquefoil flower behind my ear and rose-pink ends of my black hair, then he smiles. I tighten my jaw. He must have found something about me amusing.

Without warning, he sweeps up my free hand in his, gently, so my fingers are barely resting in his palm, and brushes his other against my lower back. A summoned flurry of wind sails us through the air like the yank of a fishing pole. I squeeze my eyes shut as the world blurs, a bellow in my ears and a rush in my stomach.

A moment later, my feet hit something solid and the warmth of Willoh's hands disappears. I open my eyes and gasp. Ahead is a clearing, wider and more open to the sun than I could ever imagine. It's a vast stretch of grass on top of the trees, supported by the tangled thicket below. Blue sky spills endlessly in all directions. I twist round to the south and my throat catches. The stone walls of the citadel are a distant grey shadow past the sea of forest. To the west lies a sparkling ocean, and to the northeast, the snow-capped peak of the Spinal Steppe Mountain stands at the forefront of the mountain range that curves north to Senred and farther east to Dreah where Bash's younger brother, Prince Merit, lives.

I turn to Willoh.

'H-how . . .?' I stammer. How could something like this exist? How could I not know this was here? How can I be standing above the trees and walking on fresh grass?

He shrugs.

'Magic,' is all he says, then sets off.

I hurry to keep up, captivated by the squish under my feet, and it isn't until I tear my eyes from the ground that I realise where he's heading – *what* he's walking towards.

In the centre of the magical meadow, a singular flower grows. Its tall saffron-yellow stem supports leaves that bleed into a magnificent fiery red and, gods, the petals . . . Long thin triangles burst out like the sun itself in rich gradients of pink and coral. It's the sunset, the sunrise, and all the light between. The fully bloomed afternoon sun. A golden, shimmering daylight, aflame with light and life and an intense brilliance that has me falling to my knees beside it. I lift a trembling finger to the petals. The raw magic greets me with a burning smile, but there's no discernible emotion or meaning contained within. It soaks into my skin like basking on a summer's day and I would absolutely be telling the truth if I said I'd never felt a flower containing *this* much power before.

It's impressive.

And dangerous.

I pull my finger away and stare up at Willoh, speechless.

'Satisfied, Princess?'

'I'm . . . I . . .' I truly do not know what to say, what the truth is. This is the greatest flower I've ever seen and I'm going to hand it over to a complete stranger.

'I think I'm jealous,' I say, and Willoh snorts a laugh.

'Why?'

'Because I don't get to keep this. I have to give it away. Actually, I'd rather let it be. I'd rather let it grow and thrive here, but . . .' I trail off.

'Then do that,' Willoh says, with a shrug. 'Just say you couldn't find it.'

I shake my head. 'I can't.'

I realise what I've just said. I can't do as he suggested because I can't lie. But he doesn't know that. As I scramble for an excuse, for something of the truth to cover my tracks, Willoh simply crouches down beside me. A wave of hair falls over his eyes as he studies the Feiyan. From the pinch between his eyebrows, I'm sure he can feel the magic pouring from it.

'Well,' he muses, 'at least make sure they pay you generously, then.'

I don't mention that the request hadn't provided a price range for my services, or that I was so curious about this flower that I would have come regardless of payment or not. I simply watch him examine the Feiyan a little longer until he drags his eyes to mine and grins.

'Don't worry, I won't charge you for my help.'

Even in the brightest of meadows, Willoh Vane manages to infuriate.

The Feiyan comes out of the grass easily enough – roots and all – and after it's safely nestled in my flower basket, I enchant it to retain enough water to last the journey home, where I can pot it and spend dedicated time working my magic to keep it fresh. Not that I think it needs much magical assistance from me – I can already feel that the flower is powerful enough to survive much longer than the common flora I usually work with.

Willoh floats us back to the forest floor and I dust off my dress before quietly following him back through the trees. How am I supposed to thank him for this? Worse, how am I supposed to *not talk* about this to anyone else? The mention of his name sends both Queen Fern and Bash into a spiral, and if I tell Card, Bash will be able to sense that he's hiding something. With six weeks until their wedding, I would hate to cause any extra stress.

'Here you are, Princess,' Willoh says, startling me back into reality.

I trip on a branch and he catches my elbow, helping me out of the tree line and onto the gravelled path. When I'm stable, his hands disappear into his jacket pockets.

'Um,' I mumble as we face each other on the path. I should thank him. I should say something . . .

From seemingly nowhere, the white cat I saw before I fainted scampers towards us.

'It's that cat!' I say.

Willoh groans as the cat paws at his leg.

'What?' he says to the cat, who changes tactics to butt its head against his boot. 'I told you not to come this far out. Ugh, *really*?'

Willoh gives in and lifts the cat into his arms.

'That's *your* cat?' I ask as it puts its front paws on his shoulder and snuggles a fluffy head under his chin.

'Yeah, he's so needy. *Gill*, my guy, *really*?'

The cat tries to clamber onto his shoulders and I cover my laugh.

'Don't let him get attached; he'll never leave you alone,' Willoh says.

'Gill?'

'Yeah,' he says, and the cat continues to wriggle around his neck. 'I found him in a stream nearby when he was just a kitten, so I called him Gill. He must have held his breath a long time – *Gill*, oh my gods.'

Gill rests around Willoh's neck like a scarf and finally decides he's comfortable.

'Cute,' I say with a smile.

Willoh rolls his eyes.

'Yeah, until you want to breathe,' he says, but there's something different about his tone, a fondness I've never heard before. One that certainly hasn't come out anytime I've heard him talking to Bash. '*Anyway*, this path takes you back to the citadel. Just keep going in a straight line.'

'Thank you.'

Willoh's eyes flick to the flower in my hair. He spins on his heels and waves a hand.

'Sure. Later, Princess.' As he walks away, he lifts Gill from his shoulders and scolds him. 'Seriously, bud, we've talked about this.'

With a soft chuckle, I turn in the direction of the citadel having completed my customer's request *and* survived the company of formidable sorcerer Willoh Vane. The success is a sunlit fiery buzz in my chest that has me glowing all the way home. ASAP, the request said. I thought it would be impossible, but I've delivered in a day. Reliable to a fault.

When I'm home, I choose a pot for the Feiyan, douse it with my usual flower feed, and use the rest of the sunlight hours inspecting it in every way possible. When exhaustion reminds me to eat and sleep, and my journal is full of new sketches and annotations, I finally wrap the Feiyan in protective paper and place it in the collection box, sad to see it go. The flower disappears overnight without any clues as to who the customer could be, and the surprising sum of ten gold is left behind in payment. No amount had been specified, but I charge five gold for my most expensive bouquets with all additional enchantments and accessories, so ten is a more than generous payment for a single flower.

I hope that whoever the customer is, whatever they use it for, they take good care of it. It's what beauty like that deserves. And if any more requests for unique flowers come in, I'll find them. I'll never fail to deliver. Perhaps then people will trust me, and I'll be safe from an outcast's fate. I won't end up like Willoh Vane, alone in a forest with only a cat for company. Although, he didn't seem to mind it . . .

No. I can't allow myself to think that way. I have to pretend our meeting never happened. There are already far too many reasons for people to be wary of me. I'll keep my mouth shut and words locked tight and pray I never have reason to meet him again.

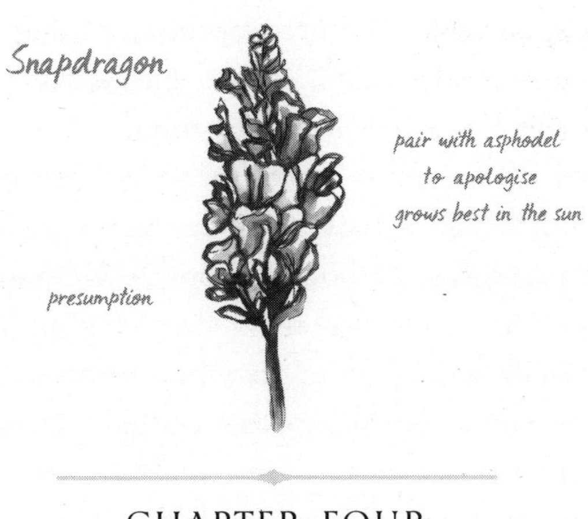

CHAPTER FOUR

A week later, when I get home from stocking up on marigolds, I check the anonymous request box out of habit and am surprised to find another form there from the same customer who ordered the Feiyan. This one, likewise penned in unusual calligraphy, names another flower I've never heard of, the Odyssa, alongside – again – only two other words: *Collection. ASAP.* However, this time they haven't included a helpful map – not even a *hint* – meaning I have nothing to go on and no way of delivering with the same speed as last time.

Hmm. I wonder why it's so urgent. Have they already used the Feiyan for something? It can't have wilted already, not with that much power inside. And if they know more about rare flowers than I do, why would they ask me to collect them instead of going themselves? Whatever the reason, knowing the customer was willing to part with ten gold for the first flower shows they are serious about their requests.

After several days of rifling through my mum's old textbooks and asking everyone who might know at the castle, I decide to look for information in Card's second home – the castle library. If there are hours in a day and no urgent wedding planning taking up his time, Cardamine can be found among the bookshelves and dust.

I heave a pile of books onto the table where Card is sitting, crunched over a large textbook with a forgotten ink-dipped quill in his left hand. When I'd asked for his advice, he'd waved me in the general direction of the botanical books without raising his eyes from the page – not even when I'd clambered up a shelf, cracked it, and accidentally pulled an entire string of books onto my head. Luckily, the librarian forgave me fast enough once she saw who I was with. Card's presence *had* come in useful then.

'Hey,' I say, slamming the books down. 'I found a few.'

His eyes skim the page he's on, full of characters that have no meaning to me.

'Hmm?'

This is one of those times I wish I could use sarcasm. *I said I've decided to blow the castle up. I said I'm running away to live in the forest among the fairies.* Whatever I say, Card's not paying attention to me. He'll snap out of it in a minute or two. It's futile to fight against his obliviousness when he's caught up in a book.

I plonk myself down opposite him and open the first book, titled *Wild and Weird: Flowers Beyond the Garden.* The green angelica flower embroidered on the cover represents inspiration and imagination. Based on that alone, I expect the author of this particular book to embellish a few facts, but it's still worth a flick through.

A few pages in, I come across a beautifully illustrated vine of clematis, each violet-inked flower detailing eight long petals, open like a giant star. I've never actually seen one in real life before, but I've heard the name and know that if it's paired with rosemary, it makes a good luck charm. I'd love to have them for the front of the shop. They'd look so pretty growing around the door.

'Check it out,' I say to Card, regardless of if he's listening or not. 'The clematis represents problem-solving and cleverness. That could come in handy. Shame it doesn't grow in Alrick.'

Card shakes his head. 'Sorry, I'm reading in ancient Berian. What did you say?'

'Why are you studying ancient Berian? I thought you only started learning Wyean the other week.'

'Wyean was *so* easy; I've pretty much got it down already. Besides, if any ambassadors from those outlying kingdoms come to the wedding, I want them to be able to gossip with someone.'

'That someone being you.'

'Exactly.' Card grins, his blue eyes sharp with success. He finally notices my tower of books. 'Oh, nice. Have you found anything useful?'

'Nothing about the Odyssa,' I tell him, and turn the page. 'I'm glad they included a map to find the Feiyan last time. This time . . .'

'Looks like you'll be spending the day inside with me, then. Quality fun!'

'Can't we take these outside to read? It's such a clear day and the field by the lake is still full of daisies.'

Card snorts. 'Oh yeah, *sure.* You ask Librarian Yun if you can take her hundred-year-old books into the sun and see how she reacts.'

She already has her eye on me after the shelf fiasco. I'm not sure she'd forgive me for desecrating these books any further.

'Fine.' But unlike Card, I can't read anything for too long. His focus far outmatches mine, and in the stuffy silence, I find my mind wandering. I reluctantly wonder if Willoh Vane would know where to find the Odyssa. He knew where the Feiyan was instantly, *and* he studied at the Library of Heris, whose collection far surpasses this one's.

The thought makes me want to test the waters, to see if it's safe to tell Card about what happened in the forest – something I'd initially decided against.

'Do you know anyone who studied at the Library of Heris?' I ask. Mentioning the Library is an infallible way to crack Card's concentration. Although I haven't heard much about his obsession with the place lately because of all the wedding planning.

'I wish!' He sighs. 'Occasionally there's a visiting professor or student to see the king and queen, but I've yet to corner one of them, despite my best efforts. Why do you ask?'

His eyes lift from his page long enough to have my face squirming to stay straight. I have to be *so* careful here.

'Someone like that might recognise the Odyssa. Do you think Bash knows anyone?'

Someone like the sorcerer he frequently argues with?

Card brushes the end of his quill against his chin in thought. 'Hmm, maybe. I can ask him later on if you like?'

I decide to go for it.

'What about Willoh Vane?'

Card's lips pinch together, like he's seen me sprout wings and wants to clip them before they can grow too big.

'*What the*— Felicity Farrow, have you gone mad?'

Ah. Okay. Perhaps a retreat, then.

'Never mind. I just . . . Well, he has magic, so . . .' I pretend that a paragraph in the book has suddenly enticed me.

The scoff in his voice is clear. 'Yeah, magic that he uses to put people in harm's way on a regular basis.'

'*Someone* knows where this flower is, but no one I've asked so far has any idea.'

'Yes, but if you're genuinely considering asking *that pest* for help, then I fear you've lost your mind. Bash *hates* him; you know this. He wouldn't be happy about you inviting Willoh over for tea and a chat about flowers. Good gods, *imagine*.'

I let out a short laugh. Yeah. Imagine . . . I force away the memory of Willoh's fingers skimming the palm of my hand before he swept us into the air.

Pest. Is that how I would describe him? Not really. It *is* true that he's caused Bash an immense number of headaches and can do so easily with a few scathing words and swift flashes of magic. And yes, apparently he was the one who caused the tree in the north to die, which blighted the northern villages and threw them into tension with the citadel. But does that make him so dangerous that even suggesting a conversation is too much? I didn't feel threatened when I spoke to him the other day.

'It was an idea,' I say, and shrug, like it wasn't the only lead I had to find this flower.

'A crazy one. *Wow* . . . you must be really desperate for information to consider—' Card bursts into a laughter that echoes off the dusty stone walls. He wipes the corner of his eye. 'My gods, sorry, that's just— Wow. Amazing. *Sure*, let's go ask Willoh Vane. Ha! You're so funny sometimes.'

My fingers rest on a page about snapdragons, an exotic plant from a distant kingdom. Their cylindrical petals are curled like a mouth being squeezed shut, and there's a label next to the illustration that reads *presumption*. Snapdragons are famous for sending messages about oversights and misread situations. Is there something I'm missing here? Willoh Vane went from being Bash's best friend to bickering with him and occasionally drawing blood, and everyone just assumes it was because he poisoned the tree. But why would he have done that? What did he have to gain?

I've purposefully turned away whenever I've come across him in the past, simply to save myself from having to inform the queen, but now my lack of information has become a hurdle. I can't ask a sorcerer about a magical flower I need to find because said sorcerer likes to rile my best friend's fiancé every once in a while. *How annoying*.

I'm taking my time thoroughly combing through my thoughts as I often do, when the scuff of metal against metal grinds through the library doorway. A sound that unfortunately only means one thing. The Guards of Alrick are here.

'Ava!' Card greets the captain over my shoulder. His face hardens. 'Lark.'

No. My stomach plunges. Two sets of footsteps stop behind me. I clench my hands into fists and stare at the snapdragons in the book.

'Felicity. I'm glad we found you here,' Captain Ava says. 'The queen requests your presence.'

'She's busy,' Card says, with the authority of someone protected by Bastion's status. I don't have that same leeway. I collect myself as best I can and turn to face Ava with what I hope is a steady expression.

'Of course.'

Ava rests her hands on the leather belt of her armour and offers me a sympathetic smile. She has closely cropped brown hair and dark skin, and despite being only a little older than Card and me when she took over as captain, I told her truthfully that they couldn't have chosen a better fit. It has nothing to do with the crush I had on her when I was younger either. She's genuinely a good person. Unlike the guard at her side. Who I don't look at.

The push of my chair scratches across the stone floor.

'Are you coming back?' Card asks.

'It depends,' I say. On what the queen wants. On how much information she wants to wring from me today.

I step away from my snapdragons. Let's get this over with.

'Felicity,' Ava says, and gestures to the door.

There's no way to further avoid Lark. My eyes fall on him and I'm back to that night all over again, my chest heaving from crying so much. My arms tired from clinging to Card. My heart crumbled like dried, distrustful lavender. If Ava is a steady olive tree, Lark is rue. *Regret.*

'Fliss,' he says. My name on his lips makes nausea rise to my throat. He inclines his head ever so slightly to let me pass, and when his dark blond hair falls over those lime-green eyes, I can't stop the twitch in my fingers.

I used to run my hands through that hair.

Gods, I hate that I get these flashes of memories. I hate stumbling upon him around the castle so often. No, I simply hate all of him. Here he is acting like everything is fine – like I didn't cry until I lost my voice, like he didn't remind me all too well that my curse can be a knife. I haven't forgotten. He's fickle, and I don't need to say it out loud to know it's true.

Ava falls in beside me as we exit the library, her blue-and-silver one-shoulder cloak billowing behind. Lark brings up the rear, out of sight. Good.

'How have you been?' I ask the captain. A question like that from me is usually a cause for averted eyes and vague answers, but Ava is not so suspicious.

'Busy. I meant to thank you for Simon's flowers, Felicity, and I apologise for not doing so sooner. We're still attempting to secure safer trading routes to prevent further rebel attacks, but unfortunately, they know the forest better than we do. It's imperative that Prince Merit can travel back safely for the wedding. There's five weeks to go and I'm sure it will fly by, so we're preparing in advance as much as we can.'

'It'll be nice to have Prince Merit home,' I say, knowing Card loves it when Bash's younger brother distracts the queen. While Merit gets to escape his mother's watchful eye by living in the Kingdom of Dreah for months at a time, Bash is under constant scrutiny. That's part of the weight of being crown prince, I suppose.

'It will. He plans to arrive in just over two weeks, and then it'll be three weeks until the ceremony so I'm sure his help will be greatly appreciated.'

'These are plans that are kept *secret*,' Lark interrupts from behind us.

Ava's smile becomes tight. She knows what happened between the two of us. Everyone does. Loudly breaking up at Card and Bash's engagement party ensured that.

'I'm sure no harm will come of Felicity knowing that *someday*, in the near future, the younger prince of Alrick will be travelling home. The wedding is on the horizon after all,' the captain says, artfully putting him in his place.

'We don't want the rebels finding out.'

'Are you suggesting I'm in cahoots with them?' I spit out.

The clunk of his metal armour stops.

'No, that's *not* what I meant,' Lark says, his tone changed. I know that when he puts this voice on – the smooth one, the silky one, the one that is supposed to reassure me that I'm wrong and he's right – that I should get as far away as possible.

'We shouldn't keep the queen waiting,' I say, and march down the corridor.

I know Ava has given Lark a silent warning look behind my back. That's just who she is: a peacekeeper, a leader.

If only the same were true of the queen who awaits me.

Queen Fern's quarters are always kept dim, with heavy velvet curtains that block out the natural light and more candles than I can count. The wooden doors to her private chamber open hungrily, and all at once, I'm hit with an overwhelming musk of foxgloves that makes my eyes water, as if there's a pinch of something spicier in the mix. The purple flower, to me and other florists, carries the meaning of insincerity and riddles. Secrets. But putting that interpretation aside, it's also used as an aroma oil to regulate the heart. I've been summoned by the queen enough in the past five years to know that she has regular panic attacks and days consumed by the irregular beat in her chest. It's no wonder she would want to use a child who could only tell the truth to soothe her fears.

My mother had always kept us at a distance from the royal family, probably to give me a sense of normality in what was already a highly unusual childhood, and her dislike of the queen shut down any questions I had. But shortly after the incident in the north, knocks came at our door with a royal command not subject to refusal, and my mother could no longer keep me – or my curse – out of the castle. Whether she went to Queen Fern and fought against it, or even considered leaving our family home and moving out of the citadel, I doubt I'll ever know. If there's one thing about my mother, it's that she'll always keep her mouth shut and pretend things are fine.

'Felicity.'

Queen Fern snaps my attention to her. She sits poised upright in a plush chair by the lit fireplace, wavy black hair pulled over her collarbones, her brown skin a shade paler than her husband and sons' from all her time indoors. She's in a fur-lined green silk gown and has her usual fluffy blanket on her lap. Across from her is a similar chair that she gestures to with a manicured hand. 'Please.'

I curtsy as always, then take my seat.

'So,' she begins. Her dark eyes study me.

I know better than to relax. This is usually when she asks me to fill her in on every detail since we last spoke, and I try to convince myself it's for the good of the people. I tell her about the townsfolk in the lower town – whose business is taking off or struggling, who's quarrelling with whom, which families are abuzz with celebrations of marriage or pregnancy, and so on. At the end, she always makes a point of asking if I've seen anything suspicious. When my response is no, her shoulders relax as if the muscles around her ribs were clenched tight, suffocating her heart until she's reassured by the truth that all in the citadel is at peace.

Today, however, she surprises me.

'I know you've been looking for a particular flower,' the queen says.

'You do?'

The laugh she gives is barely a breath. 'Felicity, I know everything that happens in this kingdom. Of course I know. You asked every one of my gardeners and physicians. In fact, I was dismayed when you didn't ask me for help personally. You know you can come to me for anything, dear.'

I hesitate.

I've never quite trusted her – how can I, when all she wants from me is information about others that they don't consent to give? But she does this often. She floats words of kindness and attempts to make us sound close. When I was younger, I was more easily swayed. I know better now. I know what she wants from me: my curse and my silence.

I bow my head, as I can't truthfully agree or apologise.

'The Odyssa, is that the name?'

'Yes, Your Majesty.'

'Well, then, I can help.'

I shoot my eyes up. From the pulled smile and tilt of her head, my eagerness has pleased her.

'How . . .?'

She waves her hand. 'We've known each other for years now, Felicity, so you know how this goes.'

Oh, of course. I hadn't doubted it. She'll want some truth in return. Information. Ah . . . I do have something. I have my meeting with Willoh Vane in the forest. But he *helped* me. It wouldn't feel right to snitch on him to a queen who hates his existence almost as much as her son does.

'Anything to share?' she prods.

'Yes,' I say. 'This isn't the first unusual request for a rare flower I've had recently.'

I decide to tell her about the anonymous request for the Feiyan, that I found the flower in the northern forest (without mentioning Willoh), and that the request for the Odyssa seems to be from the same person. When I finish my expertly worded tale, she hums.

'Interesting,' she says. 'And you have no idea who wants the flowers or what they want them for?'

I plaster on a smile. 'Your Majesty, I admit I was curious. They seem to have more knowledge than me, but with respect, it's not professional to pry into the identity of my anonymous customers. I do my best to strive for a reliable, trustworthy reputation.'

The glow of the fire flickers in her eyes.

'Of course, dear, but please come and tell me if you feel concerned at any point,' she says, then reaches to her side table. With bony fingers, she lifts a battered hardback book. 'Here. A good friend of mine was able to source this at the Library of Heris and send it over promptly. I hope it will help you deliver this flower just as efficiently as the last.'

She passes the book over and I read the title: *From Bud to Bloom: Mountain Regions and their Wildflowers*. This is a debt she'll hold over my head. She'll want to know how this story ends, how it could affect the kingdom she so desperately tries to keep stable without her husband at full strength to share command.

For now, at least, all she says is 'Good luck.'

CHAPTER FIVE

The Spinal Steppe Mountain in the northeast of the Kingdom of Alrick is no place for a florist. I traipse up a slope, thoroughly underdressed in a few measly layers of cotton, clutching a cloak under my chin with wind-burned fingers. A short while ago, the rocky path gathered dustings of snow, and now, with only the wool around my shoulders for protection, I'm faced with an endless expanse of white. A steep climb towards a clouded summit.

It occasionally snows in the citadel in winter, but it's a light coating, the barest kiss of ice on the cobbled streets. This, I am unprepared for. This is a deep bitter bite under my skin, a cold that claws into my bones and makes my joints struggle to function. With a wolven howl of wind around my stinging ears, I drag my feet forward, heaving my sodden slip-on shoes through inches of snow, and pray to the gods I'm still on the right path. If the gods even exist in this bleak, infinite nothing.

The book the queen gave me said that Odyssa flowers only grow here on the Spinal Steppe, on the edge of a precipice not too far up the mountainside. Great, I'd thought. No problem. I like walking, I like nature, it shouldn't take that long. From the citadel to the mountain, I can hop on the back of a travelling cart for an hour or so, and from there, I just follow the road up until I reach the cliff. Simple.

Then snow started falling faster than I could anticipate – far faster than any ordinary blizzard – and the path before me disappeared, like the flower is being protected by the mountain itself, sending snow and wind and storms to keep people away. Now icy rocks grow from the ground like the goose bumps on my skin, and somewhere to my left, an ashy abyss waits, a drop so severe that it descends abruptly into darkness.

I should turn round. I should go home and come back more prepared. Maybe with thicker clothes. Or a fire-lit torch. A hot drink. Something to thaw the shivers in my veins.

But I can't. I know the flower is near. I can feel it. There's a certain nip in the air, an energy that shivers from the sky – something louder than the wind, stronger than the chill. It's the blue hour, the in-between. Magic.

A shuffle nearby freezes me in place. From the stillness, a white hare bounces over the snow with the lightest of leaps. It pauses, resting on its hind legs, and sniffs the air, twitching an ear. As fast as it appeared, it scampers away, blending into the snow like the water bleeding into my socks. I hoist a foot up and try to follow its tracks. If there are small animals here then it should mean I'm not in danger of meeting any bears, or worse. White rabbits are animals blessed by the gods. It should mean that there's food and water nearby, a cave, a burrow, *something*. *Anything*—

A hidden rock trips me up and I'm sent sprawling into the quilt of snow. Powdery ice seeps into my chest like a cold poison. My cloak, now heavy and useless, weighs down my shoulders, as does the flower basket strapped to my back.

A sob cracks my dry throat.

I'm going to die here.

I'm going to freeze and die and be forgotten and be buried in a blizzard until a bear comes and has me for dinner.

Or—

My head shoots up, the wet ends of my hair stuck to my cheeks. Something just called to me. Nudged me. Roused my magic like all flowers do.

I listen intently, lying flat and still.

What is that?

My eyes focus. Right before me, on a canvas of cloudy grey sky, twin flowers sway on the very edge of a precipice that pokes out like an arrowhead. I whimper in relief. The deep blue stems of two Odyssa flowers twist around each other, softening out to a pastel blue that gives way to blooming heads of white petals. Unlike the showy, pointed petals of the Feiyan, both Odyssa are soft and round, balls of inward curls that protect a gleaming cerulean centre – exactly like Card's eyes, sharply aware and persistent. Resilient. As I must be to collect them and get off this godsforsaken mountain.

I crawl my way to the flowers, biting my lip to resist the cutting cold. I don't know how strong this precipice is . . . If I remember from the times the lake behind the castle froze over, I should balance my weight, move slowly and steadily. My clothes are a waterlogged burden, but I manage it. Splayed out on my front, I grasp the bottom of the Odyssa stems. And they smile. For a brief moment, I get the barest waft of warmth, the faintest memory of a deep navy sky and deathly silence as the sun sleeps under the horizon. Just as I read in the book the queen gave me, this flower lives in the seam between day and night like the stitches separating light and dark. It's volatile and elusive, hiding out here in the mountains, in the quiet, in the snow, not bright like the sun, or beautiful like the moon, but a vivid, fleeting moment in between. And I *found it.*

I wiggle my basket off my back and use the tip of my trowel to make minuscule jabs at the icy dirt, slowly, carefully digging out the two Odyssa with at least some of their roots intact so I can pot them later. After a quick enchantment to give them sustenance for the journey home, I delicately place them inside my basket where they're cushioned and safe. Next, to find some safety for myself. The wind bashes the air, almost angry to see its flower friends gone, but I'm able to roll onto my shoulder and tug my basket securely on.

The mountain behind me groans.

There's a crack.

A creak.

'*Oh, g—*'

Where there once was rock beneath me, a torrent of snow slides like a waterfall, sweeping me in its current and pulling me down over the edge of the cliff and into the emptiness beyond.

My scream is a splinter in my throat as I fall, tumbling through the shower of snow with nothing to grasp, nothing to keep my stomach from convulsing. I crash into a sloping pile of snow, pain spiking in my shoulder, and barrel down farther, rolling with thunder in my ears. My descent slows, and I have barely a second to register my surroundings and fling my arms to my face. A rock juts out of the ground just ahead and I'm hurtling towards it, fast. I tuck my knees up just as my right ankle collides with the raw edge of stone and forces out another shriek.

Finally at a halt, I curl inward on the snow, gripping my hands around my ankle and shuddering for breath. *Gods. Fuck. Ouch.* The throbbing in my ankle tells me it's probably broken and there's an awful twinge in my left shoulder. I'm so stupid. Why didn't I ask anyone for help? Why didn't I make Card come with me?

I know why. Because I would've felt guilty about taking up so much of his time. He's got his wedding planning, language learning, *important* matters. Anyone who I'd have brought here would have told me I'm mad. They'd have called it a heedless quest. They . . . they just wouldn't have understood. They don't have to walk through life constantly proving themselves like I do.

With a sniff, I shuffle up to sitting and press my fingers against my left shoulder. Under the wet cloak, the muscles are tender and aching, but I can rotate it. Slightly. Just a little. So it's not dislocated. But my ankle . . .

Taking stock, I flip open my basket lid to check if the flowers survived the fall – thank the gods they look unharmed – then cast my eyes around to find myself on a slope that stretches towards a grove of pine that cascades down the mountainside. With the cliff at my back and frozen clothes, I'm stuck. Stranded. Panic creeps in like the chill. What can I do? Could I crawl my way to the pine? Would there be any healing flowers in the cluster of trees? Or any birds? Could I somehow get a message back home or—?

Gods, I don't know. I can't think. My ankle spasms and I can't breathe and there's no relief or comfort or saviour or warmth or miracle, there's no one coming, no one—

'Hello?' a voice calls from within the pine.

I *weep*.

It comes again. 'Is someone there?'

'Hello! Over here!' I cry, and hastily wipe my face to see clearer.

A girl jogs out from the line of trees, her brown hair in a long braid down her back, bow in hand and countless satchels and pouches attached to her thick outdoor clothing – much more suitable than what I'm wearing. She spots me and sprints over the snow with ease, tossing her bow aside as she kneels next to me.

'What on earth are you doing out here?' she asks me, rooting in her leather side satchel.

I'm so stunned by her arrival that I can't answer. The girl raises her caramel-coloured eyes to mine and presses a glass vial of amber liquid into my numb hands.

'Drink this,' she orders. 'You're frozen stiff.'

Fighting the rattle in my bones, I lift the drink to my dry lips and tip it down my throat. Like the clouds parting, warmth seeps into my veins and the shivers retreat. I swallow every last drop desperately, and when the remedy has reached the tips of my toes, I exhale and find my words.

'Th-Thank you,' I stutter, then lick my lips to get my mouth working again. 'Gods, thank you. I thought— I— Thank you.'

The girl sits back in the snow with one knee raised, as comfortable in these conditions as a deer. She doesn't look too much older than me but there's an edge to her posture like she's ready to flee at any second, and from the dagger at her hip and the arrows strapped to her back, she doesn't look like anyone I know from the citadel. She's familiar with these mountains. *Thank the gods.*

'What are you doing out here?' she asks again as I pass back the empty vial.

'I was looking for a flower on the mountainside and I fell.'

'In *those* clothes? *Are you crazy?*'

I expect more of a scolding, but she lets out a laugh that dances on the breeze and leans back to take me in – the basket on my back, my damp dress and cloak, my outstandingly obvious lack of preparation.

'I, um, I didn't know what to expect. I don't usually come out here . . .'

'Clearly! *No one's* going to believe me back at camp. When I think I've seen everything!'

'Would you . . . Would you be able to help me get back to the citadel? I think I've hurt my ankle and shoulder.'

She pauses.

'What's your name?' she asks with an extra lilt of kindness.

'Fliss.'

'I'm Pigeon,' she says, and motions to the ankle I'm gripping. 'Can I take a look?'

I nod and let her inspect my foot.

'I think it might be sprained, perhaps a tiny fracture,' she says, then glances at the cliff. 'You fell from *up there*?'

'Yes.'

Pigeon chuckles, strands of hair falling from her braid. 'Who knew the citadel folk could be so hardy? I thought you were all dull and stuffy.'

What does she mean? Perhaps some aren't as used to the outdoors as Pigeon, but . . . Wait, come to think of it, I've never met anyone who lives outside the citadel before. (Besides Willoh Vane, who does not count.)

A thrill of excitement runs through me. That means Pigeon doesn't know I'm cursed. I'm a clean slate.

'Why do you think that?' I ask.

Pigeon roots around in one of her satchels again and brings out a roll of bandages. She peels off my shoe and sock and starts to wrap the fabric around my foot.

'I mean, those tall walls, the big, tough guards at every entrance. You live in a cage.'

'Oh . . . I've never thought about it like that.'

She sighs, her hands working swiftly. 'It didn't use to be so bad, but those musty uptight royals share less and less with us as time goes on, believing we're a bunch of miscreants who bit the hand that fed them. Anyway, it means I have to come up here to hunt or head over to the coast to get by. That's why I'm here today – lucky for you, I guess!'

Hesitation grips my throat. She's from the north. If what the rumours say is true, then shouldn't Pigeon be corrupted by the tree? Shouldn't she be threatening and hostile? Isn't that what they say all the northerners have become?

The discrepancy brings to mind a man in the town square, not long after the incident first happened. I'd been thirteen at the time, coming home from school with Card, when we'd noticed guards detaining a man, perhaps in his forties, with greying hair and dirt-splattered clothing.

'Tell us what happened!' he'd yelled, struggling against the grip on his arms. 'Tell us why the land is turning barren! The harvest . . . We can't—'

I had grabbed Card's hand in surprise. The queen herself was in the mix, chin raised in refusal to meet the man's eyes and flanked by guards. At that point, she'd summoned me to her chambers only a few times, but it was enough to have me petrified of her.

'We sent you aid. Food. Supplies,' she declared, a slight tremor to her tone, and took a step away.

'We can't rely on handouts forever – we've told you this! We need to stop the spread and restore the land. It's making people sick, it's . . . My wife . . . She—'

The man had lunged at the queen in desperation, and before the guards could subdue him, he ripped a tear in the queen's sleeve. Immediately, the guards hoisted him away, probably to the dungeons, and the man's shouts had turned to sobs. His pleas had turned to accusations. 'Isn't anyone coming to fix it? Won't anyone tell us what happened? You're murderers! Murderers!'

Around me, whispers were already spreading. *What a scene. Did you see him attack the queen? There must be something wrong with him. How violent! Gods, those northerners are ungrateful. After all the help they've been given . . .*

It was the last time the queen had been seen outside the castle walls.

And it was the reason behind the citadel changing sympathies towards the north.

Despite witnessing that, and despite all the rumours I've heard, Pigeon doesn't seem dangerous to me.

'Do you live in the mountains, then?' I ask her.

With my ankle snug in her bandages, she puts my shoe back on and smiles.

'We live wherever we want. When the land started to wither, the citadel shared plenty of food with us at first, but they never wanted to investigate further and resolve the root of the problem. Maybe they can't resolve it. It's some pretty dark magic, after all. But either way, more transparency would have been nice, and having to live off limited rations instead of being able to fend for ourselves, well . . . hungry people make angry people. Generations of farmers had their entire livelihoods grind to a halt. It was devastating, and we were told by the royals to be satisfied with the provisions they gave us and not ask questions. Anyway, after some of the villagers started to get sick too, people abandoned their homes and moved farther south. A few of us stayed. Mostly we camp in the forest. I don't mind it actually, but it'd be easier if we had enough to go round.'

The king and queen had assured the citadel that they would send aid to the affected villages. I've seen carts heading out of the citadel loaded with supplies, albeit less so these days. So if what Pigeon says is true, why did their help come with limitations? How could Bash let this slide? Surely Card can't be barrelling into a commitment with someone who would sit back and allow people to be displaced, to go hungry?

'If I'm from the citadel, then why are you helping me?' I ask.

'Fliss, you climbed the Spinal Steppe in a *cotton dress.* You're made of strong stuff, but no one should be left to fend for themselves. My help costs nothing.'

She thinks I'm . . . strong? It sinks in that I haven't made a new friend in a very long time. I haven't been able to. Even when I was young, it was impossible. Back in school, anytime there was an argument, the teachers would always make me tell them what happened, even if I wasn't involved. I had less control over my words as a child, and I discovered quickly that staying silent got me in trouble too. So I snitched when someone broke a glass window with their ball. I ratted out who stole all a teacher's candles. And when it was time for the summer solstice dance, I accidentally let slip who one of our classmates had a crush on. Then promptly got slapped. I'm not like Card, who glows with confidence and converses with ease. People don't flock to me. I'm a wary acquaintance, someone to be polite to in case I go running to the queen.

Gods, I really want Pigeon to like me.

All I can manage is 'Thank you.'

Pigeon stands and dusts snow off her coat. 'Come on, let's get you out of here.'

I hobble up. She hooks my good arm across her shoulders, then holds me around my waist for support. With a squeeze of my hand, she smiles.

'Can you try to walk?'

I attempt a step on my injured ankle and pain shoots up my leg like a punch to the nose. It has me reeling, so I inhale and focus on the pine scent of Pigeon's coat. Keep a cool head like her and I'll be home in no time.

'Okay, good job,' she says, unperturbed. 'Slow is fine. I have a horse at the bottom of the ridge, and I can take you to a healer who'll fix you up. Once we're down the mountain, we'll head there.'

We shuffle forward in the snow, Pigeon carrying most of my weight. With her around, I'm confident I'm not going to die anymore. It takes a while, but we eventually reach her horse, and she rides in front as we make our way down the mountain, until the snow fades to stone, and farther on, until the trees welcome us back to ground level. The overcast light beyond the canopy casts hazy shadows as she encourages me to keep talking to distract from the pain and cold. I'm telling her about the white flowers I've been researching for my best friend's wedding (with five weeks to go, it's a little too soon to cut and bunch them yet) when I notice we're heading west, and this particular line of trees looks suspiciously familiar. *Run*, something tells me. *Flee.*

Wait. Was I wrong to trust her after all?

'Oh, crap, I forgot about this—' Pigeon says.

My vision suddenly spins, and like falling off a mountain precipice, I plummet into darkness.

CHAPTER SIX

I become aware of a warmth against my forehead and the comforting scent of flowers. Pigeon is next to me, gripping my waist to keep the weight off my ankle, but the dampness of my clothes is no longer causing me to shiver. Instead, I'm dry and warm and— Did we . . .? Wait, *where are we*? Weren't we just in the forest on her horse? I'd been telling her about different types of wedding flowers when – *what*?

'Look who it is,' Willoh Vane says, taking his hand off my forehead. He stands in front of us with that infuriating smirk. 'You ended up getting past my wards after all.'

I whip my head to Pigeon.

'*This* is the healer you meant?' I ask her. My eyes dart back to Willoh in a flutter of agitation. 'Wait, *your wards*?'

'Sorry, you know I can't take her back to the citadel,' Pigeon says to him. 'I assumed someone would be home to heal her.'

'It's fine,' he replies. 'Need any supplies while you're here?'

Pigeon shakes her head, then unhooks my arm from around her neck. I wobble and Willoh reaches out to take my elbow. There's no other choice than to lean into him as Pigeon steps back and fixes her satchel straps. I'm blindsided. Has Pigeon heard the rumours that Willoh's magic destroyed that tree? He might be the cause of all her problems. *How are they friends?*

'I need to ride back to the mountain before the light disappears,' Pigeon says, then gives me a reassuring smile. 'You'll be okay from here, Fliss. Maybe invest in some warmer clothes though, and perhaps some proper walking shoes.'

'Thank you, Pigeon,' I say, 'for everything.'

She laughs. 'If you ever venture this far out of your cage again, maybe we'll cross paths. I'd best be off. Take care, you guys.'

She jogs into the line of trees, bow already in hand.

I look anywhere but at Willoh. In the centre of the wide clearing we're in, there's a beautiful pastel-stone cottage with a sloped roof and ivy clambering up the walls, the two floors separated by thick wooden lining. Beside the front door sits an idyllic bench and, in front of the downstairs window, bunches of chamomile flowers hang upside down to dry in the afternoon sun. On either side of the gravel path, wildflowers and grass grow freely across the large stretch of land. It's overrun with a lush rainbow of flora that carries a bouquet of aromas on the breeze, a sweet tangy cocktail of flowers, but there are certain sections that are tended to, organised. There's a wooden stable by the line of trees far to the left, and – is that a herb garden over there, too? Those look like planters and trellises. I'm intensely curious to further inspect this magnificent garden, but Willoh Vane tilts his head to the side and draws my gaze to him.

'Well,' he says, and quirks an eyebrow at me, 'what did you do this time, Princess?'

'Your wards were the ones that made me faint?' I bite back, not letting the topic go just yet.

He shrugs, that hand still tight around my elbow. 'Yeah. We like privacy. Usually people avoid the area, but you . . .'

He trails off and I hear what he doesn't say. I blazed right into that spell and knocked myself out. And now I turn up at his door chilled to the bone and unable to walk. He must think I'm out of my mind. Well, *fine*. I try to put weight on my ankle so he doesn't have to assist me, and a sharp stab of pain shoots up my leg. I can't help the wince that escapes.

'All right, up you go,' Willoh says, then scoops me under my knees to hold me in his arms.

'W-What are you doing?' I ask, clutching the straps of my basket and absolutely avoiding relaxing into his chest. A wave of hair falls over his eyes as he glances down at my face, just inches away.

'Huh, looks like you ended up in my arms after all.'

'Put me down!'

'Can you walk by yourself?'

'No, but . . .'

He carries me towards the cottage with ease. 'Is that another magical flower in your basket?' he asks.

'. . . Yes.'

His laugh vibrates in his chest.

'Well, let's see the damage,' he says, and a gust of magical wind opens the front door of the cottage.

Before he can carry me over the threshold, a black cat with long fur and narrowed eyes pads out and plonks itself down right in the doorway. It tucks its paws under itself as if to say it's perfectly comfy *right* here.

'Mustard, my guy. Really?' Willoh says with a groan of frustration. Mustard doesn't even blink. 'Excuse us, Your Majesty.'

Willoh does his best to step over the cat without knocking me into the doorframe.

The inside of the cottage has my mouth gaping open. It's a wide-open area bearing wood-panelled walls strewn with dried plants, various scenic oil paintings, hung lanterns, and, by a door at the bottom of the stairs against the left wall, a well-loved straw cat tower from which Mustard had perhaps just relocated. At the back of the room, a fireplace and kitchen unit hug the wall behind a large hand-carved dining table, the legs sculpted into intricate rootlike shapes, around which are four similarly engraved chairs, each with a brightly patterned cushion. Above the grey-stone fireplace, a few unlit candles sit beside small, whittled objects – including two cats, a horse, and three figures, and a smaller portrait painting that I'm nosy enough to want a closer look at.

Willoh carries me to the right, through an archway that sections the right side of the room off from the rest. This area is lined with bookshelves full of textbooks and well-organised vials and jars that have interesting wax dots on the labels. There's a simple examination bed in the centre of the space and a desk with tools reminiscent of those in Creon's apothecary.

'Where's Gill?' I ask, tucking my elbows in so I don't knock any of the vials out of place.

'Probably doing his best to avoid that nightmare on the doorstep.'

'Aw, poor Mustard.'

'Don't pity him. He's a demanding old grump.'

'I think he's cute.'

'*Ha ha,*' Willoh says sarcastically, then places me on the bed in the middle of the workshop. 'You won't be saying that when he's scratched your arms to ribbons because you're *one minute* late to give him some breakfast.'

'Don't be late for breakfast, then,' I suggest, and Willoh snorts. I drop my cloak and flower basket to the floor, but not before peeking inside to check on the Odyssa. It's a relief to see that they're holding up better than I am.

Willoh straightens the pillow on the bed and motions for me to lie down.

'So, Pigeon said you've screwed up your shoulder and ankle?' he asks. I settle back and twist my fingers together. 'You wanna tell me what happened?'

'I, um, fell down a cliff.'

Willoh cocks his head to the side. His earrings gleam in the sunlight pouring in from the windows.

'You fell down a cliff?'

'Yeah.'

'Right. Of course you did. How did you manage that?' he asks, moving to the end of the bed.

'Um, I was picking Odyssa flowers on a precipice and . . . then I wasn't.'

'Odyssa? You're really into these unusual flowers, huh?'

'It's my job,' I say.

So he *does* know where to find the flower. Card was wrong. It *hadn't* been a crazy idea.

Willoh rubs his palms together and whispers a spell. His hands spark with light, and it tightens a knot in my chest.

'What does that spell do?'

'It helps me see your injuries. They kind of . . . glow,' he explains, then hovers his hands above my right ankle. 'May I?'

I hesitate.

'Sure.'

Willoh's eyes flicker closed as he rests his fingers on Pigeon's bandages around my swollen ankle. He hums slightly as he prods and presses the area, gentler than I expect, then checks my other ankle too. I wish I could know what's running through his mind. My knowledge of healing magic is limited to tea blends and certain types of herbs, so it's fascinating to watch him furrow his brow slightly and know exactly which areas to examine.

'Is healing magic difficult?'

He glances at me, and there's a small smile in the corner of his mouth. 'For some. I can't just snap my fingers and cure you instantly. Like any magic, it requires concentration and knowledge. You have to gather information before choosing which spell to use – I'm not a mind reader.'

'Is there a spell for that? Mind reading?'

'Thinking of using dark magic, Farrow?'

'No.'

With a soft chuckle, he flattens his hands around my injured ankle and a flood of warmth soaks into my muscles. The pinch of pain eases like getting into a hot bath, and I let out a breath.

'Healing magic isn't actually my speciality,' Willoh says, double-checking the muscles around my foot with his fingertips. 'This is my mum's workshop. She says my magic is a blunt instrument and healing needs a softer touch, a steadier hand.' I'm about to reply that his hands seem soft enough to me, but I catch myself before my mouth opens. I'm glad that his attention is on my ankle because a flush surges to my cheeks.

'A sprained ankle is easy enough though,' he continues, oblivious, 'and Pigeon did a good job wrapping it up. Just don't come running to me if you need surgery. Can you rotate it?'

I do as he asks and find that my ankle feels completely healed, if not better than before.

'It's great. Thank you,' I say. He takes a step round the side of the table to lightly tap my right kneecap, just above the hem of my skirt.

'Do you kneel down a lot?' he asks. 'There's some tension here too.'

'Um, I spend a lot of time picking flowers, so . . .'

'Do you mind?'

I wave my hand for him to go ahead, if only because I'm curious. And not at all because watching him work is enthralling. A sentence I probably couldn't say out loud.

'So, you and these flowers . . .' he begins.

'What about it?' I ask, very aware of the defensiveness in my tone.

'You're really willing to faint and fall down cliffs for your customers? Do they pay extra for that?'

I scowl, but it doesn't last long, as that magic warmth diffuses into my skin again.

'I have my reasons,' I say, then find I can't keep my mouth closed. 'I like being helpful in a way that doesn't use my – well – I know I go to extremes to deliver, but my bouquets can help my customers connect, or heal, or move on. I want them to trust I can do a good job. I want them to trust *me*.'

I flush with embarrassment at what I just admitted. Willoh takes his hands from my knees and walks round to stand at my head. He presses gently into my shoulders and says nothing to rebut my confession. Is being trusted a sentiment he's also had concerns about? I'm not popular, but he's even less so.

The silence continues as he examines the muscles around my collarbone, then lifts the back of my neck off the pillow to smooth his thumbs down the top of my spine. My heart skips a beat. It's fine. It's *nothing*. I'm just not used to anyone touching me so gently. This is a professional, medical situation. That's all. I let him test the rotation in my shoulders and lift up my hands to check my wrists, and when he's healed my remaining injuries and the heat of the spell is fading, his fingers brush the side of my neck again. There's a flicker of something in my stomach that I'm determined to ignore, because when I tilt my chin back to look up at Willoh, his eyes are closed and creased in confusion.

'What is that . . .?' he whispers to himself.

'What?'

'Hmm . . .' With the barest graze, his fingertips move to my throat and all the breath goes out of me. 'You have like a . . .'

A few seconds pass. Beneath his fingers and my pounding pulse, I can feel his magic diving into my skin, into my muscles, into my voice box – *oh*.

'Wait—' I warn. In the same instant, Willoh leaps away.

'*Fuck.* Gods, Farrow – *Fuck, fuck, fuck.*'

I bolt upright.

He staggers against the nearby desk. His fingers twist, magically summoning a vial of blue liquid to his palm, and without waiting, he downs it, then slams the empty glass on the table. I catch the smell of Saint-John's-wort, a flower used to ward off evil.

'Gods above, that hurt! Fuck. Gods. *Fuck*.'

I stay quiet until he wipes his hair back and leans against the edge of the table, breathing hard. He's looking at me like I stabbed him through the stomach.

'Are you okay?' I ask.

'I've just been blasted back by a dark curse, but, *sure*, yeah, I'm great . . . Farrow, why on earth do you have . . .? You have, like, this *lock* around your throat. It did *not* like me getting close, I can tell you that.'

'I'm sorry.' He doesn't know how much I mean it. 'I, um . . .'

He massages his forehead but doesn't push for answers. I don't have to tell him. I can choose silence. But there's an urge, an ache to share, to finally talk freely about my curse with someone who *understands* magic.

'A sorcerer cursed me before I was even born. My mum said it's her fault but won't tell me why,' I say, keeping my eyes locked on him for any reaction. All he does is wait. 'Sometime after I started talking, it became evident that I . . . I can't say anything that isn't true. I can't lie.'

There it is. The big confession. The truth of my life that twists every conversation into an all-consuming torture and keeps me at arm's length from others.

Willoh runs his eyes over my face.

'The truth can be subjective,' he simply says.

I attempt a smile and a shrug. I'm not sure if it comes off as confident as when he does it.

'I've tried to find ways around it – ways to word things, like phrasing sentences in certain patterns but . . .'

Willoh folds his arms. There's a glint of something in his hazel eyes like he's stumbled across something unusual, something surprising. Something that he's never seen before. I can't hold his gaze for long and drop my chin to stare at the hands I'm twisting in my lap.

'That's why I take time to reply,' I say, and pick at a hangnail. 'I think through every sentence, every word, before I speak. My ex used to get annoyed with me. He'd say things like, "Are you listening? Did you hear me? Why can't you just spit it out?" Then he'd get mad when I said something he didn't want to hear. The truth has the ability to hurt and I have to be careful.'

'He sounds like an idiot.'

'Well, we're not together anymore.' The heaviness of Lark wraps vines around my ribs. I don't usually talk about him these days, even with Card. He's worse than a sprain in my ankle, did more damage than a fall, and I don't want to let Willoh see those injuries. There's no spell in his textbooks that can heal them. If the sorcerer notices the plummet in my mood, he doesn't show it.

'How's your ankle and shoulder now?' he asks.

I stretch the memories away. 'Much better, thank you. What do I owe you?'

'Hmm?'

'What do you usually charge for healing?'

Willoh pushes off the table and closes the distance between us, standing only an inch from my knees. My mouth goes dry as he tugs that smirk across his face.

'How about a promise?' he asks, and I have to wonder if he's teasing me on purpose. He reaches out a hand to tuck the cinquefoil flower snugly behind my ear. It must have been falling out of its clip. I'm surprised it survived the avalanche. 'You can say no. I don't know how promises or conversations about the future work with your curse, but next time you get a crazy request for a flower, promise that you'll ask me to come with you first. Only so you don't end up injuring yourself further. It does seem to be a skill of yours, and I'd hate for your loyal customers to lose their dearest florist.'

I swallow away the flutters. 'Um, I . . . um.'

'Well, don't say it out loud. Just think about it and we'll call it even.'

He reaches for my belongings, and I take them from his hands gingerly.

'Why?' I ask, and follow him to the door.

'Why not? Besides,' he replies, and throws me a wink, 'my mother would kill me for abandoning a princess in need.'

A bristle runs down my spine. *He always ruins it.*

Willoh pulls open the door again to find that Mustard has not moved an inch.

'Hey, you. Budge.' He crouches to poke Mustard's fluffy back. The cat twists his head round slowly and gives him a glare that would put Bastion to shame. 'Or stay there. Fine. Come on, Farrow, I'll walk you out.'

We step over the door guardian and out into the flower-filled garden where Willoh tucks his hands in his jacket pockets.

'You know, you can get past the wards now – that's what I was doing when you woke up; I have to press a spell to someone's forehead to give them permission to enter without fainting. But the magic protecting this place means you can't point to it on a map or tell anyone the location,' he says, leading me past some shy daffodils and through the same gap in the trees Pigeon disappeared into.

'Don't worry, I'm used to choosing my wording carefully.'

He frowns, but says nothing. Sometimes this happens when people find out about my curse. They become reluctant to reply. Reluctant to share. Besides Card, who upon finding out about my curse a few days after we met, simply shrugged, told me that words are only one way to communicate, not our whole identity, and that language changes so much over time that, in years to come, historians will argue over how many interpretations there are of my truth. He had squeezed my hand, not one to linger on sensitive topics, and immediately changed the conversation to tell me about his grandparents' recent trip to the deserts of Ject. I suppose not everyone can be as self-assured. I have to wonder if Willoh's regretting letting me in at all.

Soon the trees widen, and I spot the wild crocuses that bloom outside the citadel, adding colour to either side of the dirt path. They're wilting slightly today, which is strange for spring.

Willoh comes to a stop. 'You know where you are now, Farrow?'

'It's Fliss. Felicity. Farrow is my last name. Um, thank you for your help, Willoh.'

'Ouch, so formal. Will is fine.'

'Then thank you . . . Will.'

I open my mouth again. Close it. I find myself wanting to stay, wanting to ask a thousand questions I shouldn't. Why do Bash and the queen hate him so much? What exactly happened five years ago? Why does he have wards around his house, and why can Pigeon get through them? Also, off topic, but who whittled all that cute furniture? Because I'd truly love some for myself.

I say nothing, as usual, and take a step away.

'Try not to injure yourself on your way home, Princess,' Will calls. I shake my head, and he turns back in the direction of the cottage.

It isn't until after I've greeted Godfrey at the gates to the citadel that I realise the questions in my mind are a bud unable to bloom. Questions I've actively avoided for years. They're going to gnaw away at me from now on. Right beside them, the memory of Will's hands on my skin refuses to shrivel, digging a home like the roots of an oak tree. I know that I'll be keeping the promise he asked of me.

It's almost disappointing to find the submission box empty.

CHAPTER SEVEN

The air in my tiny greenhouse is thick, like a fever under glass-walled skin, but it might be one of my favourite places in the world. It's nice to get back to some familiarity after working with the unusual power of the Odyssa all of yesterday. I'd studied the twin flowers for as long as I could allow myself, enchanting and inspecting and sketching until my fingers ached, but eventually, I had to pack them up and leave them in the collection box. I was worried they would wilt without the winter weather conditions, but neither flower showed any signs of weakening. And just like with the Feiyan, the welcome sum of ten gold was left behind and nothing more.

I'm clipping away at my collection of coloured roses when the chime of the door pulls me back to reality.

'Just a moment,' I call out, placing my pruning shears next to the jug of sugar water I've balanced between pots – just another reminder that my flowers will be fighting for space if I can't invest in a bigger greenhouse soon.

I leave behind the overpowering smell of roses and enter my shop through the back door. There I find Marceline, my part-time delivery girl, bouncing on her toes, her auburn hair in two braids beside pink windswept cheeks. It surprises me that she's here already. It must mean it's later in the day than I thought. Time often distorts in the greenhouse, like it's on a different beat from the rest of the world.

'Got anything for me?' Marceline asks, unable to still the energy in her limbs.

'I do,' I say, fetching a bouquet I'd prepared this morning. It sleeps in a thin blanket of pastel-blue paper, tied together with a white ribbon. 'I have this for Drew Maccan.'

'Oh, he lives next door to the bakery, right?'

That's why I trust my deliveries to Marceline. She has an incredible memory and can recite addresses to perfection. Marcie has been helping out for a few months now, after our mums got to talking at the tearoom. She needs practice interacting with people, her mum had said. I need not mention how relieved customers must be to see a face other than my own.

I pass over the bouquet of deep-purple gladioli, dainty forget-me-nots, and white wind anemones – a bouquet that speaks of a heroic love and the hope that it isn't unrequited – especially after I worked my magic to bring out the emotions.

'Yes, it's from the baker's son, Rane. There's a card in here, so make sure it doesn't fall out.'

'Of course, miss.'

'And remember to go straight home after.'

I tuck Marceline's flyaway hair behind her ears so it doesn't get in her eyes and open the front door for her. She skips down the street in the direction of the bakery, and when her animated frame is out of sight, it's time to get back to my roses. I'm reaching for my shears when the bell above the front door rings again. She's probably forgotten something.

'Back so soon?' I ask, stepping back into the shop.

I stop dead. It's not Marceline. Gods, I wish it was.

Lark stands before me, not in his usual guard armour, but in a green cotton shirt that matches the hue of his eyes and the sickness that twists my stomach. He brushes his blond fringe to the side.

'I wouldn't call this soon,' he says, and it has me wishing I'd kept the shears in my hands. Just in case. You never know.

'What are you doing here?'

He takes in the flowers that line the edges of the room with a small smile. How dare he take any sort of joy in *my* flowers? I'd rather they wilt away than suffer his presence. No, I don't mean that. They don't deserve to wither because of him.

Then again, neither did I.

'Can we talk?' Lark asks, and takes a step forward.

I take a step back.

'We are open for *paying customers*,' I say, determined to keep my composure. He'll never see me break again.

'Fliss, I only want to—'

'If you have a business transaction to make, then yes. Otherwise, get out.'

Both of us are surprised at how fast I reply. I hadn't lied to Willoh the other day; Lark used to get so annoyed at my slowness to speak, my methodical, mindful word choices. However, now that I think about it, it was probably his increasing pressure that caused my response time to get worse. Without the fear of pleasing him holding me back, I can talk just fine.

Lark studies me, then strides to the nearest pot, plucks out a flower, and holds it out.

'Then I'll take this one,' he says, and places it on the wrapping table in the centre of the room.

'Really?'

'Really,' he says, and gestures for me to approach the table.

'Do you even know what that flower means?'

'It means that I can keep talking to you.'

I clench my jaw. He's not wrong. Still, the flower lying on the table has me struggling to keep a smirk off my face. I take slow steps and pick up the stalk of asphodel. *Unceasing regret. Despair.* Usually used in mourning bouquets. Well, if he wants to feel that way, then I shouldn't refuse him.

'Enchanted and wrapped up, please,' Lark says, knowing it will take longer.

'Five copper.'

The coins are placed on the table and begrudgingly, I pinch the end of the stem, winding my magic into the flower and feeling for its connection to the earth, to the emotion, searching for the thread. I've made a lot of bouquets with asphodel in my time, so I know just how to hook out the magic inside. Asphodels are sharp. The sorcery inside them feels like a barbed shell, imprisoned by its own grief. It takes a patient hand, the soft brush of their white petals, and an understanding of the cage they keep themselves in. If I wind my magic just right, I can coax the asphodel's emotion to the surface and create an enchanted flower that cries out in regretful agony. As I work, half my mind meanders in the flower's magic, and half keeps a watchful eye on Lark.

'I heard you went north recently,' he says.

'And?'

'You need to be careful.'

Gosh, thank you, I want to say, but I don't want to genuinely thank him for his concern, so I can't. Lark folds his arms. He knows what my silence means.

'Did you go alone?' he presses.

'I left the citadel alone, yes,' I say, to avoid revealing I met Will and Pigeon out there. 'Card and Bash are busy these days, so I didn't ask them to come with me.'

Lark's broad shoulders rise.

'*Prince* Bastion and his consort have duties to attend to,' he says, with a drop of bitterness. It's not my fault he has to address them like that. Lark used to join us outside the citadel too. He was there for hot, lazy summer walks in the grass, winter evenings in Bastion's chambers with wine and wild stories. Now he has to treat Bash like the rest of his subjects do – with a distance and respect that Card and I can bypass.

When I drag the last of the asphodel's power to the surface, Lark moves round the table and closes the space between us. I flinch away like he's fire, scorching every defence I've built.

'Fliss, I'm being serious. You can't be going off into the northern forest alone anymore,' Lark says. He takes my shoulders and his sandalwood scent washes over me. I *hate* how nice it smells. It was the first thing I'd noticed about him that day in the training yard, when I'd hung back waiting for Card to finish flirting with Bash. Lark had wandered over, a rookie guard-in-training from the south, and done what many people are reluctant to do with me – smile and say hello.

'Let go of me.'

He does. A sting of tears threatens the back of my eyes. *Just concentrate on working, on choosing some wrapping paper, on folding it around the flower.* I select a ribbon (the cheapest one) and tie it to the bottom, flooding the package with a spell that will keep the flower alive and healthy for much longer.

'There are rebels out there,' Lark continues, his hands now clenched at his sides. 'They've been attacking the trading wagons more frequently, and you know what happened to Simon. That explosion might not be a one-off. You have no idea what kind of security we're putting in place to prepare for Prince Merit's return.'

'I've come back unharmed so far,' I say. I don't mention the injuries that were gained and healed *while* I was gone, but my point still stands.

'Fliss, you're not listening to me.'

'I don't need *you* to tell me what to do.'

'I'm only trying to help.'

'I don't want your help!'

The truth of it knocks at Lark's persistence. He runs his eyes over the tight press of my mouth.

He drifts into that velvety tone. 'Fliss . . . how long will it be until you stop looking at me like that? You need someone to protect you.'

'Protect me? I don't— You—' My tongue trips over all the curses and exasperation I can't find the words for.

He thinks I'm *weak*.

Lark skims a finger over a petal of the asphodel in my shaking hands. The enchantment must sink in. It doesn't take much for the emotion to bleed out once I've triggered the magic. Unfortunately for me, unceasing regret and despair are just what prompts Lark to lift a hand to my cheek and gaze deeply into my face. His skin is rough from years of sword training. Compared to Willoh's hands, they're—

'Fliss, I'm *sorry*. I can tell you every day if that's what it takes. I shouldn't have—' He cuts himself off.

'No, go on. Tell me exactly what you *shouldn't have* done.' I push him back, twisting out of his grip. Let him squirm. Let him suffer. He only wants the attention and applause. The boost to his ego. The proximity to the royals. But he can't handle my honesty. His pride can't take the hits. That was our breaking point after all.

Ten months ago, Bash and Card's engagement celebrations around us, drinks in hands and music playing, he'd flipped. Exploded. Irrationally, I'd thought at the time. I didn't see the signs until it was too late.

Earlier on when we'd been getting ready, he changed into a dark suit bought with his new earnings and asked me how he looked. I said he looked nice, how he always looks, and didn't understand why he got annoyed at that. I reminded him that I couldn't exaggerate. I literally could not tell him he looked like the falling stars, or whatever romantic compliment he was fishing for.

Later on, at the party, we were mingling with a few of his guard friends, and one had made a joke about missing his kid's bedtime story, saying how he'd have to ask his wife to catch him up on the plot. I opened my mouth before I could think about it.

'Yeah, Lark didn't want to come either,' I said, which was the truth. He'd had a hard day of training and had a slight headache.

The look I got from him was acidic.

I knew I'd said something wrong but didn't want to ruin the party, so I excused myself and clung to Card's side for a while. When Lark caught up with me, he was sulky and needy, complaining I was spending too much time around my best friend. I gave him a confused frown and said that the point of the party was to celebrate *their* engagement, not *us*.

'Gods, why are you so difficult?' he yelled, loud enough for onlookers to hear.

I jerked back.

'What are you talking about?'

'I mean, you and your *fucking* words.'

'My . . . *what*?'

'You just can't say anything supportive, can you? *No*, you have to be a fucking nightmare! You take every chance to embarrass me. It's like you *want* people to be uncomfortable around you!'

My world had plummeted. All the anxious thoughts I'd had about us were coming true. I was hard to be around. I was hard to communicate with.

I was hard to love.

So I shouted back. Told him he was controlling. Told him he was too arrogant, too critical of his peers – things I'd previously kept to myself for fear of losing him. I couldn't see through my tears when Card pulled me into his arms. Bash dragged Lark out. Threw him out of the party and sent him to Ava for a behavioural assessment. And by the next day, the whole citadel knew.

The whispers that agreed with Lark hurt the most.

I shove the flowers into his chest.

'Get out of my shop. You can help me by staying as far away as possible.'

'Fliss—'

The chime interrupts and Tarin, dressed in leather armour, short dark hair tucked behind their pale pointed ears, opens the door with one hand. As a guard-in-training, Tarin immediately hesitates, thrown off by finding their senior here. Lark's jaw is clenched and he's gripping the asphodel.

'Miss Felicity,' they say, their eyes jumping between the two of us.

'Tarin, please come in,' I reply, delighted to have any other company.

'I only came to deliver this from Master Cardamine,' Tarin says, and brings forth a yellow elecampane flower, its thin trails of petals not too dissimilar from a sunflower.

Elecampane means one thing.

I snatch the flower out of Tarin's hand, my pulse rocketing.

'Are you sure this is from Card?'

'Y-Yes,' Tarin stutters.

Forgetting everything else, I fly into action, dashing forward to turn the shop sign to CLOSED and grabbing my keys. I yank open the door and wave my hand urgently.

'Everyone out,' I order. I'm so panicked I'm hardly able to see. Elecampane from Card is an SOS. A call that I should run to him immediately.

'Fliss—' Lark begins, but Tarin hoists him out. I don't care what they do once I've locked the front door. It's not as important as Card being in distress.

I race in the opposite direction Marceline went earlier and head towards the castle, practically running over the drawbridge and through the courtyard. Howell is there at the large double doors and with the experience of a longtime guard, he opens them for me with a hand clenched in a fist over his heart. Even now, after years of being granted entry to the castle without question, I can't help but think about how this is not a privilege most have. I often wonder if my access adds to my 'otherness', or whether it might be one of the few places I'm accepted – even if it's on the queen's orders. I know where the hallways and stairwells lead, and when I reach Card's quarters, I don't even knock. I throw the door open and stand there panting, the elecampane drooping in my hand.

'Fliss!' Card sings with a grin. 'Come on in, my darling.'

I heave a deep breath and stare at him. He's lounging on a sofa in his parlour, a goblet in hand and no emergency to be seen. Nettle, resident tracker and Captain Ava's partner, reclines in a chair to the side, eyeing me as she always does, with a haughty indifference. I told Nettle she had food in her teeth when we first met, and she's hated me ever since. One of Card's wedding planners stands by the fireplace, holding what seems to be a type of cravat, next to a variety of fabric squares laid out on a low table. Card leaps up and pushes a spare goblet towards me. I catch a waft of wine, and prickle.

'Card, I closed the shop for this.'

'Good, we'll have all afternoon, then. Sit, sit.' He tugs me down onto the sofa and gestures for the wedding planner to continue. 'Eurain here was just showing us some fabrics and I want your opinion. Which shade do you think I should choose? Should I go for a cravat or a tie?'

I'm still reeling from the whiplash of his signal, so I blink at the samples. I hear a small snigger and when I look over, Nettle is hiding her mouth behind her drink. Her brown skin reflects the gold of the goblet, and when she catches my eye, she shakes back her tightly coiled hair as if she couldn't care less if I were here or not. It's at times like these that my envy over Card's collection of friends rears to the surface. Swiftly followed by guilt for feeling that way. It's not anyone's fault that he's better at socialising than I am.

'Yeah, Fliss, what do *you* think?' Nettle says, and crosses the legs of her hunting trousers, revealing a small knife sheathed on her thigh.

I sigh.

I take a sip of wine.

I stow my annoyance away.

'Go on, then, show me the choices.'

Card's beam stretches across his wine-flushed cheeks. I smile. I won't tell him about Lark – just like I didn't tell him about Pigeon or Will. This is my best friend's wedding after all, and there's just over a month left until the big day. I can put myself aside for him for that long. It's not like I haven't done that before. And with the guilt of ruining his engagement party – no, of *Lark* ruining his engagement party – I owe it to him to make his wedding the most perfect it can possibly be.

I end up being persuaded to try on my maid of honour dress to check for alterations, and with pins in place, I twirl myself in front of a large ornate mirror. The skirt is beautiful – magnificent, even – made from layers of shimmering periwinkle fabric that twinkle in the light. It's fit for a princess. Like Will called me. I can't imagine what he'd make of this dress. Would he make a typical sarcastic remark, or would he do what Lark wanted me to do, and tell me I'm a star fallen to earth?

A sudden blush spreads across my cheeks, and I glance at Card and Nettle. For once, never being the centre of attention works in my favour. They don't notice my panic. Well then . . . maybe they also won't notice if I take another trip into the northern forest.

CHAPTER EIGHT

I wait a week. It's less of a choice and more that it's the earliest I can get out of the citadel, what with Card summoning me to the castle every day on top of my usual workload. There's always something else to plan for the wedding – now less than a month away – and he *always* wants my opinion. There's the decor, ranging from the flowers that he's given me full control over, to the table decorations, napkins, ribbons, and abundance of formal tableware that I have no experience with; the handpicked guest list that includes royals I've never heard of who need specific seating arrangements (I don't understand how Card expects *me* to be able to offer insight on that); the orchestra arrangement, what instruments they'll play, where they'll sit; and the food, which actually hasn't been that frustrating to help out with. I'm more than happy to sample different flavours of wedding cake, and there's plenty left over for me to fill a basket the morning I plan to visit Will.

It sends a thrill down my spine to use 'Will' and not 'Willoh'. Will.

I wake up extra early so I can get ready before Card can send one of the guards to my door, and even though I'm yawning the whole time, I'm out of the house before Mum comes down for breakfast. She doesn't have a shift at the tearoom today, so she can take care of any customers, like she does all the other times I need to leave for the day. I hope the short note I left for her suffices. Although my curse doesn't allow me to speak lies, there are no restrictions when it comes to writing, which I suppose makes sense after Will confirmed that the curse is wrapped around my voice box. My hands don't freeze up like my throat does, but whenever I've tested it out, gestured or written something untrue, it always gives me this nagging, burrowing guilt in my stomach. So instead of making something up, I simply wrote that I'll be out all day and left it at that. No details.

Dawn is a haze of pastels and sleepy shuffles as the citadel wakes around me. I pass the bakery, inhaling the smell of fresh bread from the dimly lit kitchen, and smile. The bouquet I'd had Marcie deliver from the baker's son had been a success. I'd caught wind that Drew, the recipient of the bouquet, had stormed right into the bakery, flowers in hand, and gone on a rant, saying that he assumed they were already dating and that Rane was a complete idiot for thinking otherwise. The rant had lasted until Rane interrupted him with a kiss. Gods, I love my job.

When I leave the citadel, I glance back at the formidable stone walls and armoured guards posted at the northern gate. Hmm, I guess if I were Pigeon and if I'd only ever lived in a small village surrounded by trees, I suppose that sight *would* be pretty intimidating.

I continue into the forest though nerves start to nibble at my insides. I've been desperate to do this all week, but now that I'm on my way, I wonder if this is a good idea. I know I can get past the wards, but would Will feel comfortable with me turning up without warning? The barrier is there for a reason, and he said he liked privacy . . .

In the clearing, the cottage is as beautiful as ever, and now that we're in the middle of the morning, the wildflowers are open and swaying. Bees and butterflies flit around my knees, and ahead, at the end of the pebbled path, the sun paints half the slatted roof tiles in light. To the left of the ivy-framed front door, a fluffy white loaf snoozes on the bench in a patch of sunlight.

'Good morning, Gill,' I say to the cat, and scratch between his ears. He raises his head and blinks slowly. 'Anyone home today?'

Gill unfurls his paws and has a long, arched-back stretch before deciding he'd like to see what I'm up to. He hops down off the bench and winds himself between my feet.

'Coming too?'

If Will is in a bad mood, having Gill here will hopefully make him less annoyed that I've come out of the blue.

I knock on the door and wait. There are a few seconds of silence, and when the door swings open, a woman around my mum's age stands before me in a stained navy apron over a simple blouse and long skirt. Her hair is the same warm brown as Will's, cut short like a pixie and her eyes – I hold in a gasp. Perhaps they were hazel once too, but the irises have clouded over to a soft beige like a milky tea, and instead of trying to focus on me, she closes them all together.

'Hello,' I squeak, gripping my basket in both hands. 'I'm sorry to disturb you. I, um . . .'

'I don't think we've met before,' the woman says, her voice resonant and reassuring. 'I assume you're the one my son let through the wards recently?'

'Yes . . .'

After all the anticipation, I'm unsure what to do next. This is Will's mum and really, it should be his choice to let me in on this part of his life. I don't want to overstep. Gill pads through the open door into the main room and curls up in front of the fireplace. It looks cosy. Inviting.

'Would you like to come in?' Will's mum asks, pleasantly. 'Willoh's out at the moment, but he should be back shortly.'

'I don't want to interrupt. I can come back another time if you're busy.'

'Oh, you're not interrupting at all,' the woman says, and gestures me in. 'I'm Ruth, it's nice to meet you. Please, come on in. I've just brewed a pot of tea.'

I guess I am a little tired after walking all the way here . . .

'Thank you.'

Ruth closes the door behind me, then I follow her over to the carved wooden table near the kitchen. To the right, in the organised workshop where Will healed my injuries, the tools on the desk show she's in the middle of measuring out a selection of dried yarrow – a common cure for bleeding and fevers. After seeing her eyes, those wax dots on the jars start to make more sense.

'Make yourself comfortable, dear,' she says, and checks on a steaming kettle on the kitchen countertop. I place my basket on a chair and open the lid.

'I brought some flowers,' I tell her, bringing out the bouquet of delicate sweet peas and begonias I'd prepared last night. It's a classic gift to say thank you for hospitality and to repay a favour – and besides that, it's one of my favourite blends of pink. 'And cake. A lot of cake.'

'How kind. It smells wonderful! I'll fetch some plates. If you like, you can choose a vase from over there,' Ruth says, and waves a hand towards a shelf in the workshop area. I pick a thin glass one to support the fragile stems while Ruth pours out two cups of tea. Over the strong scent of sweet peas, I catch hints of berry from the teapot. An excellent pairing for all the different flavours of cake I brought.

'Have a seat,' Ruth says. 'You know, Willoh didn't tell me your name. He only said that he'd let someone new in.'

'Oh. I'm Felicity. You can call me Fliss. Either is fine.'

Ruth's mouth tightens for the briefest of moments.

'Are those cinquefoils in your hair?'

'Yes,' I say, and Ruth smiles. Almost in relief.

'I thought so. I'm glad you're here, Fliss.'

She means it. After a lifetime of noticing people's tells, Ruth's facial expressions are as open and honest as a daisy in summer. She feels like a midday sun, a warm breeze, a steady hand to hold. Much, much less prickly than my winter thistle of a mother.

I sit down opposite her, facing the front door, and hug the cup of fruit tea in my hands. Gill, not wanting to be left out, leaps up onto the table and sniffs at the liquid. I talk Ruth through the different flavours of cake on offer, that the chocolate in this slice was traded from Lucan, the citrus fruits in this one from Dreah, and even though I assumed her clouded irises to mean she's fully blind, her eyes focus on each of them with delight – perhaps she's partially sighted then. I choose a slice of strawberry cream cake, made from homegrown ingredients in the castle greenhouses.

'I brought these as a thank you to Will,' I say. 'He's helped me out twice recently.'

Ruth runs her clouded eyes over the flowers in my hair, my dyed-pink ends, and my floaty blouse. She smiles like she knows her son far too well. He did say his mother would kill him for abandoning a princess in need. Apparently I'm just the type.

'I asked him to make a delivery this morning. There's an elderly woman who lives not too far away that I make preserved sugar cloves for,' she says.

I sit up straighter and find my words flow out. I tell her how I use cloves in bouquets sometimes, and how I think it's interesting that its red flower looks like a tiny claw but people like to order them for dignified, classy celebrations. Ruth raises her eyebrows like she's impressed and counters with her own medicinal knowledge. I'd heard that the guards sometimes add it to tea before training, but she teaches me that it can help with digestion and muscle ache too. There's something about Ruth that makes me lower my guard. She knows plants. I can talk to her about flowers and have her actually *engage* with me on the topic.

'One plant can have so many uses and interpretations,' she says. 'We can always look to nature for inspiration, whether it be for a bouquet, a healing herb, or something as simple as a cup of tea.'

'Exactly!' I say, and surprise myself with how fast I react. 'My mum says the same thing. She was the one who taught me how to focus my magic and enchant the bouquets for our shop.'

She pauses and sets down her cup.

'You wouldn't happen to be Lilibeth's daughter, would you?' Ruth asks, a lightness to her tone. Her milky eyes rest on mine.

'Yes. You know my mum?'

'I do.'

'She's never mentioned you.' Well, of course not. She never tells me anything.

'We grew up together,' Ruth says.

'*What?*'

'Yes, we had a very tight-knit group, the four of us. Unfortunately, it was not meant to last, and I'm sorry to say I haven't spoken to Lilibeth in a long time. How is she?'

'She's— Wait, the *four* of you?'

I'm so eager to hear something about my mother's past, about *anything* she's been reluctant to tell me, that my heart pounds behind my ribs, cake left forgotten on the plate.

'Yes, four. Lilibeth, Morgana, Fern, and I. You'll know her as Queen Fern now.'

My mother and the queen? *Friends?* Then why does my mum refuse to talk about her?

Wait. *Morgana?*

My hand shoots to my throat.

'What happened?' I plead. 'Please.'

'If Lilibeth hasn't shared any stories with you, then I shouldn't either. It's not my place.'

'No, *please.* She's barely told me anything, even when I ask. I only know that Morgana—'

I stop. If the four of them were friends, but now live like less than strangers – one overwhelmed with paranoia, one protected by magical wards, one living in mystery outside the kingdom . . . and my mum, guilt-ridden and secretive. There had to have been a catalyst. A catalyst as big as a dark curse.

'It all fell apart after Morgana cursed me, right?'

'A lot happened,' Ruth says. 'We all made mistakes and lost things we held dear. Sadly, the rift became too vast to heal. I'm glad you came here today, Fliss. I'm grateful for this chance to get to know you now.'

My chest pangs. It must have been awful . . . I couldn't imagine falling out with Card to the point where he isn't in my life anymore. I mean, it's hard to get rid of him as it is.

'Um, I know that the difficult times might be hard to talk about, but I'd quite like to hear some stories of my mum and her friends before the fallout. If that's okay.'

Ruth beams.

It must be an hour later, certainly after midday, when Ruth finishes up a story about Mum and Fern climbing a tree so high that they got stuck and had to shout for the guards to come and help. I'm helpless with laughter and there's a joyful pink glow to Ruth's cheeks.

'It wasn't until they were back on the ground safely that Morgana told us she knew a spell to float them down. Fern went ballistic. Garland, the current king, had summoned a magical bubble to get her out of the tree while all the guards watched on. He was crown prince at the time. We all knew Fern had a huge crush on him and she was mortified. But Morgana was always like that, tricks up her sleeves that she didn't reveal until the last moment,' Ruth says, finishing off her second slice of cake – blueberry jam and vanilla sponge this time.

'My gosh, I can't imagine the queen stuck in a tree.' I laugh. 'That's amazing!' Definitely something I'll call to mind next time she has me stuck under scrutiny in that foxglove-filled room. She wasn't always so stern. She was once a teenager in a tree.

Ruth starts to top up our cups.

And the front door opens behind her.

Will strides through the doorway in a brown leather jacket, his hair windswept and a sheen on his skin from the midday sun. He kicks the door closed with his heel and doesn't notice me until he's taken a few steps into the room. His eyes meet mine and he halts like he's been caught off guard, like he's unsure if he's imagining me. Gill, who fell asleep by my feet a long time ago, instantly pads towards Will and taps a paw on his boots. It's not enough of a distraction.

'Fliss,' he says. 'You're here.'

'Yes. I am,' I reply. Then kick myself. *Obviously*.

Thank the gods for Ruth.

'Would you like some cake? Fliss was kind enough to bring some over for us, along with these beautiful flowers.'

Will pushes his hair back and I find myself watching the way the waves fall into place behind his pierced ears.

'Of course there are flowers,' he mutters loud enough for us to hear, then heads to the kitchen. He downs half a glass of water and leans against the kitchen counter, one ankle kicked over the other.

'Do you not want them?' I ask, with what I hope is a bite of mockery.

'I couldn't wish for anything more,' he replies melodramatically, then finishes the rest of his drink. 'There's cake?'

'Join us. How was Wendy?' Ruth asks.

Will takes a seat to my left and Gill hops onto his lap.

'She's fine. *Please* don't make me go again soon, though,' he complains. 'She wouldn't stop showing me her antique collection. I've heard the same stories a *thousand* times. And then I had to dodge a patrol of guards on my way back. I'm surprised I made it back before sunset.'

'She's very proud of that collection,' Ruth says, and passes Will a napkin of cake.

It's so surreal to see him here, with his mother, slouching at his own dining table, picking at a dent in the wooden tabletop and venting about chores. All the gossip and commotion, the way Bastion treats him like his worst enemy . . . it's all very at odds with what I'm witnessing here. The thought that Bash could be wrong about so much doesn't fill me with comfort.

Will lifts the napkin and looks at the contents with quizzical eyes.

'Where on earth did you get this, Farrow?' he asks.

'I . . . I know some people who had plenty of leftovers.'

'Well,' he says to Gill on his lap, 'we must be grateful that Felicity fell down that cliff, then, if the end result is a mountain of cake.'

Cocky little—

'Will,' Ruth warns, with a fondness that I've rarely heard when my own mother scolds me. He shoots her a sheepish grin.

'Have you remained injury free recently?' he asks me.

'Somewhat.'

'I was actually thinking about you the other day.'

I have to catch myself from tipping my cup over and burning myself with hot tea.

'You were?'

'I heard Reed's supply wagon was heading to Mithian from Hemlor. It's en route through Lucan right now,' he says. I wait, unsure what this has to do with Will and his thoughts of me. I would very much like to know.

'Oh, wonderful,' Ruth says. 'I hope he has some stock left. Queen Clover might buy it all up for her garden again.'

'What kind of stock?' I ask.

'Every now and then a trader brings foreign flowers to Mithian,' Ruth explains. 'Do you know it? It's a small village on the edge of the northern mountains, just before the border to Senred. The trader is old friends with the florist up there, so he occasionally loops around to drop some off.'

I frown. I've never heard of such a wagon.

'Why doesn't the trader stop off in the citadel?' I ask. The queen is always promising the best deliveries of flowers in exchange for the use of my curse. Not that I can refuse her calls, but at least I occasionally get something in return.

Will picks a white strand of cat hair off his jacket.

'Funnily enough,' he says, 'people in Mithian don't have a lot of warmth for the citadel these days. The trader would rather travel all that way himself to ensure his products actually make it up there.'

It reminds me of what Pigeon said. That our royal family hasn't been sharing as many supplies with the north of Alrick as they used to.

'How far away is Mithian?' I ask, clasping my hands together. 'Is it within a day's walk? Do you know how to get there? When will the wagon arrive?'

Will looks at me with an amused smile in the corner of his mouth, like he'd predicted my questions. The strangest feeling washes over me, like gravity took a breath to lighten its weight. The workshop behind him is out of focus. It's only Will and that stupid annoying smirk that knew I would do almost anything to get my hands on those flowers.

'Will, why don't you take Fliss up there one day?' Ruth suggests. 'You're always saying you want to be more useful.'

My heart rate rockets. A day with Willoh Vane. A whole day.

'Sure, why not?' Will says, then leans an arm over the back of his chair. I shoot him a look. Is he serious? He's actually fine with this? 'If you think you can survive a two-hour walk without injuring yourself.'

Oh, there's the witty remark.

'I think I can manage,' I say.

'Great,' Ruth says, and stands up holding the empty teapot. 'Would you like to stay for dinner, Fliss?'

I shouldn't. Coming here in the first place was a risk. Bash would kill me if he knew, but the more I learn about Will, the less I trust Bash's side of the story. And the less I want him to marry my best friend. Not to mention that the queen would torture me to find out every detail of my time here, even if it only involves sitting and having tea with one of her childhood friends. If I stay longer, I'll have more to hide. And Card knows me too well. If I get back too late . . .

I'll never be able to keep this day a secret.

I open my mouth to politely refuse, and the truth comes out.

'I'd love to.'

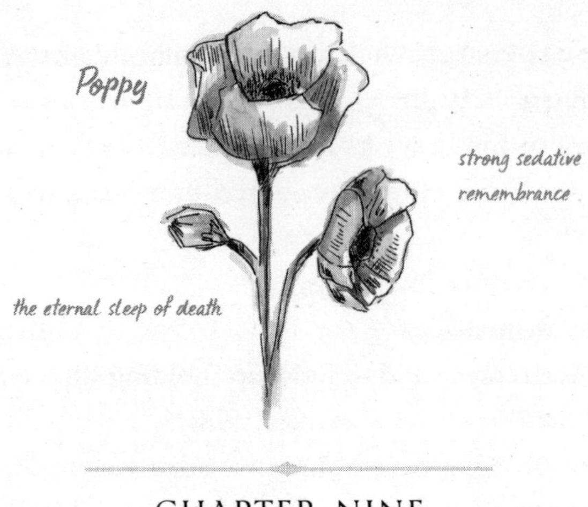

CHAPTER NINE

'Where were you?' Card asks, twirling the stem of a bright red poppy between his fingers. He's leaning against a wall in my shop and not helping at all.

'When? You'll have to be more specific for me to answer,' I say, and keep my eyes on the flowers I'm sorting into bunches. There was another attack on the trading wagons this morning and the castle requested as many herbal remedies as people could spare. Fortunately, this time no one died, but some of the guards sustained burns and grazes from an exploding trap the rebels had set.

'Yesterday,' Card says. 'I sent Tarin for you. Your mum told them you were out.'

'Doesn't that answer your question?'

I tie some string around a cluster of poppies and place it on top of the other bunches I've made. They can be used as a sleeping aid and hopefully calm any headaches or ringing ears the guards have. I've managed to fill two boxes of flowers – some dried, some fresh, all with some kind of medicinal use. I know that Creon down at the apothecary will be more useful in a crisis, but I want to help as much as I can.

'According to Godfrey, you didn't come back until nightfall.'

'Card.' I sigh. 'Why are you grilling me?'

'I had the final meeting with the fashion designer! I needed your opinion!'

Needed my help. *Wanted* my help. I've heard this more than a hundred times, and it's only recently occurred to me that he's exaggerating. I'm sure he was absolutely fine without me there.

'It's not my wedding. It's your choice to make.'

'You're the maid of honour. You're supposed to stop me from making stupid choices,' Card says, and folds his arms across his decorated teal shirt.

'Like what?'

'Like what if the colour of my suit clashes with the ribbons?'

A disaster, I want to say, but can't because it comes under the umbrella of sarcasm. A pang of jealousy runs through me. Stupid curse.

'I'm sure it will be fine,' I say. 'Besides, it's not about the ribbons or the suit. It's supposed to be about you and Bash.'

Card rolls his eyes at me. It's his way of saying that I don't understand because he's marrying a *royal* and they have higher expectations. There's more pressure to be perfect. Yeah, like I couldn't *possibly* understand what that feels like. Ah. Someone's sarcasm is really rubbing off on me . . .

'Are you going to help me carry these boxes up to the castle?' I ask.

He pushes off the wall and picks the lighter of the two. Because of course he does.

As we make our way up the cobbled street to the castle, a passer-by bows at him, and Card nods in response. He's not royal yet, but the townsfolk already treat him that way. He certainly carries himself that way. The same person clamps their lips tight and avoids meeting my eyes. *How kind*.

'I don't know why you're being so secretive about where you went,' Card says.

'You're the one making it a big deal. I went out.'

'Where?'

'Why does it matter?'

'You're being weird lately, that's why.'

I grit my teeth. I don't want to talk to him about Will or Ruth or Pigeon or anything else that's happened in the forest recently. It's been so refreshing to have my own experiences separate from Card. Or Lark. Something that's mine, where I can introduce myself as myself, not as Card's friend or Bastion's fiancé's friend or Lark's (ex)girlfriend.

'Would you like me to tell you everything I do from the moment I wake up to the moment I go to sleep?' I ask, shooting him a sideways glance. 'Or do I also need to tell you what happens in my dreams too?'

He actually looks surprised at that one.

'Like I said,' Card scoffs, 'you're *so weird* lately.'

We enter the castle courtyard and find it bustling with a variety of townsfolk already, most laden with towels, sheets, water, and anything else that could come in handy. There are a few tables set up for supplies, and from the looks of it, the court physician's clinic on the second floor of the castle isn't big enough to house all the injured guards. A frazzled energy follows everyone except Howell, who stoically sits on a makeshift bench, tightening a blood-soaked bandage around his bicep.

'Great, you're here!' Ava says after ushering a few of the younger squires in the direction of the stables. Those explosions will have spooked the horses too.

'And with gifts.' Card grins, lifting up his box of flowers. I refrain from specifying that he had no hand in organising said gifts.

'Thank you, that's wonderful,' Ava says. 'You can set them over here.'

She shows us to one of the tables where Creon has already delivered some of his own remedies. There will be plenty to help any injured guards as long as these attacks don't become too frequent. Plants don't grow fast, even for those of us with magic to speed the process.

'I've included notes about the different flowers and their uses, just in case,' I say.

Ava smiles. It's tight-lipped. Concerned. A crack in a frozen river. If she's this worried, it must be getting bad out there. Is the forest safe enough for my upcoming trip to Mithian? Well, even if it isn't, I'll be with Will. By his side is the safest place I could be.

'Thank you, Fliss,' she says, her shoulders tense under her chain mail. 'Your kindness doesn't go unnoticed. It's my responsibility to keep this kingdom safe, and with Prince Merit arriving in a few days, I must do everything in my power to ensure nothing like this happens again.'

'Have you tried reaching out to the rebels?' I suggest. 'Aren't any of them willing to talk?'

Considering it was another trading wagon carrying food that was targeted, it brings to mind what Pigeon said on the mountain, that this cage we're in keeps the best for itself. After talking with her and Will recently, I'm inclined to believe that the rebels are more motivated by desperation to feed their friends and family. But I don't know the truth, so I can't say for sure. Literally.

Ava pats my shoulder. 'That's considerate of you, Fliss, but we tried that a few months ago. Unfortunately, the peace negotiations broke down quickly.'

'What happened?'

'They demanded a personal audience with the king and queen. We couldn't ensure their safety and feared an ambush, so their request was denied. I offered to meet with them alone in a place where they had an advantage as a compromise.'

'And it spiralled from there,' Card butts in. 'How boring.'

I want to elbow him. Ava is clearly on edge, and she's not the only one.

There's a nagging feeling about the two unusual flowers I was recently ordered to find. Both were incredibly powerful, and I still have no idea who requested them. Surely if it was someone at the castle, they'd be using the flowers' magic to help the guards somehow. For all I know, I could be passing a potent magic to the rebels and adding to the tensions. The increase in guard patrols and watchful eyes, the whispers of shop owners worried about their suppliers, children being told to go straight home after school . . . I could have helped cause this chaos.

'Ava,' I say, a twist in my gut. 'The explosions . . . Are they new? They didn't have weapons like that before, right?'

She considers it.

'I think the first time we found traces of explosives was when Simon was killed. Since then, they've been frequent but less extreme. We assume they're rationing their resources.'

Okay, that was before I found the Feiyan. It's possible the flowers aren't an ingredient in these attacks. But then, what are they needed for?

Card pinches my arm and I'm shaken out of my thoughts. His warning does nothing to lessen the nausea.

'Captain,' Lark says, marching over, 'the queen wishes to speak with you.'

He glances at me for the briefest of seconds. After this fresh attack, he'd better not continue his insistence that I need a chaperone. Actually, I'd rather not stay to find out.

'Let me know if I can be of any further help,' I blurt to Ava, and walk away from the table in a random direction. Card links his arm in mine as we squeeze past two servants carrying fresh linen, and steers us towards the castle steps.

'Ugh,' I grumble, 'is it bad that I wish he was one of the guards who got injured? That's really bad, right?'

'Ha! No. By all means, wish all the misfortune you want on that prick.'

A rush of navy blue hurries out the large double doors.

'Thank the gods you two are already here,' Bastion gushes, a wicker basket in hand and a frantic pinch between his eyes. He kisses Card. 'It's absolute madness inside and I desperately need to talk with someone *normal.* Here, I just picked up some lunch from the kitchens. Come with me.'

Around the east side of the castle, there's a secluded grassy courtyard surrounded by bushes that shelter it from passing eyes. It's Bash's favourite place to hide, and it's there he leads us, almost at a run.

'My mother is having a complete meltdown,' the prince says. 'I can't deal with her anymore. If I have to listen to her complain about me not being able to use magic one more time – like, does she think I can just suddenly start conjuring spells out of nowhere? We've been through this so many times and I've had *enough*! I have *other* skills. Honestly, Merit can't arrive soon enough. It's his turn to be nagged.'

He plonks the basket of food in the middle of the grass and starts pacing. Card, probably more than used to this, sits cross-legged and starts taking out the selection of food. I kneel down beside him quietly.

'I know magic is historically supposed to run strong in our family – I mean, Merit was making objects fly before he could even talk – but it's so naive to think it's the solution to *everything*. Especially with Dad's health getting worse. These days, he can barely light a candle with magic, but *surely* that doesn't mean he's completely useless. He's the king! Gods, it's like she hasn't even heard of diplomacy!' Bash runs clawed hands through his hair.

'We can't just blast people with offensive magic whenever we want! I've given other suggestions, written drafts of possible agreements – I even counted every bag of food in our winter stores *by myself* and drew up a plan to have it rationed fairly without relying on the trading wagons. At every stage, she overrules me. I'm losing my mind.'

'Strawberry?' Card offers up, and Bash shakes his head.

'Alrick is supposed to be built on equality, peace, and justice for all its citizens. We can achieve reconciliation without magic, but it's all my fault in her eyes. Every trading wagon stolen from, every guard injured.' His steps falter and Card's eyes flicker over the sudden anxiety on Bash's face. 'I mean . . . It was . . . I suppose—'

'Babe, sit and have some food.'

Bastion does as he's told and drops to the ground unceremoniously. Card presses a grape to his fiancé's mouth, then passes me a plate of raspberries. I hold it in light fingertips knowing I shouldn't get involved in this. I should keep quiet and let Bash rant, but Pigeon's words rattle around my brain. *My help costs nothing*, she'd said. While the citadel, the queen, does nothing to help her.

It's anger that summons the words.

'I've heard that the north has been receiving much less aid lately,' I say. 'That people have had to leave their homes or fend for themselves because the citadel hasn't been transparent with what happened to cause the pollution. And that the people up there actually *haven't* been corrupted by that tree – it's just rumour. It makes me wonder what else is false.'

I am not prepared for the looks they shoot me. Bash is washed pale, his mouth open and an unfamiliar fear in his eyes. Card is similarly stumped, a crease between his eyebrows like he's stumbled across a language he doesn't recognise.

'Where . . . Where did you hear that?' Bastion asks, breathless, like the words winded him.

'Oh. Um.'

'Fliss, I never normally do this,' he says, unblinking. I've never seen him like this before. So desperate. So scared. 'But I need you to tell me.'

Tell him the truth.

Just like his mother.

I look aside and grip the plate in my lap. I shouldn't have opened my mouth. I know better. I screw my eyes tight and take a shuddery breath. Pigeon was kind to me. She saved my life. I don't want to put her on the radar of the royals she mistrusts.

'Please don't make me answer,' I whisper.

My words roll through Bastion like an ocean wave. He sits back, a tinge of embarrassment on his cheeks.

'Of course. I'm sorry, Fliss. I apologise. I – I forgot myself. It won't happen again.'

Card glances between us. After a beat, he quotes, '"Mr Wolf, what could I possibly have to offer you, when you are strong and fast, and all in our forest know your name?"'

We both eye him, confused.

'Don't you remember, Fliss? Our junior school play,' Card says, casually helping himself to some of the snack-size sausages. '*The Wolf and the Rabbit.*'

'I remember,' I say.

'I played the wolf, of course,' Card says, grinning at Bash, 'and I persuaded the teacher to allow Fliss to be the rabbit despite her being the shyest child alive. Fliss had the cutest costume, didn't you? This little tail and fluffy ears. You should have seen it, babe. I wanted to wear a real wolf head but they wouldn't let me. My grandparents have a painting of us actually. I'll have to dig it out. Anyway, near the end of the play, you know when the wolf has visited all the other forest animals for help and returns to the rabbit, you were so focused on your lines—'

I give him a small smile and finish his sentence. 'I tripped backwards and almost fell off stage.'

Card's laugh makes Bastion's shoulders relax.

'I have *never* in my life had to try so hard to keep a straight face.'

'You were turning purple.'

'It was hilarious. One of the funniest things Fliss has ever done.'

'Well, I had to whisper "said the rabbit" after every line. Acting is too close to lying.'

'True. Anyway, the rabbit says, "Mr Wolf, what could I possibly have to offer you, when you are strong and fast, and all in our forest know your name?" And the wolf replies, "Everything, my dear Rabbit, for you are all I am not. I have much to learn and this time I will not take what is not given freely." A classic parable. One to learn from.'

He pops a grape in his mouth like he's concluded his story. Is he talking about Bash and me learning from it, or the rebels? Either way, he's clearly drawn a line under the conversation.

'I've had to memorise a lot of speeches or other texts, mainly poetry, history, legislation, the like, but I've never had to "perform",' Bash muses. 'Although . . .' There's a beat. A flash of a smile. 'There was one time Will and I stole some troubadour instruments and put on a *terrible* show for his parents. We practised for so long the night before, his dad ended up yelling at us to go to sleep. I still can't look at a lute without remembering.'

He takes a moment to chuckle to himself. It's a rare glimmer of joy. A glimpse of what once was. Then his face submits to sadness and he retreats within. Silent now, solemn, Bastion takes out a sandwich and leans on a knee, scanning the northern sky. As the prince ruminates, I try to imagine a younger Will strumming enthusiastically on a lute and Ruth clapping politely.

I bet it was hilarious.

I bet I could get Ruth to tell me more.

Card pokes my knee.

'You okay?' he whispers.

'Mm.'

He glances aside to check that Bash isn't listening. 'What you said about the north . . . Did you hear it from Willoh Vane? You didn't actually end up asking him about the Odyssa, did you? I told you it was a bad idea.'

The silence stretches past even my normally slow response time. *What?* How has he jumped to that conclusion? What did I do to make him think that? I stammer, mouth dropped open, and in my shock, am forced to confront that my heart has skipped at the mention of Will. *Again.*

Like it did yesterday, when he'd offered to clean the plates after we finished all the tea and cake we could manage. I thought it was chivalrous – until he winked at me and used a snap of magic to make them spotless. Then, when Ruth showed me around her incredible garden, the wildflowers and fauna hadn't been enough to keep me from sneaking glances over at where he teased Gill with a long strand of grass. Afterwards, Ruth explained her workshop to me, teaching me about her herbs and how, when her eyes are tired and her sight is lower than on other days, she uses sound and the small patterns of dried wax on the labels to differentiate the vials. All the while, Will sat reading a magic textbook by the fire, the warm glow highlighting the (very adorable) focused frown on his face. Every so often, he absentmindedly petted Gill's head. I helped Ruth package some of her deliveries and truly, honestly, enjoyed it all.

I didn't go home until after dinner, during which I'd finally asked about the fascinating wooden furniture I'd been eyeing all day. Ruth told me with a smile that Will's dad had been a sorcerer who used magic to enhance his carpentry, similar to my floristry, and motioned to the painted portrait on the fireplace of a man with dark curls and a glint in his green eyes. Will grew silent after that. Far away. So even though I was reluctant for such a pleasant day to end, I asked him to walk me back to the crossroads in the forest. He promised to be waiting there in three days' time for our trip to Mithian.

It's my bottle of joy, my wax-sealed secret.

Mine.

I don't want to satisfy Card's curiosity. From his reaction earlier, I'm assuming he and Bash are on the same page. Both seemed concerned that I might have heard something *true* about the north. Something that might not paint the royals in the best light.

'Willoh Vane was not the person who told me about the northerners having to hunt for themselves, no.'

Card studies me.

'Hmm. Well, I hope you'd tell me if you'd got yourself in trouble.'

I keep my face straight, but guilt laps at my insides. Card has never averted his eyes or watched his words around me. He's trusted me from the day he charged into my life, a bright-eyed chatty child, and remained glued to my side since. It's hard to consider him losing faith in me. Imagine if he knew who I was meeting and where I was heading in a few days. Imagine if he knew I was starting to trust the sorcerer more than the prince.

CHAPTER TEN

When the day of the Mithian trip finally arrives, I wear an indigo pansy in my hair for a change, the colour bleeding towards the centre like rain. They're an easy addition to any bouquet and come in a delightful variety of colours, all meaning that the sender has been occupied by thoughts of the recipient. Something very true for myself of Will. He's been gnawing at my senses like a sparrow at the window – small and subtle, but completely remarkable if you stay still long enough to pay attention.

Will is already at the crossroads when I arrive, leaning against a tree with his hands in his jacket pockets. Just the sight of him has my stomach wrapped in nettles. A sting of excitement. Or nerves. Whichever. Both. His head turns my way, and I smooth down the purple pleats of my skirt with clammy palms.

'Felicity Farrow. Did you manage to get here unscathed?'

I adjust the flower basket in the crook of my elbow.

'I *am* able to get through a day without injuring myself.'

'Apparently so. Come on, it's this way. Watch your step.'

Funny.

Will tips his head to the northern path and matches my pace. I don't know what to do with my hands, so I settle on picking at flyaway hairs of wood on the handle of my basket. A rogue word, a badly phrased sentence, and I could spoil what's starting here. However, from the small glances I dare, Will's expression is more relaxed than ever. There's something about the forest and heading north that's putting him at ease, as if the farther away from the citadel he gets, the less he has to preserve his posture, preserve the mask.

'How often do you go to Mithian?' I ask as we crest the top of a hill.

'Maybe a few times a month. My mum heads up more often to check on patients in the area and support the apothecary.'

'Isn't the apothecary in the citadel closer?'

His eyes twinkle in the sunlight that peeks through the canopy. 'Yep,' he replies succinctly.

'So . . .?'

'Mum won't go into the citadel. And I don't know if you've noticed, but I seem to stir up a bit of trouble if I go myself.' He says it playfully, with none of the aggression that Bastion has for the topic.

'Oh, I *noticed*,' I say, in an attempt to match his humour while still keeping to the binds of my curse. 'But is Ruth okay walking all this way alone?'

'Oh, yeah. She's fine. The forest is a familiar friend and there's more than one way to find a path home.'

I scan the thick line of trees on either side of us, the misshapen branches and uneven, mossy floor. Perhaps the groaning of the trees is advice, each crooked twig and forked trunk a nudge in the right direction. But even though there doesn't seem to be any immediate danger, you never know, not in this forest. I wonder if there will be more guards out patrolling – I think Prince Merit should be arriving any day now, and they'll want to get him home safely.

'The apothecary in Mithian must be wonderful,' I guess out loud, and swing my basket.

Will laughs, and it's a delightful carefree sound. 'Yes. And I suppose we'll be needing to go. I'm sure you'll gain at least one injury on the way.'

'Hey!' I jab his side, and he exaggerates a wince of pain.

'Ouch! Are all florists so violent?'

Before I can think of an impressively scathing reply that fits within the confines of my curse, we round a bend in the path and come across the unusual clearing I first saw during my search for the Feiyan – the hollow ashen-white oak tree in the centre of a shrivelled brown circle of earth, all life leeched away. The air stills – just as frail as before and just as unsettling. It constricts my lungs and sits heavy on my shoulders. I want nothing more than to walk away quickly, like I did the first time. From the silently held breath in the area, any local wildlife had the same idea.

Today though, two figures are tying a fresh braided rope around the trunk. I'm about to look at Will to gauge his reaction to the tree he supposedly cursed when I realise one of the people is surprisingly familiar.

'Pigeon!' I gasp.

She turns sharply, hand flying to her belt. Her shoulders drop when she recognises us, and a wild grin stretches across her face. Beside her is a shorter teen with blonde hair that flicks outward below her sharp jaw. She's in similar attire, aside from a few curious metal shells at her hip, which are no bigger than the head of a rose. As the blonde girl finishes tying the last knot of rope, I tread over the mud towards them.

'Well, look who it is,' Pigeon says, and sticks her hands on her hips. Her eyes jump to Will as he strolls to catch up. 'Wow, you got him to socialise? What a rarity.'

'We're heading to Mithian,' I tell her eagerly. 'There's supposed to be some rare exotic flowers in stock.'

'Pigeon. Tansy,' Will greets the girls cordially. 'Nice to see you're still in one piece.'

'I could say the same for Fliss. How's your ankle doing?'

'Great!' I say, far too fast. Calm down. Speak slowly. 'Yeah. Um, thank you again. Will did a great job of healing me.'

'I knew it,' Pigeon says with a pinch of smugness. 'And now you're on your way to Mithian together. Huh.'

'A thrilling update,' Will says flatly. 'You've just come from there?'

'Yeah, we had to stock up for . . .' She trails off and I get an uncomfortable feeling. Pigeon doesn't know about my curse, but I know all too well when people are concerned about speaking freely.

'Well,' she says, 'gotta be prepared for the day is all.'

'Sounds like a *completely normal* day,' Will drawls. 'What is it this time? Arrows or explosives?'

Pigeon folds her arms. 'You can't complain about our methods. I asked if you wanted to help and you said no.'

'Correct. I'd like to keep myself out of the dungeons, if possible. I'd hate to give the queen the satisfaction of committing an *actual* crime.'

I frown. What are they talking about?

'Don't fret, I double-check all of the phosphorus levels these days,' Tansy chimes in, tapping her fingers over those metal shells. 'There's only enough to stun.'

'Exactly,' Pigeon says. 'We didn't take that guard's death lightly. You know we're more careful these days.'

My blood runs cold. Colder than the bite of wind against my frozen limbs as I reached for the Odyssa. Colder than the mountain Pigeon found me on. My mind is having a hard time catching up. Pigeon saved my life. She helped me. But—

'You're one of the rebels,' I say.

It's the truth.

Tansy's eyebrows rise in offence.

'That's what they're calling us in the citadel, yes. Apparently, we're all corrupted with evil magic,' Pigeon says gravely. 'But we're more of a . . . volunteer group. There's about forty of us from the affected villages, and all we want is enough to survive. We're only taking back what was taken from us until we find a way to heal the land.'

I can't move.

I made the mourning flowers for Simon. I chose the marigolds and dahlias and placed them in his mother's arms. I saw her crying at the fountain for weeks.

'Fliss.'

Will's voice is outside a bubble that has me paralysed, that's shoved a dagger between my ribs as I realise what this means. I know who some of the rebels are. I know who is responsible for Simon's death. Oh gods. *Oh gods.* What do I do? I should turn them in, right? I should tell Ava. It's the right thing to do.

Is it?

Either way, the queen will find out. She'll know I'm hiding something. She'll prise it out. She'll do anything she can to wring this truth from me.

I shouldn't know this information.

I shouldn't know this.

Pigeon should have left me on that mountain.

She shouldn't have told me.

Oh gods, oh gods, oh—

'Fliss. Felicity. *Fliss. Breathe.*'

Will grabs my elbows. I blink away the sting of tears and focus on him, on that golden glint in his concerned hazel eyes. The coil of roots in my chest calms. Not for the first time, Willoh Vane is a balm, a medicine as strong as the pansy in my hair. More than anything, I want him to keep looking at me as intensely as he is right now.

'S-Sorry. Sorry.'

'You have nothing to be sorry for,' he says, his grip tight.

'I-I'm not used to people sharing information like that with me.'

I'm a liability. Pigeon just shared a huge potentially devastating truth, and she doesn't know that I'm the queen's plaything or that my best friend is soon to be part of the royal family. Neither does Will. There's so much to hold inside, the pressure of the secrets stretches at my seams.

'Just breathe. You'll be okay, Farrow,' Will whispers.

He releases my elbows, brushing light fingers against my lower back until my weight is balanced again. Then his hands are gone, tucked back in his pockets, and where he touched becomes an empty, cold breeze.

Pigeon gestures to the newly tied rope, a circle of protection for the fraying bark underneath.

'We come here every now and then just to . . . remember, I guess. To pray that the life here heals, that the north heals, and that we don't have to steal to be heard,' she says, defiant tears threatening the corners of her eyes. 'We know loss. We've lost houses, farms, livestock, healthy soil, entire villages. *Fine*, we can rebuild. But we've also lost people, loved ones, and those can't be replaced. This talisman of rope is an old custom. It's a prayer for the god that died here and a prayer for those lost after. I have siblings who need to eat. Tansy has grandparents who can't walk well. What are we supposed to do? Just sit around and wait to die? The food in those trading wagons won't be missed in the citadel. There's plenty to go round.'

'They sent us a decent amount of supplies in the beginning: food, clean water, soil to place over the infertile land . . .' Tansy says, bitterly twisting her boot in the mud. 'But when we tried petitioning the royals to send for sorcerers or scientists to investigate further and find a cure, the provisions they sent started to become scarce. There were pathetic excuses at first. Accusations that we were ungrateful and hostile, as if it was *our* fault that we were angry about our livelihoods being destroyed. Eventually, they ignored all our requests, and the professionals in the citadel we contacted were more focused on the king's health. No one was listening. We had no choice but to resort to something more drastic.'

I can understand their story, but—

'Simon,' I breathe.

The girls exchange a flash of guilt.

'Was that the guard's name?' Pigeon asks quietly.

'Y-Yes . . .' I stutter, struggling to untangle the threads of who knows what, of what I can and can't say. 'Yes. He . . . He was twenty-three years old. His mother asked for orange marigolds at his funeral. He—'

I break off. The heaviness of the clearing sinks deeper into my bones. Pigeon places her palm flat against the chipped white bark.

'This talisman we make, it's for him too. It's for you too, Simon,' she says. 'I'm so sorry.'

All eyes fall to the battered oak tree. Pigeon's lost friends and family are remembered here. Simon is remembered here. Like the bouquets I put together, this tree holds his memory and mourns him.

I step forward to squeeze Pigeon's arm.

'I'm sorry for all you've been through,' I say. 'I'm sorry you've lost so much. It's not right that they didn't listen to your petitions. But, Pigeon – the captain of the guard, I know her. She's reasonable and fair. She'll hear you out. I'm certain of it.'

Ava said she feared for the safety of the royals if a meeting was arranged, but if she came herself, if she spoke to Pigeon, I'm sure they could come to an understanding. Pigeon gives me a small smile, a small shrug. 'That's kind of you to suggest, Fliss, but I don't think all in the citadel have your good intentions.'

Tansy checks a strange contraption on her waist.

'We should get going. It's almost time,' she says.

Time for what? Is there more I can do? Is there more I can say?

'Pigeon, *please*,' I urge, 'be careful.'

'Don't worry. The explosives are only to slow them down. No one needs to get hurt.'

'People have already been hurt!' I remind her, thinking of the cuts and burns I saw in the castle courtyard the other day. Thinking of Simon.

'It'll be *fine*. We'll be in and out in a blink,' Pigeon assures me.

Tansy bows her head goodbye. Pigeon starts to follow but thinks twice. Stepping close to Will, she wraps a hand around his forearm and peels up on her toes to reach his ear. A few whispered words later, he flushes bright red. *Wait*—

'Take care, you two,' Pigeon says, and hurries back to the path, 'Oh, and Will, maybe take the coastal route back to the citadel, just in case. It would be inconvenient to accidentally frame you.'

Will snorts. 'Get out of here.'

Pigeon waves and scampers after Tansy.

Are they—? Does he—? I mean, Pigeon can get through the wards. How long have they known each other? What did she say to him? I've never seen Will blush like that. I mean, I've only known him a few weeks, so I don't *really* know him—

I don't care.

Nope. That's a lie.

Oh my gods, *I care*.

'Coming, Princess? I would very much like to leave this tree as far behind as possible,' Will says.

I try my best, but I can't quite fix the smile on my face. It's the knowledge of Pigeon's rebel identity. It's the fear of what she's running off to do and the hurdles that await me back at the citadel. It's this frustrating knot Willoh Vane has my head in.

No. It's this place.

The immense gravity forcing my feet farther into the barren earth, the twisted broken squeeze in each breath. The grieving twists of rope. It's too much.

'Do I need to carry you?' Will asks. He's trying to joke but it doesn't ring true. Not here. Not in this clearing. 'Come on, let's get this filled up with flowers.'

He takes the basket out of my limp hands and gently guides me back to the path. Each step I take away from that tree is easier, lighter. Eventually, I chuckle and rub my eyes to shake off the lingering feeling.

'There we go,' Will says, and smiles down at me. 'That place will do that to you – especially to anyone with magic. It's best to avoid it.'

'You felt it too?'

He doesn't glance back. 'More than I care to admit.'

I don't know if I should dig further. I don't know if I can handle any more harsh truths today. From the way they were talking back there, the rumours that blame Will for the tree's death seem less and less likely, but the only way to know for certain is to ask. And if he wasn't at fault, then where did those rumours start?

'What happened to it? The tree?'

For once, it's not me who takes a long time to answer. A shadow falls over Will's eyes and I instantly regret asking.

'Ego and desperation. That's what happened.'

'It feels like death.'

'It does.'

'Was it dark magic?'

'Yes.'

These short answers are most unlike him.

'Did anyone try to restore it using magic? Like the king or someone?'

He attempts a laugh. 'I did, actually. Several times. Clearly, I was unsuccessful. A few people who lived nearby tried too, to no avail. It's a spell that cannot be undone. Only time will tell if the earth will recover.'

Does Bash know that? That Will tried to heal the tree? It doesn't seem like a topic Will wants to talk about . . .

I chew my lip. 'Do you think Pigeon will be okay?'

'Most likely.'

'Is she from Mithian?'

'No, she's from Oxburg. It's a small village in the forest a short walk in that direction. No one lives there now though.' He sighs. 'Most of the spell's impact is kept to that clearing – that's the epicentre – but over time, the dark magic bled out to the surrounding areas. A few months after it happened, a nearby village noticed rot in their wood. Then their harvests started to sour, and the soil became too acidic. Some people fell sick. I think most places within a half-hour walk of the tree were affected badly, while the rest of the forest saw minor damage. Pigeon's village was one of the worst hit.'

That's awful . . .

'It sounded like she was going to attack the trading wagons again,' I say. Meaning I could get back home to find an injured friend. On either side of the conflict.

'Let's stay out their way, then, shall we?' Will says. 'I prefer my days guard free.'

I anxiously rub my fingers down the pleats of my skirt. I actually agree with that. Especially one guard in particular.

'I don't want anyone to get hurt . . .'

When I look back up, Will grins at me, and any hint of my sorrow is flung to the wind.

'Anyone? Worried about me too, Princess?'

I fold my arms with a scowl.

Not at all.

'I decline to answer that question.'

Will laughs and it's sweeter than any fruit I've ever tasted.

'As you wish, my lady.'

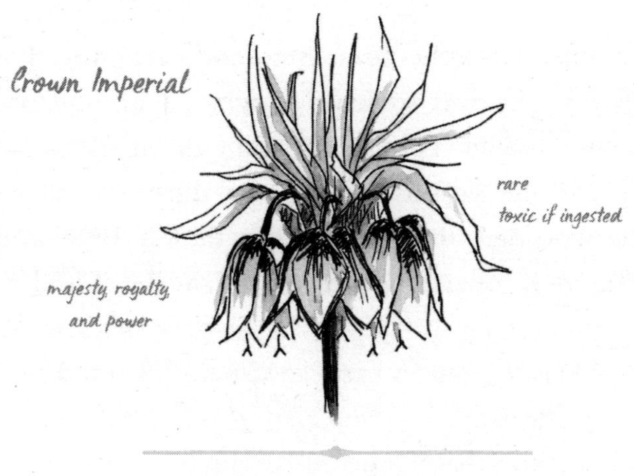

CHAPTER ELEVEN

Mithian sits on the edge of the forest, the boughs forming a leafy gateway to a village that consists of barely more than two dozen buildings. Some have an abandoned quality, with boarded windows and misplaced bricks, clinging to life like a cluster of frozen shrubs in winter. In the centre, there's a well where a thin woman hoists a bucket with too much ease, like there's barely a drop within. I hug my arms around my waist to shield myself from the frost that's trapped at the bottom of this valley – so abruptly cold, I wonder if there's magic at work – and peer towards a small bonfire at the far end of the street, near where an open-air blacksmith works in his forge. Beyond that, the fields hold shrunken wheat and a handful of cattle. Not enough to feed everyone, I'm sure.

It's just like Pigeon said.

A rustle of anger runs down my spine.

Mithian is still part of the Kingdom of Alrick. It might be close to the border, on the cusp of the outlying mountains, but these people deserve just as much as we do in the citadel. How can

Bastion let this be? Has he been here and seen how little they have? Is this why he was so worried when I brought it up the other day – because he knows and can't do anything about it? Although . . . he did say that his mother disregards all his ideas. *She's* the one who fuels the rumours that these people are beyond help by hiding away instead of showing an ounce of leadership – a failure that wouldn't be so stark if the king wasn't also absent of late. But why? Has the queen barricaded herself behind castle walls to avoid seeing the truth of the kingdom in wilful ignorance, or does she really believe that the people of the north are to be feared?

'Most of the people here are older,' I point out, and Will nods.

'That's why my mum comes up here often. They can't survive alone. I mean, sometimes a wagon makes it through the mountain pass, but the Kingdom of Senred can't give too much without stepping on Alrick's toes, and no one wants to go to war over an outlying village. They make do with scraps and support from Pigeon's group.'

'I don't understand why this has gone on for so long.'

I'm not even asking Will for an explanation. I simply can't believe, for all her anxiety and paranoia, that Queen Fern would let her people suffer like this. If she craves peace and stability, surely that means for all. I know she's been under a lot of pressure since the king's health started worsening, but there must be something I'm missing. A piece of information that would help me understand her motivations.

Will presses the small of my back towards a bungalow with a long-petalled daisy engraved on the wooden doorframe.

'A big question. One to ponder later, after we've looked at these flowers you were so eager to see.'

Will holds open the door and I shove my worries to the side for now. This is why we came, and if my purchases will bolster this village, then I am ready to shop.

The wood-walled store is smaller than my own, with less than a third of the stock, but the reassuring aroma remains the same. I take a deep breath and scan the neat rows of flowers. There's the common flora found in the forest: daffodils, crocuses, and daisies, but on a table in the far right corner next to a door leading to the rest of the house, I spy something special – a potted plant with an unusually long stem that supports a drooping orange flower and sprouts leaves from its head like messy emerald hair.

'Oh my gosh!' I say, and rush over. 'Is this a crown imperial? Will, look!'

From the back room, an elderly hunchbacked man shuffles in and steadies himself with a wrinkled hand on the doorframe.

'It is indeed,' he says, his voice croaky from age. 'A rare one.'

'I've only read about them in books before!'

Crown imperials are native to the Kingdom of Hemlor in the far south due to the land's rocky mountains, way too far for my usual supply. I reach out a hand to inspect the leaves. The magic inside greets me with a boldness that common flowers wouldn't dare. Power and nobility live within, ordering me to bow down and bask in its majesty. There's a vividness to the orange petals that reminds me of the golden band Bash wears around his head for formal events. It's rare, all right. Rare and royal. *A perfect wedding gift.* There's three weeks to go until the big day. If I keep it potted or plant it in my garden, then add some enchantments, it'll certainly still be thriving by the ceremony. And ancient Hemlorian was one of the first languages Card mastered, so to be given this native flower . . . he would lose his mind.

The old man wobbles a smile and glances over my shoulder.

'Who have you brought to my shop, Willoh? Where have you been hiding her this whole time?'

I hear a chuckle, then Will is beside me, shaking the old man's hand.

'Nice to see you again, Reed,' Will says. 'This is Fliss, and I assume she'll be wanting to take that flower off your hands.'

I pull away from the flower's magic and clasp my hands around the crook of Will's elbow. His promise of exotic flowers has not disappointed.

'Yes, please!' I say. 'How often do you get deliveries like this? Do you know where to find more? I've heard they can be poisonous under certain conditions. I should plant it outside, right?'

Reed laughs and it folds the wrinkles of his face like a newborn puppy.

'What a breath of fresh air,' he says. 'A friend of mine came by last week, and lucky for you, he had one left. Most had already been sold in Lucan to Queen Clover.'

'It's travelled so far!' And it's fit for Lucan's queen. Card will be pleased to hear that.

'Clearly it was meant for you,' Reed says. 'Here, let me find some paper. I can write down what I know.'

He scuffs his slippers towards a cabinet and searches within it with shaking hands. I look up at Will and tug on his arm.

'You are amazing for suggesting we come here. Thank you, thank you, thank you,' I say.

Will's eyes dart to my hands on his jacket, then back up to meet my own, and I'm *certain* he's blushing. I wonder if my enthusiasm is the cause or if he's just not used to being thanked. Or perhaps it's just warm in here compared to outside . . . A second later and the softness in his gaze retreats.

'I am amazing. Thank you for confirming that truth to the world,' he says, and smirks.

I roll my eyes and bound over to help Reed instead, desperate to pick his brain and perhaps get the contact information for this trader he knows.

I barely notice the time passing as we discuss growing conditions, pruning techniques, and how I use my magic to enchant even the most common flora, with a demonstration to match. Reed tells me that most of his stock is used for healing aroma oils that Ruth often buys, like lavender and sage to treat mild headaches, as well as paints, inks, and perfumes that he can sell to the small number of traders that make it up this far. It turns out he has heard of my shop, although he's not able to make the walk down to the citadel himself. I can't wait to tell my mum that I've found someone else who loves flowers as much as we do. I wonder if I could ask Bastion to let me borrow a horse and carriage so Reed can visit.

But then I'd have to explain – never mind.

A thought occurs to me partway through our chat.

'Reed, would you happen to know anything about a flower called the Feiyan? Or the Odyssa?'

He furrows his wispy eyebrows. 'Hmm . . . I can't recall anything about the Feiyan. I think I've heard tales of a twin plant called the Odyssa or something similar growing in the mountains, but as far as I know, the stories are more folklore than truth. I've never seen one myself.'

'I had a customer request both recently. Is there anything else you remember?'

'I'm afraid that's all, my dear. Perhaps Creon down in the citadel knows more?'

'I already asked him . . .'

His answers don't scratch the ever-growing concern I have about these flowers. No further requests have come, yet there's been no show of power, no flourish of magic that has utilised them. They wouldn't have withered by now either, not with their raw power and my added enchantments. Whoever wanted them is either long gone or sitting on them for another purpose. The fact that Creon and Reed, similar in age and wisdom, know very little about them tells me that only someone like Will, who studied at the Library of Heris, could have any information about these flowers. I wonder if the requester asked the Library's professors for information or sought out anyone else who might know before coming to me. Maybe the Feiyan and Odyssa were taken back there for further study. They seem to be rarer than rare. Rarer than this crown imperial from a distant kingdom.

Much later, my flower basket contains the carefully wrapped crown imperial, cushioned with a selection of coloured tulips that always come in handy, and some large white daisies that Reed insisted I take for brightening his day. I tuck his written recommendations safely inside the basket and pay him generously. I wish I had more to give.

We say goodbye to the old man, stepping once more into the cold. The sun has moved since we arrived but with the thrill of my time at Reed's buzzing in my chest, I'm reluctant to head home right away.

'Do you . . .' I start, then glance to the tree line, trying to word my question as subtly as I can manage. 'Do you think the forest is safe enough to go back yet?'

Will hums. 'Perhaps we should stay a little longer, just in case.'

'Maybe that's for the best.'

'We don't want to get caught up in Pigeon's mischief.'

'Right. We could . . .?'

Will points across the street to the widest building in the village. 'Hungry?'

The sign above the inn reads THE VALERIAN. The flowered herb is known for sleep, accommodation, and healing – a perfect name for a respite among this austerity. Inside, the basic wooden tables and chairs are almost all empty, with a tarnished bar over to the right and an open door that, from the smell and steam, leads to the kitchens. I follow Will to a small table by one of the windows. He pulls out a chair for me – chivalrously, which doesn't have any impact on me in the slightest – places my basket on the floor, and takes the seat opposite. The few other patrons are mostly elderly people sitting slouched in corners, taking slow spoons of broth as though each mouthful should be savoured, no matter the contents.

'Are we taking food away from the village if we eat here?' I ask in a hushed tone.

'Not at all,' Will says. 'I've found that the people with less to give are usually the most willing to share.'

He says nothing about the opposite side of the coin. About how he probably thinks someone like Bastion, with so much wealth and security, could be more generous, especially towards places like Mithian. I wonder if that's why they fell out, considering all I've learned about the royals recently.

'And besides,' he adds, because of course he has to, 'we walked a long way. You wouldn't make it back without something to eat and then I'd have to carry you *and* the flowers.'

I pout at his grin. Why was I warming up to him again?

A stocky middle-aged woman exits the kitchens in a stained apron and heavy knit cardigan, her blonde hair bundled on the top of her head and cheeks flushed from the heat of cooking. Will waves and her face lights up like a buttercup in summer. Within seconds she's trotted over to our table.

'Willoh, darling, I didn't know we'd be seeing you today!' she says, then beams at me. 'And who is this? *Gosh*, aren't you beautiful.'

I was about to introduce myself, but her compliment has me faltering. Me, beautiful? Is that something my curse would allow me to say out loud?

'Anhora, this is Felicity Farrow, Alrick's most renowned florist,' Will says for me. 'We just popped over to Reed's.'

'Nice to meet you,' I say.

Anhora rests her hand on Will's shoulder, and it strikes me to see someone touch him so familiarly. There's usually a sword swinging for his head.

'Well, it's lovely to see our Will with someone for once,' she says. 'He always hides away in the back corner there. It took some time for him to come out of his shell when he first started visiting with Ruth. He was such a shy wee lad back then.'

'Oh, really?' I reply and raise my eyebrows at Will. It's his turn to look away. I can't imagine 'shy' being a word associated with him at all. Luckily for the both of us, just like Card, Anhora has the sought-after talent of being able to keep a conversation flowing.

'I tell you, we'll never forget when he saved our Truffle from falling off that ladder after my blasted roof had been blown off by a storm. I have so many stories, Felicity, but' – she looks between us – 'you probably have so much to talk about without me blabbering on, so what can I get you both? We're running low on vegetables and the soup is a little watered down, but it's hot.' She says it like the promise of a warm meal is as pleasing as all the riches in the castle vault.

'We'll take whatever you recommend,' Will says, and his embarrassment is more entertaining than I expected. Anhora pats his shoulder and heads back to the kitchens.

'Huh . . . shy Willoh Vane . . . Do tell me more,' I say.

'There's nothing to tell. I've been dashingly confident from birth.'

I snort. *Sure.*

'Why didn't you choose your regular table?' I ask.

'Well, this one has—' He stops suddenly and gestures to the window. 'I guess you can see the village and the flowers from here. And. *Whatever.*'

'Wow, that wasn't very eloquent,' I tease, but he's right. From my seat, I have a view of the whole street, the people passing by, and even better, the potted daffodils on the windowsill. Aw, did he choose this table for me? How interesting . . .

Anhora brings out two bowls of slate-coloured soup for us and insists we share some of the freshly baked bread before she bustles away again. I blow the soup on my spoon and take a mouthful. It's surprisingly good, if a little weak. I decide to say so.

'It tastes better than it looks.'

Will barks a laugh and shakes his head. 'I do enjoy your bluntness,' he says.

'What else can I say? Cursed, remember?'

'That's a good question. What *can* you say? Have you figured out all your restrictions?'

I eye him carefully. 'Why do you want to know?'

'I'm curious. You aren't exactly common and it's intriguing.'

My chest flares alive. He just means my curse, surely. He wants to know more from a sorcerer's perspective. But he also pulled out my chair for me and carried my flower basket and I want him to want me around for more than my curse. I think through my sentences and try to explain.

'It depends on how I learned the factual information. If I read it or heard about it, perhaps it's not the truth, just an opinion or it's been misinterpreted, so I can still repeat it if I start with "I read that" or "I heard that." Questions are useful if I'm not sure if I'm correct, like, um . . . Anhora cooked this soup, didn't she? Maybe she did, maybe she didn't, but I can make an educated guess that is potentially wrong. What else . . .? Oh, I can say my own opinion too even if it's not true for other people. Like, for example, grapes aren't delicious.'

'What? You don't like grapes? After all those trade agreements with Dreah . . .'

'No, they taste weird. I don't like the texture.'

'They're *grapes*. Just shove them in your mouth.'

'No, thank you.'

Will laughs, then rests his chin on the back of his hand and looks at me so directly, my mouth goes dry.

'You really are unique, Farrow.'

A flush radiates across my cheeks, and I squeeze my spoon tightly. Oh no. I don't know how to navigate this. It's the first time I've felt like this since Lark, and I think I'm starting to really like him. He needs to stop. He can't keep saying things like that.

No, I want him to. *Compliment me. Call me unique and fascinating and intriguing and keep your eyes on me.*

'But,' Will continues, giving his soup a stir, 'on behalf of all grape eaters, I have to tell you that you're lying. Grapes are very delicious.'

'I can't lie,' I say with a weak smile, like it's not the chain that binds my every breath.

I look out the window at the daffodils doing their best to endure the unusually cold weather. They're not so much thriving as surviving, just as I've been doing for possibly my entire life. For as long as I can remember, I've been shoving down my feelings and pretending everything is fine. It was better than drowning in despair, I'd thought. Exist and persist, stare at nothing but the future, the next step, the next order, the next bouquet, don't let anyone down, be reliable, be polite, smile, help Card with his wedding planning, do what the queen wants. Stubbornly stare past Lark. Put everyone else before myself. Hold my tongue. Then Willoh Vane obstructed my path. He helped me off the forest floor, and now I'm here, in a new village with new flowers and a person who doesn't find my curse annoying, who doesn't nag me to speak faster, who not only supports me but also encourages my passion for floristry.

It feels like I'm claiming back the pieces of me that I lost. I'm reaching inside and remembering myself. I'm listening to my own wants and needs, not Lark's or Card's or the queen's, and for the first time in a long time, I don't care what they think. I don't care. I'm choosing myself and I'm not willing to share.

CHAPTER TWELVE

'So, what truth will you concoct to explain where your new flowers came from?' Will asks.

We stroll south on the coastal road, the thick forest on our left and patchy fields that stretch towards the ocean on our right, as per Pigeon's advice. We've been walking for some time and I'm running out of ways to stall. I don't want this day to end.

'I got them from a village in Alrick,' I say, peering up at the hawthorn blossoms that border the tree line. Their tiny white flowers are almost fully bloomed, like scatterings of snow on thin frosted branches.

'It's that simple, huh?'

'Why do I need to elaborate?'

'You don't.'

I wander left to inspect a low branch of blossoms. Maybe I can cut a sprig off. Hawthorns are always very open to magic. They brim with hope and optimism, and I could make some of the flowers into hair accessories for days I need a little of that light.

'Do you have a knife or something to cut this?' I ask, standing on my toes to pull the branch towards me.

'I do not, but that can be easily solved.'

'What do you mean?'

He flourishes his empty hand. Between blinks, a pair of gardening scissors appear. He spins them around a finger, then ostentatiously presents them to me in both hands, my flower basket sliding to his folded elbow.

'For you, Princess.'

I come back to the path to inspect them. The scissors are as real as I am, no magic or illusion.

'How did you do that? You did the same thing with the Saint-John's-wort potion the other week.'

'It's one of the first spells we learn at the Library. It's not that difficult. You'd probably be able to do it.'

'Really?'

'Yeah,' Will says, and steals the scissors back. 'You wanna learn?'

'Absolutely.'

I've never learned an actual spell before. All my magic comes from intuition and my mother's guiding hand. The flowers I work with speak to me and together we create an enchantment. This is different – this is taught spells and incantations. This is *sorcery*.

'Okay,' Will says, and moves a step closer. He bends his head so it's mere inches from mine. I swallow and let him arrange my palm face up, his fingers just as gentle as the time he healed my ankle. 'So, the spell is "*encho kaveh*".'

'You didn't say anything when you did it.' My dry mouth betrays me. He's *so* close.

'I don't need to. I'm incredibly talented.'

I glance up at his face and he grins. I almost buckle. Gods, that smirk is growing on me.

'So, um, *encho kaveh*,' I say.

Will hums, his hand resting under mine. '*Kaveh*,' he corrects me. 'Like *kah-vay*, don't add an *r* sound.'

'*Encho kaveh*.'

'Good. Now you have to focus, and you can't just summon anything. You have to know exactly where it is and exactly where you want it to arrive. It's easier if it's closer or if the item belongs to you. Oh, and this is only for small items. You can't summon something like . . . a bookshelf or a horse.'

'Where did you get the scissors from?'

'My mum's workshop. She always keeps them on the same hook so it was easy to summon. Let's hope she didn't want to do any gardening this afternoon.' He chuckles and my stomach tightens. 'Okay, try these scissors.' He holds them in his palm right next to mine. 'Focus on where they are, where you want them to be, then say the spell.'

I do my best. I stare at the scissors until my eyes sting, but it's hard to focus completely when Will's hand is brushed up against mine and his soft chamomile scent has me enveloped.

'*Encho kaveh*,' I say.

Nothing happens.

I try twice more and yield the same results.

'Huh,' is all Will says.

'It's like . . .' I think it through. 'I can't *feel* the scissors. I can feel flowers. That magic comes naturally.'

Will presses his lips together in thought. 'That's interesting. Okay, new idea. Go chop off your branch and come back,' he suggests, and I nod despite how little I want to step away from him.

I hurry back to the hawthorn tree and cut off the branch with the most blossoms on. As always, I mentally thank the tree for its gift and pat the trunk. And what a gift it is, to allow me magic lessons with Willoh Vane. When I return, Will motions for the branch and plucks off one of the most open blossoms. He spins it between his fingers.

'You wanna try the spell with this?' he asks.

'Okay. Let me just put this away.'

I bat at his elbow so I can tuck the rest of the blossoms in the flower basket. The lid doesn't shut properly and the branch sticks out but, whatever, it'll do. I'm too eager to try the spell again to care.

Will magics the gardening scissors away, then holds the blossom in his open palm, and this time, when I roll my shoulders back and focus, when I envision the blossom in *my* palm, there's an energy in my spine like the buzz of a bee – something significant, something different, something made of sorcery.

'*Encho kaveh,*' I say, and with a zap of magic, the flower sits in my hand as if it's been there all along. Oh my gods. I did it. I . . . Was it just luck?

'Congrats,' Will says, and starts to put his hand down.

'No, no, I want to do it again,' I say, and grab his palm. He laughs and lets me place the flower back. '*Encho kaveh.* Oh my gods. Oh my gods! I can do sorcery. I did it! Wait, one more time.'

Again, I summon the hawthorn blossom from Will's hand to mine and the success of it is sweeter than honey wine. I'm wide-eyed and far too thrilled to contain my triumph.

'Did you see?' I ask, hopping on the spot. 'That was incredible!'

With a laugh, I dance in the light breeze, pinching the blossom between my thumb and forefinger.

'Felicity Farrow, master of summoning flowers,' Will says with a grin.

'Shh, no sarcasm, this is amazing.'

'I wasn't—'

He cuts off the moment I trip backward over a rock in the path. My heart skips and I brace for pain, but before I hit the floor, there's a sudden strong wind against my back. Instead of falling back, I stumble forward and smack right into Will's chest. His hands catch my elbows and the magic wind that saved me withdraws.

'You really can't go anywhere, can you?' he says.

His voice is distant compared to the hammering under my ribs. The anticipation of pain to the abrupt safety of his arms has given me whiplash. I breathe hard against the front of his jacket, and he smells so . . . *him*. Thank you, clumsiness. *Thank you.*

'Are you okay?' Will asks, and I pluck up the courage to lift my chin. When I do, those hazel eyes distract me long enough to make him raise his eyebrows. 'Fliss?'

'Oh. Yeah. I'm fine. Um.'

His hands don't leave my elbows. One of us has to move. One of us has to be the one to step back. He doesn't. And neither do I. My eyes fall down his sun-kissed neck to his collarbone. Under his jacket, he's wearing a pullover shirt with an open buttonhole at the top.

'For your service, sir,' I say, and thread the stem of the blossom through the buttonhole. Will tenses but doesn't move away.

When the flower is fixed in place, I don't know what to do with my hands. His shoulders are right there. I could run my hands over them. I could see where this goes. I could find out if this fluttering in my stomach is worth the risk.

'Thank you,' Will says. It's softer than he's ever spoken before and it knocks the breath out of me. I couldn't reply if I tried.

His eyes waver between mine like he's scouring for an answer, waiting for my response. A wavy lock has fallen over his forehead and I still haven't moved my hands. There's an idea: *Tuck his hair behind his ear. Do it. Go on. It's so simple. It's right there. You can graze his jaw on the way down. You can wrap your hands behind his neck. Stop being a coward and do it. Stop remembering the last time you were in a position like this and how that relationship ended.* Will's thumbs tighten on my elbows and those searching eyes flicker to my mouth. I'm convinced he's going to kiss me. The thought turns my heart into a fast-fleeing rabbit. Will is not Lark. They couldn't be more different. I want this. I like this.

And—

He lets go of me, his expression creasing in confusion at the tree line. I stay still, stunned, blinking at the emptiness. Oh, I'm *livid.* He can't do that. He can't just reel me in like that and speak so softly and look at me that way and not—

'Fliss, don't move,' Will says urgently.

'What is it?'

He squints at the forest.

'I don't know . . .' he replies. 'Give me a second.'

There's the faintest brush of wind as Will's eyes focus on a spell. Is it Pigeon? Could something have happened to the guards? Did something go wrong? Did someone get hurt?

I hear a crack of a twig underfoot from within the tree line, then another, followed by a clamour of rustling that grows closer and closer like a wild animal lurching through the trees. Suddenly, a lean figure topples out of the brush, their dark hair a mess and travel clothes smoking from scorch marks. The person gasps, collapses to their knees, and passes out face first into the gravel. It's a face I know.

'Oh my gods, Prince Merit!' I cry, rushing to his side. I push Bastion's brother onto his back and slap his burning red cheeks. I've only met the younger prince a handful of times in the three years since Card and Bash started dating, but this doesn't feel like a time for formalities. 'Merit, wake up!'

'Fliss,' Will warns, 'you need to get out of here.'

Prince Merit is out cold. Whatever happened to him, he used every last ounce of strength to escape. I pat down the arms of Merit's thick coat, checking for blood, for injuries I can calm. There don't seem to be any big cuts, nothing surface level ailing him. Hopefully he's just exhausted and in shock. Until I check his thigh. There's a slice so deep, his dark trousers can't soak up the blood oozing out. I press down on it as hard as I can and the blood leaks through my fingers. How did this happen? Didn't Ava say they upped the security for his return?

'Will, help me. Get something to wrap around his leg.'

'Fliss, listen, there are more people coming. You need to run.'

'I'm not going anywhere.'

Will crouches and grips my shoulders. I keep the pressure on Merit's wound.

'You need to go. The guards will be here soon and you can't be caught up in this.'

'I don't understand. I'm friends with some of the guards. I'll just say I was walking home and found the prince, which is the truth.'

Will wipes his hair back. 'You're insufferably stubborn.'

'If someone should run, it's you. The guards might think you did this,' I say.

He shakes his head. 'I can handle the guards. You shouldn't have to deal with their questions.'

I start to understand his logic. If they question me about finding Merit, they'll question me about what I was doing and who I saw, and like an unstoppable waterfall, there's a chance I'll plunge Will, Pigeon, and her friend Tansy into danger, along with anyone we interacted with in Mithian. I know too much. Though . . . should I fight to protect someone who would do this to Merit? The guards are desperate for information on the rebels and if Pigeon was involved in this—

'Please,' Will says, then snaps his head to the trees. He swears under his breath and pulls me to my feet. 'I'm sorry about this.'

Before I can reply, he shoves my basket into my bloodstained hands and twists his wrists. A rush of wind swirls around my skirts and throws me backwards. The trees zip by me in a blur of earthy streaks until I land in the brush, scratches from all around trying to claw at my skin. The magic wind doesn't abandon me. It dissipates slowly enough for me to find my feet among the shrubbery. I check my hands in the little light left – hands I was so happy to have next to Will's, now covered up to the wrists in Merit's blood. Oh my gods.

I scramble around for a plant safe enough to scrub my skin with. I find a dock leaf and frantically wipe my hands. It won't all come off. Why isn't it coming off? A shout from nearby paralyses me. There's no time left. Heavy footsteps clunk in the direction of Merit and Will. It's too late. The guards are here, and Will was right. Nothing good can come of my inability or refusal to answer questions about this. But if Will gets blamed . . . What should I do? Do I defend him or let it be added to his pile of allegations?

Later. Think about it later.

'Over here!' A familiar voice cries near the tree line. It's Tarin.

'Search the area!' Howell shouts. 'Spread out.'

Okay, time to go.

I bolt away from the voices, towards the southeast and the late-afternoon sun, towards home, where I will be found doing nothing suspicious whatsoever. The trees in this part of the forest are nestled close together and I have to fight against branches and squeeze between trunks before they spread out enough for me to run. With a choking pain in my throat that has nothing to do with my curse, and a tight grip on my basket, I press on.

Just like on the mountain, one moment I'm balanced, the next I'm sprawled on the ground, pain rocketing down my legs. Gnarled roots bruise my forearms and my basket tumbles away. I stifle a cry. *Get up. Keep going.*

A startlingly cold slice of metal appears against my throat.

'Don't move,' Nettle says, pressing the hunting knife against my skin. I spread my hands on the dirt.

'Nettle—'

'Save your words. Get up and come with me,' she orders.

'Where to?' I ask, moving as slowly as I can manage with her knife hovering so close to my neck.

'Where do you think, Little Miss Perfect? To see the queen.'

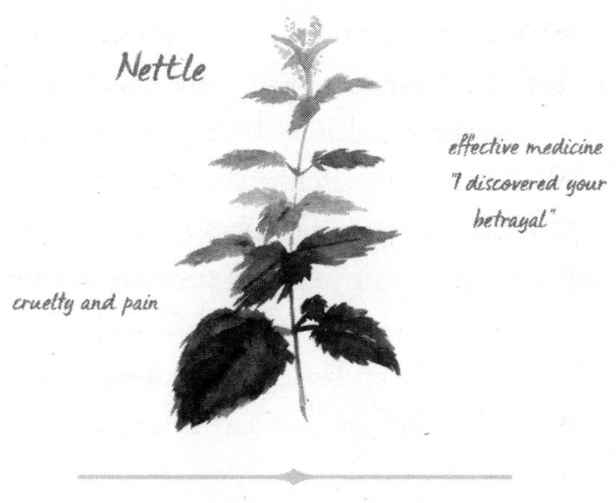

CHAPTER THIRTEEN

Nettle keeps her blade against the small of my back until the citadel gates come into view. Godfrey nods in greeting but the grip on his sword belt is tighter than usual. He knows something is in the air, something in the forest that has his guards on high alert.

'Try to run and there'll be a knife in your back,' Nettle says into my ear, then shoves me towards the fountain.

'Where do you expect me to run?' I bite back. She's acting like she caught me in the middle of a crime. Surely she doesn't have any evidence I was with Will. Hopefully.

By now the sun is dipping below the horizon and candles are being lit as stores close up for the evening. I should be doing the same. I should be potting the flowers in my basket and tending to them. Instead, Nettle marches me to the castle without any detours, right over the drawbridge and into the entrance hall.

'Not so polished and perfect now, are you?' she says.

'You sound jealous.'

She scoffs. 'No, I find you nauseatingly sweet. It's about time I caught you messing up. Move.'

I'm guided left into the Grand Hall, usually reserved for important ceremonies and petitions. In fact, it's where Card and Bash's wedding will be held in a few weeks, although there's no sign of preparations yet. The spacious stone hall is empty as we barge in, nothing but floating dust and two thrones on a raised dais at the far end, on which the king and queen sit in thick robes that suggest they were getting ready for bed before – well, before they caught wind of whatever caused Merit to collapse at my feet. Queen Fern shoots to her feet and the blanket on her lap crumples to the floor.

'Nettle! Is there any news?' she cries.

'Your Majesty,' Nettle says, and curtsies. Her hand on my shoulder forces me to do the same, as if she thinks I wouldn't have shown them respect without her assistance. 'I found Felicity in the forest near the site of the attack.'

The acute relief on Queen Fern's face has my stomach sinking. She thinks I have answers. She thinks that my curse will put her mind at ease once again. I'm her remedy to any worry – except this time, I have nothing to give her. Nothing I'm willing to give anyway. Not until I learn what truly happened. Pigeon didn't tell me her plan earlier, so if she was involved, I'll have some degree of control over my words because I don't know the details. I truly do not know what caused Merit to be injured. If Pigeon wanted this violence, then I need time to decide what to say. Now is not the right time to open my mouth without thinking it through, not with emotions running so high.

King Garland's dark eyebrows pinch together as he regards me. His wide jaw and built shoulders would have been intimidating were it not for the sickly green cast to his skin. From the sheen of feverish sweat on his forehead, to the ever-present tremor in the fingers that rest on the arms of his golden throne, I can tell that the rumours of his worsening illness hold some truth. I haven't seen him out in the town since before Simon's passing, and even then, he was becoming more and more of a recluse as the months went by. We've never been well acquainted, certainly not on the level I have been with the queen, and perhaps the stories about his failing memory are also accurate, as he doesn't recognise my face right away.

'Speak,' the king commands. 'What did you see? Miss . . .?'

'My dear, this is Felicity Farrow, Lilibeth's daughter,' the queen says, with a warmth I don't expect. I'd never considered after all our 'chats' that she'd actually have any sort of fondness for me, that her niceties weren't just faked to keep me on her side. I figured I was a tool to her. A balm. As necessary as the foxgloves that fill her room. Except now I know from Ruth that the queen was once friends with my mother. I wonder if that helped or hindered any true affection.

'I gather that what I'll hear will be the truth of it,' the king says.

'Of course,' the queen assures him. 'Felicity, please. What happened?'

My first tactical choice is to move my hands behind my back, holding my basket there to hopefully hide any remaining stains of Merit's blood.

Okay, I can do this.

'I don't know what happened,' I say.

Nettle tuts. 'You were running away from *something*.'

Okay. I was. How can I word this?

'I was walking home.' True.

'Then?' the queen presses.

'I heard shouts in the forest.' Also true. I heard Tarin and Howell looking for Merit. 'It scared me.' Also true. 'I ran and tripped. That's when Nettle found me.'

I hold the queen's gaze so she doesn't know just how much I omitted.

'Before that—' the king says, then coughs into a handkerchief produced from his sleeve. The empty hall is silent while his short barks turn to wheezes, then deep breaths, before the king speaks once more. 'Did you see anyone? Hear anything? What were you doing in the forest?'

I bite down on my tongue. Okay. *Okay*. This is exactly what Will wanted to avoid. His spell was supposed to save me from this interrogation. Was he able to get away safely? I shouldn't have left him. Merit was bleeding and I should have tried to help more. I should have—

'Felicity, please,' Queen Fern says, her pitch rising. She's tiptoeing towards a hysteria I'm familiar with and I can't get distracted by Will here.

'I bought some flowers up north,' I start with. 'Like I said, I was walking home. I took the coastal road—'

'Why would you take that route when the forest is quicker?' Nettle butts in.

'I . . . Uh . . . There are hawthorn blossoms that way,' I say, which is not exactly the reason why, but is still a fact in itself. Thankfully, the branch of blossoms is still sticking out of my basket to back my story up. 'I heard shouts. I ran.'

Short. Sweet.

'I asked if you saw anyone in the forest,' the king says in a tone that implies he's not happy he's having to repeat himself.

Ooh, *in* the forest. Will wasn't *in* the forest. He was outside on the road, as was Merit. Hmm, however, before that I met Pigeon and Tansy *inside* the forest, so I'll have to stick to talking about the homeward journey. Also, I didn't *see* any guards, I only heard them. Gods, how will my curse allow me to answer here?

'On my way home . . .' I say, and swallow. If my throat closes up, if I choke on my words, they'll know I'm trying to lie. 'I saw no one but Nettle in the forest.'

I exhale. *Thank the gods.*

My relief is short-lived.

'Then,' Nettle says, and grabs one of my wrists to hold my hand up to the royals, 'why are you covered in bloodstains?'

I yank out of her grasp and take a step back.

'I fell.'

'And you saw no one? How convenient,' Nettle drawls.

Before she can push me further, the doors behind us swing open.

'What's going on?' Bastion asks, marching into the hall with Card behind him, both in clothes that look hastily thrown on. Card's collarbone is on show and has the burgundy tinge of a fresh love bite, but either he doesn't care, or they got ready in such a rush it slipped his mind to cover up in front of his future in-laws. I'd probably guess the former.

Bash strides towards the thrones and eyes me strangely, as if it's unusual to find me here. It is, I suppose. This is not the time or place for florists.

'Merit's company was ambushed on their way back from Dreah,' the king says.

Card reaches my side and nudges our elbows together. It's a comfort, a solidarity I need to keep myself together.

'And? Where is he?' Bastion asks.

'The captain set out with a search party but they've yet to return.'

'Why are the girls here?'

'Nettle found Miss Farrow near the explosion site just north of here.'

Bash whips to me and places his hands on his hips. He presses his lips together like it'll stop his emotions from bursting out. I know that look. It's actually not too dissimilar from the way he looks when someone brings up Will.

'Fliss? Why didn't you tell us you were going north today? We could have come with you,' Bash says.

Both Card and Bash look at me expectantly. *Oh, I was just meeting your worst enemy for a cute day trip to buy flowers and eat soup and learn sorcery and have the most agonising almost-kiss moment.* Luckily, I don't have to say any of that. I have a suitably truthful answer.

'I bought you a wedding present,' I whisper and motion to my basket, the sprig of hawthorn a sad reminder of how my day was going before this.

Bash does that thing that only happens around Card. His temper thaws and the rigid chains keeping his shoulders tight loosen their grip. He softens.

'Are you okay?' Bastion asks me.

Am I?

'I don't know . . .'

My answer is drowned out by the arrival of grinding metal footsteps. Ava leads a group of guards into the Grand Hall, including Tarin and Howell who I heard in the forest. In Howell's arms, Merit lies as unconscious as I last saw him. I immediately eye his leg and clasp a hand to my mouth to hide the shock. The slice in his thigh, the one that stained my hands and threatened his life, is completely healed over. Merely a simple red line on an otherwise unharmed prince. His trousers are still ripped and soaked through, but— *Gods, Will. You healed him. You used what little time you had before the guards arrived to save him instead of saving yourself and I can't tell anyone.*

'Oh! My baby!' the queen cries, flying past Bash, Card, and me to take Merit's face in her hands. She pushes his black hair back anxiously. 'Is he okay? What happened?'

'Your Majesty,' Ava says, beginning her formal salute by forming a fist over her heart where—

An uncontrollable surge of surprise forces a laugh out of me. Oh, Will. The *cheek* of it. There, tucked right in the top plate of Ava's armour is a hawthorn blossom. Is it the same one I gave him, or would he want to keep that? Either way, it has my heart soaring. He must have taken note when I told Pigeon that I know Ava. Is it a message? Does he know that the hawthorn blossoms mean hope?

Card shifts at my side.

'Prince Merit needs rest, but he doesn't have any serious injuries,' Ava continues. 'However, we found him in the company of Willoh Vane.'

'Will? *Of course*,' Bash spits out.

'We don't know if it was a coincidence. He wasn't willing to cooperate,' Ava says.

Of course he wasn't. But I'm sure he was willing to stall and give me time to get as far away as possible.

'Howell, take Merit to his room. Tarin, call for the physician,' the queen orders, then ushers Ava forward. 'Please, Captain, tell us everything.'

Ava dismisses her guards and joins us by the thrones. When she finds me among the group, her eyes sweep up and down my body as if checking for any wounds. I must look a state then. I'll probably find tears in my clothes and leaves in my hair when I get home.

'When we searched the site of the attack, we found metal and phosphorus debris but no trace of the rebels. A few of the guards accompanying the prince were unconscious and some sustained minor injuries. They were able to tell us that the caravan of Dreyan food supplies en route with the prince had been raided. However, there had been a larger explosion when a leaking barrel of alcohol caught fire, after which, the rebels retreated.'

That sounds like an accident . . . a bad one. After seeing what the explosion did to Merit, I hope Pigeon is okay. I'm glad I was able to keep quiet about her.

'One of the guards was able to point us in the direction that the prince fled. We eventually found him unconscious on the coastal road with Willoh Vane.'

'Did he say anything? Was he involved in the attack, do you think?' Queen Fern asks with stark focus.

'I'm not sure, Your Majesty. He said he was out enjoying the splendour of northern Alrick when the prince stumbled out of the forest. After that, he said that the prince interrupted what had been a very pleasant day, and that if you wish to invite him to the wedding, next time it would be wiser to not send Prince Merit with any invitations.'

Bastion swears so violently that his mother slaps him around the back of the head.

A very pleasant day, he'd said.

I work hard to dim the glow in my chest. Not here, not now.

'Perhaps the sorcerer was telling the truth,' the king says, slumped in his throne. 'It matters not. We must focus on bringing Merit back to full health first and foremost. Once he is awake, he will be able to tell us more. Captain, in the meantime, provide the injured guards with whatever they require and set up more patrols in the forest. Sweep a wider area and bring in anyone found wandering. We need more intel on these rebels before we can consider a strong countermove.'

Ava nods, bows, and makes her leave.

'Dad, if Will was involved—' Bastion starts, but the king raises his hand, face heavy with exhaustion.

'Let it be for now. Your brother needs you.'

Bastion grumbles, and in the silence that follows, Nettle clears her throat from where she's taken to sulking against the wall, her knife twirling between her fingers.

'Just reminding everyone that the prince was found with Vane on the coastal road. The same coastal road Felicity took,' she says.

Crap.

All eyes are on me – including Card, who looks at me with a curiosity usually reserved for his textbooks. Queen Fern approaches and places her delicate hands on my shoulders, that sweet foxglove scent wrapping me in its tendrils.

'Felicity, are you sure you have nothing else to tell us?' she asks. When I struggle to think of a quick answer, she bores her dark gaze into mine like she wishes she could bury herself in my mind and discover the truth for herself. 'If Willoh Vane has threatened you or told you to keep silent, know that you are safe here. You can share what you know.'

'I didn't see the attack and Willoh hasn't threatened me. I'm glad Prince Merit was found safely, though. I hope he recovers soon,' I say, and pray the quavering in my voice doesn't betray me.

The queen rubs the sides of my arms. If I'm not wrong, she's disappointed in me. Disappointed that her tool didn't function as it's supposed to.

'Okay,' she says. 'Go home and get some rest, but if you remember anything else, come and find me immediately. You may leave.'

I curtsy and cross the hall with echoing steps. Don't hurry too fast. Don't match pace with the pounding in my chest. Keep it slow and steady, a calm mask of chamomile.

Outside in the empty entrance hall, I gasp and lean against the cool stone wall, my basket almost slipping from my shaking fingers. Relief cascades through my chest. Oh my gods. I managed it but it was close. Too close. Will got away unharmed too, which is more than I could have hoped for. Hope. That blossom. It is possible that—

'Fliss, wait up,' Card calls, jogging out of the hall. I straighten, slipping the mask back on as he comes to a stop in front of me. He exhales deeply. 'What are you doing?'

I glance down at myself confused, like he's caught me in the middle of something surreal.

'What do you mean?' I ask.

'You know what I mean.'

I'm taken aback by the weight of his seriousness. Card has a lifetime of reading me, knowing my word patterns, hearing what my silence says. Could he know I was trying to shield information back there?

'Can you be more specific?'

'I saw your face.'

'Uh . . . when?'

'Your reaction when the guards came back safely. I saw you looking at the flower in Ava's armour.'

'Card, I'm a florist. I like flowers.'

'It's not just any flower though, is it?'

I don't reply. I'm unsure what he wants from me. Ava didn't say that Will put it there and I don't see why Card is so intent on pushing the subject.

'You're hiding something,' he says. 'You literally have the same flowers in your basket. I'm not stupid.'

'It's . . . it's a common flower.'

'Then why is Ava wearing one?'

'Why do you need to know?'

'Because you're keeping something from me!' Card bursts, voice raised. His sharp blue eyes scrutinise every inch of me. 'You're acting weird and distant and constantly leaving the citadel and you're supposed to be *here*. With me. You used to tell me everything, but I don't even know who you are recently!'

I stare at Card.

'*Excuse me?*' I dig my fingernails into my palms. 'Are you saying you want me to revolve my entire life around you? Is that it?'

'You know what I mean. There's so much to do for the wedding and—'

'Oh, the wedding!' I reply, louder than I mean to. 'Yes, of course, because it's the *biggest, most*—'

Like tripping backwards without Will's magic to save my fall, my throat seizes up. The sarcastic sentence I wanted to say gets stuck and forces out a wheezing cough instead. I splutter and cover my mouth as pain scrapes down my neck.

Card takes a step back.

'What did you want to say just then?' he asks, deadly serious.

I heave in a breath and fight against the agonising scratch in my throat.

'Nettle says you don't even want to be my maid of honour,' Card continues, quiet and still. 'She says you're not interested in any of the planning, except when you can work with flowers. That you're selfish that way. That you're not even excited for me, or for Bash.'

'Nettle's never liked me,' I whisper hoarsely.

'But you're not saying she's lying. Tell me. Tell me she's wrong. Please.'

He's surprisingly pleading.

Like he's clinging to a thread he knows is worn and frayed.

But I can tell. He already believes her.

I wipe my mouth and take a step forward, trying to conjure up some bravery.

'*Tell you?* I shouldn't be forced to tell the truth all the time! Why does everyone else get to choose? Why would I tell you if I had concerns about the wedding if you're so happy about it? Do you want to know what I've been thinking? *Truly?* Do you *really* want to hear that I was shocked to see you accept the royals as family so easily after the way the queen has treated me? Or how I think they're not to be trusted, *including* Bash? That maybe, just maybe, the rebels have cause to fight back, because your new family aren't bothering to help them in their time of need? You're planning a lavish wedding while they fight for food. Any of that? Or do you want more?'

Card's jaw drops open. For once, he's speechless. No language he knows has any words for him.

I need to leave before I do any more damage. Before I burst into tears.

My lip wobbles.

'I've been interrogated enough today. I'm going home,' I say, and spin on my heels.

Card doesn't stop me.

I wonder if this is how Will felt when he and Bastion fell out, if his most important friend broke his heart like Card is breaking mine. I'm so sick of being treated like I'm only worth something when I'm telling the truth. I have to be an open book or I'm discarded in the waste pile. Well, Nettle can have her victory. She can take my place if she likes. See how she likes being called upon every waking moment of the day.

After that night, I hear nothing from Card. The wedding looms closer as the days tick by. Three weeks until the big day turns into two, and no emergency elecampane flower arrives. No guards request my presence. I don't bother to reach out either. I snap at my mum. I hide in my greenhouse. I plant that damned crown imperial in my tiny garden and tend to it with ferocity. Nothing calms the torrent of anger in my stomach.

Not until I check the anonymous request box and find a third form from the same person who sent me into the forest, up mountains, and right into Willoh Vane's path.

Lunarie. Collection. ASAP.

CHAPTER FOURTEEN

The pouch of money accompanying the request form was a sum unlike any other. It was double what they'd given for each of the previous two flowers, then doubled again. Forty gold. More than a whole season's worth of salary. *And* they paid in advance this time, so I take it as an unmistakable hint that ASAP means as soon as humanly possible. Which is fine by me. This time, I don't ask Creon at the apothecary or check the library for information. I don't need to. I've heard of the flower they're asking for and know it needs the cover of nightfall to bloom. What remains is the exact location.

I wait until the citadel is dozing under a blanket of darkness, until Mum has blown out the candles and the guards have patrolled past my house. Until I can't wait any longer. I give in to the frenzy in my veins and gear myself up with a fleece-lined coat, lantern, and basket of gardening tools. I creep down the stairs and sprint through empty streets like there's a tether pulling me on.

The gates are locked and guarded at night, but there's a guard-house to the right that's empty until the shifts change – something I only know because I occasionally snuck out to meet Lark when he got off duty during his sentry days. I tiptoe through the candlelit space, haunts of my past self in every corner. Every table and chair, every wall he had me pressed against. Every kiss that we tried to keep silent. Every lie he whispered into my ear.

I hug my arms around my waist like a shield, but the hurt doesn't hit as hard. These memories don't matter much anymore. There are other people whose betrayals cause more pain. I just never thought Card would be one of them.

Out in the cold air once more, I stride into the forest. The discordant shadows that move out of sight don't scare me. The pounding, drumming beat behind my ribs drives me forward and doesn't let up until the cottage comes into sight, the ivy silver in the moonlight.

There's a dim light in the window to the workshop and when I peek through the glass, Ruth is dozing on a chair by the fireplace. There's only one other light on in a room on the upper floor, so I pick up a small pebble and chuck it. It hits the window with a pathetic tap, less than the peck of a bird's beak, and I cringe. So much for a bold move.

While scanning the wildflowers at my feet for something else to throw, the window opens and Will leans on the frame, a loose white shirt rolled up to his elbows.

'Farrow, what on earth are you doing?'

I startle and almost drop my lantern, which would be a very bad idea with all this dry grass around.

'Trying to get your attention. Come down here.'

Will angles his head. It's too dim to read his expression.

'Right . . .' he drags out.

'Are you coming or not?'

'Give me a minute, Princess,' he says, then disappears from view.

It's only then that the panic creeps in. I smooth down my skirt, my stomach squirming with every passing second, but thankfully, I don't have to wait long. Without warning, Will leaps out of his window and softens the landing with magic. He shrugs his hands in the pockets of a black jacket, that white shirt now buttoned up and tucked in some leather trousers. A flicker of a breeze, and the window closes.

Will ambles towards me, the warmth of my lantern lighting fires in his eyes.

'To what do I owe the pleasure?' he asks.

'I'm paying my debt.' It comes out harsher than I want it to. I don't mean to be so bitter but tonight, thoughts of both Card and Lark have me battered and bruised.

'What debt is that?'

'I owe you a promise,' I say, and tug the anonymous request sheet out of my pocket.

Will holds it close to the light to read. 'Lunarie, huh . . .'

'Do you know where they are?'

He scans my face.

'I do,' he says, but doesn't elaborate. 'Are you okay?'

'I'm—' I start to say that I'm fine but I can't. Because I'm not. I swerve around the sentence. 'I don't think that's important.'

'Fliss.'

'Let's go.'

Will holds my determined stare for a few seconds, then nods. He gestures for me to follow him into the forest.

'Did you avoid questions about the princeling?' he asks as I set the pace, striding like there's something at our heels.

'I managed.'

I can tell he's watching me carefully. I've never been this snappy before. I don't want to be. I don't want to sour what time we spend together. I want to go back to flowers in our hands and teasing smiles.

'Okay,' Will says. That's it. No sarcastic quip.

I don't realise I'm almost running until he jogs to catch up and grabs my elbow.

'All right,' he says decidedly, then bends down and throws me over his shoulder. I kick a leg out but he holds me tight.

'Hey!'

'Nope. You're going to trip over something at that speed. This'll be quicker,' he says, and summons the wind around us. Once again, the trees blur and Will sprints through the forest with magical assistance. I close my eyes and grit my teeth against the rushing in my ears. In almost no time at all, he lets me down in a different part of the forest, an area with thin, dark trees snaking in unusual bends towards the sky. The leaves are like large green dinner plates and there's an overwhelming smell of musty humid citrus. I've definitely never been here before.

'See? Easy,' he says with a grin, and I narrow my eyes.

'Maybe some warning next time?'

'You'd hate it if I was boring and predictable.'

I say nothing. It's true, I would.

'This way, Princess.'

Will pushes back one of the leaves and treads farther into the thicket. Just like when we found the Feiyan, I follow him through the trees until we reach an interesting cluster of branches, tangled together in a knotted wall blocking our way forward. He spreads his fingers towards it and, with the whisper of magic, the branches relax and extricate themselves, shifting and unravelling until they make a small doorway.

'What would you do without me?' Will jests before ducking his head through.

When we enter the hidden grove, we leave the night behind. The air shines with sparkles of gold dust, and although the high ceiling is pitch-black, the ground glows a vivid green – a radiant reflection of the flowers that bloom across the stretch of grass before us. My breath catches. There must be more than thirty Lunaries here! Each one comes up to my shin, standing strong with a purple stem and lime-green almond-shaped petals that *crackle.* There's an energy within that's unlike any flame. It's intense and glimmering and beyond anything I could imagine. I don't need to use my lantern here.

'Oh, Will, thank you,' I say, and bend to brush my fingertip over a stem. The magic inside burns with vitality and zest right down to the roots. It radiates through my skin and warms my bones, alive and very, *very* powerful. Just like the other two rare flowers. Hmm . . . A prickle of wariness tickles my mind once more. 'How many people do you think know about this place?'

'Probably only the people at the Library who studied botanical magic, but most would have a tough time getting through the thicket.'

'I think this must be the most powerful flower I've ever come across.'

I take a few steps towards the centre of the grove. The trees that enclose it are impenetrable. If I hadn't asked Will for help, could I have got here by myself? What would the requester have done if I had failed to find it?

'You don't know what they want it for?' Will asks.

'No . . . I'd never even heard of the Feiyan or Odyssa, let alone know what they're used for, and Lunaries are the stuff of legend. I remember reading about them in a fairy-tale book when I was a kid. It said that they bloom at night, as bright and potent as the magic of the moon. I didn't know they were real.'

Will shrugs. 'I've never learned about the three flowers being used together. What do you want to do?'

'The magic reaches into the roots, so I suppose I need to dig one up.'

I kneel by the closest one and tug a trowel out of my satchel. Will settles down opposite me on the other side of the flower, one arm lazily resting over his knee. He watches me plunge the trowel into the ground.

'You can take your anger out on the soil there,' he says pointedly.

'I'm not—' I choke, and my words can't come. Damn it. 'Fine. Yes. I'm angry. Happy now?' I say, and shovel away some of the grass.

'Why would you being angry make me happy?'

'I'm . . . I just . . . *Argh.*'

I dig in silence and Will says nothing. A few roots unearth before I crack.

'I'm tired of people taking advantage of me,' I say, but don't look at him. I sink the trowel into the dirt and burrow deeper to find the words. 'I feel like . . . like my curse is the only thing people think is worth something and it's getting harder and harder to let go of the resentment. When I find someone I think I trust, who I think trusts *me*, they still end up letting me down.'

I release the handle of the half-buried trowel and rest back on my heels. Like the soil disturbed at the flower's base, my face crumples. For so long, I've shoved everything down – my mum and her guilt, her secrets, the queen beckoning me at any moment, the heartbreak of Lark, Card and his inability to notice that I've been drowning. Everyone expects me to be fine. They expect me to open my shop and complete my orders and be a good friend and good daughter and – I can't keep this up anymore.

'I argued with my best friend last week and we haven't spoken since. I . . . I don't have any other friends. I've *never* had any other friends and – and I'm so scared that I've ruined it by saying the wrong thing and no one else will put up with me and—'

My voice breaks, but I need to release the pressure on my tightly capped chest. The rift fractures and I'm unable to fight back the torrent of tears that follows.

'I feel so broken and I don't know how to stop. I don't know when it'll end. Some people want to use my curse for their own gain. Others are terrified of me snitching. I try to do what I think is the right thing but everything I do, everything I say is already decided for me. I can't say what I want or make my own choices. I don't even know who I *am* without this curse. It's probably why I'm so clumsy – because I'm *constantly* thinking about what to say. I'm just – I'm so tired of feeling trapped. The other day, when they questioned me about the forest, I did my best, but why should I have to? Why is navigating something as simple as a conversation such a big hurdle?'

I choke out a sob and press the balls of my palms into my eyes until purple and green blotches pulse in the darkness. Gods, I must look pathetic.

Not a second later, Will is there. He pulls me to his chest and hugs me tight. His fingertips dig into my coat, and he holds me there like armour against the world. I'm buried in him, as sheltered and shielded as the flowers in this grove. The queen can't summon me now. Card can't find me. No one can touch me with Will here.

'I'm sorry,' I say, and press my face into his chest. 'I'm sorry that I feel like a mess and I can't say exactly what I want to. I'm sorry I dumped this all on you.'

He leans his chin on top of my hair, quiet and gentle, like those hands on my sprained ankle all those weeks ago.

'Felicity, you don't owe anyone anything,' he says. 'You don't need to defend yourself. You don't owe anyone an explanation. It's not your fault.'

It's a difficult truth to hear.

Will pulls back to hold my shoulders, his knees touching mine. I don't want him to see me like this, all puffy and red, but those eyes I've grown so fond of are soft and genuine, no judgement or snark or expectation in sight. I heave a few breaths and mop my wet face.

'You have nothing to be sorry for. If anything, you're the one that needs to be apologised to,' he says, and clicks his tongue. 'They don't deserve you.'

The grove glows behind the waves of his hair like an emerald halo. He reaches up to my cheek and brushes away a tear. When he's done so, he doesn't take his hand away. His fingers skim my skin, grazing my jawline towards my chin, then back up again to cup my face in his palm. I'm speechless and staring. Tingling in all the places he touched. What did I do to deserve this tenderness? I've spent the evening snapping and venting and crying, yet here he is. Here's the sun, his golden glow and warm eyes, touching me like a precious petal, like I'm something to be cherished. There's none of the anxiety I felt trying to please Lark. This affection I have for Will, this yearning, it's spring flowers in full bloom, open and simply *wonderful.*

'Did you put a hawthorn blossom in the captain's armour?' I ask quietly.

Will chuckles and moves his thumb a final time across my cheek. Now that my tears have stopped, he drops his hands to his lap, inches from mine. I miss the warmth of his palm already.

'Yeah. I figured if you hadn't got away in time, it would at least make you laugh,' he says, and a small smile breaks through my sadness.

'It did. But—' I clasp my hands on my skirt. If a truth goes unsaid for too long, sometimes people think I've been tricking them or keeping secrets. It's a thin line. Will still doesn't know just how close I am to the prince who hates him. I haven't told him.

I want to.

I want to tell him everything.

There's a tightness in my chest that feels like I've buttoned up a shirt that's too small. It'll crush my lungs until the truth blurts out.

'Will,' I say, and grasp the collar of his jacket. He glances down at my hands in surprise. My eyes squeeze shut. It'll make it easier to say it out loud. 'I don't want you to be angry that I didn't tell you something sooner.'

I hear his smile. 'Fliss, I've told you. You aren't obligated to tell anyone anything.'

No, he doesn't get it.

I take a deep breath.

'Cardamine is the best friend I was talking about. Prince Bastion's fiancé. I'm even supposed to be Card's maid of honour in two weeks, but then we had this falling-out and I don't know what to do about it, just please know that I didn't try to keep it from you at all. It never seemed like the right time, and I've spent so much time talking about what Card wants and needs that with you, I never – I didn't want him to take up the space when I was with you.'

It comes out in one unrelenting breath, and I wait until I finish to open my eyes. Will is staring at me. His mouth has fallen open slightly and, gods, if I could pull that mouth to mine in any other circumstance, I would. But like revealing the truth, now is not the right time. I cling to his jacket.

'Nothing has to change,' I say. 'I like spending time with you, and I don't care what Bash thinks.'

It's only when I say Bash's name like that, without all the titles and royal respect, that Will hardens. He pushes himself to his feet and paces away, frantically running a hand through his hair. Desperate to not let him get too far away, I leap up and follow him to the edge of the grove.

Suddenly, he crouches to the ground and exhales like he's been punched.

'Will—'

'I'm not angry at you. Just give me a second,' he says, breathless. He grabs a fist of grass and lets out a furious, guttural growl. '*Fuck*. That *fucking*— After everything I've fucking sacrificed, he gets to— I can't have just *one* thing without him—'

For all the times I've seen Bash ranting about Will, this is the first time I've ever seen Will react this way. Never before have I caught him so deeply incensed. From all the jokes and smirks, I've always assumed Will considered his fallout with Bash a petty squabble, a teasing thorn in Bash's side. Not whatever this is.

I let him breathe it out until he stands up in front of my pale, paralysed frame.

'Your best friend is Bash's fiancé. *Of course*,' Will says. 'Every single time I think he has everything, he finds another way to one-up me.'

He bursts out laughing.

It's a sour, acidic laugh that tastes like bitter tea.

'I'm sorry I didn't tell you sooner . . .' I say. 'I was worried you'd think I believed all the things he says about you.'

'Felicity,' he says. He brings up both hands and tucks my hair behind my ears. In any other situation, I'd be tugging him closer. 'You've had a thousand things to worry about. Don't worry about me. I am more than used to it.'

'I don't, by the way. Agree with him – with everything Bash says.'

'I wouldn't blame you if you did. That's the whole point of their plan.'

'What do you mean?'

Will looks off to the side, considering something. Eventually, he sighs and holds a hand out, palm up.

'I suppose it's easier if I just show you. If you're interested in a trip down memory lane. Uh, literally.'

I hesitate. He's offering to show me what happened between him and Bash five years ago. Something I have tried so hard to dodge, something I have so often walked away from.

Not this time.

I nod and link my hand with his. He intertwines our fingers and relaxes his shoulders.

'Don't let go,' he says, stepping closer with intensity in his eyes. I realise he's focusing on a spell. 'Ready?'

My heart hammers a heavy beat.

'Yes.'

The grove around us desaturates and disappears until it's just Will and me and a large brown oak tree in the middle of a prospering forest.

CHAPTER FIFTEEN

'Wait up!' a voice echoes around the moonlit clearing.

Right on cue, a rosy-cheeked Bastion rushes onto the scene. He's bundled up in a long coat to stave off the early winter frost and his shorter hair sticks up in odd directions. Clearly, he ran the whole way here. The memory of Bash doesn't pay us any mind. He paces around the oak, creating circles in the grass and peering up at the bough. We're ghosts here, an audience unable to intervene.

Somewhere, an owl hoots.

'Is this five years ago?' I ask Will in a whisper.

He nods, his fingers gripping mine like unyielding vines. He stares down the path as if waiting for something, for someone.

Fourteen-year-old Will sprints into the clearing and leans over at the waist, panting. His hair is longer, half tied back in a short ponytail and instead of the leather jackets I'm used to, he's thrown on a baggy knitted sweater.

'Idiot. I told you to slow down,' he says, his voice a slight pitch higher than it is now.

Bash walks by and Young-Will kicks his foot out towards the prince's shin.

'You could have used your magic,' Young-Bastion says, sidestepping the attack and continuing his inspection of the oak. 'Some of us don't have that privilege.'

'It's past midnight. Excuse me if my brain isn't working,' Young-Will says. He rubs his eyes and groans. 'Gods, if my parents wake up and find us gone, they're going to murder me. And then you. And then your mum will murder them both, so I hope you know what you're doing.'

'I told you,' Young-Bastion snaps. 'I overheard them.'

He stops surveying the tree to dig a screwed-up ball of yellowed paper out of his coat pocket. He chucks it at Young-Will, who catches it with ease and flattens out the creases. I tug my Will closer so I can glance at the page. It seems like a botanical illustration of an oak alongside a few unusual runes, perhaps a spell written in an ancient language. Card would know.

'Okay, so what? Oak trees have been used in rituals for thousands of years. What makes you think it'll suddenly grant you all your worldly wishes? You've never been able to do even the easiest of spells and I'm too tired for this,' Young-Will complains.

Young-Bastion plants his feet, a glimmer of the swordsmith yet to come.

'Mum's friend told her. Some blonde lady. She said that she'd been searching for years and this could be the answer. She said that if I tried this spell, I could *finally* use magic. They didn't know I was outside. I snuck in after and ripped this page out of the book they were looking at.'

'Oh, so not only are you trusting the word of a strange woman, you're also vandalising books. Sounds great. Truly the makings of an honourable king.'

'Shut it. It'll work. I know it will. Why are you being so grouchy? Are you still pissed off that I beat you at cards earlier?'

'I don't know. Maybe because you woke me up and dragged me out to the middle of the forest? It could have something to do with that.'

Young-Will angles his head, and it's such a familiar move that I press back a smile. I want to tell my Will that he's so cute when he's sulking like this, but he's frowning at his past self, barely blinking.

I squeeze his hand.

'Hey, you okay?' I ask, keeping my voice soft. It doesn't feel right to break the silence of the forest, this deeply held breath.

'I should have stopped him,' Will mutters next to me. 'I should have convinced him not to.'

I look back at the boys.

'Can you read it? The spell?' Young-Bash asks.

'Duh.'

'Teach it to me.'

'It says to repeat this incantation three times, then place your palm on the bark. If you feel a pull in your chest, it means you've created a magical connection to the gods within the tree that will allow you to siphon away some of the magic. Damn . . . *siphon* is such a strong word. Are you sure this is legit? Normal spells don't mess around with the gods. Maybe I should check with my professor first . . .'

'Will, stop moaning. You're supposed to be excited for me. We could go to classes at the Library together!'

'I'll be excited when I'm back in bed, asleep.'

Despite his words, Young-Will sighs and ushers Young-Bash closer.

The Will beside me can't watch. He turns his head aside. 'This is how the oak tree died,' he says. 'This is how the north was blighted. It's our fault, Fliss.'

The memory shudders like the flickering of a candle and when it settles into place once more, both boys stand in front of the tree sharing the paper. The boys chant together like a funeral march, and as the seconds tick by, gleams of magical light gather in the heart of the tree. The blades of grass in the clearing start to shrivel. Twitch. Like they're suffocating. Like they're in agony. And there's something on Young-Will's face I've never seen before – pure, abject terror.

'Bash, wait. Stop, it doesn't feel right,' Young-Will warns. The glow of magic begins to fade when Young-Will stops the incantation, but Young-Bastion pushes his friend away in desperation.

And places one hand on the bark.

The memory of that moment hangs in suspense. The unused magic shimmers, waiting to be told where to go. If performed correctly, that power should be entering the person making contact with the tree. But I know Bash. This didn't work. This didn't grant him any magic. Instead, his sudden interaction with the tree redirects the magic like a flock of birds fleeing from a predator.

Young-Bash gasps, horrified.

For the smallest of moments, I catch a spark of green around his wrists like the locked chains of a prisoner.

Then the clearing explodes.

I flinch and lean into my Will, screwing my eyes shut until the blast of light fades. Both boys have been flung back. Young-Bash crawls over and shakes Young-Will, who writhes and punches the air like he's being attacked by invisible spirits.

'Hey! Will. *Will.* Stop. We gotta go.'

The tree is rotting now, flaking and crumbling with awful crunches, moaning in distress as it pales. From the roots, a perfectly circular patch of darkness creeps out, slowly, like a drop of poison in a pond. Young-Will rolls onto his knees, shaking, and unclasps an amber gem from his ears. He punches it into the ground, and a shining sphere of gold shields the boys, just in time. All this time, I've been fascinated with his earrings. It's no wonder. They're *magic.*

The death continues to spread until it becomes the clearing I'm more familiar with, the one with rotted grass and unhealthy air and a devastatingly ethereal white tree in the centre.

A final branch rips off like a crack of thunder.

And the clearing falls still. Silent. Dead.

No owl hoots in the distance. Not a sound.

'W-What did you do?' Young-Will stammers.

Young-Bastion can't answer. He's speechless. Scared. Twisting his palms before watering eyes.

'Why didn't the spell work?' I ask my Will.

Will is choked up and has to swallow to reply.

'I don't know. It backfired,' he says. 'Whatever power it was supposed to grant imploded when Bash touched the bark.'

I wait for him to drop the memory, to move us on, but he lingers, his eyes on the forest path. Galloping hooves greet us as the dark-haired man from the portrait on their fireplace rushes into the clearing on a grey horse. Will tenses. His fingers are taut, almost painfully so.

Will's dad – who else could it be? – slides effortlessly from the saddle and, after only a short glance at the horror of the tree, runs over to the boys. He drops to his knees and Young-Will immediately flings his arms around the man's neck.

'What on earth happened here?' he asks, pulling his son away to check for any injuries.

'I-I'm sorry,' Young-Bash stutters. He doesn't look like royalty. He looks like a shell-shocked child in an oversized coat.

'Okay, okay,' Will's dad soothes. 'Never mind for now. Both of you ride back. Quickly.'

'Dad—'

'Willoh, go home; we can talk about this in the morning. Your mother is waiting for you. I'm going to check everything is safe.'

They share another hug, then the man helps both boys onto the back of the horse. He remains in the clearing as they ride away, facing the tree with hands on hips, only now letting his full concern show. The scene shimmies out of focus as Young-Will rides farther from view. Soon, it'll be over. Soon, they'll be back at the cottage. Beside me, Will jolts forward. He lifts his free hand towards his dad.

'Wait—'

His voice cracks.

His hand drops.

The memory fades to an ocean of grey.

Will stays silent for a long minute. Finally, he lets out a short, quiet laugh.

'Let's move on, shall we?' Will asks, forcing a brimming smile.

'Will . . .'

He gives my hand a quick squeeze and takes a step. The scene around us whips in a whirlwind of colours until it settles on a large stone room with a dais of twin thrones at the end: the Grand Hall. Queen Fern stands on the raised platform, her arms wrapped around Young-Bastion like a smothering blanket. Her face is twisted in crimson fury at Ruth, who is ferociously straight-backed with her hand on Young-Will's shoulder. It doesn't seem like much time has passed.

'I *specifically told you* I wasn't happy about it,' the queen spits. Young-Bastion focuses on the floor, unable to meet his friend's adamant stare. 'He's supposed to be here. Not running amok in the forest! Now look what's happened!'

Ruth's face is set. She's not allowing herself to be bullied.

'Did you ever think to consider *why* he prefers to spend time with us? Perhaps he finds our home more welcoming than this dusty castle?' There's a pinch of outrage to Ruth's tone that I wouldn't have thought possible. 'Instead of pointing the finger—'

'Do not tell me what I can and can't do. *I* am the queen. *I* am the one in charge here.'

'Get off your high horse, Fern. I would say Bastion is the one responsible for this, but I know better. Who was it that put the idea in his mind? Was it Morgana?'

My throat tightens at the name. Morgana. The one who cursed me, now involved once again. It's always her.

'Your son is a bad influence. He has been from the start. I knew it was a bad idea to allow them to be friends.'

'Stop changing the subject. You have a crisis at hand. Whatever dark spell Bastion found has turned the area unliveable. The wildlife have abandoned it, the plants are dying, the soil has dried up . . . What if the ruin spreads? What about the nearby villages? You and Morgana *have* to answer for this. You need to do *something*.'

'It's not her fault! She was only trying to help. Which is more than you've ever done!'

'I told you what happened the first time I tried!' Ruth raises her voice. 'I'm surprised Lilibeth stayed in the citadel after what Morgana did to her and that poor girl. Once again, you're blaming others, Fern. There's a dark magic spreading in the north and it won't be long until the people find out. When they ask who is responsible, what do you think they'll say when they find out it was their own prince?'

The queen clutches Young-Bash tighter.

Her rage peaks.

With a simmering low voice, she says, 'They won't. Because they'll never know. The only people who know what happened are our husbands and the people in this room. Morgana will investigate the area the next time she visits and fix it. In the meantime, we're sending extra supplies to the people. They'll be fine. Everyone will have forgotten about the whole incident by the next solstice. So if you breathe a word, if I catch the story spreading, I'll know who it was, and I'll have your entire family killed. Don't test me, Ruth.'

Ruth blanches in disgust. She pulls Young-Will closer.

'Fine. Have it your way. Let's go.'

Young-Will hasn't once taken his eyes off Young-Bastion. As his mum tugs him towards the doors, he blurts out, 'Bash—'

The prince flushes in shame. His jaw clenches but he doesn't look up.

'Coward,' Will says from my side.

'If the queen asked Morgana to fix it, why didn't she?' I ask as the colours bleed together again.

'I don't know,' he says. 'Maybe she couldn't. No one else has been able to. I guess the queen believed that if she denied it long enough, it would go away and heal itself. Instead, years later, it brought rebels and explosions to her doorstep.'

That does explain her paranoia, her desperation to keep an eye on everyone and everything in the citadel. Just in case any whispers begin that this was Bastion's doing.

'Something makes sense to me now.' I grimace. 'It was very soon after this that the queen summoned me to her chambers for the first time. I was thirteen. She must have been checking for any rumours about what Bash did.'

'*What?*'

'She asked if I'd heard anything suspicious, and in return for my truth, she would give me something I wanted.' I stop to hold back a pained laugh. 'I told her that my best friend loves reading, and he wanted to use the castle library. She agreed, but asked again: *What do you want?* I then answered that I wanted my mum to be happy, as she sometimes looks sad. She asked what would do that, and I said flowers. The best flowers in the whole kingdom. Since then, the queen improved the trading routes with Lucan and Dreah to include more varieties of flowers. And in return, she gets to question me anytime she wants.'

'Fliss . . . that's awful. You were a *child* and she used you like that?'

'Actually, it's what allowed Bastion to meet Card, so I suppose some good came of it. Card and I wondered why the prince was suddenly spending so much time in the library when he was supposed to be in the training yard. Now we know.'

Will scoffs.

'Here, this is a few months later,' he says.

He pulls my hand, and we step onto a cobbled street in the lower town, the fountain at our backs and the castle standing tall below a strong summer sun. We see Young-Will passing a group of townsfolk who whisper and throw side-eyes his way. He yanks a hood over his head and marches on. Shortly ahead, Young-Bastion laughs alongside Ava, who has not yet made captain. They pause before a stall selling a variety of summer fruits when Young-Will catches up. He tugs on Young-Bastion's sleeve and the prince's face falls.

'I'll just be a moment,' Young-Bastion says to Ava with a strained smile. She nods and continues her conversation with the seller.

Once out of sight down a nearby alley hidden in shade, Young-Will grabs the prince and presses him against the wall with his forearm against Young-Bash's throat.

'Where have you been? I haven't heard from you in *weeks*,' Young-Will says. 'The guards in the castle courtyard won't tell me anything.'

At least the prince has the decency to look ashamed.

'Mum thought it would be for the best if we weren't friends.'

'*What?*'

'She . . . She doesn't want you hanging around anymore.'

'And you?'

Young-Bash doesn't answer.

'*Wonderful*. So, what? I'm getting cast aside because you can't keep your ego in check for *five* fucking minutes? Was trying to get a smidge of magic seriously worth all this?'

Young-Bastion surges forward, trying to push Young-Will's arm away but Young-Will holds him in place.

'You don't get it,' Young-Bash growls. 'The pressure of being next in line. I have to—'

'You don't *have to* do anything, idiot. *You* make the rules.'

'Of course you think it's that easy. You can do anything you want with magic!'

Young-Will sighs and finally lets the prince go. He falls back against the stone wall opposite and wipes his hair back.

'Not everything. Have you been up there since?' he asks.

'. . . No.'

'It's a mess. One nearby village had their entire spring harvest die. The soil is ruined, and it won't be long until they're forced to move. I tried but I couldn't . . . You need to help them or find someone who can. It's your fault after all.'

'What am I supposed to do? If magic can't undo it, what do you want me to do?'

Young-Will wrinkles his nose in disgust. 'You're pathetic.'

Red creeps up the prince's neck. He straightens his shoulders.

'Don't come near me again, Will.'

Just before he makes it back to the street, Young-Will lunges forward and slaps a hand to Young-Bash's forehead. There's a short glow of magic.

'Get off me, jerk. What are you doing?' Young-Bash says, pushing him off.

'I've revoked your privileges,' he hisses. 'You can no longer get past the wards to the cottage. Enjoy your loneliness, *Your Royal Highness*.'

Young-Bash doesn't quite succeed in seeming unbothered.

The scene spins and we're in the cottage. Ruth stands solemnly beside her husband, a hand on his shoulder. The man looks gaunter than before. He hunches in one of the wooden chairs he made, as both parents watch Young-Will rant, kitten Gill trailing behind his every step.

'How do we know the tree didn't cause this?' Young-Will seethes. 'It killed everything else, and you were there *right* after. Bash and I must not have been affected because of my shielding spell.'

'It's the hand we've been dealt,' Ruth says.

'Don't give me that,' Young-Will says, spinning on his heels. 'There has to be something we can do. You're a healer.'

His parents exchange a glance.

My breath catches as I realise what's happening. This must be how Will's dad passed away. He must have got sick not long after the incident. *Oh*, gods, *Will*.

'Marc . . .' Ruth says to her husband, 'talk some sense into him.'

My Will squeezes my hand and smiles down at me.

'We can speed through this part,' he says, like it's not important. The strain in his eyes tells me he doesn't want to witness this twice. He doesn't want to watch and not be able to change a thing.

There are flashes of memories around us. Young-Will watching his dad lose strength. His father needing to lean on him to go up the stairs. Becoming bedbound. Pale. Young-Will pacing his room. Destroying his desk one day in anger, then sobbing over it the next. Young-Will sitting, arms crossed, before a paper-cluttered desk in a glittering navy room. *Are you sure, Willoh?* a greying man asks. *You have so much potential. Never mind the rumours. Please reconsider.* Young-Will pushes his chair back and leaves. The endless monotonous hours that follow. Young-Will trawling the forest from boredom and discovering the Feiyan's meadow. Begging his mum to give him something useful to do. On a delivery for one of his mother's patients, a scrawny Pigeon tries to steal his backpack. They share lunch in the forest, but Young-Will declines the offer to join her cause. Back home, his dad lies in bed with half-closed eyes as his son reads to him. The days are idle and slow. Agonising. We overhear a conversation between Ruth and Marc. They're resigned that it won't be long now.

Moments later, Young-Will bursts out of the cottage door and runs all the way to the citadel. He dodges the guard on sentry duty and heads left to a shop I'm familiar with. Shortly after, he leaves Creon's apothecary with a backpack full of tonics. *Anything*, he'd said. *I'll try anything to save my dad. He can't die. Give me all the healing tonics you have.*

On his way out, he's not watching where he's going. He shoulders a guard by accident, who stops him and grabs his arm. Young-Bastion is there too, right in his face.

'I told you you're not welcome here,' the prince says – something I've heard said multiple times before.

Young-Will lashes out. He has somewhere more important to be. He has to get these to his dad *now*, before it's too late.

'Get out of my way, idiot!' he shouts.

'You can't talk to me like that,' Young-Bash replies.

'Oh, *sorry*, am I supposed to be keeping my mouth shut? We wouldn't want anyone finding out about how you destroyed—'

The prince shoves him.

I gasp.

Young-Will hits the floor and the backpack catches his fall. Glass splinters. A pool of liquid drips from the corner of the bag. I hold my breath. Young-Will freezes. His hands curl into fists. A torrent of wind blasts outward as he jumps to his feet. Young-Bastion pulls out his sword. It ends with the guards pulling them apart and Godfrey ushering Young-Will out of the citadel, advising him it's best to stay away for a while. Back in the cottage, Young-Will weeps in Ruth's arms.

'You didn't need to,' she says.

'I had to try.'

She hugs him tight.

The memories fade to grey.

'After that, all the arguments went down a similar path,' Will says. 'You probably caught a few of them. Sometimes I'd go on purpose to rile him up, if I was bored or wanting to lash out. Sometimes I just wanted to be left alone. But that's about it . . .'

The green glow of the grove blooms so suddenly that I lose my footing. Will steadies me.

'Careful, it can be disorienting.'

'Will . . . I'm so sorry about your dad.'

He lets out a long breath.

'I wonder if it really was the dark magic that made him sick. And if I hadn't smashed the tonics . . . would he have lived longer? Or was it just random happenstance? Did I doom him myself by performing that spell with Bash?'

'Oh no, Will, no.' I take his collar. 'It's not your fault. He loved you so much.'

Will smiles at the glowing grass.

'That's true,' he says. Exhaustion overcomes him. 'Bash has everything. He's always had everything – wealth, protection, status. Education, opportunity, his fairy-tale prince, his happily ever after . . . The reason he gets so angry when he sees me is because he knows he's at fault. He's guilty. He knows that if I really wanted to, I could take all of it away. He can do whatever he wants with no consequences, and I have to spend every day living with his choices. He gets to go home to his fiancé and his castle and put his feet up and I . . .'

His expression buckles. He's unfocused and sweltering, breathing unsteadily, overwhelmed by the memories we witnessed. He's been fighting a losing battle for so long that he doesn't know how to win. My gut had been right. I'd known Bash was hiding something. So much for peace.

I stand on my tiptoes, yanking on Will's jacket.

'Well, I'm not letting you go easily,' I say.

'Oh, they'll find a way.' He laughs sourly. 'I'd be surprised if the queen doesn't already know we've been meeting. She's been keeping tabs on me for years.'

The night catches up with me and weariness seeps in. We've been out for so long, I don't even know what time it is. Will notices my stifled yawn and smiles.

'Come on, Farrow, let's get you home safely.'

The trowel I'd been using to dig up the Lunarie is still shoved in the dirt nearby, my task unfinished like the score between the two boys. In tired silence, I scoop the flower out, give it the usual brush of enchantments, and place it carefully in my basket.

We choose the quick way back to the citadel, which once more involves Will carrying me and the wind as our guide. He leaps us up, over the citadel walls, and I force myself to leave his arms. In no time at all, we arrive outside my shop.

'"Farrow's Flowers",' he reads from the sign.

'Now you know where to find me,' I say, and stand on the front step so we're almost at eye level.

Will pauses.

'Fliss . . .' he says, his eyes flicking up to the castle. It's hard to read him in the dim light but there's a heaviness in his shoulders. 'You know it's only a matter of time before I get you in trouble. Bash won't be happy about this.'

My chest ignites. 'Since when do you care what he thinks?'

He'd better not be giving me up and letting Bash have his way again. I'd better not be another thing he loses because of Bastion's guilt. But he's saying *this* like there's something here, like he's been feeling the same as I have, and he's looking at me like no one ever has – like the sun could rise at any moment and it wouldn't be as captivating as me on my doorstep.

The castle watches over us. A reminder of who wins, of who rules.

Willoh Vane takes a step back.

'Good night, Felicity.'

No. No. Don't go. I don't want us to leave it like this, suspended in a potential, a could-have, the kindling of our flame left forgotten.

'Will, wait . . .'

I stand on my tiptoes and at the last second shy away, dodging his mouth and kissing him lightly on the cheek.

'Thank you for helping me find the Lunarie,' I say.

He blinks, then regains his smirk.

'Go on, Farrow,' he says. 'You've got a flower to take care of.'

Regretfully, I turn my key in the lock and stand in the open doorway.

'Good night, Will,' I whisper and shut the door slowly, keeping my eyes on him until there's no sliver of space left.

My head rests against the wood. There isn't an inch of me that isn't screaming to throw open the door, to tell him not to go, to continue the magic of this evening into the sunrise and forevermore, but I need to get the Lunarie prepared and into the collection box before Mum wakes up.

I don't know what to do. Everything stems from Bash's mistake. *Ego and desperation*, that's what Will had said on our way to Mithian. Not his, but the prince's. Bash had wanted magic so badly that the entire north got destroyed in the process. These days, he does everything he can to avoid relying on magic. Maybe Card's indifference to it rubbed off on him. Or maybe magic and guilt have become so intertwined, Bash can no longer differentiate between the two.

But would they even listen if I explained Will's side of things? If I have the ability to use the truth as a way to clear the air and smooth things over, shouldn't I try? Bash needs to know how his actions affected Pigeon and her fellow villagers. As of now his sympathies have yet to turn into action. He needs a brutal dose of honesty or nothing will change.

Then, after it's all worked out, Will and I . . . We wouldn't have to . . . We could . . .

Well, I never want Willoh Vane to sacrifice anything ever again.

CHAPTER SIXTEEN

I outdo my usual clumsiness. First, it was the dropped plate of crumbs after breakfast, then I walked into the corner of the wrapping table on my way to open the shop, and just now, Mum watched me drop my pruning scissors by my left foot. Any closer and I'd be missing a toe.

'What is with you this morning? It's a good thing I'm not working at the tearoom today,' Mum says from the kitchen table where she's checking the accounts. The audit book is surrounded by the latest shipment of ribbons that I need to organise. For now, I'm pruning any brown leaves from the single-stemmed flowers available for sale. Well, I had been, until I almost dismembered myself. I shake my head and scoop up the fallen scissors.

'I'm tired,' I say, and don't elaborate. Last night, after I'd finished preparing the Lunarie, with the sun rising and the world outside still snoozing, there had been nothing to block the spiral of thoughts that kept me awake. Like an enchanted portrait, every time I closed my eyes, I saw Will. He brushed my hair behind my ears as the glow of the grove glistened with magic. I couldn't stop myself from taking the memory in a different direction. What if I'd run my hand up his neck and brought his lips to mine? What if he'd kissed me? How would he have done it? What would it feel like to have his breath on my skin and his hands all over me? Because gods know, I've thought about it more than once. A lot more than once.

'You should go to bed earlier. I've told you a thousand times,' Mum says.

I ignore her and inspect the branches of pastel-pink apple blossoms that are almost fully bloomed, inhaling their delicately sweet scent. Why these flowers mean *beware* is lost on me. They didn't warn me about dropping my scissors.

'I tried.'

'Maybe you should take one of Creon's sleeping potions.'

'They don't work on me.'

'I've told you to drink lavender tea too but no, all my advice goes in one ear and out the other.'

Mum scratches a number in the accounting book. She's not holding back her judgement, as usual, and unfortunately for her, I'm cranky enough to poke at a wound. To bring up a topic I'd been keeping secret to spare her any sadness. It's past time we aired this out.

'Perhaps Ruth has a remedy,' I say.

It takes a few seconds for my words to sink in.

When it does, her mouth drops open. The pen in her hand clatters to the tabletop. All the while, I don't drop her gaze.

'H-How . . .?' Mum struggles, then composes herself with a roll of her shoulders. 'I don't know what you're talking about.'

Liar.

'Oh, really? She seemed to know you *quite* well.'

'Felicity, you shouldn't be going that far into the forest.'

'Ha! So, you do know each other,' I say, and march to the table. I slam the scissors down and scowl at her over the boxes of ribbons and paperwork. 'Another secret you didn't tell your daughter.'

'Ruth and I haven't spoken in a very long time,' Mum says, a wobble in her lip.

'Why?'

'It's all in the past now. There's no reason to bring it up—'

'I know there's something you're not telling me.'

'I'm your mother. I'm allowed.'

I narrow my eyes. She's normally good at brushing off my questions but something about this topic rattles her. Her fingers shake as she picks up the pen again.

'What did she say about me?' Mum asks, too quietly.

'Why should I tell you? You don't tell me things.'

'Fliss.' Mum sighs. 'Please.'

'I know that you were friends with the queen too. And Morgana.'

Mum slaps her hand on the open book.

'Do not mention those women in this house.'

'If you just told me—'

'No!' she snaps, her eyes ablaze. 'You don't understand. Everything I've done, every decision I've made, has been to keep you safe. From the moment I knew you existed, I loved you. I didn't care that I lost my friends and your father. I didn't care because I had *you*.'

I falter.

She *never* mentions my father.

She squeezes her mouth to try to regain her composure.

'Fliss, everything I do is for you, and if that means I don't share with you some of the more painful moments of my life, then it's for your own good. It's in the past. Now it's you and me. That's all I need, and all I'd like it to be.'

'Mum . . .' I say, a squeeze in my heart.

Before I can think through my reply, the front door swings open and Marcie trots in, her hands a tight knot over her chest. Instantly, I know something is wrong. She's pale and twitching like a spooked squirrel.

'Marceline, are you okay?' I ask, stepping towards her.

'I'm sorry. Could I stay here for a little while?' the girl asks, chewing the inside of her mouth. I crouch a little to get on her level.

'What's happened?'

Marcie glances up for the slightest of seconds. 'They're fighting again. I got scared.'

Her words strike me like an arrow. I don't need to ask who.

'*Where*, Marcie? Which way did they go?'

She hides her hands in her face.

'Okay, it's okay,' I say, and wave her to the back of the shop towards Mum.

'Marceline, dearest, come here and help me with these numbers. You're much smarter than I am,' Mum says, getting to her feet and ushering the girl over. Mum fetches a mug, and I know she'll be serving up a calming tea.

'Go on, don't worry. You can stay here for as long as you want,' I tell Marceline, then meet my mum's worried eyes. We can continue our conversation later.

'I'm going to check what's going on,' I say, heading to the front door.

'Are you sure that's a good idea?' Mum asks.

If Will's in danger, I can't hang around to discuss it further.

'I . . . I'll be back.'

I fly into the street and find a flow of people hurrying away from the lower square. I push against the crowd, a drum in my chest. There's a shout from a guard – Howell maybe? – and a woman nearby trips. I help her to her feet but keep moving. Before the fountain, a wall of people huddled in a large circle blocks my view of any action.

'How many times do I have to tell you you're not welcome here?' Bash's voice rings loud. He's pissed off. Stuck in the same cycle he gets himself caught in.

'Excuse me,' I say, squeezing between shoulders. There's so much chatter that no one pays attention to me.

A gust of wind has the crowd clutching at their hair and clothes. It gives me the chance to spot Will by the fountain. He's not hurt. Thank the gods. But Bastion is opposite him with his sword out.

For all the chaos, only Howell is here, a few feet away with his arms out to control the crowd. Knowing how this usually goes, backup will be on the way. Hopefully this confrontation will be taken for one of their usual squabbles if we can cool it down. Maybe I can help with that. I look left and right for any gaps to slip through and try shoving between some shorter people.

'Bash, the world doesn't revolve around you,' Will says. 'I'm not here for you. I couldn't care less, to be honest.'

I push to the front in time to see Bastion swing his sword. A shriek gets caught in my throat, but Will dodges so easily he doesn't even take his hands out of his pockets.

'Then leave,' Bastion growls, his cheeks poppy red.

I try to make a run for it, but that grabs Howell's attention. The guard blocks my path and keeps his arms outstretched.

'Felicity, please stay back for your own safety,' he says.

Behind Howell's arms, Bastion slashes his sword through the air so forcefully that the tip smashes into the floor. Sand dances in the air. That could have been Will.

'You know I don't need a weapon to beat you,' Will says, still relaxed. He's circled around to my left. 'You're wasting your effort and I'm really not in the mood today. I have other places I'd rather be.'

'You're afraid of facing me head-on.'

I wish I could fully see Will's expression, because I'm sure he's delighted by the challenge in that comment.

'Afraid? Gosh, you really overestimate how much I think about you.'

'When will you get it through your thick skull that we don't want you around here?'

'We?' Will laughs and it trickles down my spine. 'I think *you* don't want me around here. Perhaps I remind you of a guilty little secret?'

Bastion swings his sword, but changes angles at the last second and manages to slice a clean cut on Will's cheek.

A line of blood seeps down his chin.

I claw forward.

Howell grabs my shoulders.

Let me pass. Let me through, please. Let me get to Will.

Will reaches his fingers to his cheek. He doesn't seem to be in pain, just surprised. He dabs blood on his fingertips and smirks.

'Oh, Bash. You must be so proud.'

'Get lost.'

Will takes a step forward. A drop of red drips to the ground like a fallen petal. The cut flows freely as he advances unflinchingly on Bash.

'I used to find fun in winding you up, but I'm bored of this,' he says. 'I'm tired of letting you get what you want. You and your self-absorbed fiancé in your big, strong castle thinking you can use people and discard them as you wish—'

'Do not insult Card.'

'Why not? It's true, isn't it? That he's incapable of thinking of others? Maybe that's why you're a perfect match.'

'Shut up!' Bash swings once more.

A symphony of metal from behind has Howell breathing a sigh of relief. Reinforcements. The guards are coming. Will needs to get out of here.

'Aw, Daddy's guards are coming to save you once again. How cute,' Will says. He spins round, finally facing my way. Howell, being built like a wall, expertly blocks my attempts to catch Will's eye. 'Well, I'm done here. Have fun playing the perfect son, your lordship.'

'At least I still have a dad to save me,' Bastion spits.

His face drops immediately in regret.

His hands fall limp to his sides.

The wind halts.

As does Will. He stops in his path, suddenly hardened and shut off.

The shock of Bash's comment has me floored, has my stomach curling. I never expected he could . . . It's too low. He's crossed a line. It's—

Will whips round, bloodstained hands curled in fists. Bastion raises his sword-free hand in supplication, absolute anguish on his face.

'I'm sorry. Will, I shouldn't have— I'm really s—'

The prince doesn't get to finish because Will, a sorcerer so reliant on magic, punches him square in the nose. The sword flies out of Bastion's hands as blood splatters onto the street for the second time. Howell swears and *finally* I can slip past him.

'Will!' I cry, dashing forward. The arriving guards shout orders and the crowd combusts into turmoil. I grab the back of Will's jacket and get easily thrown aside in the tussle. A guard – I don't care to see who – tries to pull my arm away. I shake them off and crash a knee against the cobblestones.

Both Will and Bash eye the fallen sword and I know what happens next. Bastion can roll for it. Will can use his magic to block it. Round and round until one of them is seriously hurt. Or I can kick the sword out of reach. I can get between them so they don't kill each other and put a stop to this.

I jump to my feet and run.

Bash skids across the street.

Neither of us are faster than magic.

The sword flashes in the sun and materialises in Will's hand right as I— *Oh.*

The eyes I've been daydreaming so much about meet mine and all goes silent. The world around Will and me crumbles like pollen in the breeze, slowly at first, and then swiftly swept out of sight. My hands fall forward to cover his on the hilt of the sword he's holding. The one now sticking out of my stomach. Our eyes are locked tight, neither of us breathing.

Will's golden glow pales, his dry mouth open in shock, that smirk nowhere in sight. His eyes are boring into mine like he's trying to wish me away. I shouldn't be here. I shouldn't have been in his path. He didn't know I was here. If we stay here, like this, frozen in time, if we don't move, maybe I won't – maybe—

I have to cough.

The moment breaks.

Pain greets me like a weighing anchor. At once, noise and colour and movement rush back so suddenly that the street before me spins. I stumble forward into Will and breathe in his chamomile scent. Even when I press my hands against his chest and wheeze, he's stunned still.

'Fliss!' Bash's shout reaches my ears like he's calling to me from the other side of a field. Hands are on my elbow, patting me down, tapping my cheeks, trying to keep me conscious. 'No, no. *Fliss*. Wake up.'

I wonder for a moment what he means and why I can't see him and then I realise that I've slumped to my knees. My skin is on fire, boiling and pulsating like the blood that's trying to find a way around the metal through my veins. I'm a stone in a fiery well, unable to rise above the waterline to think clearly. Everything is fuzzy and distant and *ouch*, this hurts. I blink away dark spots. A splatter of blood drips down the front of Will's shirt. Is that mine?

'Arrest him!'

Wait – I want to say. Instead, I collapse into Bastion, clinging to the last thread of consciousness as the Guards of Alrick force Will to his knees, his hands behind his back. He lets them. He doesn't once stop staring at me. *Wait. Wait* – I try to say, over and over, until I can't fight it any longer.

Until the cool steel of the blade prevails and my world turns dark.

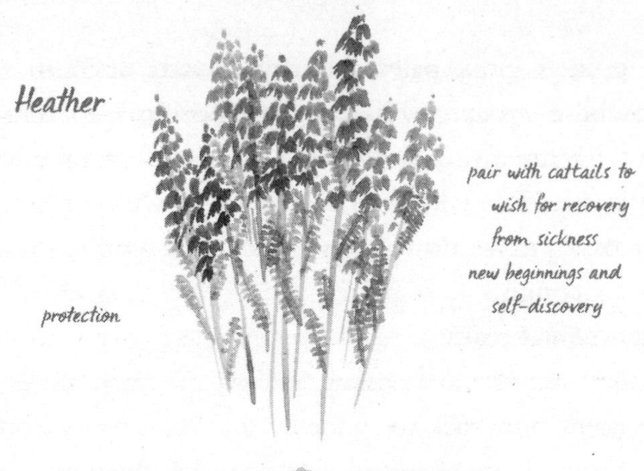

CHAPTER SEVENTEEN

'Get her on the bed.'

'Careful!'

'Tarin, find Fliss's mum. Quickly.' *That's Card.*

'That bastard—' *Bastion. He's here too. Wherever here is.*

'My lord, if you're going to kick things, please do it outside so I can work. Hold her steady.'

'Sir, we're out of yarrow.'

'Find some poppy extract.'

'There's not much of that left either.'

'Gather what you can.'

There are hands on me, pressing, prodding, then – *pulling*. My throat burns with a scream as metal slides *out* and—

I swing between nothingness and agony. They smother me, smoulder beneath my skin like an intimate burial. Seconds could pass, or years. There's no difference in the feverish in-between where I exist. Occasionally, I'm aware of a coolness against my sweat-beaded forehead, a hand pressed in mine, water dripping down my throat, a murmur of voices, the waft of medicine. For the most part, oblivion is my only companion.

In a murky moment of lucidity, I swim to the surface and squint my eyes open. It's blurry, hazy, but I'm in a room. I'm in a bed. There's a candle beside me and a blanket up to my chin. Where am I? What happened? Why can I smell a bouquet of heather and cattail? Aren't they usually paired to wish good health for someone sick?

I attempt to sit, but a wall of pain hits me so hard, I black out.

'—done what we needed her for. Why are you visiting again?'

'You don't need to be so cruel. I've grown rather fond of her.'

Is that the queen?

'Fernie, you have me. I have all the magic you'll ever need.'

Who is that? She sounds far away. Fragmented.

'I know, my dear, but this is Lilibeth's daughter. Don't you think she's suffered enough?'

'She certainly has an unexpected strength to her. I was actually pretty impressed she managed to find the Odyssa. Most who've tried have perished. Maybe she'll make it through this as well.'

The queen sighs from my bedside. 'Maybe. I'm doing everything I can to save my son from a doomed fate, Morgana. I can only imagine Lilibeth feels the same way.'

There's a soft brush of a hand against my cheek. I can't open my eyes, let alone move away from it. *Morgana. She said 'Morgana'. The Morgana who cursed me.*

'You know there's nothing I can do for her. I'm good at many things, but healing is not one of them, and besides, I'm all the way in Berian right now. Let's focus on the positive: we have all of the flowers. They're enchanted and ready to go, so at least we can save your son. Did you tell them that you've planned something magical for their vows?'

The queen hums softly and strokes my cheek again. After a quiet moment, she says, 'Not yet. If she dies, they might be too devastated to go through with the wedding ceremony. That cannot happen. There might not be any other opportunities.'

'Ah,' Morgana says, like my death would be something of an inconvenience to her. *Like it wouldn't take much for that to happen.* 'Aren't your fancy physicians up to the job?'

The queen adjusts my blanket.

'They're running out of supplies because of the rebel attacks, and none of the healing spells they're trying are strong enough,' she says. Then adds, 'I've considered calling for Ruth.'

Morgana snorts. 'She'd never help us.'

'I have her son locked in the dungeon. She'll do anything I ask. When he doesn't come home, she'll have to come looking for him eventually. And when she does . . .'

Will. Oh my gods, Will. He stabbed me. He's in the dungeon. We're both as good as dead. I'm dead. Dying.

I stir slightly and the queen presses a hand to my shoulder. Not a moment later, there's a sudden bang, like a door crashing against the stone castle walls, and Morgana's flicker of magic vanishes. Even that can't rouse me from my inertia.

'Get away from my daughter,' Mum says, loud and unwavering.

There are stomping footsteps and the comforting smell of carnations as a hand takes mine.

'Lilibeth,' Queen Fern says. 'I was just—'

'I don't care what you were doing. Get out.'

'You can't address me like that.'

'I said *get out.* I don't want to see you here again.'

The pulsing in my limbs throbs louder and louder. It won't be long until I'm back in the arms of unconsciousness. Whatever battle of wills is happening over my bed is a strain bigger than I have the energy to comprehend, so in the safety of my mother's care, I slip into the darkness once more.

A muffled shout makes me aware of my body. I'm trapped in my aching bones, unable to open my eyes, unable to twitch even a fingertip. I know this feeling now. It's the effects of poppy. Probably the ones I prepared the other week. The physician must be trying to keep me under, which is a terrifying realisation. It's usually reserved for patients who don't have much hope, and from the unceasing cramp in my stomach and weakness in my veins, I'm most likely still bleeding out. Over the terror pounding in my ears, Card's voice comes from my left.

'What was that about outside?'

A chair scrapes across stone to the bedside.

'Lark. I've just decided to relieve him of his duties for the time being,' Bastion says, sounding like he's sitting down next to Card. 'He almost punched me for telling him to stop trying to see her.'

'Prick. Fliss would rather die than have him allowed in here.'

The silence hangs.

'Don't joke about that happening, please,' Bastion says, with a sternness he usually never uses to address his fiancé.

'Sorry. I'm . . .'

In a rare occurrence, Cardamine runs out of words. He doesn't know what to say. Clothes rustle as if Bastion has moved to comfort him.

'She's going to be okay,' Bash says quietly.

'Is she?'

'The court physician told me that he sent two apprentices out looking for more yarrow this morning. That should help clot the blood around the wound.'

'But what if they're too late?' Card's voice barely reaches my ears. 'Fliss and I never smoothed things over between us. I'd been sulking for a whole week. It's so stupid now. *I* was so stupid.'

'Then when she wakes up, you can tell her what an idiot you are,' Bash says, a smile in his tone. 'You've been under a lot of pressure, my love. Feeling overwhelmed is not a crime.'

'But it's *Fliss*. If I'd have told her how insecure I've been feeling lately, she would have listened. I've been so out of my depth with all this formality, and she makes me feel . . . normal. Myself. I know it's expected of royalty to have a big ceremony, so I want – I *need* her with us at the wedding. It's in twelve days! She *has* to get better before then.'

'I'd marry you with rings made of parchment, dearest.'

'I *know*. I know that.'

'I should have been helping you more. I'm sorry I've been so busy.'

'No, the council needs you at those meetings. Your dad needs you. And your ideas are what the kingdom needs too. I just—' Card growls in frustration. 'I don't understand why she suddenly became so distant. It can't just be the wedding stuff, right? I hate not knowing things.'

'People aren't as easy to learn as a language,' Bastion says, then tuts like he's hesitating. 'Merit told me he remembers hearing her voice that day. She *was* on the coastal road where he was found, which means she knows more about it than she let on.'

'What are you saying?'

'I don't know. But Merit heard her, his leg was healed, and then Nettle finds her fleeing the scene covered in blood. She said she wasn't threatened, but . . .'

It's Card's turn to consider his words.

'Has he said anything?' he asks. From the venom in his voice, I know that the 'he' in question is not Merit.

Bash shifts.

'Not a word,' he grits out. 'I should have *known* something like this would happen. This is my fault, and when Fliss wakes up, I'll apologise to her too. I shouldn't have let anyone be put in danger because of him. This has gone on for too long.'

'Do you still want to . . .?' Card trails off.

Bastion doesn't answer for a long time. I catch the smell of his soap as he leans closer.

'That depends,' he says, colder than the damp towel he presses to my forehead. 'What happens to him is in Fliss's hands. If she doesn't make it, then neither does he.'

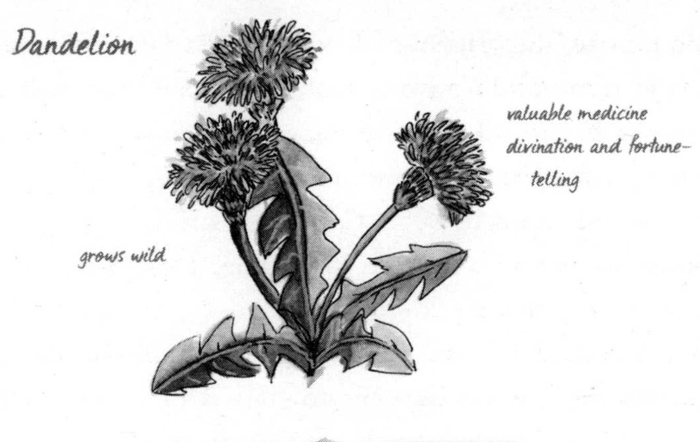

CHAPTER EIGHTEEN

I come to in a room of twilight darkness and melted candles that cast ghostly shadows along the ceiling. The moonlight streams in through the balcony window and for the first time in however long it's been, I open my eyes and turn my head. On the wooden bedside table, there's half a stopper of poppy extract. The physician must have forgotten to give me the full dose today. Whenever today is.

I'm feeble and shaky as I use a hand to peel back the blanket covering me and lift the long shirt I've been dressed in. I hold in my shock, knowing it would hurt to gasp. Across my stomach is a tight wrap of cotton bandages. With a fingertip, I gingerly press the wounded area and the sharp twinge forces a hiss out of me. Even in the dull light, it's easy to see that the layered bandages won't stop the flood of red that's oozing through. Didn't I overhear someone going for more yarrow to stop the bleeding? When was that? Ruth has yarrow. I helped her with it the other day. Day. Week. Whenever.

Oh my gods, Ruth.

Will.

They're going to kill him if I don't survive.

I attempt to sit and feel weaker than I've ever felt in my life. It's like I've forgotten how to move, how to connect thoughts to my limbs, like my muscles are retired veterans, lost to the fight. I just about manage to get my legs over the side of the bed and sit there for a while to collect my strength.

I refuse to believe I'll die here. If the castle physicians have run out of supplies, then I'll go somewhere else. Somewhere safe with a healer I can trust. I've seen Ruth's workshop and know she has the skill. I recall Will fixing my ankle and saying *Don't come running to me if you need surgery*. I need Ruth for that. And I'd be protected from questions by the magical barriers. Yes, the cottage is the right move. But how? I certainly can't walk. I have no way to contact Ruth, and I don't know if Mum can get past the wards.

Or . . . Perhaps it's the lingering medicine that gives me such an outlandish idea. Perhaps it's my belief that he didn't drive that sword into me on purpose. Without a doubt, I know that Will is the only one who can get me to Ruth in time.

In time.

Before.

Getting him out of the dungeons is the only way to save both our lives and if I don't try . . . well, I'm dead anyway.

I pull myself up using the bedpost, and my stomach screams in agony. The wet pool under the bandages drenches through the shirt I'm wearing. Oh gods, okay. Better tuck the poppy extract in the pocket of the shorts just in case. My entire body thrums. I'm hot and sweaty and every thought, every laboured breath, every inch shuffled forward is sluggish like I'm dragging myself through mud.

At the door, I rest my forehead against the wood, just like the night in my shop after Will and I collected the Lunarie. Back when I was full of hope and longing. My shop. Oh my gods. Wait. Can I . . .? I swallow and hold up my palm thinking of my home, my sanctuary. My flowers. Which one can give me the boost I need?

My dry throat cracks as I summon all the magic I can. '*Encho kaveh.*'

In my palm appears a single yellow dandelion. Its gentle magic tingles down my spine. *It's okay. I can protect you. You can find a way forward.* It whispers a lullaby of encouragement and healing before the cluster of petals shrivels inward. It leaves no life left for itself and wilts in my palm.

If I was feeling stronger, I'd burst into tears.

My flowers don't usually wane so fast, but the dandelion knew I needed all the energy it had – its short life for a chance to save my own. And from such a common, overlooked species. Taking what it has offered feels like a betrayal. *I'm so sorry.*

I find myself in the east wing of the castle where the court physician works. There are lanterns lining the carpeted hallway but with the citadel asleep, there's no one to be seen. I pinch my mouth to stave off the strain and hobble past the court physician's chamber door, past the mumbles of a mind that works late into the night. I pray he doesn't want to check on me anytime soon.

The way to the dungeons will be arduous. It's down a few corridors and three flights of stairs. That's if I don't encounter any guards. Or bleed out. I cling to every tapestry I pass, lean against the cool stone wall when my vision starts to flicker, and on the second set of stairs, when a stream of blood drips out of the bandages and down my thigh, I summon another dandelion. Another sacrifice. Another burst of magic to keep me going.

My luck runs out at the door to the dungeons. I have only a second to throw myself behind an alcoved bust of an ancient queen before a pair of guards turn the corner, and I pay for it with a dizzying pang of pain.

'You reckon they'll just let him rot in there?' a guard says. It's not one I'm familiar with. 'At least until after the wedding.'

It's Tarin who replies, their usual stammer under control.

'I think he's being charged with attempted murder,' they say.

'Attempted,' the other guard scoffs. 'If that girl survives, I'll make captaincy.'

'Borage, if you crack one more joke—'

'Come on, Tarin, you've seen the look on the prince's face the past week. There's no hope there,' Borage says bluntly. 'And Lark said—'

'Lark doesn't have a say in this. He's suspended, and last I saw him, he was neck deep in whisky.'

The guards pass my hiding place without suspicion. It's interesting to hear how Lark is reacting to my brush with death. Perhaps that asphodel I gave him really got the message across.

'Well,' Borage says as they disappear from earshot, 'either way, that sorcerer down there is screwed.'

Not if I can help it. The bandages chafe as I force my body to move again.

In the dungeons, there's a set of torchlit spiral stairs down to a square entry room where two guards sit at a table with flagons of drink, dice, and the emergency horn. From there, corridors stretch straight ahead and to the right, suggesting they loop round in a square. One of those cells has Will in, and I have one trick left. I take out the poppy extract used to sedate me and summon what's left of my magic. The poppies in this liquid are not freshly cut or planted, like most flowers I work with. They've been dried, boiled, and strained – but at their core, they're the same. Which means I can still pull out the emotions within. I concentrate on drawing out the drowsiness of the poppies and pour the liquid over the guards. One of them pats his head as he notices a splash, but I quickly fall back against the wall out of sight, a hand on my stomach. The shirt is sticky now, like a smear of berries, and my adrenaline is losing grip, so it's a thankful relief when two slumps hit the table and I can brave the stairs down.

A few drops of poppy are only enough to lull someone into a light sleep, so the snoozing guards won't be out for long. I peek around for any sign of the keys and realise I've screwed myself over. The keys to the cells are hooked around one of the guard's belts, and he's bent right over his colleague, squishing their hips together. There's no way I can get them. That's okay. I won't be discouraged. Will is a sorcerer. He can get out. He always has a plan. He'll know what to do.

I stumble right, using the rusted bars of empty cells for support, and pass one containing a sleeping man that reeks of alcohol. More empty blocks. Then more. He *has* to be here. I'm not going to die. The blood running down my leg means nothing. It's fine.

I reach a fork in the corridor and catch my breath, hot beads of sweat sticking to my already soaked shirt. Left would take me back to the guard room. Right, the cells look different, *feel* different. The bars on them are a striking silver, reflecting the torchlight and dampening something inside me. Oh . . . *gods*. These are iron cells. Cells for magic users.

'Will,' I squeak, and limp forward.

He must be in the last one. Of course. Bastion wouldn't take any chances. I throw myself on my knees before it and clasp the bars with bloodstained hands. The cell is a square prison of iron walls and a cobbled stone floor, with not even a window for fresh air. Will sits against the far wall, his head tilted back and eyes closed. He's pale, dishevelled, and from the discarded tray of uneaten food by the bars, he's found no comfort here.

'Will,' I repeat desperately. I need him to save us. I need him to have hope.

His purple-ringed eyes shoot open.

'Fliss?'

I let out a short sob.

'Fliss, you're alive!'

He crawls towards me and grips my hands on the bars. *He's alive. We're still alive.* Will's lips shake as he bores his eyes into mine. Gods, I've missed those eyes.

'I'm so sorry. I didn't know you were— I didn't mean to—' He gasps, struggling for breath.

I shake my head, forcing the tears to stay inside. I can't break down right now. *Just hang on a little longer.*

'Later,' I whisper. 'Later. We need to go.'

Will scans my bloodstained shirt, the red on the iron bars, my fever-flushed skin. He flinches away from the bars like lightning struck.

'Fliss, I can't – I can't heal you. I can't use magic here. I can't do *anything*.'

'Shut up and listen. Your mum can heal me,' I say. He can wallow later. I need that arrogant confidence back or we're both dead. 'We need to get out of here or they're going to kill you. I couldn't steal the keys, so think of something. Fast.'

I pant for breath. Gods, talking hurts.

Will takes a moment to digest the situation. The sight of me. The way I'm barely able to keep my eyes open. The puddle of blood forming at my knees. He nods.

'There's too much iron – I can't use magic from inside the cell,' he says, with a clearer head. He kneels before me and undoes the clasp of a red earring like the one I saw him use in the memory. 'But you can. Take this. All you need to do is activate the spell inside the gemstone.'

I lean my forehead against the bars to steady myself and pinch the crimson gem with shaking fingers. It has a hum, an energy to it, but not one I resonate with. I'm not a sorcerer. I don't know how to use this kind of magic. I wheeze through my dizziness. The dark spots in my eyes want to pull me under, want to return me to that cold, dark oblivion.

'Fliss, you can do this,' Will says, and reaches through the bars to take my jaw. He pushes my hair back and holds my face in warm hands. 'I've got you. You're going to be okay. Stay with me now.'

He takes my hand with the earring in and interlocks our fingers, the gem a spike between our palms.

'Imagine it's the seed of a flower,' he urges. 'It wants to grow. It wants to open. All you have to do is give it permission. Make it bloom, Fliss.'

I close my eyes and focus on the magic in my hand. It's not alive like a flower, not speaking to me like a flower. But it is of the earth, and there's a vitality to it that feels similar. Familiar. It has the same punch that Will's sorcery has, like the summoning spell he taught me. And it's *his*. It's his magic. Under the hard surface, it's bold and curious and longing to be useful. To be opened up and loved.

I squeeze our hands and try. The magic is there, I'm just – I'm just—

'I'm so tired.'

His free hand pulls my chin up, his fingers digging in to keep me awake.

'Don't you dare,' Will says fiercely. 'Don't you dare leave me.'

I flutter open my eyes briefly. The world is swimming. Chamomile and the remains of the dandelions that I drained drift in the air.

'Fliss, stay with me. Fliss, *please*.'

He's pleading now. Desperate. Terrified.

Will swears and pulls my forehead to his against the bars.

'Okay. Fuck. Let me try and help. Be brave, Fliss. Stay with me. Please.'

He grips me like it's the last chance we have. It *is* the last chance we have. He grits his teeth, suppressing a shout, and there's a strike of magic in my veins, pulsing like the stinging of a nettle. It soars down my limbs, down my spine, up and into our linked palms containing the earring. Will hisses in agony and the earring cracks in two. A flash of heat ruptures. The bars separating us dissolve like the burning of a match and I'm thrown back against the dungeon walls. The iron curls upward, leaving a door-size hole and Will behind it, who wipes away a stream of blood from his nose.

'Huh,' he says, like he's nothing more than curious. 'That was stupid of me.'

His eyes roll back and he slumps, motionless. Lifeless.

My heart stops.

No. No. No. Will. No. All this. I've come all this way. We tried so hard. Don't. Don't leave me. Don't leave me alone here.

'Will,' I cry, crawling towards the hole in the bars, *heaving* myself on. My chest is a heavy stone. I'll get to him even if every second is a roar of agony. Even if it takes everything. I'm not leaving him.

'*Will.*'

The flood has broken me and I'm bawling, gasping through tears. Please. I don't want to die. I don't want him to die. *Please.*

Will's limp hand twitches. He pushes himself up on his elbow and chokes on a cough. Blood splatters on the stone floor as I wail in relief. The sight of him breathing, moving – I'd trade anything for it. He ignores his injuries and throws himself through the gap, wrapping himself around me immediately. I whimper, too exhausted to cry anymore. Too relieved to say a word. His chest is pounding. Alive.

'I've got you. You're not dying on me today,' he rasps, and picks me up like he did the day he carried me into the cottage. In his arms, I reach up and use my thumb to smudge the blood flowing out of his ear.

'Will, you're bleeding a lot,' I mumble.

'It doesn't matter,' he says, and smiles down at me, attempting a glimmer of his usual self. 'Don't worry.'

I'm a frayed floss of cotton, unable to speak or think or move so I bury myself into his chest. He can do it. He can get us home.

We get as far as the nearest side entrance when the emergency horn destroys the quiet. Will startles and grips me tight as the clockwork of the castle churns to life – the distant echoing of the emergency bell, shouts from rallying guards, that metal grinding on metal.

There's a waft of magic that sputters out and Will's voice strains. 'Stay awake, Fliss. Just a little longer.'

The cool night air is a welcome gift as he sprints, not towards the castle courtyard, but straight for the surrounding wall.

'Halt!' It's Ava.

Will keeps running. He summons a breeze. It fades away. It dies like snow on a fire.

'*Fuck*.'

A few feet from the stone wall, Will whips round and faces the handful of guards who caught up to us. They stand in a curved formation, blocking any escape.

'Evening,' he greets them.

I wonder what they see. A boy, the ends of his brown curls matted with blood and terror beating in his chest? The trembling in the hands that carry me?

Or someone to be hunted? Feared?

'Put Fliss down right now,' Ava orders. There's the sound of a sword being drawn.

'Come now, Captain. That wouldn't be sensible,' Will teases, but I can hear the edge to his voice. He's almost as starved and spent as I am.

Bastion runs free of the line of guards in an oversized coat, just like the night in Will's memory. In his hurry, the prince must have forgotten his sword. Regardless, Will takes a step back. His heart hammers against my ear and the wind starts to weave itself around us like Gill between our feet, building slowly while Will recuperates his strength.

'How the fuck did you get out?' Bastion seethes.

'You forget that I'm incredibly talented.'

'Let Fliss go.'

'Oh, her?' Will says, like he hadn't even noticed he was holding me. He uses the moment to adjust his grip and lift me a little higher, stalling for more time. 'Huh.'

'This isn't a game, Will. She might die!'

'I know that,' Will says, his inflection suddenly sharp. 'Don't be an idiot. What do you think I'm doing? Do you want *more* death on your hands?'

Bash, interestingly, isn't spurred to anger. Through heavy lids, I watch the realisation dawn on him. He knows where Will plans to take me, and knows Ruth might be my best chance.

The prince holds a hand out to still the guards.

'Your Highness—' Ava starts, but Bash shakes his head, eyes locked tight with Will. I can almost hear his threat. He's trusting Will to save me. And there'll be consequences if he fails.

'Lower your swords.'

'But, sir—'

'Do what I said.'

A splash of blood – mine or Will's, I don't know – hits the earth. A groan escapes me. *Hurry.*

'I'd love to stay and chat,' Will says, more pep in his tone now. The magic around us whirls to life. 'But as you can see, I've got my hands full.'

Will leaps up and a gust catches us in gentle arms. We make it to the top of the wall just as Card sprints out the side door, his hair a mess and his eyes hollow.

'Fliss!' he yells. 'No! FLISS!'

Bastion grabs him around the waist. Card fights and scrambles and pushes, grappling against Bash's arms, and it's the last thing I see before my eyes fall closed.

'Still with me?' Will asks, jumping off the other side of the wall and making for the northern forest. He runs through the air with the wind supporting every step.

'I'm with you,' I whisper.

'Stay with me.'

'I will.'

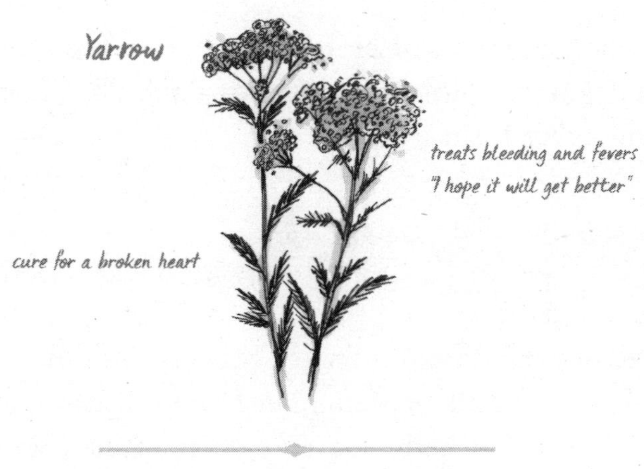

CHAPTER NINETEEN

My back collides with something hard. It's Ruth's workshop bed.

'I tried but—' Will gasps. He *sobs.* 'Mum, I couldn't— It happened so fast and then – and Bash – and—'

'Willoh, breathe. You're hyperventilating,' Ruth says, and her careful hands peel off the layers of cotton around my stomach.

'No, I have to help. She can't die, Mum. Please. I have to— It was my fault and—'

'*Willoh.* You are no help to Fliss like this. Clean yourself up, take that draught there, and get some sleep first. You can tell me everything when you've had some rest.'

'What? No. *No.* I'm staying. I'm—'

A cry escapes me as Ruth's magic seeps into my stomach like the relief of soaking in a hot bath. As the twinge of pain retreats, my head lolls to one side. Maybe now I can sleep. Maybe now I can let go.

'I have it under control, Willoh. Clean up. Sleep. Then let me check you over. You've got iron poisoning.'

'I'm fine,' he says. But he knows he's not. His footsteps disappear, and I settle into the softness of Ruth's healing, hushed to sleep in a safety I can trust.

Gill nuzzles my face.

'Hello, mister.' I yawn. I scratch between his ears, and he purrs. I've woken in a small bedroom, but I know where I am this time. I know the smell of herbs and tranquillity of the cottage, *and* I've woken without any searing pain. I shuffle up with ease, adjusting the white pillows at my back. As far as I can tell, I have fresh bandages and clothes that aren't covered in blood. A good sign. Gill hops onto my legs and kneads his front paws against me.

'Are you my nurse?' I ask him, and he butts his head against my hand. With a laugh, I comply with his demands and pet his chin.

There's a gentle knock, and the door to the bedroom opens. Holding a tray, Ruth steps over Mustard, who was apparently sitting right outside with his back to the door. She smiles at me, her eyes a paler white than last time.

'You're awake. Good. How are you feeling?' she asks, and comes to sit on the bed. She places the tray on my lap. Gill sniffs to see if the soup and water are to his liking.

I think about it – what the truthful answer to her question is.

'I'm not in any pain,' I reply. 'I think I'm in shock, mostly.'

Ruth nods in understanding.

'You went through something terrifying; it's okay to need time,' she says evenly. 'I was able to heal the wound to your stomach. You had an infection and a large amount of internal bleeding, but I've knitted everything back up and given you an infusion draught to restore the lost blood. You'll be a little sore for a few days and I'll give you some more medicine to take, but no lasting damage done.'

I swallow. I'd been right to put myself in Ruth's capable hands. If I'd stayed at the castle . . . I might not be here right now.

I take her hand.

'Thank you.'

I can't find the words to tell her how deep my gratitude goes, but from her expression, I think she knows.

'Here,' she says, and holds out the spoon for me. 'Have something to eat. Don't worry if you can't finish it all, just take it easy. Everyone recovers at their own speed, Fliss. You can stay here for as long as you want.'

I stir the soup.

'How long has it been?'

'Since you were injured? A week. You spent five nights in the castle and two here.'

'Oh. Okay. Um . . .' My cheeks turn hot. 'How is Will?'

'He's fine,' Ruth says. 'Do you want me to go and get him?'

'Oh, uh . . .'

Gill headbutts my elbow, as if reminding me to eat.

Ruth smiles. 'I'll let him know you're awake. Would you like me to get a message to your mum too?'

I nod. Mum knows Ruth. She'll know that I'm safe here.

'If you can,' I say, 'send a cinquefoil. She'll know what it means.'

Will never comes to see me. In fact, he never shows up at all.

I spend the next few days resting around the cottage with Gill as my constant companion. Ruth told me the bedroom I'm using is for her patients and it's just to the left of the stairs on the ground floor, so if I'm in there napping in the bed or sitting in the corner reading one of Ruth's books, the white cat is there too, by my feet, on my lap, or snoozing nearby. If I take a short walk round the garden to remind my legs how to hold my weight, he follows and plays with the butterflies. If Ruth and I have a meal together at the dinner table, Gill paws at my leg for some of the meat. Even Mustard keeps his eye on me from a distance, although he'd hate that I noticed.

The only one missing is Will. Every time I seek him out, he's nowhere to be found. He circles to the other side of the house or disappears for hours at a time. It wouldn't be sensible for him to leave the wards, so he's definitely still here. Somewhere. Wherever he is, he seems determined to avoid me. After lunch on the third day, I bring up Will's absence to Ruth before she heads out to make some deliveries.

'Don't tell him I told you,' she says, and points over to the stable that sits on the far side of the field. 'He's been in there since dawn.'

My heart rate shoots up. *Finally.* Finally I can corner him.

'Good luck,' Ruth says with a smirk so reminiscent of her son that I realise how much I've missed him. I've wanted to talk about what happened, sure, but I've wanted his company too. I want to spend time together. I want *him.* That hasn't changed.

Once Ruth leaves, I smooth down the violet dress she found for me and steel myself. He is not evading me this time.

I find Will in the stable surrounded by an immense amount of hay, the sleeves of his shirt rolled up. I linger by the barn door for a while, just watching. He shovels hay into a stall with an old grey horse in it, who occasionally sniffs and prods Will with his nose. Neither of them notices I'm here, which is fine by me. Compared to the last time I saw him, it's nice to see him with a healthy pink tinge to his cheeks. And not covered in blood. I've never had this much time to take him in without him knowing. He's wearing those leather trousers again that do wonders for his slim frame, and without his usual jacket, I very much enjoy watching the strain in his arm muscles as he works. His eyes are far away, and from the way he stabs the pitchfork to and fro repeatedly, he hasn't realised that he should have stopped shovelling a while ago.

'Are you stress-haying?' I ask from the doorway.

Straws of hay jump into the air.

'Good gods, Farrow!' Will says, and holds a hand to his chest. 'You scared the life out of me.'

I wander over. Gods, I'm nervous. I'd be great if the anxious twist in my stomach wasn't so similar to being stabbed. That would be wonderful.

'Horsey there has enough hay for a family of five,' I say.

Will leans on the pitchfork and raises an eyebrow at me, a gleam of sweat on his brow. There's a piece of straw in his hair that makes me smile.

'What did you call it? Stress-haying? What the heck is that?' he asks, with that delightful cynicism.

'It's what you're doing,' I say, then hold my hand out to the grey horse. 'May I pet you?'

The horse nickers in approval and I pat his neck.

'I'm not stress-haying,' Will says, stretching his shoulders. 'Jeremy only deserves the best.'

'Jeremy?'

'Yes.'

'I only know old men called Jeremy. How about Jemmy? Jezza? Jembino?'

When I glance over at Will, he's staring at me strangely.

'What? You don't like those nicknames?' I ask. Jeremy snorts happily. 'See, he likes them.'

Will walks away without a word and leans the pitchfork against the stable wall. He turns round and opens his mouth, closes it. Takes a step forward. Stops. Flexes his fists. Runs his hand through his hair. I wait for him to go through whatever he's going through.

'Jemmy, do you want some flowers in your mane?' I ask. 'You'd look so pretty.'

'Fliss, stop it,' Will says sharply. He stands there with those wide hazel eyes and ruffled clothes.

'Stop what? Jemmy and I are bonding.'

He starts to speak again but clenches his teeth and looks aside.

'How can you—?' Will starts to ask then breaks off. There's a flush of shame on his cheeks and it occurs to me that he hasn't been avoiding me because he doesn't want to see me. Maybe he hasn't been able to shake the guilt.

I take slow steps to stand right in front of him.

'Will, it's okay. I'm okay,' I say.

'How can you act like everything is fine?' he growls. 'I almost killed you.'

His hands jerk like he was going to reach out for me but thought better of it. Like he doesn't trust those hands to not hurt me.

'Will, look at me. I'm fine,' I say, and brush sawdust from his shoulders. The movement finally forces him to bring his eyes to mine and they sweep me away like the wind that brought us here. If only I could rid them of that remorse.

'Fliss, you crawled down three flights of stairs, leaving a river of blood behind you,' Will says. 'You almost died trying to break me out of the dungeons.'

'I would have died if I hadn't.'

'Only because I put you in danger in the first place!'

'I would do it again. If I got you out alive. If it meant you were safe.'

'You shouldn't have to!'

I almost stamp my foot in frustration. I can't tell if the buzzing in my veins is from anger or from how close he is. I tilt my head up farther to glare at him.

'You spent five nights in an iron cell and almost killed yourself helping me release the gemstone's magic,' I remind him.

That pinch between his eyebrows doesn't ease. 'Oh yeah, that's *really* comparable to almost bleeding to death.'

'Maybe if you stopped hiding and talked about it—'

'What is there to talk about? I stabbed you!'

'Yes – but . . . Well, did you even want to stab Bash?'

'No!'

'Then, what were you thinking? Why did you pick up the sword?'

His eyes flicker wildly. '*I don't know*, Fliss! I don't know! I was just – I just was so angry, and I saw him glance at it and – I didn't think—'

'Exactly! You didn't do it on purpose, right?'

'Of course not! But I still hurt you! You could have died—'

'I didn't. Your mum said I'm almost fully healed.'

'That doesn't change what you went through. Because of me.'

'Will—'

'You recover from this, and then what? What could possibly make up for almost killing you, Fliss?'

There's barely a breath of distance between us and it wipes my mind blank.

'I-I . . .' I stammer, incapable of finding the words.

The flutters in my stomach dance against the bandages.

He's as close as he was that day on the coastal road home from Mithian. He's right there, warm breath and searching eyes. Desperate for an answer. He should be able to see it on my face. Surely. He must know what I want. Who I want. How I want him to shut up and kiss me and forget this whole ordeal. His eyes fall to my mouth. I watch him swallow. Watch his eyelashes flutter. My heart pounds in my ears and *oh my gods, please, finally*—

I catch the exact moment he decides against it. There's the barest twitch between his eyebrows, a flicker of hesitation, of . . . fear.

Willoh Vane steps away.

The disappointment is a plunge into an ice-cold lake.

He leans on his hip and that ridiculous mask of sarcasm takes over.

'I suppose it was only a matter of time. I have quite the track record of destruction,' he says, but he doesn't sound so confident this time. I think he really believes it.

'Will . . .'

'You're about to tell me that's not true, aren't you?'

'It's *not*.'

'Just because you think something is true, doesn't make it true for everyone, Fliss. You told me that you're able to voice your opinion. This is one of those times. I mean, look at the facts. You, Bash, Pigeon . . . all of you and more have ended up hurt because of me.'

A hazy memory knocks at the edge of my mind, and I screw my face up in concentration, determined to remember. Bash stilling the guards and holding Card back. A rush of wind and the night sky. A lot of the past week is a jumbled blur but . . .

'Wait. Bash let you go. He let you bring me here.'

'Yeah,' Will scoffs. 'Probably the first sensible thing he's done in years.'

The words pour out through the gaps in my memory. 'No. He knew it was the right call to make. Deep down he still trusts you. He knows you're a good person at heart and was confident you'd do the right thing to save me.'

Will starts to shrug but freezes the same moment I do. He stares, wide-eyed, at the fact. At the truth.

'Oh my gods,' I exhale. 'Will, see! This is what I'm trying to tell you! Even Bash doesn't think you're completely at fault! That's the truth.'

Will turns towards the horse to hide his expression and pats Jeremy's nose without a reply. There's a weight to the air, a deep hurt that has him guarded and distant. After so long apart, having one minuscule moment of reprieve with Bash, one hint of the friendship that once was, gods . . . I can't imagine how confusing that must be. It sinks in that this is how Will copes. He hides behind magical wards to avoid the pain and guilt. Covers them up with jokes and smirks. Only lets his feelings show when he's here, alone, with animals that won't abandon him. The loneliness after falling out with Bash must have been suffocating. Then to lose his dad shortly after . . . He's convinced himself that he's going to lose me too.

'If you're feeling better, you should go home,' Will says.

What?

'Why would I do that? I'm safe here.'

'I can contact Pigeon and get her to escort you back. There are plenty of supplies and you can just say you don't remember what happened. I'm sure that'll be true in some way.'

No. No, I don't want to go. I don't want to leave things like this. He can't push me away and hide in here forever. I won't allow it. I won't do it.

'I want to stay.'

'It's for the best. Besides, the wedding is really soon, right? Cardamine will be wanting his maid of honour back.'

But how soon? The wedding was in just under two weeks before I was injured, so if I was in the castle for five nights . . . then asleep here for two . . . and this is the third day I've been awake, then that makes the wedding – oh my gods, it's in two days. The day after tomorrow. Card must be freaking out.

'Will—' I say.

'I need to get cleaned up. I'll pack up some medicine for you to take home afterwards.'

He adjusts a bucket of horse feed and strides out of the stables.

In the silence that remains, Jeremy nudges my shoulder with his nose. I rest my fingers on the soft bristles of his neck and sigh. If I go back to the citadel while things are still so fresh, I don't know how I could explain everything. I'm pretty sure breaking a fugitive out of the dungeons is a crime, and my curse won't allow me to feign ignorance. Even if Bash let us go, he'll be wary. He'll want to know the details. As will the queen. There's nothing for me there but stomach-churning questions upon questions that I don't want to answer.

I stroke Jeremy's mane and chew on my lip. There's an unease in my chest like I've forgotten something. A fog is draped over me and the shadows in the mist have their teeth bared, waiting for the curtain to be pulled back. My brain must be feeling bruised from all the adrenaline, that's all . . . Aside from that last moment of our escape, all other conscious memories of my time in the physician's room have vanished without a trace. I don't remember a single second. Probably for the best . . . right? Maybe if I try hard enough, I can convince myself it didn't happen at all. No good can come of looking back. I can only look forward. To the future, to Will, and make him see that he is worthy of being loved. I have a good idea of how to do that, but it'll be the most nerve-racking truth I've told so far.

CHAPTER TWENTY

Back inside my room at the cottage, I practise everything I want to say to make sure my curse will allow it, and when I hear Will come back down the stairs, I stop pacing. I stop rehearsing and force myself out the bedroom door. He stands at the workshop desk in a clean button-down shirt, tipping some crushed ginger into a glass vial. My heart rate spikes at the cute crease of focus on his face.

'This won't take long,' Will says, his eyes on the task at hand. 'We've got a variety of remedies to keep you going. I'll pack all of them just in case.'

My footsteps are slow creaks across the room.

He reaches for a jar of eucalyptus leaves, pops open the lid, and holds one out over a small bottle. I devour the way his breathing slows, and his eyelashes bat together. Gods, he's beautiful. How I want him to be mine. He casts a whisper of a spell, and the leaf melts into oil in an instant of fragrant steam. It's that time of day when the sun is setting and the world is grey, when the birds stop singing to settle in their nests, and there's a hint, a magic, a *potential* in the evening mist. Even in this spacious candlelit room, the night is suspended, allowing me this moment to cherish how, even in the desaturating light, he glows. As the last drop of eucalyptus oil settles, I reach his side, close enough to smell the fresh soap on his skin. I'm ivy, clinging to any moment together.

'Will,' I say, my voice scratchy.

He twists on a wax lid and sets the bottle aside, then reaches for another empty vial.

'Will, stop.'

I place my hand on top of his.

He pauses, a lock of hair hiding his eyes.

'I'm not leaving,' I say.

I summon all the courage I have and trace my fingertips up to his wrists, barely grazing his skin, and lift his hand away from the bottle. His hazel eyes struggle to meet mine, and when they do, he scans my face, lips slightly parted and a tug of disbelief between his eyebrows. Gods, if I could pause the world . . .

'I'm not leaving you.'

I'd prepared my speech while he was getting cleaned up. *Will, you have nothing to feel guilty about. I would come for you no matter what. If I was bleeding, if every bone in my body was broken. If I'd been carved up and beaten, if every single breath was poison, I'd come for you. If anyone stood between us, I'd claw my way to you if it was the last thing I did. To keep you alive, to keep you safe, I'd break you out of a thousand prisons. Drag myself over any obstacle.* I'm going to be bold and determined so he understands that I won't abandon him. He'll know that there's nowhere else I'd rather be than by his side.

But now he's here, in front of me, and the longing I have for him is a forest of aspen trees, not allowing anything else to flourish where they grow. It rattles and laments in the wind and—

'Why haven't you kissed me yet?' I blurt out.

Will blinks, stunned.

I can't stop the words from tumbling out.

'That day we found Merit, I thought you were going to kiss me. Then in the Lunarie grove that night, and when you took me home, it was perfect and, even just earlier today in the stable I thought— Actually, I don't know what to think and it's tearing me up not knowing. When I thought you'd— When I thought I'd lost you, I was terrified and, well, now that we survived and we're okay, I just— It's something I've been thinking about, a lot. Since we met, actually. I think about you. A lot. Um.'

I take a breath.

Fuck.

I hate telling the truth when it's so clunky. I'd planned this out. I wasn't supposed to say it like this. I've ruined this for sure. The silence stretches and Will doesn't move and when I can't take it any longer, I drop his hand. *Okay, never mind, forget it,* I want to say. But I can't. I whip round as the heat of embarrassment burns my face. It's a frustrating truth to know that I was a fool to hope so freely. I suppose he did tell me to leave. I didn't think he was being serious. I thought—

'Fliss.'

It comes out so sober, so gentle, that I halt.

Will takes my elbow and turns me back round. His eyes are golden in the candlelight, and they flicker with a vulnerability that squeezes my chest tight.

'Fliss, it's not easy for me to . . .' His eyes dance across my face. 'There's so much we haven't talked about. So much *I* haven't talked about. And I learned my lesson. The one time I decided to be selfish was the morning I almost killed you. I'm not risking a repeat. I will *not* be the reason you get hurt again.'

'You . . . you were coming for me?'

'Yeah. And instead, I put a sword through your stomach. As things go, not a great turn of events.'

Hope blooms behind my ribs.

'It was an accident,' I insist. 'I willingly put myself at risk and the sword appeared in your hand at the exact moment I reached you. There was no time to avoid it. Don't forget that you also *saved* my life. I needed your mum's help, and you got me here in time. There's nothing to forgive.' I reach up and cup his jaw. 'Please. Believe me.'

Under my palm, his skin is soft and warm, and when I move my thumb against his cheek, he leans against it and closes his eyes, seemingly fighting an internal decision. Finally, with a deep breath like he's about to dive into water, he grabs my waist.

'Oh, fuck it,' Will says, and tugs me flush against him. I squeak and grab the collar of his shirt. His eyes flare in panic that he might have hurt me, but I shake my head adamantly at the worry and rise up on my toes. Closer. I need to be closer.

His voice is a soft breeze, inches away from my mouth. 'Those times you mentioned . . . Did you want me to kiss you?'

'You know I can only tell you the truth.'

'How about now?' he asks, and walks me backwards.

He presses me against a bookshelf, and I let him, melted like candle wax in his grip. My heart is a thundering mess. I'm dizzy, unable to think straight, breathe right, let alone reply to his question. He has me captured and he knows it.

'If I kiss you, that'll be it for me,' Will whispers. I lick my lips. 'It'll be all I want. There'll be no going back. I've wanted to kiss you more times than I can count. Lain awake on sleepless nights consumed by it. You were everywhere I went and running through my dreams as if I'd willed you into existence myself. Gods, Fliss, of course I want you.'

His confession floods through me like a winter downpour. He *was* holding back. He likes me. He wants me. Like the first kindling of a bonfire, I switch from silent pining to a satisfied triumph that I've been right this whole time.

'Then do it,' I dare him, and lift my chin.

His hands shoot up to catch mine and pin them against the books on either side of my head. But it's my turn to take revenge for holding out on me. It's my turn to play. Will lingers in that in-between, his eyes on my lips and hitched, heavy breathing. He can't resist for much longer. It's a marvel that I can have that effect on someone. On him.

'What are you waiting for?' I tease as his fingers intertwine with mine and hold me firmly against the book spines. Will nudges my nose and I grin. He's seconds from caving. I lower my voice. 'You're hot when you're desperate. Like in the dungeon. Fliss, please. Fliss, stay with me. Fliss, don't leave me. Begging. I want you to *beg* for me.'

My words do the trick. He growls and grabs my jaw. There's a split second when our eyes meet, both alight with challenge.

'Trust me,' Will says, 'you'll be the one begging when I'm done with you.'

He kisses me. It's urgent and determined, desperate. Exactly what I want. I grasp the waves of his hair and surge against him, kissing him back with just as much fervour. Gods, *finally*.

Everything else disappears. There's only Will and his mouth on mine and pleasure humming in my veins. His tongue brazenly sweeps against mine and I reel. I'd be swaying if it weren't for the bookshelf and Will's body keeping me upright. I'm completely tangled in him, overwhelmed by the gods damned taste of him. His hands skim the curve of my backside, and I can't help the gasp that escapes me.

He stops, his cheeks flushed and lips tinged pink.

'Do that again,' he orders.

I shiver. 'Make me.'

Intensity gleaming in his eyes, Will lifts me up by my thighs and carries me over to the workshop desk. There's a gust of magic as he sweeps the books and herbs off the table and sits me down, yanking me close by the backs of my knees. Then he's kissing me all over again as if he can't bear another second apart. I hook my legs around him and roll my hips forward. It provokes a delighted hum from his throat that has me kissing him even harder, devouring him even more. Consciously or not, he's whipping up a magical wind around us that's really ruining Ruth's organisation, and it's not long before vials are clattering to the floor around me.

'Your mum won't be happy about that,' I say between kisses.

Will digs his fingers into my thighs, eyes closed.

'Please don't talk about my mum right now.'

His indignation makes me laugh.

'What should I talk about, then?'

'Your mouth should be otherwise occupied.'

'Any ideas how?'

Our hands meet at his collar.

'Fliss, wait—'

'We can stop,' I say.

He shakes his head, those waves ruffled from all my traversing.

'No, it's just . . . There's something I haven't told you.' Will's voice cracks. He places his hands over mine, paused at his top button, and squeezes. 'I, um, I've had a couple of procedures to help me become more . . .'

The words feel important to him, weighted, and I know well the fear that comes with rushing to explain.

'Take your time,' I say.

Instead of replying, he undoes his top button. Then another. I notice he's trembling.

'Allow me,' I whisper right against the earrings that decorate his ear. The ones that saved our lives. I undo one more button and check his expression.

'Please. Go on.'

It's a request. A plea. *Please.*

I open the rest of his shirt slowly, carefully, giving him plenty of time to stop me if he wants to. All the while, he skims his eyes across my face. He's worried. Nervous. And when the shirt parts, I understand more. The first thing that springs to mind is the bouquet I made a few months ago: pastel-blue morning glory for future happiness, white edelweiss for courage, and an eye-catching singular protea in full bloom, with triangular pink petals surrounding a bulbous white centre, that carries the meaning of transformation. It wasn't the first time I'd made a bouquet of that kind for customers who wished to celebrate the change in someone's identity, but this time, when I delivered the flowers, I could hear the momentous party from the far end of the street. Over the strumming of the live band, the recipient of the bouquet had thanked me for their first gift addressed to their new chosen name and then asked for the name of the tailor who made the dress I was wearing. I remember thinking that I'd never seen that neighbour smile so widely before.

I glance up at Will with a question. *May I?*

He nods.

I trail a fingertip down the middle of his chest, passing two horizontal surgery scars that curve towards his armpits. The lines have faded to a soft pink and don't look raised. I've only read up on herbal flower-based medicine so I can't know for sure, but I'm guessing that the procedure wasn't recent. Perhaps it was done around the age I saw in the memories.

Will clears his throat.

'Magic can do a lot but . . . I chose to get the tissue removed when I was fifteen,' he says. 'Perks of having a healer as a mum is access to all the transitioning treatments I want – and the Library has a ton of experts in identity-affirming care too. My parents supported every choice I wanted to make pretty early on. They didn't mind adjusting to having a son instead, so . . .'

'It makes no difference to me either.' I fell for him as he is, and although he's rare and exceptional in my eyes, the procedures he's talking about aren't unheard of in Calla. My tongue trips over the question I want to ask. 'Do . . . do they hurt? The scars?'

'No. Mum made some really good moisturising balms at the start that helped them heal well. It's been so long, sometimes I even forget they're there.' He ropes a hand in my hair. There's a vulnerable pinch between his eyebrows, but he has nothing to doubt. 'Fliss . . . Being with me . . . I don't know what expectations you had, or . . .'

'You're Will,' I say. 'Nothing changes that. And it doesn't change how I feel about you. Although some more questions might come to me later on. I want to make sure I understand fully, when – or if – you feel up to it.'

'Yeah, of course. I mean—' He grins, his nerves swept away. It's been so long since I've seen that smirk that I almost keel over and off the desk. 'I'm sure it's hard to believe that I haven't always been a devilishly confident and handsome guy.'

I snort. 'Didn't Anhora say you used to be "shy" in Mithian?'

'You're remembering wrong. She said nothing of the sort.'

I inch my mouth towards him again. 'Hmm . . . is that so?'

'Well, if you need convincing . . .'

This time, when he kisses me, it's cautious, conscious, as if every tiny movement means the world. His touch sweeps over my lower back, my waist, my hips, my thighs, then up my jaw, into my hair, deliberately, unhurriedly, like he's intricately memorising the way I feel, noting each quiver down my spine. I do similarly and I relish every second of it. I've been so obsessed with those hands, but this is better than any wishful daydreams.

After some time, Will chuckles against my mouth.

'This is not how I imagined this day would go,' he says, red to the very tips of his ears. It's adorable.

'I hope it's turned out for the better,' I say, and curl a lock of his hair around my finger, letting it unravel lazily.

'Oh, certainly,' he says. His laugh turns into a soft sigh. 'You've been on my mind since you stubbornly – and stupidly – marched into the wards and knocked yourself out. It was those flowers in your hair and your cute, frowny expression.'

'Frowny?'

'Yeah, you have a tough little scowl. Your eyes get all narrow and you pull your chin up. Ah, just like that.' He beams at my reaction. 'It's so at odds with the way you dress; it threw me off guard from the start. I didn't realise someone so short could cause me so much trouble. You're a persistent little wildflower.'

'Stop teasing me!'

'I'm not! These are compliments!'

'Stubborn and stupid?'

'I'm trying to tell you the truth!'

'Well, I don't think you're doing a very good job of it.'

'Perhaps I need a teacher. Know anyone?'

'You're—' *The worst.*

A sentence I can't say.

I glower and his laugh is a cherished prize.

'Cute,' Will says, and kisses the tip of my nose.

'It's your own fault for being so gentle with me when you healed my ankle.'

He raises an eyebrow. I should have known he'd revel in hearing that, but it's still a surprise when he suddenly wrenches me close and hovers his hot breath over my neck. I cling to his shirt, unable to contain my squeal.

'Oh? I'll be rougher next time, shall I?'

Gods—

I'm dazed. Flushed. A complete mess.

'How would you like me to atone?' he whispers against my skin. He presses his lips to my throat in an achingly slow kiss that has me struggling to find air. 'I'm completely at your mercy, Princess.'

I don't speak.

I grab his jaw and kiss him.

I wrap myself up in him and soak up the taste of his tongue, the quiver of his eyelids, the hammering of our pulses under exploring hands. His earlier openness and vulnerability about his transition – his trust in me – makes me cherish each moment. I lose myself completely in the spell of him. It's enchanting. *He's* enchanting. Truly a sorcerer at work.

It's fully dark outside when the front door opens and both of us jump. Ruth closes the door with a slam at odds with her usual care. Will straightens up in panic.

'Don't mind me, your *very* blind mother who can't *possibly* see what's occurring in my workshop right now,' she announces, louder than she needs to. The smug smile on her face tells me otherwise.

I snigger as Ruth drops her basket near the front door, then takes off her coat and hooks it on the wall. Will's heart pounds under my palm. She's making her way up the stairs when she pauses, hand on the rail.

'Willoh, when you have a minute, do pick up my fresh rosemary from the floor. If you're not too busy.'

He chokes. Ruth grins my way before leaving us alone. Will's head falls to my shoulder.

'She's going to be a nightmare,' he says, muffled. I pat his curls.

'I'm sure I can think of a way or two to make it better.'

His head shoots up, and he cocks an eyebrow.

'Oh, yeah?'

I move my mouth towards his as if I'm going to kiss him.

'Gotta pick up those herbs first.'

Will narrows his eyes, then grins – that stupid, beautiful one that messes me up every time.

'I'll hold you to that.'

Honestly, he can hold me any way he likes.

CHAPTER TWENTY-ONE

I kneel on the path to the cottage coaxing out the daffodils that sleep there. Ruth had told me over our breakfast together that they hadn't bloomed well at the start of spring, and with the season almost over, it would be a shame to see their potential wasted. I brush my fingertips up the wilting petals and delve around their connection to the earth. Hmm, it feels like the colder winter left the bulbs a little starved. An easy fix for me. I send my magic down the stems and it's not long before the yellow petals are open and proud. Just as a delivery of daffodils represents new beginnings, so do these flowers begin life anew.

A hasty crunch of footsteps from the forest calls to my attention and my mother breaks the tree line, her black hair dancing behind a large travel sack and the puffy pink cheeks of someone in a hurry.

'Fliss!' she gasps. Her bag hits the floor, and she breaks into a sprint, arms wide open.

'Mum!' I fly down the path and she hugs me tight, her carnation perfume easing both my mind and body. She's *here*. I grip her like the slightest breeze will sweep her from me.

'Oh, my baby. Are you okay?' she asks, and takes my face between her palms.

'I'm okay. I'm all right. Ruth healed me wonderfully.'

Her dark eyes glisten in the corners. 'My darling. I was so worried. When I heard – and then when Ruth sent me— Well, thank the gods you're okay. I'm here now.'

'Lilibeth, is that you?' Ruth calls from the cottage door.

Mum seems to wobble slightly.

'Let me get your bag,' I say, peeling myself out of my mother's arms. 'Go ahead.'

She takes a second, as if mentally preparing herself, then stretches her smile. I know that smile. It's the one she uses to fake resilience. The one she uses to tell the lies that I can't. With a purposefully straight back, she heads down the path.

At the front door, Ruth holds out her hands and Mum doesn't hesitate to take them.

'My old friend,' Mum says. 'I can't thank you enough for what you've done for my Fliss. I'm sorry it's taken me so long. I'm sorry it's taken this to bring me to your door again.'

Ruth's foggy eyes close with a smile. 'There's nothing to forgive, Betty. You're more than welcome.'

Mum's lip trembles and I glance between the pair with uncertainty. What does she mean? What did my mum do? Mum tugs Ruth into a hug and squeezes her like a lost child being returned home.

'Thank you. Thank you a thousand times over,' she says into Ruth's shoulder.

'Still using the same perfume, huh? You haven't changed,' Ruth says. The two women let go and Ruth pats Mum's cheek familiarly. 'Come on in.'

While a pot of fragrant tea leaves waits to be brewed, Mum goes into her bag and brings out an incredibly suspicious bouquet. Periwinkles, to represent childhood memories, sweet peas to thank a host for hospitality . . . and hyacinths. To ask for forgiveness. She seems determined to ignore my questioning frown, so I go over to Ruth's workshop shelves to find a suitable vase instead. The vials of herbs are back in their usual organised state after Will and I tidied up last night (it took longer than it should have for, uh, reasons), and out of the corner of my eye, my mother takes in every inch of the cottage like it's a miracle. *Why?* It tickles my thoughts like a stray strand of cat hair.

'Mum,' I say, harsh and final. I slam my chosen vase onto the dining table a little harder than I should.

'Yes, dear?'

'How are you here?'

She blinks at me. 'What do you mean?'

'How did you get through the wards by yourself?'

'Oh.'

Mum and Ruth exchange a glance.

'You've been here before,' I say, and because I can say it, I don't need it confirmed. It's the truth.

Mum dallies, giving me one of her small laughs that usually come before I get brushed off for being 'silly'. Luckily for her, Will appears at the top of the stairs and halts like he knows he's come at a bad time. Even so, our eyes meet and it tosses my insides like a wave at sea. Is it me, or has he put more effort into his appearance today? I could swear that his hair looks perfectly tousled. *Interesting.*

'Morning, Will. Could you take Lilibeth's bag into the other spare room? She'll be staying awhile,' Ruth says, getting out some teacups.

'Uhh . . .' He surveys the room and comes to the decision it's best to do as he's told. 'Okay.'

'Mum, how many times have you been here? When?' I ask. She's so intent on watching Will duck out of sight, a glossy sheen over her eyes, that I doubt she hears me.

'Ruth . . . he's all grown up . . .' she breathes, a hand on her heart. She probably hasn't seen Will this close up since before the transition he told me about yesterday.

The boiling kettle bubbles as my unanswered accusation hangs in the air.

'Hello? Answers please.'

Steam shoots out of the kettle's spout. Ruth gently guides Mum to the dining table, and says, 'Let's sit and talk, shall we?'

I glare at the fresh bouquet with folded arms. You know, the one of *hyacinths*. Seeking forgiveness. For *what* exactly? Will returns and takes a seat to my left as Mum looks at Ruth with rosy shame.

'I should have come after Marc passed away,' Mum says. 'I should have sent a letter, flowers, something . . . I should have been there for you, after all you did for me . . .'

Ruth places her teacup down seriously, and says, 'I do not regret trying to heal her, Betty.'

I sit up straighter, a hook in my throat.

'Heal who?' I ask. 'When? What happened?'

'Well, I suppose . . .' Mum says, and wipes under her eyes with a single shaky finger. She takes a deep breath. 'I was always a little jealous of my friends. Ruth and Morgana had incredible magical talent, and Fern was destined to be with King Garland. When Ruth and Fern got married and both had kids on the way, my envy got the better of me.'

My heart leaps to my ears. Is she finally going to tell me? After all these years? Her guilt, her secrets, her sadness? I've never known anything besides *Don't talk about Morgana. All you need to know is she cursed you, and no, I won't answer more of your questions.* I freeze in my chair like there are restraints around my wrists.

'One night,' Mum continues, 'after I vented to Morgana about how I felt, she saw an opportunity to try something no sorcerer had ever succeeded at before. She told me she was working on a spell to make someone fall in love. If all went well, she would be hailed as the greatest sorcerer to ever live, and I would have the family I craved. Needless to say, we rushed into it without thinking. I pointed out the first man I found attractive and within the week, she'd cast her spell. It was . . . well, it was a whirlwind. I could hardly believe it had worked, despite Morgana's ego being unbearable. Yet . . . After a few weeks passed, I started to wonder if I'd made the right decision. I'd tricked this man into my life without a second thought to his own – what did *he* want before Morgana cast her spell? Did he have his own aspirations? Would he have chosen me without magic? Then, Fliss, my baby, my darling, then I found out I was having you.'

A tear splashes down her pale cheek. Her history washes me to shore like a hollowed-out shell. Jealousy and magic. *Lies.* That's what made me.

'The spell on your father soured the instant I told him I was pregnant. The news was too big for the spell to maintain its hold. He became disgusted with me, with us, and left the citadel without a word. I never heard from him again. Right after, I ran to Morgana, who said it must have been my fault the spell didn't work correctly. I begged her to help me, to find him again, to fix it, but all she said was that with a baby on the way, at least I'd have one person who might love me. Fern took Morgana's side. She shut me out.'

Mum smiles at me, both pained and proud. 'I didn't care once you were born. You were everything to me – and more. Years later, when you started talking, I realised that part of the spell must have passed down to you. Magic as strong as that always has a price. A child born of magical deceit, cursed only to tell the truth. It restored the balance after we so arrogantly tried to manipulate the rules of magic in our favour. I'm so sorry, baby. It's all my fault. I should have been the one punished, not you. I tried so hard to remove your curse. I tried everything. I even asked Ruth – and it took her sight and . . .' She glances at Ruth ashamed, and words fail her. She can't go on.

I look between the two women, a trickle of ice in my veins. Surely she can't mean . . . ? Ruth's eyes. She had been blinded because Mum asked her to try to heal me. I recall that day I collected the Odyssa when Will brushed my throat and jolted away. That's what a mere second of contact with my curse did. Gods . . . how much pain did Ruth tolerate before giving up?

And Mum has carried the guilt of it since. Of what her request did to Ruth, of how her lies ruined a man's life, of how her choices bestowed on me an unyielding curse. So much hurt ricocheted and hit all those people because my mum wanted what so many want: to love and be loved in return. I don't know how to feel, like there's an orchestra of emotions trapped within my ribs. Each cresting wave is another truth I have to carry. Each crescendo a heavier burden.

Ruth turns to me, concern etched in every groove of her face. 'Curses cannot be broken easily, least of all without significant sacrifice. Don't feel any guilt, Fliss. I was more than willing to try, and I'm sorry it didn't work. Shortly after, Fern and I had our own falling-out, so Marc and I decided to raise the wards around the cottage, thinking it would protect us from being Morgana's next target. He gave Lilibeth access when they ran into each other in the citadel, just in case she ever wanted to return. He was never one to give up on people.' She smiles at her old friend. 'And here you are.'

The hyacinths sit between them, a bridge of forgiveness, but something . . . something isn't right. There's something in what Ruth said . . .

My spine prickles.

Morgana's next target.

Wait. There was a conversation. At the castle. Morgana was there. Or . . . no, she wasn't there, but the queen said – or was it – when . . . with . . .

Like the first coal of a blacksmith's fire, my memories spark to life. The sediments of my lost days stir. I remember.

To everyone's surprise, I stand up. The chair tips back and crashes against the wooden floor with such a crack that I'm glad there aren't any cats nearby.

'They're planning something,' I announce.

No one moves, waiting for me to find the words.

'The queen and Morgana. They were talking when I was in the physician's room,' I say. '*They* ordered the flowers. The rare ones.'

I look down at Will. I can tell his mind is already at work, spinning to put together the pieces. There's a cute crunch of concentration between his eyebrows and – no, *focus*.

'Will knew where they were because he studied at the Library. That's also where Morgana lives, so she could have easily accessed the same information and sent the book over for me to find the Odyssa.'

'She's coming to Alrick for the wedding tomorrow,' Mum says, and exchanges a nervous look with Ruth.

The wedding.

My hands fly to my forehead.

'*Oh my gods*,' I blurt out, causing a twinge in my gut. 'They— She was worried the ceremony would be cancelled. But why—?'

Mum stands and reaches a comforting hand out. 'Okay, honey. Settle down, it'll be okay.'

'Have you seen Card at all while I've been gone? Did he come to see you? Ask about me?'

'Fliss, sit down. Breathe.'

'*Did he?*'

'As far as I know, he hasn't left the castle.'

What? Her answer grazes my chest like a sharp thorn. The last time Cardamine saw me, I was half dead, curled in Will's arms and dripping blood. He screamed my name. I can't imagine he'd be sitting idly by. Hasn't he tried to find me?

Still, there's only one thing to do.

'We have to warn them.'

That's what I do best. I tell people the truth. Problem solved.

'They won't believe you,' Will says. 'Not without proof.'

'I'm cursed to tell the truth. They have to believe me.'

He shakes his head. 'You've spent too much time here with me. They'll be suspicious if you suddenly return and start accusing the queen of plotting.'

'But Bash knows you were saving my life.'

'Yes, but most people in the citadel believe I'd do anything to tear him down, regardless of if it's true or not. Sending you back as a mole wouldn't be that far-fetched.'

'I hate to agree,' Mum says, 'but he's right. After you fled, every available guard was ordered to comb the forest looking for you. That's why it took me a few days to arrive. I'm sorry, Willoh – I didn't know when the best time to bring it up was – but there's a warrant for your capture, for your . . . execution.'

I harden, but Will simply rolls his eyes. 'They can try.'

'Perhaps it would be better for you both to stay inside the wards for the time being,' Ruth says. 'Especially with Morgana returning to Alrick.'

'We can't do nothing,' I say, and look beseechingly at my mother. 'We have to tell them!'

'Morgana brings nothing but calamity,' she says. 'You will stay as far away from her as you can.'

'Mum, please. We show them that Will saved my life. We tell them the whole story. If the rare flowers are dangerous and there's a chance they'll be used at the wedding ceremony, then we have to warn them!'

'You're not going anywhere.'

'Stop trying to control me!' It leaves my mouth like a clap of thunder.

Mum doesn't reply. Her silence says everything and from her taut expression, she's not willing to budge. But there's a frothing anger in my chest that won't cease. Too long. I've been playing this game too long, and the one situation in which my curse can actually help, she refuses to let me.

'Never once have I done something without considering how others will be affected,' I say. 'I choose the right words, choose which secrets to keep and which truths to share in order to keep other people happy. Card called me a people pleaser once and he was right. But I'm the one who collected those flowers, so I'm partly responsible for whatever happens. I want to do something about it.'

'Fliss, sit down,' Mum says, her voice an arrowhead. 'You're not yet fully healed.'

'The wedding is *tomorrow*.'

'You are going to stay here and rest. That's final.'

'Rest?'

'Yes, Felicity. Staying out of it is the best thing for you.'

'If they use the flowers and it hurts Bash in some way, if it hurts *Card* in some way—' I can't finish my sentence, because truthfully, I don't know what I would do in that situation. I have no idea what it would push me to do. Despite all they've done, all the betrayals and accusations, neither Bash nor Card deserve whatever chaos Morgana is bringing.

'Honey,' Mum says, but I'm done listening. I stomp out of the cottage, out into the wind and the flowers that don't try to control me.

'Is this your version of stress-haying?' Will asks from over my shoulder.

My fingers pause from tearing apart a group of weeds I'd found by the bench at the front of the cottage. My blood is thrumming. To learn that Mum and Morgana's manipulation is why I'm cursed, and then to have Mum refuse to let me use it for good is outrageous. I can't believe her.

'I'm very irritated right now,' I say in warning.

'I can see that.'

I throw down the weeds and clamber to my feet. Will's face is impassive, his hands tucked in his usual maroon jacket.

'Why aren't you freaking out?' I ask. 'There's a warrant out for your death.'

'I figured one of us should try to keep a cool head. I'll take my turn after you,' he says, and gods forbid, gives me a huge grin.

I grasp the air like I'm battling with it and yell. Will waits, and when my throat cracks and exhaustion waves in, he takes a step forward and wraps his arms around me. I bury my face in his chest. Gods, I could linger here forever, surrounded by his warmth and that soothing, familiar scent, clinging to his back like moss on bark.

'I don't want to go back inside,' I grumble into his jacket.

'You don't have to.'

'Good.'

We hold each other in the wild grass, accompanied by the rustling forest leaves and distant birdsong.

'What do you want to do about the wedding?' Will eventually asks.

I groan and knock my forehead into his chest. 'I don't know.'

He pulls back and rests his hands on either side of my neck, his thumbs cupping my jaw, then presses a light kiss to my forehead. It makes my heart stumble, like tripping over a branch in the woods.

'Felicity, you are exceptionally endearing for always wanting to do the right thing,' Will says. 'Whatever you want to do, I'm by your side. I'll follow you anywhere.'

'Charging in isn't the best idea, is it?'

'Logically speaking, I think we need some evidence,' Will says.

'I only have the anonymous requests, but I never caught the delivery person.'

'Then we go straight to the source.'

'Sounds like you have a plan,' I say, and purse my lips, impressed. I love the way the movement makes his eyes dance to my mouth. Somehow, and seemingly without much effort, Will has swept away my previous annoyance. *Damn, he's good.*

He moves his hands to my waist and pins them in place there. Just like he did yesterday when he'd had me writhing under his mouth. After cleaning up the workshop, he'd kissed me good night at the door to my room, several times, all while intending to leave. We'd been unable to drag ourselves apart even after I'd yawned in his mouth. It took Mustard jumping onto the top of the cat tower and hissing for us to head to sleep.

'I told you,' he says, closing the distance. The air between us crackles. 'I'm at your mercy, Princess. Anything for you.'

'Oh? Is that so?'

I'm close enough to see the gradient of his eyes, each artisan's brushstroke of gold. With a smug hum, Will runs his thumbs around the inside of my waistband. The breath of his chuckle tickles as he indulges himself, as he dips his hand over the curve of my bare waist, then hovers, an inch away from my lips, not kissing me, but setting off a swarm in my stomach. *Idiot.* He thinks he can tease me like this. He thinks he can just—

He presses his lips to mine and my legs almost give. Okay, maybe he can. I'm going to *shatter.*

'I think . . .' Will breathes, then dives to kiss me once more.

'Mm-hmm,' I reply, against his mouth.

'We should' – he kisses me again – 'go to' – and again – 'the Library.'

It shouldn't be a surprise that I can't reply, because he decides to run his tongue along my bottom lip and kiss me even harder. It's intoxicating. Devilishly satiating. It has me flattening myself against him and gripping fists of his hair. He seems to lose his train of thought for quite some time.

'Will—' I manage to choke out.

'Hmm?'

'Your idea?'

'Huh? Oh.'

He licks his lips, struggling to come back to reality.

'The Library,' he pants, and catches his breath. 'Maybe . . . Maybe we can find out what kind of magic they're planning to use the flowers for. I know a professor who'd be willing to hear us out.'

'So we can work out their plan.'

'Exactly.'

Without warning, Will scoops me up under my knees and seizes me in his arms. My hands fly out behind his neck for balance so we don't tumble into the weeds, but I shouldn't have panicked. There's nowhere safer.

'A classic Fliss-and-Will move.' He grins. 'If we take Jeremy, we'll get to the Library by mid-afternoon. It's too far to go on foot, even magically assisted. You can get answers about the flowers before heading back to the citadel in time for the wedding.'

My heart catapults towards the sun he blocks.

'You want to sneak out?' I ask, so excited that I almost yell.

He has a reckless glint to his eyes that crinkles the corners.

'I mean, it wouldn't be the worst crime I've committed in the past week.'

'Let's do it.'

'That didn't take much persuading.'

'Would you rather go back inside and play house with our mothers?'

He raises his eyebrows at me like I've gone mad. 'Absolutely not.'

'Then,' I say, pulling him closer by his collar, 'whisk me away.'

In almost no time at all, we're in the stables with Jeremy saddled up and a satchel of supplies strapped to him. Will conjures some warmer clothes and offers me a fleece-lined jacket and some stretchy trousers more suited for riding than my long skirt. My mother's warning about the forest gives us a moment of pause, but Will promises he can magically send a message later on, letting our parents know we're safe. Our near deaths are not something Mum or Ruth should have to consider happening again. It's *not* something that will happen again.

Will swings onto the saddle in front of me and then turns his head.

'Ready?'

A lump in my throat, I nod, and he leads Jeremy off in a trot towards the forest, towards answers and an entire army of guards out for blood.

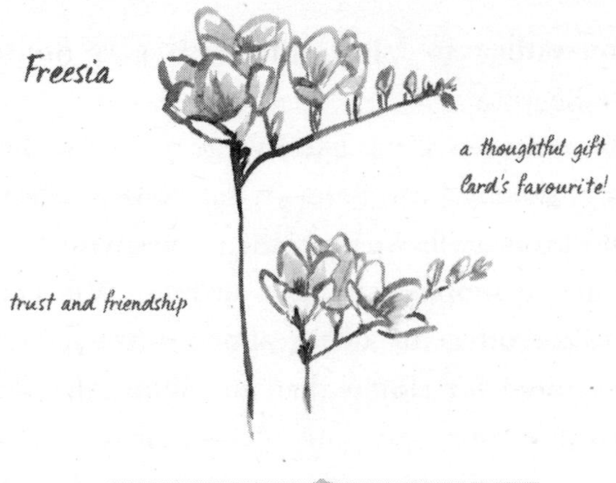

CHAPTER TWENTY-TWO

We avoid the roads and artfully weave between the trees, the horse's hooves a drum beat to the dance of my heart against Will's back. He knows this forest and has more than enough experience eluding the guards. Mum was right, though. There are glimpses of blue and silver lurking among the greenery that we bypass carefully, and just when I don't think my anxiety can take any more close calls, Will pulls back on the reins and slows Jeremy to a quiet walk.

'What is it?' I ask, hushed.

'The fastest way to the Library is over that bridge.'

From our position within the bark and branches, I peer round Will. Past the scatterings of leaves, the tree line gives way to a wide, fast-flowing river and a sturdy grey-stone bridge with waist-high walls. At first, it looks empty, until the midday sun catches a flash of metal. There are guards ahead.

'They've set up a checkpoint here,' Will mutters.

My instinct is to try to ride past them as fast as possible but my mistakes have been made plain recently. I've been rushing in too fast, charging forward and hoping for the best. Each time, someone's been hurt. *I've* been hurt.

'We should scout it out,' I say, and Will agrees. He slides off the saddle and helps me down before tying Jeremy around a nearby tree. The horse happily munches on some patchy grass near the roots. If only we could be so easily satisfied.

'I can do a silencing spell, just in case,' Will says. 'It'll hide our footsteps and voices, but we won't be able to talk to each other until I lift it.'

'Good idea.'

Safe and quiet. That's how we should approach this.

Will swipes his hand between us like there's a pane of glass, and a tinny high-pitched buzz washes past my ears. Magic shivers down my spine but my startled gasp is silent, not even a breath of sound. I test it, try to speak but no noise comes. Weirdly, it feels similar to how the curse locks my throat up. Will must see that in my frown as he gives me a thumbs-up in question. I calm his worries with a nod and motion him mutely towards the river.

When we reach the final row of trees, Will presses his back to a wide trunk and I tiptoe to the next one over, no crunch of leaves under my feet. With my palms against the rough bark, I risk a glance at the bridge.

Thank the gods for Will's foresight.

I whip back behind the tree, balling my hands into fists. I clench them with all my might and scream. Because I can. Because no noise will come from my mouth to alert the two guards at the base of that bridge. Because, gods, it feels good to do so. My soundless scream is as silent as the fury in my chest. Why is it always him? In the bliss of being with Will, I – oh my gods. I'd actually forgotten about him.

I didn't think that was possible.

'He did this on purpose, sending me all the way out here,' Lark says with a huff I know all too well.

'Good. Hopefully you'll learn something,' Howell replies.

There's a short march of metal footsteps and each step closer is a stab of fear. *Please don't find us.*

'About what? How many trees this forest has?' Lark shoots back.

'Just be grateful the prince lifted your suspension after the way you acted.'

As always, Howell is level-headed and calm. And also incredibly skilled and experienced. There's no way we can fight past him.

A brush of wind against my cheek brings my face in the direction of Will. He's staring at me, wide-eyed.

You okay? he mouths.

I shudder a breath. How can I explain? I gesture to myself, then Lark, then cross my forearms to make an X in hope that it gets the message across.

'I should be out there looking for Fliss, not babysitting a bridge,' Lark complains.

'We all have our part to do, and as a Guard of Alrick, no job is unworthy if it protects our people. It's your duty to be here, Lark,' Howell says. 'We must trust our colleagues are doing their best to search for Felicity. Besides, it was good for you when your relationship ended. This situation has you slipping back into bad habits.'

Will quickly drops my gaze to spy on the guards. I watch him study Lark up and down, and when he turns back to me, he tilts his head to the side with a pinch of smugness. The edges of his mouth tug and he hovers his hand side to side, as if to say *not bad.* He points a finger to himself then to the sky, and mouths *I'm better.*

Stop, I reply, but he's cracked my anger, drawn out a laugh, and when Lark speaks again, his voice is a blunt edge.

'How was it good for me?'

'You were such an arrogant ass when you were in training,' Howell says. I peek round the tree again to see him pace to the edge of the bridge, alert even when conversing. 'A rookie from a small southern village thinking you knew best. Having an in with the prince through Felicity made your ego even worse.'

Lark faces his senior, arms folded. 'I wasn't that bad.'

'You were. That's why I was so hard on you. You needed to learn that teamwork and loyalty would take you further than pride. It was only after you and Felicity broke up that you knuckled down and threw yourself into training seriously. You proved yourself with hard work. That's the only reason you became a fully fledged guard. The captain wouldn't have passed you otherwise.'

'Well, what else was I supposed to do? Everyone knew what happened at the party. I saw the looks I got. People hated me.'

It's been almost a year since our attempt to talk about what happened and we'd both been so emotional, so angry and hurt, that predictably, it had ended in tears. In all the months since then, I've been doing my best to avoid him. But it's a lie that I haven't been curious about how much it had impacted his life. I'd noticed the side-eyes and whispers in my direction. The gossip that the truths I'd yelled at the party had been too harsh, too disrespectful, and *Poor Lark for even giving her a chance, what a scene she'd made.* He thought everyone hated him too? Maybe, but none more than me.

I wonder where that hatred went.

I wonder when it softened from a blaze to a breeze.

Howell's gruff face turns stern. 'You learned the hard way that prioritising reputation and status – personal gain – won't do you any good in this line of work. It's a lesson you sometimes forget, which is why the prince and captain give you jobs like this, in the far corners of the kingdom "babysitting" bridges. There is more to being a guard than being best friends with royalty.'

'Prince Bastion hardly talks to me these days anyway.'

'You have no one to blame but yourself.'

Lark falls silent.

'Take that frown off your face,' Howell says.

'What more can I do, Howell?'

'You can shut up and do your job with dignity. Do you see me complaining about being here? No. Because I do not look down upon it. It's an honour to serve.'

A short birdcall echoes three times from farther within the forest, something I wouldn't have noticed if Will hadn't straightened so suddenly. He waves a hand to get my attention and points back the way we came. I push off the tree and follow him, my shoulders curled inward. Am I glad I heard all that? I don't know . . . I never thought I'd move on from the pain Lark caused. I thought it would be a thorn in my chest forevermore.

A hand catches mine and Will interlocks our fingers. I never thought I'd be able to love again. Love someone more. Gods, I'd been so very wrong.

When we get back to Jeremy, someone is feeding him a carrot. Will snaps a finger and the tingle of magic leaves my skin.

'How did you find us?' he asks, able to speak again.

Pigeon whips round with a wild grin, her bow slung across a shoulder. Across the right side of her jaw and creeping up her cheek is a faded pink burn mark that licks her skin like fire.

'I've been following your tracks for about an hour. You've gotten sloppy,' she says.

I break away from Will to march over and yank her into a pine-scented hug. She freezes in my arms and chokes out a short laugh.

'What did I do?' she asks.

I let her go, then jab my knuckles into her arm.

'Ow!'

'Last I heard,' I scold, 'you'd hurt Prince Merit on his way back from Dreah and got caught in an accidental explosion! What on earth were you thinking? He almost died! You're lucky I gave you the benefit of the doubt and kept my mouth shut!'

Pigeon laughs and taps a light finger to her scarred skin.

'Oh yeah, it was a shocker. Didn't know there would be extremely flammable alcohol inside that particular wagon. I got a cool battle wound out of it, though.'

'Pigeon, it's not a joke! I told you to be careful!'

'Ah, sorry. Everyone is on the mend on our side. How about the prince? Was he okay? He ran off before we could check, and to be honest, it was pretty chaotic.'

'He collapsed in front of us! Bleeding!'

'Yikes, sorry about ruining your date like that . . .'

I stutter a wordless reply. Moments later, Will's hand brushes my lower back.

'I told Will he should go for it,' Pigeon explains coolly. 'I assume that happened? Considering you're now on the run together with a crazy number of guards hunting you?'

'It took a while longer,' Will says, 'but I appreciate your attempt to meddle.'

Pigeon winks. 'Anytime. Now you can talk to a human being instead of always talking to your cats.'

'Thank you, Pigeon,' Will drawls, a tinge of embarrassment slipping through.

'I imagine you're wanting to get past those guards?' Pigeon says. Jeremy prods his nose into her shoulder, and she digs around in one of her pouches for another carrot.

'Yeah, we're trying to get to the Library,' Will says. 'There's some information that might come in handy before the prince's wedding tomorrow.'

'Oh, that's right.' Pigeon nods, her eyebrows knitting together. 'We were trying to come up with a plan to disrupt it but there's too many guards to go at it safely. That big one on the bridge there is particularly infallible.'

'Howell,' I say. 'He's one of the most senior guards. Definitely not to be underestimated. And the other . . .'

'The pretty blond one?' Pigeon asks.

'Hmm,' Will says with a held-back laugh. His hand slips around my waist protectively. Possessively. 'Not sure that's the adjective I'd use to describe him.'

'Are you kidding? Those shoulders? I've never felt attraction a day in my life, but I'm sure he's a popular one.'

I grit my teeth together. 'That's, um . . . That's my ex.'

Jeremy snorts into Pigeon's open palm and the last of the carrot disappears.

'Oh,' she says. 'Huh.'

'Judge me later,' I say. 'We need to get past them. Can you help?'

'Yeah, that's why I'm here.'

Will takes a step round Jeremy and strokes his mane.

'I have a handful of ideas,' he says, focus sharpening his face. 'I'm not sure any of them are actually feasible. The issue is, we still need to travel by horseback after the bridge, otherwise I'd let Pigeon take Jeremy home. It'll take too long without him.'

He flattens his palms against the horse's neck and closes his eyes. His mouth moves in a whispered spell and before my eyes, Jeremy starts to disappear, the forest filling in where his neck once was. The invisibility spell bleeds out from Will's fingers, but as it travels down Jeremy's shoulders to the main bulk of his body, Will hisses. His face screws up.

It reminds me too much of the dungeon.

'Will, stop.'

Will flinches and blinks rapidly. I rush to take his elbow as all the visibility floods back to Jeremy.

'Okay, scrap that one,' Will says, his breaths a little haggard. 'He's too big. The spell is only meant for humans.'

I dig my fingers into his arm. 'Don't do that.'

'Sorry, Princess.'

'Plan B?' Pigeon asks, hands on hips and ready for action.

'Uh . . .' Will looks down at me, hesitant. 'I'm not sure anyone will like it. *I* don't like it.'

'Go on,' I say.

'I can use the invisibility spell on myself to sneak past the guards. Once I'm on the other side, I can create a fog that will cover you as you bring Jeremy over. Pigeon can stay on this side of the bridge and if need be, distract the guards.'

'I have a little phosphorus left,' Pigeon says. Will shoots her a look. 'I said *a little.*'

'Don't use it while Fliss is still on the bridge.'

'Wait—' I interrupt. 'We have to go separately?'

Will smiles sadly. 'A lot of spells require concentration, so I can't do the invisibility spell and anything else at the same time. We need a way to get Jeremy over to the other side and using fog might be the best shot to do that. I told you I didn't like it.'

'Neither do I,' I say.

'I've got your backs,' Pigeon says, pulling her bow into prepared hands.

'Will . . .'

He grins at me. 'Let's give it a go. See you on the other side?'

I grab his collar. 'Promise.'

'Promise.'

He kisses me, the lightest brush of his lips, then he's striding to the bridge and fading from view. I wait for Howell to shout, for the sound of metal scraping from a sword being drawn, but it doesn't come. Pigeon brings Jeremy's bridle to me, and I curl tense fingers under the leather as we head back to the tree line.

'He'll be okay. He always has a knack for getting out of trouble somehow,' she says, and leaps onto a tree root to peer ahead. 'The first time we met, I'd been stealing from travellers in the forest and ended up bumping into some guards. Will helped me out of it and only asked for the medicine back. We shared the food.'

I'd seen that in Will's memory. She'd looked so gaunt at the time.

'I hope living like that becomes a thing of the past, not just for you, but for everyone.'

Pigeon's braid swings sideways as she jumps onto a lower root. 'I do too. Sometimes. But it's not something I allow myself to get hung up on. I have my family to feed, which means being pragmatic rather than idealistic. I can't indulge in hopes and wishes.'

When we're back in the citadel, I should put Pigeon's pragmatism into practice. Keeping my mouth shut for so long has only upheld the pretence of peace. No longer.

'Here we go,' Pigeon says, pointing to a thick layer of fog that creeps over the bridge and spills into the river like a cloudy waterfall.

Howell unsheathes his sword.

'What is that?' Lark calls, running to position himself at Howell's side. The canopy-high block of smog swallows the two guards.

Pigeon squeezes my shoulder.

'One foot in front of the other, Fliss,' she says. 'Keep to the edge and use the wall to make sure you're going straight. Don't stop.'

Jeremy whinnies softly. We can do this.

'I owe you again,' I say.

She shrugs. 'What are favours between friends?'

'Friends.' I smile, then step towards the cloud of fog.

My eyes struggle to focus as the world turns white. I can see only a few inches in front of me and have to work to find the edge of the bridge. When the cool stone is under my fingers, I lead Jeremy on, walking slowly, as quietly as a horse can be, but with the fear-filled urgency of Howell and Lark being nearby. One more step. To Will. Keep going. One more.

'Found anything?' Howell shouts.

'Nothing!'

'Keep looking! Spread out!'

'I can't see anything in this damned—'

Jeremy and I cross the peak of the bridge and start on the downward slope.

Almost there.

Almost back to Will.

Almost.

The crunch of metal is the only warning I have before a hand flies across my mouth from behind.

'Halt,' a voice I used to love growls in my ear.

I panic, unhook my fingers from the bridle, and slap a hand against Jeremy's shoulder just before Lark slams me into the stone edge. Thankfully, Jeremy gets the message and canters out of view. Lark leans me so far backward my hair dangles above the gushing river. His green eyes meet mine and his face pales.

'*Fliss?*'

'Please let me go,' I say with a strike of pain through my abdomen. He's stretching my stomach, stretching my scar. 'Lark, please.'

He pulls me back to standing and clasps both hands around my arms. I try to wrestle out of his grip, but he keeps me pushed up against the wall.

'Fliss, you're – you're *alive*? How?' he asks, frenzied.

'Yes. Lark, please. Please let me go.'

'You were dying. You were *dead*.'

'I was healed. Please.'

'When I thought you weren't going to make it I tried to – I looked for more herbs. I sent a message to the healers in my village but—'

'Lark.' I say his name so forcefully, so resolutely, that he meets my eyes again. I don't look away, like I often have. I don't avoid him. The anger I had for him is feeble now, it's almost pathetic. I was clinging tightly to a poisonous hatred that never did me any good. 'It's okay.'

I mean it.

He takes a deep breath in and his shoulders relax, like he'd been needing to hear that, like he'd been holding on to the pain just as tightly as I was.

'It's okay,' I repeat. 'Let me go.'

'You're . . .' he says in disbelief, 'you're not looking at me the same.'

I study him, his eyes that match the colour of the Lunarie's petals, that dark blond hair that means nothing to me now. No, I don't suppose I am.

'I'm sorry,' he says, and it's heavy, a storm denser than this fog.

'It's okay.'

It's the end of us, our story. From strangers, to lovers, to loathing. To nothing.

His hands loosen.

The woosh of an arrow shoots between us and my weight shifts back, almost toppling me over the edge of the wall. Lark reaches for his sword.

'Run!' Pigeon shouts from somewhere in the mist.

'I've got her pinned,' Howell bellows.

The shake of an explosion jolts the bridge and has me stumbling to a knee.

'QUICK, RUN!'

I don't take one last look at Lark.

I lurch up and run headlong into the dissipating fog.

When I break through, Will is pacing. Tense. Almost ripping out his hair. Jeremy toes the grass in the open plain on this side of the bridge. I see them both and my heart aches, melts, gives way, and surrenders. I run right into Will's open arms and breathe him in. He envelops me like I'll vanish.

Behind us, as I plant myself in a safe embrace, rocks crunch and slide, and the bridge crumbles into the water, swept away like the remnants of the fog in the wind. Neither Pigeon nor the guards are to be seen. Only a crater of rubble parting the river remains, the fingerprints of waves already finding a new path onward, already moving on.

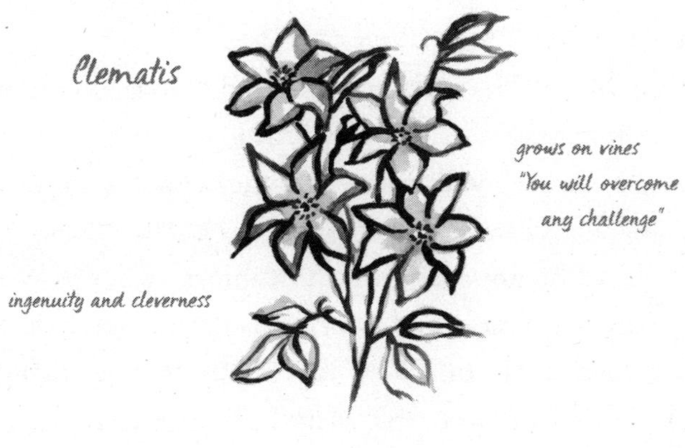

CHAPTER TWENTY-THREE

I'd stared at the water until the ripples remained behind every blink. Will had plunged his hands into the river, searching, trying to locate any sense of them, but said that water is an element not easily persuaded, and he'd never had an affinity for it like he has with the wind. If they survived, the current was strong enough to sweep them far, far away by now. Eventually, we agreed we needed to move on. If we find out what the queen and Morgana have planned for the wedding, perhaps we can save at least one person. Even if we couldn't save those three. *No. Don't think like that.*

Back on the saddle, the silence of the aftermath follows every hoofbeat.

'Pigeon will be okay, won't she?' I whisper, my head slumped between Will's shoulder blades. A question and not a question. A truth I don't know.

'She's survived much worse,' he says, but there's a forced lightness to his tone, a concern he's not letting himself dwell on. 'That river leads to the citadel anyway, so we can always check on our way back, ride along the bank.'

'Yes, please.'

For any sign of her or Lark and Howell. Gods, in their metal chain mail, I can't imagine how they could swim . . .

'We're almost there,' Will says, and kicks in his heels to spur us on.

It feels wrong to be approaching the Library of Heris with such gloom in my chest. Knowing Morgana resides here has never made me eager to visit, but I've had a lifetime of listening to Card and his obsession with the place. He painted the grandest visions of tall domed ceilings that glistened like the stars on a crisp winter night; of bookshelves that grew like mosaic-decorated branches of a tree, crammed with all the knowledge one could possibly imagine; and more. Where the students could study and thrive and access the deepest, most intimate archives, and residents could dedicate their lives to research. He talked about it over and over, until it was imprinted on my mind like an impossibly impressive legend, growing more and more nonsensical as the years went by.

He was exactly right.

The Library stands like a bold mountain under a late-afternoon sky, surrounded by open green fields that make sure it isn't obstructed. It's possibly three, no four, times the size of Alrick Castle, and wildly more interesting. Where the castle has grey-stone walls and four smooth turrets, the Library has at least ten colossal domed towers, shining like the bricks have been stamped with golden sunlight, and pierced with windows in all kinds of shapes – some paper-thin strips of glass, some rainbow-filled circles, and one large dome in the centre that holds a giant bronze telescope perfect for reading the sky.

Will rides us directly towards an open-air stable in a cream-stoned courtyard, vacant of people. I'm not sure what I expected, but I didn't realise it would be so quiet. He ties Jeremy into an empty stall while I stretch my legs to work the feeling back into them.

It's such a relief to not be sitting. To be moving. To be finally *doing* something to make a difference.

'Thank you for bringing us here, Jemmy.' I sigh and wrap my arms around the horse's neck.

'Jemborino,' Will adds, throwing me a small smile.

Ah. He must have heard it in my voice. The heaviness. The worry. My beautiful, darling raft at sea. He's trying to lighten the load and cheer me up.

I tug my mouth up.

'Jeronimo.'

'Jezzlebee.'

Will cracks a grin at the giggle he gets out of me. The horse seems to not care what we call him and helps himself to a bucket of feed.

Side by side, Will and I walk over the cream gravel, no chatter of voices covering the crunch of our footsteps.

'Where is everyone?' I ask, tilting my head back. From the entrance, the Library takes up most of the sky.

'Uh, I guess folk at the Library aren't really outdoorsy people. We – they tend to get stuck in a project and forget about the outside world.'

I hear his slip-up and note how his hands have disappeared back into his pockets. I've spent enough time around him to pick up that hiding his hands is his way of protecting himself. Of seeming arrogant and uninterested to mask his insecurities.

Something occurs to me that I should have thought about sooner.

'Did you ever meet Morgana when you studied here?'

'No, my mum warned me to stay out of her way when I first started attending. She didn't have to worry though – we never crossed paths. I heard that Morgana's always away travelling, and if she is here, she rarely leaves her chambers.'

'Will they know about the warrant for your arrest?'

'Uh . . . probably.'

'Won't that be a problem?'

He sucks in air through gritted teeth.

'Depends on how much trouble we make,' he says. 'The Library of Heris prides itself on neutrality. They welcome anyone, regardless of background, as long as you don't break any rules while you're on the grounds. Actually, I knew someone who worked as a chef here who had a pretty long list of crimes to his name back in Senred. I guess this place can be a second chance.'

'Okay. So we just have to behave.'

He throws me a wink. 'You know me, Princess.'

We reach a set of towering bronze doors engraved with a script I can't read, and Will places a palm flat on the metal. Like an invitation, the door swings open and he waves me in.

The aroma is a world away from the musty air of the castle library. This place is luscious, like a field of roses in summer, or a grove of jasmine – exquisitely unique and refreshing. There's a pinch of something sharp too, like the tinge of burnt metal and magic that fizzles on my tongue. I step forward on marble floors made of the richest navy and silver, mouth agape. Past the sparkles in the air, bookshelves grow in colossal rows towards a twinkling turquoise glass dome ceiling, not in sharp wooden lines, but in crooked curved grooves that house books of all sizes and shapes. The foyer we're in heads in a few directions, but each path ends in a deep blue shadow, from which shuffles of turning pages and whispered conversations float.

Card would be *so* jealous I'm here. I wonder what he'd say. Gods, I miss him. *No. Stop it. Focus on the now. Not the bridge. Not the wedding. Only the next step.*

'Which way is it?' I ask.

'See the silver in the floor?' Will says, setting off down an aisle. 'It reacts to the direction you want to go, so you won't get lost. Clever, right? Very handy when you want to find a specific book. My professor's office is this way.'

Will leads me into the maze of bookshelves, past twisting spiral stairs that reach an upper balcony level and wooden ladders that shift along the shelves of their own accord. Every now and then, a book leaves its place and floats into the air as if waiting to be rescued – or, rather, collected. As we walk, shimmering silver lines in the floor guide us onward.

'How long did you study here?' I ask, unable to stop turning my head in every direction possible. There's too much to marvel at.

'Uhh, about eight years. Until I turned sixteen.'

'So you started coming at eight years old? That's so young. Did you travel here alone?'

'No, at the start, Mum occasionally came with me. Actually, she took a few classes early on to learn more about identity-affirming care and to help with my treatments. I take this monthly potion to keep my chemical levels balanced. She learned how to make that here.'

Monthly? It's a good job he wasn't held in the dungeons for that amount of time. But I believe Bastion would have got Will the care he needed, even if he wanted Will dead.

'That's amazing of your mum.'

'Yeah, although it was kind of embarrassing to have her hovering nearby when I was trying to seem cool in front of my classmates.'

'That doesn't sound bad to me. I love spending time with your mum.'

His short bark of a laugh turns into a sigh. 'To be honest, the last year and a bit weren't great, what with the whispers from Alrick. When my dad got really sick, I decided to leave. I wanted to be at home.'

I can tell he's clenching his fists inside his pockets. Being back here must be flooding him with memories, and not all will be pleasant. It makes me wonder if him hiding his hands away so often is related to his transition – if there is any leftover anxiety regarding the shape of his hands. I've had them on my mind since the day he healed my injuries, so I want him to know that they're a part of him I adore. I bat at his elbow and get a frown of confusion in return.

'Take your hands out of your pockets,' I order. 'I want to hold your hand.'

A laugh of surprise bursts out of him.

'Never subtle are you, Princess,' Will says, and holds his palm out, thin fingers stretched wide. Perfect for mine to interlace with. I lock our fingers together, satisfied. The moon and sun in an eternal embrace. *That's better.*

'Cute,' he mutters.

'Shush. Focus.'

We turn again, and for the first time so far, the aisle is occupied. A woman in white-and-teal robes peers at a bookshelf from behind thin-rimmed oval glasses. Her long white skirt, embroidered with gold leaves at the hem, is paired with a teal headband resting on long silver hair. One of her sleeves is pinned where her arm ends at the elbow, while her other is extended, keeping a stack of books afloat with a spell.

'Hanya?' Will says, and halts in his tracks.

The woman looks up.

The books clatter to the floor.

'Willoh!'

There's a moment where she can't decide whether the fallen books or Will's appearance demands her attention more. Will twists his hand and the books fly back to their suspended stack.

'Will, you shouldn't be here,' she whispers, glancing over her shoulder.

'Oh,' Will says. His grip tightens in mine.

The woman checks behind her again. 'Alrick told us to contact them *immediately* if you're seen. What did you do?'

'Nothing! I mean, I accidentally stabbed this darling princess here,' Will explains, 'but as you can see, she's fine. Well, she keeps insisting that she's fine.'

I twitch my fingers in a wave.

'Um, hello,' I say.

'There are already guards posted along the border to Alrick, thanks to you, and this is a library, *not* a battleground,' Hanya says. She shakes her head so her silver fringe dances side to side. 'In all my time here, I've never heard of a kingdom so suddenly interfering with the Library. You must have *really* crossed the line.'

'Hanya, come on, you've known me since I was a child. I'm harmless!'

She sighs at Will – something I get the feeling she's done a lot over the years.

'Right . . . Well. Good luck on whatever nonsense you're up to. Not that I said that. Do *not* get me involved.' She twirls a hand under her books again. 'And when you're done being a wanted criminal, I'd better see you back here in classes again. You never finished your alchemy assignment.'

Hanya shakes her head one last time and disappears into the misty shimmers.

Voices come from behind us. People we should avoid. People that might snitch on Will. Not all might be as friendly as Hanya.

'Come on,' I say.

We stride down the aisles, slightly faster than before, slightly more on edge. Soon enough, we stop at a wooden door nestled between bookshelves. The name plate reads KEEPER EINAR.

'What's a Keeper?' I ask. There's so much about this place I don't know, it's overwhelming. I'm starting to feel like I'm caught in the same current that dragged Pigeon away.

'The Keeper is the highest position at the Library. It's like a head teacher of sorts. If anyone knows about the flowers, it's him.'

Our eyes meet as Will lifts his knuckles. After Hanya's reaction, I can tell his belief in finding help here has been shaken. But we've come all this way. There's no going back. He waits for me to take a deep breath, to nod. Then he knocks on the door.

'Enter,' a voice from within calls, and the door magically opens.

Will and I set foot in a square office lined with navy star-covered wallpaper that stretches over the ceiling. The constellations float across it slowly as if moving in real time, but I don't get much chance to study it because a stocky old man behind a cluttered rosewood desk springs to his feet. It's the professor I caught a glimpse of in Will's memory – the one who told him he had such potential. The man rushes round the desk to take Will's shoulders in ink-stained hands. His robes are similar to Hanya's, with his own twist of long bell sleeves. A curious bronze pin in the shape of an open book with a sword thrust down the spine rests over his heart.

'Willoh!' the old man says, eyes wrinkling.

'Hey, Prof. Bad time?' Will attempts a grin.

'For you, Willoh, never,' he says. 'Please.'

Relief sweeps over both Will and me as the Keeper ushers us to two plush chairs in front of his desk. Once seated, the old man smiles at me.

'Hello, I'm Keeper Einar. Welcome to the Library of Heris.'

'Felicity,' I say. 'Nice to meet you.'

Will crosses an ankle over his knee. 'This isn't a social visit unfortunately.'

'Nevertheless, I am glad to see you. How long has it been since I've had you in my office? It must be . . .?'

'Three years.'

Keeper Einar settles in his tall-backed chair opposite us and presses his fingertips together. His expression is a crestfallen wave.

'Willoh, I must admit, I received a rather alarming message from Alrick recently concerning you. It was supposed to be kept a secret between the professors, but you know how this place is – everyone knew before nightfall. However, I'm certain there is a reasonable explanation. Is that why you came? To seek sanctuary?'

'To seek answers,' Will says, and taps a finger on his leg. 'The warrant you heard about is legit, but unimportant for now.'

'Unimportant? Willoh, they told us to hand you over, dead or alive. I've never heard such a request! *Here* of all places. As if we'd break a thousand years of neutrality.'

'I'm sure it'll blow over. Fliss has questions,' he says, gesturing in my direction.

The Keeper looks at me, a piercing study that has me clutching my hands in my lap. 'Questions, my dear?'

'I collected some rare flowers, and we want to know what they could be used for . . .' I trail off, nervous now I'm here.

'Please, go on.'

'There are three – the Feiyan, Odyssa, and Lunarie. I collected them over the past month and a half and delivered them unknowingly to the queen of Alrick.' Now that I've started talking about flowers, my confidence blooms. 'I'm familiar with the magic of flowers, but these three were the most powerful I've ever come across and there's very little information about them available. We have reason to believe that they'll be used together at the prince of Alrick's wedding ceremony tomorrow. Is there anything you can tell us about them?'

Keeper Einar hums thoughtfully.

'Those flowers certainly are rare . . . How curious that they bloomed at the same time. Sometimes decades pass without so much as a bud, then the gods give life to all three at once.' He leans his wrinkled chin on his fingertips and studies me. 'You're right that these particular flowers have incredibly potent magic, but what's not widely known is that not just anyone can find them. Yes, we have information about their locations in books here, but knowing is one thing. Doing so is much different. In fact, even if one were to find them, it would be a trial for most to remove them from their soil. You must have a strong affinity for botany, Felicity, to have found and retrieved them.'

'They felt no harder to pick than any other flower for me,' I say. Sure, getting to their locations had been a near-impossible feat combined with luck and stubbornness, but actually removing them had been the easiest part.

The Keeper smiles.

'Only those with the deepest respect for the flowers, who do not wish to use their power for personal gain are able to pick them. It sounds like you were most suited to do so.'

His words are meant as a compliment but my heart sinks. Morgana couldn't have collected the flowers herself. She'd said in the physician's room that she'd been impressed I had found the Odyssa. That most usually . . . perished. That I'd done what they needed me for. Gods, they'd used me knowing I'd be betraying the thing I love most.

'So what do they do? Together? If you use them?' I ask, my head buzzing.

'Simply put,' Keeper Einar says, 'the Feiyan, Odyssa, and Lunarie form a cycle. They're a sequence, a rhythm that represents the movement of time – of the day.'

'I felt that,' I say. 'The Feiyan is daytime, the sun. The Odyssa grew in a pair and felt like . . . like the in-between, like dawn and dusk, sunrise and sunset.'

The Keeper nods, and if I'm not wrong, purses his mouth, impressed.

'And the Lunarie?' he prompts.

'The night. The moon's glow. The energy that lies in darkness.'

'That's correct. Put together in order, the Feiyan in the north, Odyssa to the east and west, and Lunarie in the south, they create a forever moving circle, an unbreakable loop, just like the cycle of days. Circles are often used in magic to amplify, as they're an incredibly powerful conduit. A spell with those ingredients certainly would be impressive, dangerous even. You say they will be used at the prince's wedding tomorrow? Hmm . . .'

He pauses, deep in thought.

'I wonder . . . The flowers and the ceremony . . . I suppose the queen has always been extremely perturbed about her son's curse. Perhaps that is connected somehow . . .'

There's a beat of silence where I think Will stops breathing.

I grip the arms of my chair.

'I'm sorry, did you just say Bash is cursed? Prince Bastion?' I ask.

Keeper Einar nods.

'Oh . . .' Will exhales.

He turns to me, pale, awash with shock.

'*That's* what they meant,' he says. 'My parents always said the wards around our house were so the queen couldn't find it. It makes sense now – the queen wanted Mum to try and remove Bash's curse, and after what happened when she tried to remove yours, Mum must have refused.'

'I thought you and the prince used to be friends, Willoh,' Keeper Einar says. 'With your level of magic, couldn't you feel it?'

Will slumps in his chair. He's drawn out, a world away, eyes flickering like he's scanning a library of memories. 'I just . . . I didn't think . . .'

'So, what is it? His curse?' I ask.

'The prince's curse renders him unable to use magic of any kind, not even the most basic of hedge magic. In Calla, even those who are born with a low level of magic ability can study and improve their skill if desired, so a complete absence of magic is highly unusual – near impossible, in fact. When the prince was an infant, he failed to display the early signs of magic intuition often found within the royal line, so the queen sent for me. Upon examination, I discovered a strong – and unremovable – curse blocking and repelling any use of magic, fixed in chains around his wrists. I told the queen my results, but I fear my assessment of her son offended her. Since then, communication between Alrick and the Library diminished greatly. Even when we sent inquiries about the situation developing in the kingdom's northern forest, the queen prohibited any of our researchers from investigating.'

I blink away the spots in my vision.

'The tree,' I say, recalling the flash of green I'd seen around Bash's wrists in Will's memory. 'Bash tried to gain a boost of magic from the oak tree, and it backfired. It didn't work because of his curse.'

Ruth's words echo in my mind: curses cannot be broken easily, least of all without significant sacrifice. Her bid to heal my curse damaged her eyesight.

For Bash, the north was the payment. The health of the forest and the livelihood of Pigeon's family. That was the consequence of his failed attempt.

If the queen and Morgana plan to use the flowers to remove Bash's curse at the ceremony tomorrow, what will be the price? What will be sacrificed this time?

'Now, I'm not personally familiar with any specific spells, especially not dark magic ones, that the flowers are used for,' Keeper Einar says. 'Lady Morgana is the expert on such subjects. Luckily for you, she got back from Berian yesterday, but she never stays long, so you'll have to try and catch her before she leaves.'

My blood runs cold. An ice bath of fear.

'S-Sorry,' I stammer. 'Morgana is here? Now?'

'Oh, are you acquainted? She's had a residency since she was a postgraduate student. Not that I see her much – she's forever off travelling around the kingdom for her research projects. But she's an expert on exotic flora and has written extremely detailed papers on dark curses, including those similar to the prince's. I recommend you speak with her. You can find her in the northwest tower. Just knock on the door; she should be in.'

'Hang on – she wrote about curses?' Will asks. 'She *submitted* those papers to the archives?'

'Yes, I've read a few myself. They were very intriguing. Most of them centre around a spoiled spell that corrupted over time into dark magic. Apparently it can manifest through generations. She certainly sees all sorts of things on her travels.'

I feel like I've been plunged into the ground.

She wrote about *me*.

'Oh, I'm sure,' Will says, his jaw taut with a rare anger. 'Considering she was the one to cast it.'

Keeper Einar's eyebrows disappear.

'Willoh. That . . . That is a very serious accusation. The use of dark magic is strictly forbidden to any who wish to stay here. I admit, Lady Morgana can sometimes be . . . vigorous in her approaches, but she's supplied this library with keen research.'

'It's the truth.' He spits it in such a way that I have to strain to keep my lips from wobbling. 'Never mind. We don't have time. Fliss, let's go.'

I take Will's hand and use him to find my balance.

The Keeper of the Library doesn't know. He doesn't know that Morgana cast her spell on my parents and passed it down to me. The person with the highest possible position in the most knowledgeable place in all of Calla *doesn't know*. All this time, she's been benefiting from research and academic papers about me. My curse. My life. While I carried the weight of it.

'Sir, thank you for your help,' Will says politely, and grips the back of my coat.

Their further farewells sail over my ears as I follow Will blindly to the exit. The queen and Morgana. Hand in hand, like Mum said. Did the queen feed Morgana details about me? Were those chats the queen and I had in her chambers another ground for Morgana to snoop, to dig for data? I've long been the queen's tool.

Her snitch. Now I find out that I'm also a test subject in an archived paper that anyone can read.

The door to the office closes behind us and Will looks at me sharply. The marble at our feet swirls, waiting.

'Where to, Fliss? What do you want to do?'

She's here. She's caused too much harm already. She's hidden in the shadows and laughed at our misfortune. We have to stop her. She can't make it to the wedding. If we cut her off here, if we get the truth out of her now, we can avoid taking the fight to the citadel.

The silver marble sharpens towards our next destination: towards the northwest tower, towards Morgana, the sorcerer who cursed me.

CHAPTER TWENTY-FOUR

The bookshelves and sparkles stop suddenly in front of an enclosed spiral staircase. Grey-stone steps lie ahead, illuminated by intricate black torches of magical firelight. The air is quiet and dry here, like it's not permitted to breathe.

'Up we go,' Will says.

I follow him with growing anxiety as the homely mumbles of the library fade farther and farther away. My entire life I've tried to shoulder the burden Morgana gave me, and sometimes, I managed. Sometimes, there was a lull. I was able to blindly make it through the day without torment – days when I made bouquets and didn't squabble with my mum, when Card and I took long walks in the countryside and I could unwind. I could relax. I could stay silent.

Then I'd turn a corner, hit a step, be dragged into a conversation, and the heaviness would slam me into submission. No matter what, the truth was always needed. People were always telling lies that needed my verification. The queen was always calling me. I was constantly reminded that I'm trapped. I'm cursed. That tight pinch in my throat will always be there. And the person at fault is right up these stairs.

After passing a few other chambers, we stop at a mahogany door with black gemstones embossed in the surface. Will inspects a large gargoyle door handle beside a nameplate with Morgana's name on it.

'Einar said to just . . . knock, right? I mean, should we go in with some kind of plan?' he asks.

My teeth have begun chattering so all I can do is nod for him to go ahead. I can barely hear my own thoughts, let alone scramble together a strategy. I've spent my life imagining Morgana as a clouded mystery. Whatever woman waits behind these doors is inconceivable.

Will raps against the wood.

There's no call from the other side, no sign of life.

'Uh, okay. Maybe we just . . .?' He shapes his hands into a sphere like he's preparing to use a spell. 'If she's not here, we could see if she's left anything behind?'

'Trap?' I manage to say.

'Good point.'

Will flicks his fingers. With a glow of white magic, he traces the doorframe carefully, as if he's checking for the thinnest of hairs, until he confidently takes the handle. A spell flashes, and with a click, the door creaks open. Almost at once, the sweetness of fresh flowers mixed with the sour, aged scent of soil wafts out.

'Nothing out of the ordinary,' he says. 'Although, if she was hiding something, she wouldn't want it to be obvious to the other residents.'

Will goes in first, his steps slow and quiet. We find ourselves in a small antechamber with an open doorway on either side of the room. In front of us is a tall stained-glass window of a castle under a full moon that casts colours on our feet as we move farther in. It's warm and humid, like the inside of my greenhouse. Despite that, I hug my arms to myself while Will peeks his head into the room on the right.

'This looks like her bedroom. I don't think she's here,' Will says.

I go through the door on the left into a wide study adorned with purple drapes and unlit glass lanterns, each step a silent vigilance. Anything here could be a hidden danger. To the right is another window, this one clear and facing northwest, with a view of the now setting sun. On a clear day, I imagine you can see all the way to Alrick Citadel. Not today. Before the window sits a work desk overflowing with books, vials, goblets, metal accessories, and various ornate instruments I've never seen before, while around the rest of the room, bookshelves hold roughly shoved-in scrolls of parchment and collections of plants – only some of which I recognise. It seems Morgana doesn't share Ruth's organisational skills. I tiptoe over to a hanging vine and restrain myself from caressing the leaf, unable to trust its safety.

Will heads towards the desk and flicks the corners of a few stacked documents.

'To be honest, Fliss, I don't know what to look for,' he says.

'Let's think about what we know,' I say, turning around the room. 'Morgana was the one who found the spell Bash used on the tree. She knows he's cursed, as does the queen.'

'Bash definitely doesn't know,' Will says with a frown. 'It's like it's . . . concealed magic. Like how I only felt your curse when I actively searched your throat.'

'Right. It could make sense that the queen asked Morgana to break Bash's curse, just like she asked your mum, and after years of research, Morgana suggested using the oak tree. I think it was just timing and coincidence that pushed Bash to try the spell by himself. When that didn't work, what would the queen do?'

Will scans a bookshelf for anything amiss, a finger trailing a line of dust.

'Try something else?'

'I imagine spells that break curses are hard to come by. I wonder if that's why Morgana travels so much – she could be searching all eight kingdoms for a cure,' I say, and sigh. 'But at the same time, I think it's plausible to assume Morgana was the one who cursed Bash in the first place – who else would have? So if that's the case, why is she trying to undo it? Why would she go to such great lengths for the queen but not my mother? If it happened around the same time I was born, it would mean she placed two curses on two friends' children in a very short time frame.'

'I was thinking the same thing. It's strange.'

I pause in the corner of the room where a portrait-sized mirror hangs on the wall. Below it is a metal stool holding a thin box covered in a black velvet cloth, several goblets with dregs of wine and tea, and a pot holding a shrivelled flytrap. The spikes on the lobes may look spent, but I know better than to trust it. Deceit, deception. Lies. That's what the flytrap's magic sings.

'It's more than likely that the flowers are going to be used at the wedding to try and break Bash's curse,' I say. 'He's complained so many times about his mother nagging him. He said that she seems to think he's useless without magic, despite having other skills.'

Will hums in agreement. 'Yeah, he's said something along the same lines to me.'

'No wonder he gets so worked up about your magical abilities. You're flaunting his biggest weakness.'

In the reflection of the mirror, Will tears his eyes away from the bookshelf he was inspecting to grin at me.

'And I have great fun doing so,' he says, then adds, 'Although I admit there have been too many broken windows and roofs for my conscience to be fully clear.'

'I just don't understand why Bash not having magic is such a terrible thing? Card doesn't care about magic and he's one of the smartest people I know. Yes, he is; don't give me that look.'

I glance down at the flytrap on the table. Morgana should water it more. My attention is pulled to the cloth-covered box beside it. The velvet hasn't gathered any dust, so I assume it's been moved recently to study the item underneath.

'I can feel something magical over here,' Will says, wandering over. 'Found anything?'

'I think it's this,' I say, pointing to the cloth.

He sends a flurry of wind to whisk away the black velvet and my heart shoots to my throat. All at once, the air turns stale. An unsettling disturbance radiates around the room as an open book stares up at us, calling out to be read, wanting to be held. To be trusted.

It's lying.

Will grabs my hand quickly.

'Don't touch it,' he warns. He takes a breath like his chest is being crushed.

'Are you okay?'

There's a flicker behind his eyes that throws me back to the dungeons. The way he flinched away from me, afraid of how much damage he could do. Afraid of himself.

'Fliss, this book. It's dark magic,' Will says shakily. It's not often I see him so unnerved, and it terrifies me. 'Sometimes books like this . . . they're more than words. They're magic itself. They corrupt and enchant and whisper in your ear until you're lost to madness.'

The late-afternoon sun hides behind a cloud and the study turns grey. The energy pouring from the book is an itch under my skin. But we *have* to know what it says. I'm already cursed. What more can it do to me?

I surrender to the call and eye the yellowed pages, dog-eared and wrinkled from age. An inked illustration tempts me closer and sets my heart alight. There, in carefully painted strokes, are my flowers: Feiyan at the peak, Odyssa on the left and right, and Lunarie at the bottom, linked with intertwining patterns and words in an unknown language. It's just as Keeper Einar said. It's a cycle, a conduit.

'Will, I think this is it! I can't read it, but Card probably knows this language. We should take it with us!'

He grimaces at the wall in refusal.

'We really shouldn't touch it . . .' he says tightly, like he's forcing himself to resist. 'I . . . I shouldn't read it. I . . . Oh, fuck you, Bash.'

Will crouches forward and scans the page. I hang on to his sleeve, teeth clenched painfully. The seconds stifle me like I'm deep underwater.

'Fliss,' Will says.

His expression cracks.

He takes a few steps away from the book, out of my grasp, out of reach.

'What is it? What did it say?'

He rubs the tips of his fingers over his forehead and shudders like he's reeling from a punch.

'Will,' I plead.

Will turns to me with a smile that breaks my heart. He's forcing it. He's trying to be brave. His eyes are glossy and strained, his spine stiff.

'It's . . . Fliss, it's possible. It's instructions on how to break a curse.'

My vision blurs. Tremors cascade down my limbs, clawing at a hope I'd long, *long*, suppressed. A way to break a curse. I'd never thought it could be real. All attempts have failed. They've always taken a heavy toll, like Ruth's eyes and the withering of the north. As far as I know, breaking a curse has never been done before. I've never even considered—

Will grabs my elbow as I sway.

'Breathe, Fliss. We should get going, *fast*.'

'Why? What does it say?'

'Any magic in that book requires a serious price.'

'What is it? What does it need?'

Will's eyes bore into mine. He doesn't want to tell me. He doesn't want to hurt me. Which can only mean—

'Card,' I gasp.

Will nods.

'It says that when the flowers are gathered and the spell set in motion, a dark curse can be broken with a declaration of true love,' he says. 'Once the person has spoken the words aloud, they exchange the life left in their body to cure the one they love. It's a trade. Balance. A life for a life.'

'A declaration of love. *Like marriage vows.*'

'Exactly.'

'That must be why they were worried about the ceremony being cancelled. They need Card to give his life to break Bash's curse,' I say, my words tumbling out. 'He won't know what he's doing. Oh my gods, it's tomorrow. Card might die *tomorrow.*'

Will tries to reply – I watch his mouth open, his lungs fill. His words should have come next. Instead, he squints as if his eyes are having trouble focusing and all the colour floods from his cheeks. He places a hand on his forehead.

I blink. Did he realise something else? Is it the effects of the book?

'I feel kind of weird,' he groans.

An instant later, he bolts upright. His hand shoots towards me and I'm hit with a magical sensation that splinters my skin. Will's knees hit the stone floor like the final crash of an avalanche.

'Will!' My voice is swallowed as his spell takes over. I twist my palms before my eyes and watch as my whole body turns invisible, concealing me from view.

Not a moment too soon.

The antechamber door swings open and a tall woman strides into the study, her pale skin still radiant in the fading sunlight. Her blonde hair is styled elegantly; jewelled pins hold sectioned twists in place while loose waves cascade down a flowing mauve dress with long lace sleeves that end in wrists of silver bracelets.

Her sharp chin is high and her shoulders low like she's used to being in control. Like she'll destroy anyone who gets in her way.

Will tries to get off his knees, but she frowns and waves a hand. A tendril of purple magic dances across her fingers and forces him into a slump.

'What's this?' the woman says, leaning forward at the waist. She grabs Will's chin and digs her fingers in. Whatever spell he's under doesn't allow him to fight back as she lifts his face to hers. 'What could you possibly be doing in my chambers?'

Will smirks. The bold one, the one he uses to tease Bash. He's going to play with her to help me escape. She doesn't seem to notice me at all, but regardless, I'm frozen in place, my breaths shallow. My hand around my throat.

This must be her.

This must be Morgana.

What do I do?

'Just wanted a chance to meet the great Lady Morgana,' Will says, but the compliment doesn't even graze her. She remains still and eyes the black cloth on the floor, the open book. Her mouth tightens. Holding back rage.

'Is that so?' she growls, and throws Will's chin away.

A flash of magic strikes the air like a whip and Will winces in agony.

I don't know what to do. I don't know how to help.

'Seems to me you're a little mouse, trying to steal from me,' she says.

'That doesn't sound like me at all,' Will bluffs, like he's in no pain whatsoever. He's determined to keep that smile plastered on his face, even if the muscles in his neck stand out.

Morgana places both hands on her hips and studies Will with keen lavender eyes. 'You must have an extraordinary amount of magic to have got this far.'

'One of my many . . . ah . . . ravishing qualities.'

'Indeed . . .' She pauses, deliberating. Then a shrewd look flashes over her face. 'Magic I can put to use.'

She whips round to her desk and Will uses the second to glance where I once stood. He doesn't know if I'm safe or not. The invisibility must work on his eyes too. He wants me to run. Morgana is too powerful for us. But I can't leave him.

'I was just about to depart for a wedding,' she tells Will cordially, reaching for a vial of green liquid. She pours a few drops in a goblet that she tops up with a bubbling golden elixir. 'Your timing is serendipitous.'

Morgana walks towards me and I flinch. She reaches towards a shelf of dried flowers by my left shoulder and collects a few sprigs without any suspicion. The flowers she chooses – *oh no.* Back at the table, she crumbles a thistle between her fingers and adds it to the broth. Thistles are never used for anything but punishment. Dislike. Misanthropy. She adds a snowdrop. A bringer of bad omens. A bringer of death.

I *need* to get Will out of here.

'What are you making?' he asks.

'Nothing for you to worry about.'

'I'm not drinking that.'

'You'll do anything I want you to.'

An idea comes to me. If Will can keep her talking . . . I might not be able to stop her from making that potion, but I can add a security net. Luckily, Morgana's flower supply is well stocked. I take the smallest pinch of heather, for luck and protection, and another of dogwood, to represent love that overcomes any adversity. Just as I thought, when I take the flowers, they stay visible. I don't have long.

'My lady, you don't need to cast a spell to get me to do your bidding,' Will says, laying it on thick enough that Morgana turns her head. 'What is it you require?'

'Right now I require nothing but your silence.' There's an edge to her voice that I didn't expect, like the threads of a tapestry threatening to unwind.

I manage to sprinkle the flowers into the mixture just before she whips back round to grab it. Taking the goblet in both hands, she whispers a spell as her eyes glow gold and steam pours from the concoction. Her words echo around the stone chamber.

'*Befoire englissimox.*'

Will's composure breaks.

He must know the spell and it *terrifies* him.

'Stop. Wait!' he begs. 'I know the wedding you're talking about, and trust me, I'm not a fan of the prince. I don't have to drink that to want to ruin him. I do that of my own volition. You don't need to do this.'

Morgana leans over Will and pushes his hair back. He's panting, struggling for breath. A bead of sweat runs down his temple. *What else can I do?*

'I know who you are, Willoh Vane. Don't assume I'm not well informed. I don't know what you hoped to find here, but I don't like intruders, and I don't like people interfering in my plans. You are a stone in my wheel, and always have been.'

'Don't—'

Morgana tips his head back and pours the liquid into his mouth. 'Now you're going to do *just* as I say.'

Will's chest heaves as he tries to resist the liquid dripping down his throat.

He twitches, grits his teeth.

Then stills, like he's encased in stone.

'Good boy.'

His eyes are no longer hazel.

'I'm sending you to Alrick Castle, little mouse . . .'

They're a pure, lifeless black, deeper than the velvet cloth that covered the dark magic book.

'. . . and you're going to finish off the king for me. He's been stubbornly resistant to my poison, and you've forced me to resort to something more drastic.'

There's a tingle in my fingertips.

The invisibility spell is thawing.

It means Will's lost concentration. It means he's gone. It means I've lost him and I'm on my own. Before the visibility reaches my wrists, I'm out the door and down the stairs. I run and run and run and don't look back.

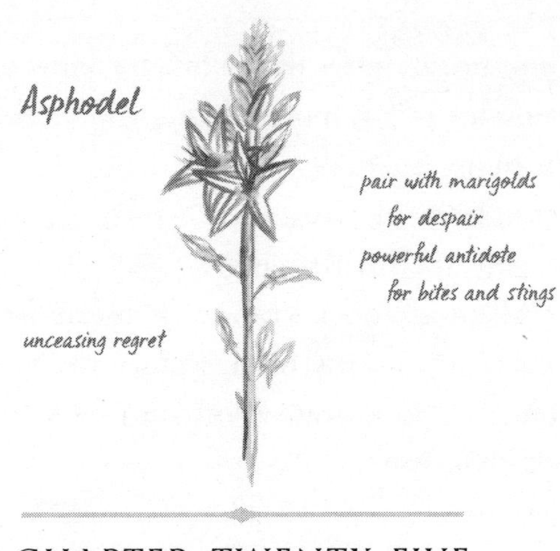

CHAPTER TWENTY-FIVE

Jeremy's hooves pound the riverside path. I gallop towards the citadel as fast as the old horse can carry me, hoping that he knows this route well enough to make up for my lack of riding experience. His mane whips against my white-knuckled fingers as the wind bites and scratches. The river rushes with us, roaring like the agony in my chest. There's no sign of Pigeon, Lark, or Howell. They're gone. Just like Will.

No. Not like Will. There's still a chance.

'Just a little farther,' I urge the horse, leaning forward in the saddle.

The hour that passes awakens crepuscular insects that flit across my face and when the citadel comes into view like the last ray of sunlight to the west, it's hope. For once, I can use my curse for good. This affliction of mine has been a lifelong torment, but this time, it's a gift. It's the only saving grace in this whole mess. I can clear the air and save everyone.

We clatter past the guards at the southern gate, the one by the lake near where I picked dahlias all those weeks ago, and into the castle courtyard where I yank back on the reins.

'Fliss!' Tarin says, rushing from their post at the main entrance to take Jeremy's bridle. They're bewildered and pale like I'm a visiting ghost. I suppose I am.

'Tarin! Where's Card? Bastion?' I frantically ask, jumping off so fast I have to grab the guard's arm to stay on my feet.

'They said Vane escaped a-and . . .? You w-were . . .?' they stutter. Clearly they haven't been given orders in case I make a miraculous return. Did no one think I would come back?

'I need to see them *now*. Please, Tarin.'

They gather themselves, like all Guards of Alrick should.

'This time of evening, they will be in their chambers,' Tarin says.

I give Jeremy a grateful pat and his grey muzzle snorts into my shoulder.

'Take care of this horse, please. He needs to rest.'

Tarin stamps their foot and pounds a fist over their heart in a traditional salute. 'I'll take him to the stable master.'

I don't waste another second and leap up the steps two at a time.

Inside, the sconces have been lit as the castle settles for the night. The flames flicker with encouragement as I race down the corridors, sweat on my neck and a foot-pounding throb around my scar. I don't pass many people. The ones I do jolt out of my way startled, and I know it won't be long before the queen is aware I'm back. She'll want information. She'll want to know why I'm not dead. Luckily, I know the way to Bash's chambers well, and when I suddenly appear before the two guards posted on that corridor, their surprise allows me to sprint right between them.

'HALT!'

I throw open Bash's door, billowing in like I'm Will using a magical gust of wind. The prince is on his feet the second I enter, surging for the sword on the dresser. Card sits on a sofa by the fire with sleep-deprived purple-ringed eyes, and a glass of wine in his hand. His whole body goes rigid as the door cracks against the stone wall.

'*Fliss?*' Bash gasps, and drops his defensive stance.

'You have to listen to me—' I start.

The two guards appear behind me, but Bastion waves them away. He strides over and wraps his arms around my shoulders securely, a tightly bound crush of a hug.

It's the most affection he's ever shown me.

'You're home,' Bash says. 'You're okay.'

Like the first cautious blossom of spring, I place my shaking hands on his back. It's been easy to forget that Bastion cares about me, and for a while now, my frustration with him has been nearing boiling point. It's a torn battle of feelings that fight for purchase in my chest as, over Bash's shoulder, Card slowly places his glass down and gets to his feet. He hasn't blinked once. His mouth is pulled tight, and it strikes me as odd that for once in his life, he's reserved, held back. Not demanding the spotlight. He's staring at me like a new word in a book, one needing a cross-examination.

'How did you escape?' Bash asks, pulling out of the hug.

'Escape?' I ask, and frown. 'I thought you knew Will's mum is a healer? Didn't you let him take me?'

Bash grits his teeth like the memory is a knife. Any victory of Will's and he *still* loses his composure.

'Yes,' the prince says. 'I was confident Ruth could heal you. But it changes nothing. He tried to kill you, Fliss. And if it hadn't been you, it would have been someone else.'

I almost choke. Will and I talked about this. We moved past it. But here, time hasn't ticked. They've been stuck reliving it without knowing the full truth.

'When you didn't return, I knew something was wrong,' Bash continues. 'What happened? Did he do anything to you? I swear, if he laid a finger on you—'

'What? No—'

My throat squeezes the rest of my sentence voiceless.

A lie.

I cover my mouth in a spluttering cough.

'I knew it!' Bash spits. 'I knew he'd use this chance to do something to you. Did he use magic on you, Fliss? It's okay, you can tell us.'

I do my best to clear my throat and when I can't prepare my answer fast enough, each passing second strengthens Bash's suspicions. He eyes me as if somehow being around Will has corrupted me. Will said this would happen. That their trust in my truth would decay the longer I spent around him. Anger catches fire in my chest. *How dare they think so little of him?*

'Where is he, Fliss?' Bash demands. 'Did he follow you?'

'Slow down and listen,' I say, rounding out my words as clearly as possible. 'You don't understand. It's Morgana—'

'Morgana?' He sucks in air through his teeth. 'I should have known he'd have gone to her at some point. Of course.'

'No, Bash—'

'I told Mother it was a bad idea to invite her to the wedding. Obviously, such a power would tempt Will.'

I grasp Bastion's forearms so tightly I can feel his pulse.

'Bash, let me talk! *Please.*'

'Fliss, it's okay, you're safe now. You're home. We can protect you.'

He needs to listen. He never listens.

Bash's dark brown eyes bore into mine. I know how I must look. A crazed animal with windswept hair, skin raw from riding. A pale withered plant that crawled through the forest, dragged itself through thornbushes. How could he ever understand in the limited time we have? Why can't I choose the correct words to make him get it? My mind scrambles to grab the most important pieces.

'Morgana's been poisoning the king!' I burst out with a wildness that feels rare. Precarious. An avalanche of unplanned words. 'She cast a spell on Will. Some kind of potion. He's not in his right mind. But I added some flowers to override it. And before that the bridge fell, and Lark and Howell might be dead, but I don't know. I rode here as fast as I could to tell you that you can't get married tomorrow or Card will die too!'

Bash exchanges a flash of apprehension with his fiancé.

'Fliss, you're not making any sense . . .' the prince says. There's a tinge of pity in his tone now, a sympathy full of sorrow. *That poor girl. Oh, how far she's fallen.* He scans my face like a question. 'What did Will do to you . . .?'

'I'm not lying! He's on his way here now!'

Bash's eyes suddenly narrow. That was the wrong truth to tell. It triggers him. Turns him impulsive and blind. He reaches for the sword again.

'I'll alert the guards,' the prince decides heedlessly, and flies to kiss Card's cheek. 'Head to the tunnels below the keep if it gets messy. That's the safest place to be.'

No. I throw my arms out to block the exit. My legs are shaking, my heart thundering towards the edge of a cliff. *Stop.* Slow down.

'WAIT!' I shout, fighting against my trembling teeth. '*You're not listening!* Why— Why aren't you listening? I told you, he's under a spell! If I come with you, I can activate the flowers I added—'

'You're not allowed anywhere near him again. Either of you. That's an order.'

A hint of Cardamine's usual charm breezes across his face. He kisses Bash. 'Come back. *That's* an order.'

I'm stammering, running low on fumes, wilting. The scar across my stomach pulls my skin like it's about to snap.

'P-Please, stop, listen, *please*,' I repeat deliriously. This isn't right. This isn't how it's supposed to go.

Bash places me in Card's arms. There's a waft of buttercups and the slam of a door. The distant shout of rounding guards. Silence. Now that my adrenaline is waning and any hope I had of making Bash understand is extinguished, I don't know if I can keep moving. Card tries to steady me.

'Come on, edelweiss. Show me your courage,' he says.

A sob breaks through. I don't want anyone to get hurt – least of all Will. He doesn't deserve this, and he's the only one who knows exactly what spell Morgana is planning to use at the wedding. Bastion is sealing Card's fate if he hunts Will down. A strangle of fear grips me, and when I open my mouth to explain everything, my truth comes out.

'I don't want him to get hurt,' I say, and burst into tears.

The thought of Will in that prison again, bleeding and barely able to stand—

Card stiffens. He takes a small step back. His fingers run down the arms of my coat, to my wrists, my palms, then let go. The firelight paints shadows on his unusually hard expression.

'You . . . you don't mean Bash, do you?' he asks, his voice low.

The flames crackle.

Outside, a guard shouts commands.

'W-What?'

'The flower in Ava's armour. The day they found Merit.'

I'm blindsided. Stumbling for balance. Why is he bringing this up now?

'Merit told Bash he heard your voice, and I couldn't work out why you didn't say anything. Merit was *sure* he'd been hit by a piece of shrapnel too, yet the physicians couldn't find any deep wounds. Just a magically healed-over scratch on his leg, which very likely quickened his recovery. He was soon back on his feet and even out in the yard training with Bash only three days after it all happened. I spent hours going over and over it in my mind. If you'd healed him, why didn't you say so? You'd already said you hadn't been threatened to keep quiet, so what happened?'

I clutch my hands to my chest, fraught, as he continues.

'I realised while you were gone that I'd jumped to the wrong conclusion about the flower. It wasn't from you. It was *for* you. You and Willoh were together that day. That's why you were acting so strange and secretive. That's why you ran to break up the fight and why he was so distraught in the dungeons. It's . . . It's been him this whole time, hasn't it?'

His shoulders are a tense rope.

I don't answer.

'Felicity, you *lied to me.*'

Lied?

No. I just . . . didn't tell him the truth. Why should I have to?

I clamp my hands to my sides and stand up taller.

'He's not who you think he is,' I say, and hearing me admit it hits Card like a hurricane. He wipes a hand through his hair and begins pacing.

'I don't care. I'll stand by Bash no matter what. You helped him escape from the dungeons, didn't you? The guards didn't notice the remains of dandelions on the stairs, but I did.'

'Yes.'

'How could you—?'

'How could *I*? Escaping was my best chance of survival! I'm alive today because of it! What about *you*? My mum said you didn't even *try* to look for me! She heard *nothing* from you!'

He gasps. '*Nothing?* I wanted to ride out for you. I wanted to burn the whole forest down to save you! Bash's mother *ordered* me to stay put. I couldn't even leave this room without a flock of guards watching my every move! You think I wanted that? You think it was easy to be imprisoned in this castle not knowing if you would live another day?'

'I think you chose Bash and his ridiculous, meaningless feud.'

'And you chose Willoh.'

Our eyes lock.

'Did Bash tell you?' I ask. 'What happened at the oak tree?'

'Of course.'

'And?'

'And *what*? It was a stupid childish mistake.'

'It was Bastion's mistake that Will took the fall for. See? That's the truth.'

'You have no idea the amount of guilt he feels about that night—'

'And what has he done to make up for it? People are starving, Card.'

'He's tried! But there's so much royal protocol he has to abide by.'

'That's a pathetic excuse. If he really wanted to do something, he should have found a way!'

Cardamine glares at me, exhaustion tearing at his seams. He's disappointed. Feeling burned like the charred wood in the fireplace. We've never spoken to each other like this before. But I'm done. I'm not wasting time arguing if the guards are out there looking for Will. I spin round and march out into the carpeted, candlelit corridors. The night outside presses against the windows as Card hurries after me.

'Where are you going?' he asks.

'Away from you,' I say, pacing fast.

He snaps at my heels. 'If you'd have told me everything, then we never would've had any misunderstandings! You kept too many secrets from me.'

'You're saying it's *my* fault?' I bite back. 'You think you're entitled to every thought I have? I don't owe you *anything*.'

'So you go running off with someone who's endlessly tortured your best friend's fiancé?'

'It's not wrong to keep some things private. If you think that's lying—'

Card snatches my elbow and spins me round. We face each other on the balcony overlooking the entrance hall.

'I just wanted you to stay in my life,' he says. 'I wanted you to feel included every step of the way, so me being here, becoming royal, wouldn't change anything.'

'No.' I throw his hand away. 'There were no boundaries – though I admit that I was at fault for giving so much of myself to you that you always expected it. You were always calling on me and demanding my time, and the moment I finally took space for myself, you lashed out. Of course I kept Will a secret. He was the first person to ever make me feel truly seen. And if Bash hurts him again, I swear I will do my best to destroy this entire godsforsaken castle. And I am *not* exaggerating. I can't.'

Card stares at me like he's never seen me before.

A blast of wind from the entrance hall soars through my ribs.

I know that wind.

Will saunters through the double doors, hands crackling with purple energy – the same magic I saw Morgana use in her chambers – and eyes a shadowy black from the potion she forced him to drink. Dust and debris dance around his boots, swirling in an ever-growing whirlwind. The magic feels off, tainted. Evil. But, gods, is it a relief he's unharmed. He reaches the centre of the room and smirks. It's not the loving, teasing smirk that I adore. It's as sharp as a crevice in a stone. I race down the stairs, hearing Card follow behind.

'Will!' I call. 'Stop!'

'I don't take requests,' Will sneers, but it's not his tone. It's Morgana's. Will is her puppet to control.

I advance towards him, each step a test of Morgana's patience. A blast of wind shoots my way and I fling my arms over my face until it dissipates. She can throw what she wants at me. I won't give up. I added the heather and dogwood. I *know* he's in there. I just need enough time to locate the flowers within him and activate the magic.

'Will, listen to me,' I plead.

I take another step. Card grabs the back of my coat.

'Fliss, don't,' he says.

I shake him off. 'I know you can hear me. Will, please. Fight this. Fight her.'

I try to sense the flowers in his system, searching for a way to pull their emotions to the surface, just like I do with the flowers in my shop. It should be easy. Except, when I'm alone and it's quiet, I can concentrate and take my time. How can I focus when Morgana is using Will like this? When her magic is infinitely more powerful than mine? I catch the faintest brush of the heather's protection and my magic scrambles to clutch it. Will laughs, harsh and bitter. It's so foreign, so out of place. And like a breeze through open fingers, I lose my grip on the flower. *No, come back!*

'Ah, was it you I sensed earlier?' Morgana says through Will. 'He was shielding me from something. *How sweet.* It serves you right for meddling!'

Will sends another gust of wind, and I decide to sprint for him. If I can get closer, get a hand on him, activating the flowers will be much easier.

Halfway there, a body slams into my side and my scar *screams.*

'Watch out,' Howell grunts as he cushions our fall. We skid across the stones to the sound of swords being drawn.

'Surround him!' Ava orders, positioning herself next to Card at the bottom of the stairs.

'Howell!' I wheeze, winded. *He's alive. Is Pigeon—?*

Howell releases me, and I scramble to get my bearings. Tarin is by the open doors, their sword raised in steady hands. Howell and I are on the left, and on the opposite side, past Will, Godfrey takes a defensive stance, his face anguished. To our right, Ava backs Card to the bottom of the stairs, her eyes fixed on Will in the middle of it all.

Howell helps me to my feet and holds out his arm to protect me from the magical cyclone picking up speed in the centre of the room. He's changed into leather armour and bears fresh scrapes on his stubbled cheeks. I almost laugh. Of course. Howell is unbeatable. Could I ask him about Pigeon without arousing suspicion? Before I can decide, the castle convulses as the purple crackles of power around Will's hands grow stronger. The guards' sudden arrival hasn't fazed Morgana.

'Come on, boy. Stop this nonsense,' Godfrey calls over the crescendo of wind.

'Howell, he's possessed! It's Morgana,' I say quickly. 'I think I can stop it. Please, let me try. Let me get closer to him.'

His staid brown eyes search my face. He knows I only tell the truth, but he's reluctant to let me walk into danger. Howell is Alrick's shield – the first one enemies see, the one who takes the hits and walks off the injuries, who remains steadfast and true so others don't panic. Who ties his own bandages. Who walks away from an explosion and survives a gushing river. Now he's faced with letting a young florist be the one in charge.

'Please.'

Howell rubs his jaw and surveys Will, then Ava. Decided, he says, 'I've got your back,' and draws his sword.

I inch towards the gale, my hands shielding my eyes from the dust.

'Will!' I shout and his head whips to me.

Like flooding a river, I throw all my concentration into finding the heather and dogwood inside him. Their emotions are wafts, somewhere downstream, but I'm determined to have them in my grasp.

'Fliss, get back!' Ava commands.

I keep pushing on. Keep closing in with my magic. Ten more steps from Will. Nine. Eight. Luck. Protection. I can feel the heather again!

There's a twitch in those black eyes.

'Howell, get her out of there!' Ava shouts. 'That's an order!'

Howell remains at my back.

The ceiling groans.

The wall of wind between Will and me sparks with Morgana's purple lightning. I reach my hand out and try to activate the hint of heather, not smoothly, thanks to Morgana's potion. It's like heaving myself through mud. I scream through gritted teeth and *pull.*

'Sneaky little—' Morgana growls through Will as she realises what I'm doing. 'Well, then.'

Will's hands shoot up and the hurricane follows his command. The blast splits the ceiling above us, and there's a second – just one – where all the breath leaves my body.

Then, like bone grinding together, the ceiling cracks.

The stones above us crunch and start to fall.

I stare at Will in the centre of the chaos and, with the fraction of time I'm granted, I yank at the flowers in the potion with all my strength. The darkness in his eyes retreats before the first stone hits the floor. He whips in my direction, flings out a hand, and it's the last thing I see before Howell flattens me to the floor, his large torso enveloping me like armour.

The entrance hall rumbles as it collapses around us and I curl inward as much as I can, throttled by terror. Shouts echo. Rocks slam against stone, bellowing booms that have me choking on a scream.

Howell's body goes limp. His arm falls away. He rolls off me and all goes quiet, like a blanket tucking in the storm.

When I eventually lift my head, the world is muffled, the air as thick as chalk. Giant slabs of rock decorate the room, dust settling like powdered sugar. Above, the star-spotted night pours in. I inhale the ash and gag, trying to push to my elbows. My eyes fall to my right.

Howell's lifeless body stares up at the holes in the ceiling, his stoic brown eyes glassy. Glassy and gone.

Dead.

I *scream*. I scream and it mangles my throat. Hurls me against the fallen chunks of ceiling. No. *No*. No – he – he survived the river – he was here – he was alive – he was fine – he trusted me – he *saved* me—

'Fliss.'

The word is quiet. Barely a whisper.

My heart shreds with relief.

Will sways where he stands, his connection to Morgana severed. I claw over the rubble to him, bruising my knees and slicing my palms. I don't care. It doesn't matter right now. He hangs his head, the waves of his ash-coated hair tickling his cheeks, and when I reach him, when we're finally together again, he slumps forward like he'll faint any moment. I catch him under his arms.

'I've got you,' I say, and hold him upright. 'I've got you. I'm here.'

I want to tell him it's okay, but I can't. His head sags onto my shoulder.

'What the . . .?'

Bastion appears at the top of the stairs. Lark is hot on his heels, with damp hair and dry clothes. He survived the river too. Pigeon *must* have as well. *I can't lose anyone else.*

Bash sprints down two steps at a time, over the destruction to where Card lies, eyes closed, on his back by Ava. They're next to a cluster of rocks. Next to. Near. Not under. *Thank the gods.*

Bastion tugs Card into his arms and slaps his cheeks.

'Babe. Babe, wake up. You're okay.'

'Ugh . . . What happened? Bash?' Card mumbles, then bolts up. 'Ava?'

'I'm okay,' she says, flapping a hand, but remaining on her side. 'Catching . . . my breath.'

At the edge of the room, Godfrey groans as Tarin inspects the old man's bleeding leg. It's oddly twisted, probably broken. Lark traverses the rubble to Howell's body. I can't breathe as he checks Howell's pulse. He looks to the prince and gives the slightest shake of his head. Bash lets out a soft *no.*

The room hangs in silence.

The powdery air ripples.

All eyes fall to Will and me.

'It's not his fault,' I say, loud and clear. No room for misinterpretation. The truth.

'Fliss, what are you doing?' Bash asks, his pitch rising as hysteria takes over. 'He just killed Howell.'

I clutch Will protectively. They are *not* taking him. He mumbles something into my shoulder and Bash's shoulders rise.

'He's done something to her! He must have!'

'It's not his fault,' I repeat.

I can say it a thousand times. It won't matter to them. Right now, with emotions running high, the truth won't make a difference. There's nothing I can say. The guards are broken, by both the fallen stones and their fallen comrade, but there's a tension in their backs like they'll come for us if commanded to. Ava, Lark, any one of them would strike us down. Separate us.

'Hold on tight,' Will mutters, and his hands creep to my waist. There's a brush of wind around my shins. He's thinking the same thing. There's nothing we can do right now.

I take one last look at Howell. Howell who saved me, who didn't hesitate to shield me.

My face crumples.

'I'm sorry,' I say.

Will exerts what little energy he has left to wrap us in wind and thrust us up through the holes in the ceiling, onto the roof he brought down. Towards the sky that Howell's unseeing eyes stare up at, to where the gods will shake his hand, his service to Alrick over.

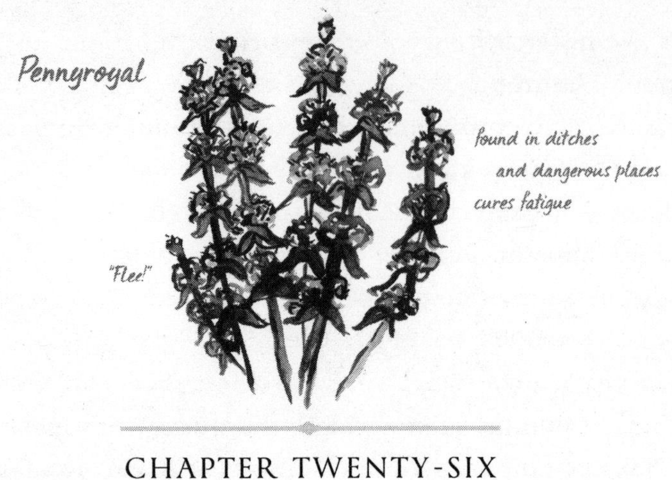

CHAPTER TWENTY-SIX

My shop feels neglected, cold. Betrayed. I've been away too long, but I'm not here to tend to the flowers. I shove Will inside and lock the door behind us with the hidden key we keep under one of the flowerpots. Hopefully we fled from the castle before they could see which direction we went in. This is the first place they'll search for us, so we need that head start. Thank the gods my mother shut all the curtains before she left to stay with Ruth. I bet they've both been beside themselves with worry, but Will isn't in any condition to be magically sending them updates right now.

'Okay, we need some wards. They'll be here looking for us soon,' I say, dashing in the darkness for a handful of pennyroyal, a purple leafy flower from the mint family. I throw down a line of them by the front door before starting on the windowsills. *Flee away*, the pennyroyals say, *nothing to see here. Flee. Run. Go away. It's dangerous, perilous. You don't want to be here.*

Will curls himself into a ball on his knees.

He hasn't said a word.

'I'm going to run upstairs,' I tell him.

He doesn't move.

I do the same for the windowsills on the upper floor – in my bedroom, the bathroom, and my mum's room – hoping it will be enough to keep the guards at bay. For now. Just until we can think of a plan. We just need more time.

Back downstairs, I kneel before Will. The curve of his back is shaking, his head tucked into his chest, and he's gasping for air against the wooden floor. I place my hand on his shoulder gently, not wanting to overwhelm his senses. I'm here. I'm here and I'm not leaving him. He shudders and sucks in a deep breath.

'I think it's my turn now,' Will says, his voice cracking.

It takes a second for me to understand what he means. We've swung, switched places. Me, level-headed and composed, like all those times Will kept cool as I fell apart.

'I'm here,' I soothe.

It's the permission he needs to surrender. Surrender and break.

Will digs clawed fingers in his hair and weeps. I sit silently by him as he chokes out sobs that mourn for so much – for the life ripped away from him all those years ago, for the freedom Morgana violated. For Howell. My own tears drip onto the floorboards. *Never again.* I'm never letting this happen ever again.

There's a sudden bang on the door that has us spooked like an ensnared rabbit.

'Fliss!' Card pounds his fist again and again. 'Are you in there? Fliss!'

'You're going to break down the door,' Bastion warns.

'FLISS? You can't do this to me! You can't leave me like this!'

The knocks slam time and time against the wood. Neither Will nor I move. He's petrified, gulping down his tears. I pray with all my might for the pennyroyals to work. *Please.* I push my magic outward and beg the flowers in my shop for aid. *Help us. Please don't let them in. Please give us this sanctuary.* There's a soft rustle and a flow of magic in the air. My flowers hear me and obey.

'We should get out of here,' Bash says. 'I doubt they'll have stayed close.'

'But—'

'Babe, come on. You've hardly slept recently . . .'

Their voices fade away.

It's just Will and me and a cold, dark room of flowers.

He shuffles upright, tears clinging to his eyelashes.

'Howell—' Will stifles.

'It wasn't your fault.'

'H-He— I—'

'Will, it *wasn't* your fault. I'm telling you.'

His bloodshot eyes scan my face. If I can say it then it's the truth whether he can accept it or not.

'I keep putting you in danger,' he says. 'I keep hurting you. I stabbed you. And n-now Howell. Who next, Fliss? I-I'm—'

'Will.' I push his ash-coated hair back. 'I choose to be here. I choose you. You are not hurting anyone on purpose. It is not your fault.'

He reaches across where our knees touch and rests the tip of his fingers where my scar is, where the sword sliced me open.

'There isn't a day, an hour, that goes by where I don't curse myself for what I did to you. What I keep doing to you,' he says, a confession of the worst kind.

My heart can't bear it.

'Stop it,' I beg. 'Stop saying that. I don't feel that way whatsoever. I told Howell it was Morgana. He believed me. He was helping me get to you and he saved my life. What she did was a horrible violation. You are not to blame, Will. She used you. This is on *her* hands.'

'I can't . . . I can't keep doing this.'

His words carry the weight of five long, lonely years.

I bite down on my bottom lip to stay strong, for him, for now.

'I keep trying and—' He shudders. 'Every time I just make it worse. They were just rumours before, but it's true. All I do is hurt people. Bash was right. I should have left like he wanted. It would be better if I wasn't here. I should have let them take me. I should have let them kill me—'

I grip him so hard my nails dig into his skin.

'Don't you *dare* ever think that. Don't you dare!'

He can barely keep his head up.

'Will. Will, look at me.'

Panic strangles my chest, my throat. How do I save him? How do I pull him out of this?

'They won't listen. Especially now. They'll never stop coming for me. You should—' He wraps his fingers around my wrists and pulls me off. 'You should go. You should hand me in. You shouldn't be here. *Why did I take you with me?* I've ruined it for you. I'm so stupid—'

'No. I'm staying right here.'

'Just leave me. Just *go*.'

'No.'

'You should hate me. I almost killed you. I almost killed Bash. Howell – I'm—'

'Will, *look at me*.'

He's choking, unable to see through the pools in his eyes, through the storm in his mind.

'I'm here and I am not leaving you,' I say.

I force his chin up to meet my eyes.

Will holds my gaze for a few watery seconds.

He erupts into tears again, this time falling onto my shoulder and clinging to my back. I hold him until his sobs retreat, until my shoulder is damp. It's what Howell would do after all. Stay calm and stoic, collect yourself to rescue others. Be a shield, a protector, taking pride in the smallest of tasks, knowing just how important it is to those who need it. I'll persevere and bear the weight so Will doesn't have to. So he isn't alone.

'Why are we even trying to help them, Fliss? Why are we bothering?' Will asks, muffled into my coat. I sit him upright and wipe his wet cheeks with my sleeve.

'Because it's the right thing to do. And you are a good person, Will. I will try as many times as it takes, until Morgana faces justice and you are free.'

His shoulders sag, like gravity itself is a punishment.

'They don't deserve your help,' he whispers. 'I don't deserve you.'

'Yes, you do. You deserve to be happy,' I say. 'I'll come for you no matter what. I'll walk beside you for as long as I can. I won't leave you.'

Will closes his eyes and exhales.

Quieter now, he says, 'That sounds nice.'

'I think so too.'

'Stay. Please. I didn't mean it.'

'I know.'

He leans his forehead against mine, and I stroke his jaw with the backs of my fingers. His grief hangs like a ceiling of wisteria, his sorrow heavy and insurmountable. We sit in sadness, in silence, and soon his tiredness takes over. Slowly, his breathing steadies.

'We should get some sleep,' I say. I don't even remember the last time we ate, let alone got some rest. The cottage seems too distant a memory now.

Will lets me pull his feet towards me. I undo the laces of his boots and tug them off with ease. He's a doll in my hands, a numb shell. When I have him standing, I kick off my shoes too and, being familiar with my house in the dark, have no trouble leading him up the stairs where each floorboard squeaks under our socks.

At the landing, I push open the door to my room. It's not somewhere I spend much time, preferring to be downstairs in the shop, in the greenhouse, or outside in the sun, so it's not much more than a simple square, a floral curtained window on the left, a pine wardrobe in the corner next to a small table with a vase of dried red geraniums, a candle, and a citrus-flavoured lip balm Card gifted me for my birthday on it. I pause and consider the bed that I've spent the past weeks in, tossing and turning, obsessed with thoughts of Will. Now he's *here* and *mine*, and yet it's no time for celebration, no place for passion.

Lethargically, Will peels off his jacket and I follow suit, dropping the coat he lent me to the floor. He flicks his fingers, and a stir of magic cleans away the ash and dirt bathing us. It's the tiniest brush of a spell but it has Will swaying with lost balance.

'Okay. You need sleep,' I say.

'Don't leave,' he croaks, voice raw from crying.

'I'm not going anywhere without you,' I say, and pull back the cotton bedsheet, nudging him forward.

Will settles down with his back against the wall. As protected as he can make himself. I clamber in too and nestle myself to his chest, the fabric of his shirt soft against my skin. I tuck my hands under my chin and close my eyes. There's barely a hint of his chamomile scent left but my flowers, this room, *him*, they smell like home. Safety. Will wraps his arms around my back, pulling me close for comfort, and intertwines our ankles. He leans his nose on top of my head and breathes deeply, his muscles slowly losing their tautness. Like loose-leaf tea soaking in hot water, the adrenaline of the day thaws. Distant clangs of armour accompany the nocturnal nightly shuffles, but we can pretend they don't exist just for tonight. Just for now, it's me and him.

After some time, Will stirs. His fingers twitch against my spine and the buzz under my skin diffuses like spilled wine.

'The wedding is tomorrow . . .' he says. 'I doubt the queen will let it be cancelled after all the effort she's put in.'

'Then we wake up early and find Bastion before the wedding starts,' I say. I shift back slightly to look into his eyes. It's dark, but I can still make out the pallor of his tear-stained cheeks. 'We force him to sit still by any means necessary while we explain everything. I tried earlier but . . . it didn't go well.'

'And Cardamine?'

I don't know. I don't understand what Card is thinking and there's no way he'll listen to me now. The trust between us shattered with a few built-up bluntly spoken truths. I slide my hands to the back of Will's neck and breathe him in to soothe the squirm of discomfort.

It's fine. Will is safe. We got out of there. We're alive and not in the dungeons. Card will get over it. It'll be a trivial thing he'll shake off and laugh about . . . right? He thinks I betrayed him by not telling him everything and aligning with Will, but at that time, there were so many reasons *not* to tell him. The grey area between the truth and lies, the layers of privacy, they've never come between us like this before. He's been my only friend, my lifeline, the one who stood by me when everyone else thought I was strange. But now, our mirrored hurt is shooting aimlessly, hitting hidden targets, and I can't help feeling like something cracked between us that won't be so easy to mend.

Will must notice my spiralling thoughts, because he tilts his head and kisses my forehead.

'Okay. We'll fix it all tomorrow,' he says. 'We'll stop the spell from being used and let the truth be known.'

'About everything?'

'Everything. If we save his fiancé from certain doom, I'm pretty sure I can persuade Bash that he owes me enough to clear my name. Like you said, let's keep trying,' Will says, and in the darkness, his mouth tugs into a small smile.

My chest lights up. *He's feeling better.* No, not better. *Hopeful.*

My fingers wander to the ends of his hair at the nape of his neck, and I twist the curls around them. I want to make him feel loved and safe and wanted. To rid him of the remorse he's carrying, the burden of all that's been done to him – that's all I want right now. He runs a hand down my side, over my hip, all the way to the back of my knee, blazing a path of fire in the places he touches. He tugs my knee up so I'm hooked around his thigh and starts trailing a finger in circles on my leg. Under different circumstances, gods know where I'd want that hand to be heading.

'What will you do,' I ask breathlessly, 'when you're free? When all this is over?'

'This.'

'I was being serious.'

'So am I.'

His finger skims the back of my thigh. With his tears wiped away and the pieces of himself reassembling, I wonder if he finds this as healing as I do. If lying together acting like the outside world doesn't exist is the only way he can summon a piece of joy. If I can make him forget, just for a little while. I'd stay here forever if it meant I'd never see him broken like that again. I'd let him do whatever he wants to me.

'I meant if you could do anything,' I say. 'I want to know.'

Will mulls it over. He leans his head back to peer into nothingness.

'Well, I don't often let myself think that far ahead, but I do miss the Library. Going back today made that clear. It'd be cool to join their alchemy department – testing the limits of magic, doing all sorts of wild experiments, being part of the first people to discover new areas of sorcery. Stuff like that. But only if *she* isn't there anymore.'

'That sounds perfect,' I say, and use my thumb to stroke under his ear, my hand still roped in his hair. 'Can I come and visit?'

He laughs, short but full of surprise.

'Felicity, if this is my dream future, then you'd be free too. No curses or obligations. You could make your own choices. So, if you wanted to visit, then I suppose I could live with that . . .'

'Hey!'

He crinkles his nose.

'Besides, those bookshelves wouldn't be half as appealing without you pressed against them,' he says, and I scoff. With his hand moving where it is and our bodies pressed together, he's playing a risky game. We came up here to sleep. He *needs* to sleep. But if he keeps going—

'How about you, Princess?' Will asks. 'After.'

'Aside from finally getting a bigger greenhouse? Hmm . . . *This.*'

His chuckle is delightful. 'Copycat.'

'I'm telling the truth.'

'So was I.'

He returns my stare and in the silence of the night, without a single sound from the world outside, I know that I've abundantly and absolutely fallen for him. There's no jolt of awareness, no cheer of applause, or resounding realisation. It's delicate and effortless, like spending a full day lying in a grassy field, only to fall asleep and wake up hours later, drowsy but changed, a glow on my skin and butterflies in my hair, the smell of daisies in the breeze and no tension, no strain to be found. Falling for Will feels simple. It's as natural as the sun rising over the citadel walls and glinting off the glass of my greenhouse, as reliable and real as the roses that grow there. Just as I do in the greenhouse, I lose time to him. He eclipses everything. And here, in this space we've built – in this trust we've created – I'm truly myself, and truly his.

Will's eyes flutter closed. The hand on my leg stills, resting around the curve of my thigh.

'We should probably sleep,' he says, and there's a tinge of regret to his words, as if dreams wouldn't bring him half as much pleasure as this right now.

'Willoh Vane being sensible . . .' I whisper, and I'd love to finish my sentence with something sarcastic, but he knows what I mean.

He smiles and wiggles around to get comfier.

'Good night, Princess.'

'Night, Will.'

'Thank you for saving me. You really are quite the florist.'

'Anytime. Always.'

'Um . . . and, Fliss?'

'Mm?'

'I . . . uh . . . thank you.'

I drift away in Will's arms, wrapped in the calmness of his slow breaths and reassuring beating of his chest. I'm one foot into sleep when I promise myself to make his dreams of returning to the Library true. But the future can wait. For now, as the night forges on, I'm sheltered and safe. He's safe. And we're together.

Together and alive.

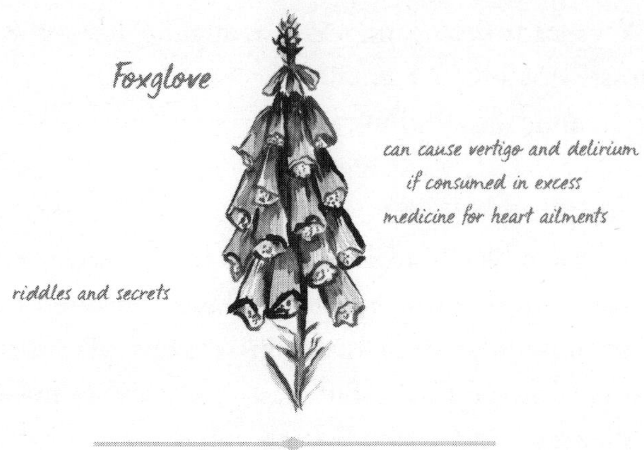

CHAPTER TWENTY-SEVEN

I wake with the dawn. The sliver of pastel yellow between my curtains brings the twittering birds to life and reminds me that the outside world – the world outside of Will – exists. And today my best friend will finally have the wedding he's been working so hard towards. Without me.

Will's arm is draped over my waist, our legs tangled together, but he's yet to stir. I carefully rub sleep from my eyes and allow myself a minute or two to soak him in, as he is, asleep and unguarded. I permit myself the sight of his long eyelashes, the messy brown waves on his forehead, a hint of stubble on the edge of his jaw. His soft breaths and slightly open mouth that has turned his lips dry. His completely serene expression, soft and unconcerned with all that awaits us. I've woken up to *this*, and find it more captivating than any flower I've come across.

I don't want to break his peace so I'm meticulous when winding myself out of the bed. I go to my wardrobe and, finally, after days at the cottage, get to wear my own clothes. The maid of honour dress Card designed for me remains in his chambers at the castle,

I suppose never to be worn. It's a drowning sadness to remember how I turned before the grand mirror and swished the long skirt around my ankles, marvelling at the periwinkle shimmer. How we chose the lace pattern of the sleeves to match the white myrtle and lily of the valley bouquets I'd decided on for their dedication, prosperity, and unabashed love. How he probably woke up and saw the dress next to his suit and burned with betrayal.

I select a comfortable white blouse, long pink skirt, and front lace rose-blush corset. If Will's red jacket and pockets are his armour, this can be mine. Letting him snooze, I tiptoe to the bathroom to fix my appearance and assemble my courage. No one is dying today. I'll see to that.

Down in my shop, I set my mind to a plan. If Bastion won't listen to us, we need a backup – and although I'm not a fighter or a rebel, I'm a florist, and I know how flowers make people feel. I *know* they make a difference. And what is a wedding without a bouquet?

I clear the wrapping table and line up a row of empty vases before assessing my choices.

I'm midway through arranging a bundle of blooming pink oleanders and azaleas (for caution, to warn someone they're about to make a poor choice) when I hear Will moving about upstairs. He spends some time in the bathroom, then appears at the bottom of the stairs in a fresh set of clothes he probably summoned from home – black trousers, a dark button-down shirt, and his usual maroon jacket. He ruffles his hair and tilts his head at me with a curious smile. Gods, he's something to behold.

'Morning,' I say. 'There's bread and tea over there if you want some breakfast.'

Instead, Will comes over, wraps his arms around my waist from behind, and rests his chin on my shoulder. He smells delightfully of soap and mint.

'Is this Fliss height?' he asks. 'How can you see anything from down here?'

'I'm holding something very sharp,' I say, waggling the scissors in my hands.

'Ah, I take it back, then,' he says. He presses a quick kiss to the side of my neck and heads to the kitchen. I grip the handle of the scissors and flush. Damn him, I'm supposed to be concentrating.

'What are you doing?' Will asks as he brings me a fresh cup of tea before settling down at the kitchen table and helping himself.

'I figured emotions are likely to run high today so I've prepared a couple of enchanted flowers – some to calm, some to warn, some to heal, and so on,' I say, and hold up one of the vases of bittersweet nightshade, a poisonous dark green plant with blood-red berries and purple flowers, its petals stretching backwards like feathers on a bird in flight, the stamen in the centre a yellow pollen beak. It's an acrid, pungent flower, but I've always kept some in stock, just in case. 'This one can compel someone to tell the truth. I'm going to leave these bundles arranged on the table here so I know exactly where they are, and if we need help, then: *encho kaveh*.'

The flower leaps from the vase to my hand in a blink. The slice of bread in Will's hand halts midway to his open mouth and the corners of his mouth tug down, impressed.

'That was the sexiest thing you've done to date,' he says, then takes the bite.

'It had better be. I've been practising.'

While I finish getting my vases ready, Will magically summons a piece of parchment and a pen to send a long-overdue message to Ruth and Mum at the cottage. He scribbles a few words, folds it in four, then flourishes it away by placing an open palm on top and then whipping his fingers back in a pinch.

'They'll know where we are at least,' he says. 'In case they want to come and throttle us for stressing them out.'

After that, there's nothing else for us to do but go. Will laces up his boots, and when he stands, I notice a tiny cut on the right side of his freshly shaven jaw. I reach up to brush a tiny drop of dried blood away.

'Oh.' Will grins. 'I cut myself while shaving, don't worry.'

'Why don't you heal it?'

'Because I cut myself while shaving. I used to dream of such a thing.'

His euphoria is a brilliant ray of sunlight. It's a small affirmation of his transition, his joy and openness of who he is now. I smile fondly and pat his cheek.

'Cute,' I say, wishing I could exaggerate, wishing I could call him sunshine and tell him how his radiance sweeps me away. 'Ready to go?'

'Almost,' he says.

Will brings my chin up and kisses me.

'Okay, now I'm good.'

Will's invisibility spell gets us through the lower town and past the drawbridge hand in hand. We have to wait for a lull in the courtyard's bustle of servants, who are all far too sombre for the morning of a wedding. The atmosphere is more fitting for a funeral. Will's hand grips mine a little tighter as we sneak through. We both know the mood is because of Howell. The news won't have taken long to spread, and the absence of his dependable long-serving presence will be as noticeable as the hole in the entryway ceiling. Even now, the last of the debris is being removed from the entrance hall by ropes and carts, to ready the castle for the wedding.

Instead of risking entering through the front, Will and I edge round the outside walls until we're out of sight by the edge of the lake, right under Bastion's balcony. He lets go of my hand and the invisibility shivers off.

'Give me a second,' he says, then leans forward and grips his knees. To catch his breath from using the spell, from seeing the destruction from last night in daylight, or from the reminder of what Morgana forced him to do, I don't know and don't ask. A few deep breaths, then, 'Okay.'

Will takes my waist and summons a wind to sweep us up onto Bastion's balcony. The glass doors are open, golden tassels holding the heavy curtains aside, but beyond that, the living room I stormed into yesterday is empty. He must be in the bathroom or getting changed.

'Bash?' Will calls, and it's the tone of a truce, a pause in their game. 'We just want to talk.'

We step into the room. The fireplace crackles to my right, illuminating the long sofas, the stacks of books Card is reading, the leftover goblets from last night. Although everything is as it usually is, something doesn't feel right.

'He's not here,' I say, resting my hands on the back of a sofa.

'No, he's not,' an unsteady voice says.

I whip to my left. In trembling hands, the queen brandishes a silver dagger as she appears from a shadowy portal in a purple dressing gown and with braided hair, seemingly partway through getting ready for the wedding. Her sallow eyes fix on Will with pure unbridled hatred.

'Queen Fern!' I gasp, and hold my palms up.

'See?' another voice says from beyond the shadows. Morgana. 'I told you they'd come for him.'

The sorcerer strides from the portal, her pointed chin high. She rests her painted nails on Queen Fern's shoulders and leans close to her ear. 'I *told* you, Fernie.'

'Where's Bash?' Will growls.

'Wouldn't you like to know, little mouse?' Morgana says, and runs her lavender eyes up and down the pair of us. 'I'm surprised he survived your vicious attack.'

'You mean *your* attack,' I bite back.

The queen glances at me for the briefest of seconds, a suppressed bewilderment flashing across her face.

'*My* attack?' Morgana says, restraining her rage. 'You see, Fernie, your son's concerns were right. That boy must have done something awful to make her say such things.'

'Felicity . . .' the queen says, her voice as jittery as the dagger in her hand. 'You're going to tell me the truth now, dear. Like you always do.'

'I *am* telling the truth. Morgana made Will attack the castle.'

'That boy has been terrorising this citadel for years,' Morgana snaps, stabbing a finger. 'He's been a menace, fuelled by jealousy and revenge. Of course, he thought to ruin your son's wedding by destroying your castle, your home.'

'That's not true—' I interrupt.

'And even worse! He murders one of your most loyal guards. An honest and hard-working—'

Will falls back a step.

'SHUT UP!' I yell. '*You* did that. Howell's blood is on *your* hands.'

'Mine? Gosh, this girl really wants you to turn against me. How did he corrupt your curse, sweet petal? I'd love to know how you're able to spread such terrible lies now.'

I throw the queen pleading eyes. 'Please, Your Majesty. You know me. You know I can't lie. You have to believe me.'

Fern stammers. Morgana places a hand on her back, moving in small comforting circles, and whispers something that sows doubt in the queen's eyes.

'I know you ordered the flowers to break Bastion's curse,' I say. 'I know about the spell. You can't go through with it. It's going to kill Card.'

'The flowers . . .' the queen mutters. 'I ordered them anonymously. How did you . . .?'

Her eyes dart to Will. She takes a step forward, stretching her forearm until the dagger is a step away from my throat and I'm doused in her foxglove aroma.

'He told you. He found out somehow,' she mutters, a wild glint in her eyes. 'He's been mocking me this whole time.'

'No, I heard—'

'Felicity, you more than anyone should understand,' Fern cuts in. 'I'm doing this for my son! Generations of royals in this kingdom have ruled with magic and kept threats at bay. Bastion will not be the exception. He will *not* bring destruction to this family. He will finally be able to use magic and never have to feel powerless again.' She swipes the knife in Will's direction. 'He'll never have to deal with *you* again.'

Will is rooted where he stands. If Morgana is believed, then there's no future for him. There's no going back to the Library or clearing his name. There's no chance for the dreams we talked about last night. He's as good as dead. Hysteria rises in my throat like bile.

'Your Majesty, please, the spell will take Cardamine's life,' I urge, flexing my open hands towards her. 'Bastion would *never* trade him for the use of magic. You should know this. You know how much he loves Card. Please. Please believe me. Bash wouldn't want this.'

She sways, suddenly disoriented, and when she blinks and tries to focus on me, her mouth hardens in disappointment. I'm no longer her tool. Just a discarded waste of time.

'No,' the queen says, matter-of-fact. She throws her head back and becomes a shadow of regality once more. 'Morgana says it'll be fine. She says you want to tear us down, make us weak. She says—'

'She's lying to you! Listen to me, she's been poisoning your husband. The attack last night was because she tried to assassinate him. Hasn't he been getting much sicker lately? Haven't you noticed?'

'What nonsense!' Morgana cries out before the queen can mull over my words, her anger shifting to desperation. She crowds Fern and embraces her. 'I'm her closest friend; I want nothing but the best for her. I've told you time and time again, Fernie, these children are not to be trusted. Lilibeth and Ruth filled their minds with lies. They want revenge. They want to take everything from you – your husband, your sons, your power. I won't let that happen.'

'You cursed me!' I jab at Morgana in a last-ditch attempt at reason. If I can finish my sentence, then it's true. 'And you cursed Bash too. It's *your* fault he can't use magic in the first place!'

'Oh, please,' she scoffs. 'More lies.'

'When your spell on my father mutated, you couldn't stand your ego taking a hit. You couldn't stand it that your magic failed. You manipulated the situation—'

'ENOUGH!' the queen yells, and the dagger dances close again. I clamp my mouth shut. 'Do *not* talk about her like that!'

Morgana glows, pleased to be defended. Then her smug smile falls flat. 'I could just kill them if you wish, my dear,' she says. 'We can't have them ruining this special day.'

For a moment, I truly believe the queen is considering it. Her jaw tenses.

'If Felicity's curse can be used again, if we can get rid of the corruption causing her to lie, then I don't want her dead,' the queen says, lowering the blade. I allow myself a breath of relief. 'I want her *useful*. Is there a way to fix her?'

'I'm not—' I try, but the queen shoots me a warning look.

'Possibly,' Morgana says. 'But we should kill the boy. Although once Bastion has his magic back, he might delight in doing that himself.'

I take a small step back and search the air for Will's hand. He locks his fingers in mine and there's a whisper of a breeze up my arm. He's going to get us out of here, like he always does. Time for a new plan. Just as Will squeezes my hand, Morgana flicks her manicured fingers. He cries out in pain and crashes to one knee, yanking me down with him.

'Nice try, little mouse,' the sorcerer growls.

He surges to his feet and goes on the offence, slashing a hand through the air and sending a blast of wind towards the two women. Morgana shields them without even blinking.

Will seizes where he stands, jerking back like he was shot by an arrow.

'Will!' I yell, and fly to keep him on his feet.

The queen stands at her full height. She lifts her nose and points directly at us. A target, a death stare. 'Send them where they can no longer interfere with today's proceedings,' she orders, as sharp and precise as the blade in her hand.

Morgana grins. 'Gladly.'

One moment I'm standing in Bastion's chambers, Will leaning his weight on me and the sun at our back.

Then the floor disappears under my feet.

Bastion's walls are replaced with blue sky and horizon, and for a fraction of a second, I hover. Shock allows me one short breath, until—

Thousands of feet above the castle, we plunge through the air.

We tumble through the sky, and I grapple with Will as he does his best to keep hold of me. A scream rips out of my throat over the deafening roar in my ears, over the overwhelming terror.

'Will, do something!'

A blast of wind rushes to greet us but does nothing to slow our fall.

'I'm trying!'

The castle is smaller than a bee but growing ever closer. In flashes, I make out the lake, the citadel walls, the forest beyond, the mountains to the north that grimace at us, knowing just how the air up here can chill to the bone.

I cling to Will's neck as our clothes whip around us.

The earth rises to greet us.

'I – I can't!' Will shouts, one hand around my waist and one attempting to magic the wind into submission. It battles against him, battering us left and right, stronger up here, unruly and temperamental. Not the friend he knows from the ground below. I sob. This is how Morgana gets rid of us. This is how we die.

'Can you swim?' Will yells into my ear.

'Yes!'

'Okay. Hold on!'

He manages to place both arms around my waist.

Nothing happens.

The castle gets closer and closer, and my thundering heart pounds faster and faster and—

'Will!' I yell, but his eyes are narrowed in focus.

The wind beats us with every passing second.

'WILL.'

I'm going to throw up.

'WILL!'

Seconds away from smashing into a castle turret, Will's arms tighten. We shift sideways, like stumbling through a door, and slow. Whatever he did knocks us off-kilter, toppling us not towards a stony death, but towards the lake beyond. The push of magic is strong enough that Will is blown from my arms and I scream for him, falling, falling, then—

I strike the surface of the water and plummet into watery darkness.

It's a fight – a silent, heavy struggle – to get my limbs moving. I wrestle against the weight of the water as it tries to drag me deeper, down into the depths. Every movement aches, *burns*. I kick my feet and something brushes against me – a plant, a fish, something worse, I don't know. Under the surface of the lake, I open my mouth and shriek.

Water heaves into my lungs and has me writhing in a frenzy. Pain becomes poison under my skin, a searing blister, ripping at every sense. Oh my gods. I can't breathe. I can't see. *I can't – I can't – I can't breathe.* My legs lash out and propel me up. I strive for the surface, towards the glistening sun beyond that watery ceiling. Just a little more. Just one more kick.

I break through and choke. Every spluttering cough is a sword in my lungs as they protest against the fresh air. Eyes stinging, I tread water and comb the surroundings for any sign of Will. I'm a fair distance from shore. The closest bank is to the west of the castle, which leads to the training yard and gatehouse, but he's not made it there yet, he's not—

'Fliss!'

I turn and there Will is, swimming for me. *He's okay. He's alive.* He reaches me and pushes back my hair, checking every inch of my face.

'Are you okay? Are you hurt?' he asks, his own hair plastered to his cheeks and dripping. 'I'm sorry. It was all I could think to do. I couldn't— Are you okay?'

I respond by hacking up more water.

My legs are so tired.

But Will's here and he's alive and we didn't die.

He starts to swim backwards, helping me stay afloat too, and after an age of agonising paddling, we scrape ourselves over the bank. I've never been so happy to lie in the mud and weeds. When we collected the Feiyan and Will asked me if I was afraid of heights, I said I didn't know. Well, it seems I have the answer now.

Once fully on the shore, Will collapses onto his back and stares up at the sky, completely drained, his arms limp by his sides. I heave myself forward on my elbows and finish coughing up the remaining lake water from my lungs.

'Let's not try that again,' he wheezes.

I make a weary grunt of agreement. It's all I can manage. There's a rustle to my left, but I'm too tired to check what it could be.

'Over here!' Ava calls, and Will groans, rolling onto his shoulder.

'Give us a bloody break,' he breathes. He pushes himself upright and lifts his palms up for peace.

Nettle and Ava approach us at a jog in full wedding attire – Ava in a cropped navy suit, a white myrtle flower pinned in her front pocket and sword scabbard around her hips, and Nettle in a short one-shoulder jumpsuit that matches the exact shade of Ava's turquoise tie. In one hand, Nettle carries her high heels, and in the other, her trusty knife. As I raise my head, she throws the knife with a spin so it lands, point down, just before Will's knee.

'Don't move,' she snaps, and Will shrugs.

Ava hoists me out of the mud.

I'm about to thank her when I meet her eyes and see the wariness there, the dilemma I pose. As captain of the guard, who am I to her but an accomplice, complicit in the murder of a guard under her command, a friend? She can't be sure, so opts for caution. After she dumps me on my knees next to Will, she decides to draw her sword.

'We can explain,' Will says, water raining from his raised sleeves. The glint of Ava's sword edges closer to his throat. Not the first time today, or even in the last hour, either of us has been threatened with a weapon. The novelty might wear off soon.

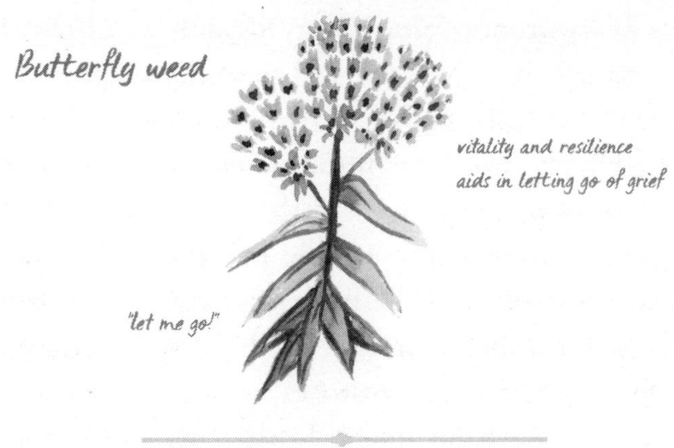

CHAPTER TWENTY-EIGHT

'Please, Captain,' Will says, no trace of his teasing temperament, 'put the sword away.'

Ava doesn't trust him. It's in her eyes. The last time she saw Will, he brought the roof down on her guards. The time before that, he carried me away covered in blood. There's no reason for her to give us any leeway.

'Why were you falling?' Ava asks, a steady grip on the hilt.

I shiver in the puddle that almost drowned me, in soggy clothes that stick to my skin. The sword aimed at Will's neck is a nerve-racking reminder of the one that ripped open my stomach, and from the jitter in Will's raised hands, it's on his mind too.

'Morgana tried to kill us,' I say.

Nettle's mouth is a hard line as she picks up her knife and wipes the mud off. Ava's eyes jump between Will and me. They're having a hard time deciding what to do with us and I don't blame them.

'Please lower the sword,' Will cuts in. 'At least let Fliss move out of reach. Threaten me all you want.'

I throw him a sharp glance. He can't possibly think I'd leave him in harm's way.

'The orders from above say I should be doing more than threatening you, Willoh,' Ava says with conviction. But this might be the first time Will's ever tried to start with peace, attempted to begin with civility, and so her hand lowers ever so slightly. 'You're wanted dead or alive by the royals, and there are many of my guards who'd like to see justice done for what you did to Howell.'

Will's expression cracks like a chip in a mirror, and I wonder if anyone but me could notice how much of a strain it is for him to keep the mask on. To keep himself from breaking like he did last night. Around these people, around possible threats, he's not letting his guard down.

'Morgana possessed him. He didn't want to,' I implore, increasingly frustrated that I'm having to work so hard to be convincing. It's never been a problem before. 'We never wanted Howell to get hurt. Can you just hear us out? Please, Ava.'

'Hear out a murderer?' Nettle bites. 'As if. We're taking you in.'

The knife in her hand spins. She flips it in the air and catches it, intending to intimidate us. She doesn't realise how jumpy we both are around weapons.

Naturally, Will startles.

From the first glint of sun against the sharp metal, he snaps his left hand in my direction and a glimmering golden shield appears before me, a wall of magic neutralising a repeat of my brush with death, and as Will moves his hand, so does Ava.

'No magic!'

She grabs his shoulder and forces him back into the muddy grass, stepping forward so the point of her sword creases the fabric directly above his heart.

'No!' I yell.

I don't even think about it. I throw myself sideways out of the safety of the golden shield and thrust the base of my palm against the flat of the sword. I shove it out of the way and fling myself onto Will's soaked chest, curling myself over him. Protecting him. Shielding him.

'Don't hurt him, please.'

Will's heart hammers unsteadily.

I raise my head to Ava. 'Please. If Howell hadn't covered me last night, I'd be dead too. He saved my life. He believed me.'

Ava contemplates the scene before her. She studies the fading golden shield, Will's supplication, the way he isn't daring to move, my beseeching, desperate plea. She's never seen either of us act like this before.

Her sword drops to her side.

'Go on,' she says, wary.

Nettle folds her arms, and insecurity creeps up my throat. I bumble out a condensed version of the truth – how the queen sent me to collect flowers for a spell that will cost Cardamine his life, and how in return, Bash will gain the use of magic. I tell them that Morgana is manipulating the queen and poisoning the king, how she possessed Will to attack the castle, and how if we don't stop the ceremony, they're more than likely going to blame whatever disaster happens on us.

'We wanted to talk with Bash alone and explain everything, but Morgana was waiting for us,' I say, and shudder at the vastness of the sky above. 'I think she's hoping we're dead.'

The women exchange a look.

'I have noticed that the queen's mental health has been in decline lately,' Ava says. 'She even dismissed all guards from her wing of the castle. And the king hasn't been well for some time now. The physicians haven't been able to find a cure, so poison could be a likely explanation.'

'Are you kidding?' Nettle says. 'You're going to believe them after what Prince Bastion said last night? He was convinced Felicity had lost her mind!'

Ava sighs. 'I do believe them,' she says. The castle casts a shadow over the lake. 'But I also cannot break my oath. I cannot disobey orders.'

'What does that mean?' I ask, and clutch Will's shirt.

'I can't help you. I've sworn an oath to the people of Alrick, and that means following the laws. Peace and order come first no matter how much I believe your story.'

'Will's innocent,' I say. 'Card and Bash are in danger. It's the truth. Ava, surely you can—'

'Or . . .' Nettle interrupts, 'we can throw both of you in the dungeons.'

'Without evidence, it's your word against theirs,' Ava says. 'If we can think of a legal way to solve this mess, then I will do all in my power to assist you.'

'We don't have time,' Will says, pushing up to rest on his elbows. As if to agree, the bells above the castle chime twelve times, each peal a foreboding threat. He sucks in a breath through his teeth. 'Add this to my list of crimes, Captain.'

He flicks his fingers against his thumbs and a silver spark of light shoots towards the women. Ava has a second to shift closer to Nettle before they both drop to the ground, sound asleep among the weeds, their wedding clothes now splattered and stained.

Will winces at me. 'I shouldn't have done that, right? I'm sorry. I panicked.'

I shake my head.

'We need to get moving. The wedding is starting,' I say. 'We can apologise later.'

On my first step, I slip in the mud. Will catches my elbow and waves his hand down my back, reducing the nip of the lake water with a magical warmth. It spreads like steam from his fingers, down my limbs, to the hems of my clothes and tips of my toes, until all the water and mud has evaporated.

'Thank you.' I exhale in relief.

Will leaves a steadying hand on my lower back and asks, 'New plan?'

We tread carefully away from Ava and Nettle, guilt squirming in every step. So close. We were *so close* to having someone believe us. I'd become so used to having my words taken as faith, it's entirely – and annoyingly – new not to have that happen. Is this really all because Bash believes Will cast some kind of spell on me? Can one small assumption really shake everyone's confidence in my curse? The *one* time I need it to work . . .

'No more talking,' I say, clenching my hands. 'New plan is to storm in and stop the wedding.'

'Sounds good to me.'

We hurry towards a side entrance and enter. It grants us swift passage to the giant doors of the Grand Hall, behind which everyone will be seated for the wedding. The bottled nerves in my stomach make my teeth clench as we find ourselves obstructed by two guards posted on either side of the doors. They watch over the entrance hall, now cleared of debris and sparkling under the sun that beams down through the shattered ceiling, but from my experience in the dungeons, I know that I can use poppies to put them to sleep. I picture the vase of poppies on my table at home and say the summoning spell. I had enchanted the flowers this morning, hooked my magic inside and drawn out the sedative, so it's a quick blink until both guards slump against the wall, snoozing, and we can make for the doors.

Just as I cross into a patch of light, Will halts me.

'Fliss,' he says softly, and I'm clay in his hands, ready to do anything he asks. 'If anything goes wrong . . .'

I take in those serious hazel eyes, my heart aching with all the possibilities that await us. There's a chance – and not a small one – that one of us won't make it. That Morgana will annihilate any hope and twist the truth. Will's mouth opens. The words don't come. His eyes flicker over my face like he's etching it into his memory, engraving me in his heart.

'Tell me after,' I whisper, and brush my thumb over the scratch on his jaw.

Will smiles and leans into my touch. 'Okay.'

We steal the second, hesitate just a moment longer. Anything that happens from now on will be worth it. It has to be. I have to believe that's the truth.

Then, with my shoulders set, I march towards the doors of the Grand Hall. Will slaps on a smirk and splays his hands. The wind hears his command and the doors burst open.

'Stop the wedding!' I shout.

The hall holds its breath. Rows of ribbon-backed chairs seal wide-eyed guests in place, surrounded by walls of silken drapes and dried white flowers that I personally picked out and bundled together weeks before. The aisle stretches before us, a straight shot to the raised stage where Cardamine stands on a thick ivory carpet in the pearly suit he's shown me several times, with a deep-violet tie, silver cufflinks gifted from his grandfather, and a buttonhole of fresh baby's breath. His ash-blond hair is swept back, his pale skin flushed and *alive*. We're not too late. As our interruption sweeps through the hall, his crisp blue eyes instantly lock on mine. *I'm doing this for you*, I try to convey. *Trust me.*

I don't know if he does.

Beside him, Bastion stops in shock, in a deep-purple suit that matches Card's tie. Without the usual sword at his hip, he seems off-balance, off-kilter. Although, that could be our entrance's fault. Farther back on the stage, in grand layers of jewels in the blues and silvers of the kingdom's flag, King Garland and Queen Fern stand with a healthy Prince Merit at their side. The queen's face twists in loathing, framed by twisted black hair and make-up that covers the sunken, stressed skin I'd witnessed earlier, while the king looks pallid, more than when I last saw him, his broad shoulders curled inward. The effects of Morgana's poisoning.

In the stillness, before chaos can crack the room, something calls to me. Something familiar and powerful and floral. I snap my head towards the back corners of the room and see two glass vases on white marble stands – one containing the Feiyan flower, its petals alert and bold and blazing like a flaming arrow; the other containing one of the Odyssa, the snowy petals shying from the congregation in a nestle of deep-blue leaves. If I'm not wrong . . . I scan the back of the stage and dread coils like a snake down my back. The other Odyssa and Lunarie hide in the other corners of the room, completing the cycle, the looped order that grants them power. Waiting.

The queen makes the first move.

'Get out,' she hisses, striding forward and shoving Bastion out of the way. He stumbles into Card over to the left side of the stage. 'GET OUT.'

The armed and armoured guards lining the room search for Ava, for command, and find her missing. I use their indecision to stride forward, past stunned citizens and mounting whispers. I get halfway down the aisle when someone on the front row rises.

'She told you to get out,' Morgana says, lifting the long sleeves of her midnight-blue gown.

'You'll have to try harder to kill us next time,' Will taunts before she can use a spell, and sends a teasing tendril of wind towards the front half of the room.

'What are you doing?' Card demands, gripping Bastion's hand.

'Saving your life,' I say.

'From *what*?'

'From them!'

I point to the flowers in the corners of the room. The tension in the room is taut, and mere seconds from snapping. But as long as Card keeps his mouth shut, there's still hope. The flower vases I prepared this morning have many uses, and one of them is silence. I summon a red flower to my open palms, just as I did for the guards outside.

'Card,' I say.

He scans my face anxiously and sees only fearless determination. *My only friend, forgive me for hurting you one more time.*

'I really am sorry about this.'

He doesn't have time to respond before I imagine the flower in his hands, imagine the magic bleeding out, and the tingle of sorcery follows my command. A beat later, Card drops to the stage, unconscious. Silent and unable to declare his love. Bastion falls to his knees beside him as the poppy crumbles into red sand.

'What did you do?' the prince cries. 'Card!'

The queen hauls herself to the front of the stage and raises a finger.

'Kill them!' she says. '*Now.*'

Finally, like releasing air trapped in a pipe, the room erupts.

Six guards stream down the aisle towards us, but Will is ready. He cuts his hand in a sharp horizontal line and the front two guards stumble to their knees, toppling the pair behind them. Chairs crash back and guests scramble to the ribbon-strewn walls. I focus on the Feiyan in the back corner. I imagine it in my hands, conjure a vision of its warmth and intensity, and say the summoning spell.

Nothing happens.

'*Go*,' Will says, lifting his hands again for another blast. He'll keep them busy.

I run for the Feiyan, past the crowds and clamouring, and just as I reach it, a burning rope of light whips around my wrist and yanks me back.

'No!' Morgana screeches.

I glance over my shoulder to find her twisting a hand in my direction, biting the rope farther into my skin.

'Stop them!' Fern yells.

'*Encho kaveh*,' I say, and summon an orange butterfly weed with tiny bright flowers that cluster like a constellation. *Let me go*, the flower sings, and the magic soars down my fingers, to my wrist. Morgana's magical light cracks apart.

I seize the chance to take the Feiyan, but my hands hit an invisible force field around the flower vase. I summon a single gladiolus with large peeled-back petals. It means sword, a piercing blow, strength. It doesn't matter. The protective border holds.

A sudden smack of wind makes me stumble into the wall. Two more guards are on Will and he ducks, a sword grazing the very tip of his curls. The chairs between us are fallen gravestones, a ghostly white destruction. He checks on me and it costs him.

A blade slices a gash down his sleeve and blood pools forth.

No!

I forget the Feiyan. I can't get to it anyway. I sprint back to Will, who cradles his limp forearm to his chest. He jerks back, dodging another strike and wipes a golden shield in place.

'*Encho kaveh*,' I say, and catch the gentle pink eglantine that appears. It fills the air with a sweetness like apples and fresh rain on stone, a concoction of healing. I press the flower to Will's arm and the wound knits together, easing the clench of his jaw, for the time being. The flower disintegrates like the dust of the damaged ceiling.

'No good?' Will asks through gritted teeth.

'They're protected.'

He nods and concentrates on the shield. Some guards groan, winded on the floor of the aisle, but two are still on their feet and there's only a matter of time until Will is too exhausted to cast anything.

On the stage, the king has an arm around Merit's shoulders. He doesn't seem to have much strength left, but what little he does, he's using to protect his son. Bash kneels over Card still, leaving the centre stage free for Morgana and Fern. Morgana rubs Fern's arms soothingly as the queen wrings her hands.

'This wasn't the plan,' the queen mumbles. 'It's all gone wrong.'

'What plan?' Bastion asks. 'Mother. Tell me what's going on. *Now.*'

'It'll be okay, Fernie. We can work around it,' Morgana replies, a surprising pinch of concern on her sharp face. She shoots her head towards the guards. 'Why haven't you killed them yet?'

'Mother!' Bastion shouts.

Over the noise, a small whine of pain escapes Will, like a cat with a thorn in its paw. A thin red trickle seeps down the arm of his jacket. And his shield spell shudders.

The guard blocking our path lifts his sword.

For a fraction of a second, I believe that we're dead. Will's dead and I'm back in the physician's room, tossing in agony and bleeding out. Instead, an arrow whizzes past my ear and pierces the shoulder of the guard's armour, sending him crashing to the floor.

'I said *non-lethal,*' Lark scolds from behind.

I whirl round.

From the open doors, Pigeon lowers her bow and grins in apology. Lark stands beside her in a dark suit, weaponless, and a look on his face like he's fighting regret. Ava and Nettle appear too, sword and knife in hand, and just as dirty as we left them.

'Why on earth would you give that back to her?' Nettle snaps.

'Because I'm excellent at disruption,' Pigeon says. 'He'll be *fine.*'

It earns her one of Nettle's most disapproving glares.

Pigeon. She's okay. Her eyes are bruised from tiredness, and her braid has all but come undone. Aside from that and her still-healing burn, she's here, she's fine. Another friend I can tick off as alive and safe. The four of them jog down the aisle, and Ava pushes through to the guards.

'What is going on here?' she barks. 'Why are half my men on the floor and not protecting the citizens? Get to it. *Now.*'

'Captain!' Morgana shouts. 'Arrest those intruders!'

Ava ignores her. She points a threatening finger at Will and me. 'You two are testing every inch of my patience. You're lucky I need to focus on the safety of the guests right now. I swear to the *gods*!'

Will's grin can't hide his discomfort. He keeps his forearm pressed to his chest to stay the bleeding as he says, 'My chance of a pardon off the table, then, Captain?'

She purses her lips so tight they disappear. 'We can talk about it later.'

'Can *someone* tell me what's going on here?' the prince shouts.

From the aisle, we peer up at the performance onstage. Morgana takes Fern's face in her long fingers. Her lavender eyes are wide as she wipes a tear away from the queen's pasty cheeks.

'Fern. Do you want this?' the sorcerer asks. 'Tell me and I will make it happen.'

The queen's eyes linger on Card's curled-up form. 'You said— You said it wouldn't—'

With the bewildered guests lined safely at the sides of the hall by Ava's command, and the aisle now clear of guards, I start moving again. This ends now. Will matches my pace, still gripping his injured arm. Fern sees us coming and her face flickers in panic.

'Bash, Morgana cursed you as a child, just like she cursed me,' I say, confirming the truth we suspected. 'They've planted a spell that will remove it, but the cost will be Card's life.'

'It's why you can't use magic,' Will says. 'Why the tree backfired.'

'*What?*' Bash scrunches up his face.

Will and I reach the bottom of the steps. I twirl my hand and, without speaking, summon another flower. Another poppy. If I can put Morgana to sleep too, she can stop interfering. Bash runs his eyes over Will. He's unsure what to make of him, unsure whether to trust him. It's been too many years since the card games and sleepovers. Just then, the sweetness in the air vanishes and my flower's healing effects wear off.

Will winces, his arm jolts, and the queen flinches. She clutches Morgana. 'Do it. Do it now,' Fern says.

The fear is a punch to the gut.

Morgana twists both her hands and the spell activates. A green circle emanates from the ivory carpet – a large glowing shape that takes up the centre third of the stage. Shimmering lines of magic pour out like molten metal in the direction of the flowers in each corner, tingeing the white wall a sickly hue. The shapes in the circle sharpen, become opaque, become recognisable as those from the dark magic book in her chambers. *This is it.* The hall hums, vibrates, *hisses*, and before Bastion can whip into action, Morgana lashes out a rope of energy and forces Card's sleeping form to his feet. His eyes shoot open the moment he's flung towards her.

'NO!' I sprint up the stairs.

Desperate, I launch the poppy, but it shrivels the moment it collides with a sliver of that green magic. The gust of wind that Will sends at Morgana bounces right off. She grabs Card's chin and the circle beneath them glows like poison. He struggles. He fights and claws her wrist, but she holds him in place.

'Card!' Bastion roars.

He's closer than me, faster than me. As is the king. He lunges forward to grab his oldest son and secures him safely in his grasp.

'NO! LET ME GO!'

'Card! Don't say anything!' I yell. 'Let him go!'

At the top step, the queen throws her arms around my waist and hoists me to the right of the stage. Her foxglove scent taints the air as I resist her, as I push and heave and try to get to my best friend, but she keeps me pinned tightly from behind. Frantic, losing hope, I search for Will. He's at the bottom of the stairs, one foot on the step like he's changed his mind about climbing up.

He looks serene, almost. Set. Decided.

Willoh Vane grins at me. That stupid smirk. That stupid, *stupid* smirk.

It's the last thing he does before a shift shakes the room, a similar push of magic like when we were falling into the lake.

He's had a backup plan all along.

In a blink of magic, Will takes Card's spot. He shoves Card out of the circle, out of Morgana's grip and for a moment, she gawks, pointed nails left holding nothing. Card skids backwards on the opposite side of the stage and gasps for breath as, around Morgana and Will, the circle of dark magic bursts like a sunspot. It shines and solidifies, burning the runes and lines into the carpet, building a glistening wall of translucent emerald green that imprisons them within, trapping Morgana and Will together.

'WILL!' I scream and buck against the queen.

Morgana grabs his throat and drives him to his knees.

'Well,' she says. 'I suppose you'll do.'

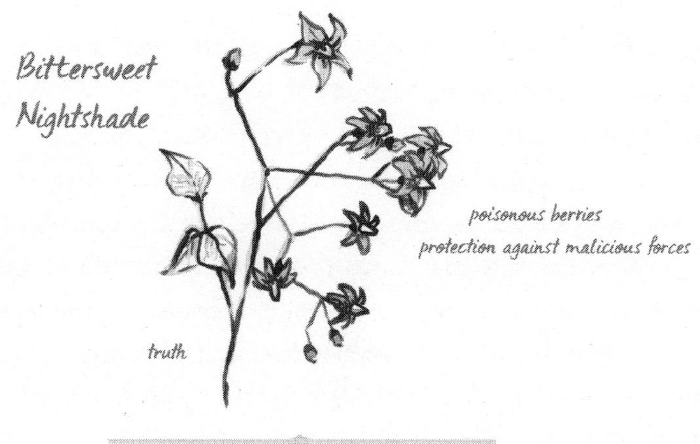

CHAPTER TWENTY-NINE

Any sound left in the room dies. It's a stunned suspended silence, struck with the fear of Morgana's next move. The sorcerer stands in the spotlight of the circle, shoulders down and chin raised, surrounded by emerald-tinted magic and the midnight-blue sparkles of her dress. Her nails dig into Will's throat as she forces him into place, onto his knees with his back to the aisle. His hair has fallen over his eyes, and from where I am on the right of the stage, I can't see if he's okay. The queen keeps her arms locked around my waist, stopping me from fleeing. Stopping me from reaching him.

On the other side of the stage, past the shimmers of green, Bastion wrestles away from the king to where Card lies on his back, sprawled and speechless. Bash carefully checks his fiancé's condition, oblivious to anything else. But Card is out of danger – for now. Below, a hundred faces stare up in shock. Most of the guests are safe by the edges of the room, but Pigeon and Lark remain in the aisle with matching haunted expressions. Weapons won't help Will here. There's only one person in this room with power.

Morgana leans forward.

'Be a good boy now and play along,' she says, a hiss to her tone. 'You know what happens next.'

Will coughs against her grip. 'Get fucked,' he says.

Morgana throws him. She hurls him backwards and he smacks into the wall of the magic circle, knocking his head and slumping down. Not for the first time recently, Will's blood splatters the floor, staining the ivory carpet like a bruise. I push against the queen. I scratch the backs of her hands. I kick my heels back and *scream*.

'Stop it, please! *Please*. Please, let him go!'

'Stay where you are, Felicity,' the queen rasps.

'WILL!'

He groans and wipes his hair back.

Morgana crouches down. 'You know I have ways to force you,' she says, 'or you can willingly sacrifice yourself for the prince. Either way, I will get those words out of your mouth. You were friends long enough to make the love count. And if not, I'll drag the fiancé back here, or the father. Even the little petal over there will do. You choose.'

Will's laugh shakes his whole body. He shuffles up to sit, back supported by the magical barrier. He angles his chin and grins. I jerk forward at the sight of blood running from his temple and the queen's nails shred my forearms in a pinch of sharp pain. I don't *care*. I told him the truth. I'll come for him no matter what. I will crawl and fight and tear myself apart. I will let the queen cut my skin open. I will *not* let them take him from me.

'Screw you,' Will says.

Morgana's face contorts. She lashes out once more, striking Will's cheek with the back of her hand. He hits the floor, the crash of it interrupted by a set of hurried footsteps.

'Touch my son one more time and you will regret it!' Ruth bellows, running through the double doors hand in hand with my mum. Windswept and breathing hard, Mum guides Ruth down the aisle, past the obstacles of fallen chairs, past Pigeon and Lark. At the bottom of the steps, they face Morgana and Fern. For the first time since before my birth, the four of them reunite. The four old friends, unrecognisable to each other now, meet again across a chasm of hurt.

'What are you doing here?' the queen asks, yanking me flat against her.

'Stopping this madness,' Mum says. 'What are *you* doing? They're just children!'

'Let them go,' Ruth says, as relentless as I saw in Will's memory. '*Now*.'

'You don't understand!' Fern screeches by my ear, high pitched and frantic. 'Morgana has always said that powerful magic is the best defence. Against our enemies. The rebels. She says anyone who tries to hurt us will be destroyed. We'll make a desert of their homes until they kneel at our feet in surrender! But when we're gone, when my children have no one to protect them—'

'Mum, they're going to kill Will!' I interrupt, to be rewarded with another deep scratch from the queen, blood dribbling between my fingers.

'How could you?' Bastion's voice is a feeble whisper of his usual command, but it still turns all attention to him. Fern clutches me like a port in a storm. 'Taking a life for the use of magic? What kind of person would that make me? What kind of king would I be? I'm the best sword master in the entire eight kingdoms. I don't need—' Bastion halts. He shoots piercing eyes at his mother and the betrayal behind them shatters my heart. 'You thought I'd trade Card? For *magic*? Mother, he's the lo—'

'DON'T!' I shout. 'Don't risk it. Don't say anything like that with the spell active.'

'Oh, honestly.' Morgana rolls her eyes. 'Can we get on with it?'

My ears chime like the bell above my shop door. 'Honestly.' *The truth*. The answer floods through my veins.

'Will,' I say, simply, steadily. From where he leans against the emerald barrier, his eyes flick to mine. '*Encho kaveh.*'

The purple-petalled bittersweet nightshade I'd shown him this morning materialises. Nightshade, to compel the truth. It reeks of a dark foulness that overthrows the queen's foxglove perfume, until, a blink later, Will summons it to himself. He claws his fingers in a sphere shape and shreds the plant into minuscule green and purple grains. The wind in his hands bursts upward, into the air, right into Morgana's face. She inhales the nightshade in her next breath.

'W-What—?' she splutters. She waves against the gust, but it's too late. A deep chesty cough wrenches from her. 'What did you do?'

'Your turn to tell the truth,' Will says. 'And I'd be quick about it. A dose of nightshade in that amount won't kill you, but you'll be feeling pretty sick soon enough.'

Her lavender eyes shoot to me. 'Y-You—!'

'Tell them!' I say, trying to heave myself away from the queen once more. 'Tell them you possessed Will. Tell them you've been poisoning the king!'

'I've been poisoning them both!' Morgana shouts.

She seizes in shock. Her eyes flare wide.

Fern's arms around me loosen a fraction.

'What . . .?' the queen says.

'No—' Morgana resists, then clutches her neck. Oh, I know that feeling. I know her throat has closed up and squeezed like a vice. A taste of her own curse, thanks to the enchanted nightshade.

'Both?' I press. 'How?'

The sorcerer struggles to keep her secrets sealed. Her pinched lips aren't enough to hold back the compulsion to speak.

'Aconite and hemlock. In the foxgloves I sent.'

Of course . . . I've always thought there was something else in the perfume, a pinch of something spicier I could never figure out. The aroma oils, the dried flowers, the layers upon layers of foxgloves hiding a combination of deadly poisons, not strong enough to kill instantly, but powerful enough to make a difference if exposed for a lengthy amount of time.

'Aconite is a hallucinogen,' Ruth says, and runs her eyes over the queen at my back, 'and can cause paranoia, fits of hysteria, nausea, and heart problems . . . Fern, your health problems haven't been natural. The foxgloves you thought were a remedy were worsening your symptoms.'

'Shut up!' Morgana spits.

'Hemlock causes anxiety too,' Mum adds. 'Tremors, memory loss, paralysis . . . Gods, it's a miracle neither you nor Garland have died!'

Fern goes limp and I use the moment to dive forward. I slide on my knees right up to the edge of the circle and plant my palms on the surface of the translucent barrier, the texture smooth like a thick pane of glass, firm and cold. Morgana stamps a heel petulantly before Will can drag himself my way.

'What?' Morgana asks, distress hammering at her confidence. 'Why are you all looking at me like that?'

'Morgana,' Ruth says, 'tell us why.'

The sorcerer seethes through gritted teeth.

'As if you'd understand,' she scoffs, and folds her arms against the force of the flower's magic. 'You and Marc, cute little school sweethearts. It was disgusting. And then you, Lilibeth, show up all mopey at my door, moaning about how lonely you are. You had no idea. I didn't know my parents. I grew up alone and the only people I knew – you, my friends – abandoned me after the smallest slights. You hated me for not solving all your problems with a wave of magic.'

I've had a lifetime of restraining myself, years to practise sheltering words. Morgana doesn't. Her words and insecurities are unhindered and tumbling in free fall.

'The love spell wasn't meant for you – it was intended for *me* – but I'm glad you tested it out first,' Morgana continues, glaring at my mum. 'What a disaster. I didn't know it would end that way or pass on to your daughter. At the time, I thought I was better than the rules of magic, but it showed me that the Library was right; there are no spells to make someone fall in love. Not forever, at least.'

Ruth takes Mum's elbow and keeps her upright.

Morgana laughs, spiteful. Hollow. 'Gods, did I celebrate when my curse put a wedge in your friendship. Finally, I thought. Finally you will know what it's like to be alone. The only person I had left was Fern. She was the only person who understood me, who *saw* me. I knew I couldn't lose that so, yes, *fine*, I cursed her baby son. I made it so he couldn't use magic. I made her paranoid. I filled her head so I'd be the only person she'd need. She'd come to me for help, me for advice, for magic, anything. She'd be reliant on *me*. You don't understand. She's all I have. I *needed* her to need me.'

The queen's knees strike the floor. I glance back. Fern stares at Morgana, her mouth open under misty eyes and messy hair.

'My . . . my son . . .' she mumbles. 'You . . .'

Morgana strides closer to the barricade of green.

'I regretted it instantly, Fernie. I've spent my life trying to undo it. I made sure that any evidence of my dark magic was hidden from the Library so I could stay, so I could use their resources, their knowledge, to find a way to undo it.' Her hands twist together as she pleads with all her might. 'I travelled all eight kingdoms of Calla – the outlying forges of Hemlor, the deserts of Ject, all the way to the Island off the coast of Berian to find a way to break his curse. And look! Look, didn't I do it? Didn't I find a way? Using an oak tree was worth a shot – one that luckily everyone seemed to blame on Ruth's kid when it went wrong – but now, this, *this* will do it. It will fix everything and then you won't have to worry anymore.'

'I-I . . .' Fern stammers. She's moments from crumbling.

'With Garland gone and Merit happily betrothed in Dreah, then Bastion can take over your duties here,' Morgana implores. 'We can be together. Finally. Just you and me, Fernie. How it's supposed to be!'

Fern looks past Morgana. She looks at her husband, at her two sons, her eyes a well of tears. Even now, his strength petal-thin, the king chooses to protect his children foremost. He's holding Merit's shoulders again, eyes watchful for anyone moving closer to Bastion.

The queen wavers.

Morgana snaps her head to the king, then back.

'*Him?* Come on, Fernie. I know you better than anyone. He's too dull for you. Too placid! I possessed Willoh for you. To help *you.* To make you see that you're better without your husband! Without him, we could—' Morgana chokes. She slams a fist on the green barrier. 'We wouldn't need anyone else. There wouldn't be anyone left to betray us.'

'What have I done?' Fern trembles. She stares at her shaking hands.

'Fern, *please. Please.* Don't hate me too.'

'My husband . . . my sons . . . I almost lost them. I can't – I've done some awful things. My – my people. All those people I let suffer . . . I'm never going to—'

'Fern. No, please!'

'My son will never forgive me for this.'

Morgana clutches her forehead, blonde wisps between her fingers. The sickness of the nightshade must be kicking in.

'Fern . . . please . . . I . . .' Her voice quavers. The sorcerer lifts her eyes to the queen. 'I love you.'

Will inhales sharply. The emerald separating us blazes like fire. The hall lights up and a piercing clang bounces off the stone walls. The energy convulses, ripples, then shoots back towards Morgana, firing a bolt of green into her chest. Her lavender eyes widen and she collapses, unconscious against the edge of the circle. The magic . . . Morgana activated it with a declaration of true love, but her love's target – Queen Fern – isn't cursed. There was nothing to break, nowhere for the spell to go, so it rebounded back on Morgana.

A hush takes over the room. The force field flickers like the flame of a candle, moments from going out. Lacking the spellcaster, the runes and lines etched in the carpet hover with potential energy, ebbing like an escaping draught.

Fern bursts into tears behind me.

I scramble for Will.

He darts his eyes towards me and sends a halting gust of wind my way. Before I can breach the edge of the circle, he slams his hand into the centre and focuses. Green magic floods up his arm, and the wall sharpens back into place just as I collide with it.

'What are you doing?' I yell.

Will clamps his teeth shut as the spell soaks into his skin and becomes his. With less experience than Morgana, he's having to fight to control it.

'Ah . . .' he grunts, straining. 'Don't want to let it go to waste.'

'Will—'

He shakes his head, his brown waves tickling his earrings. 'We've got a curse-breaking spell here, Princess. It's your only chance.'

It's . . .?

The realisation drowns me. It wraps vines around my ankles and submerges me into the depths, into a silent yawning abyss. I fall back onto my heels and stare. Like blurred figures in a painting, the world rushes around me. There are shouts. Echoes. A waft of pine.

Will keeps his eyes on me.

'I wondered how I could possibly beat your epic quest to the dungeons,' he says, just loud enough. Not for the audience, not for the show. For me. 'Here we are. I'd die a thousand times over if it meant you were free. I'd sacrifice anything, crawl down a thousand flights of stairs with a bleeding gut and it would never be enough.'

A strangled sob chokes loose from my mouth.

I can't say that I don't want my curse gone.

Because I do.

Will smiles.

'Fliss.' He says my name like it's the only word, like it eclipses the sun. 'I was lost to you from the first day. Gods, your reaction to the Feiyan was so disarming . . . I was yours then, and I am yours now, Princess.'

My heart floods, unable to find purchase. A turmoil that grips and aches. The more he says, the closer he tiptoes towards death.

'Will—'

'It's okay.' He grins, and even with the blood raining down his cheek and agony in his eyes, he's still the most beautiful sight. 'Just promise me that you'll think of me occasionally. When you lie. Think of me. And, to ask one thing in return, take care of my mum. And Gill. I'm pretty sure he likes you more than me. I'm sure Mustard won't even notice.' He chuckles. 'Don't let anyone use you ever again. Wear those flowers in your hair and be bold. Be brave. Be yourself, free of this curse. Felicity Farrow . . . You don't owe anyone the truth.'

No. No no no no no no no—

'STOP!' I screech.

Will halts, disarmed.

Tendrils of green snake up his forearm.

'*Not like this,*' I cry, and flatten my palms against the barrier. 'Not without you. *Please.* Don't do this. I don't want— *I don't—*'

I can't continue.

At the edge of my blurred vision, Bash runs to the edge of the circle and hammers a fist on it. 'Will, what are you doing?'

'I think he's going sacrifice himself to break Fliss's curse,' Card whispers at his shoulder.

The prince comes apart. He attacks the barrier like each punch is the blow of a sword.

'What? No! You are not allowed. I *order* you to stop.'

Will sighs. He closes his eyes.

'Well, I was going to do a grand romantic gesture. However, Fliss has requested otherwise so that won't be happening,' he says. He struggles to keep his hand planted against the floor as the spell bucks like a startled horse. 'If you could both get lost while I figure out how to deactivate this spell without losing my head, that would be great.'

'Wait!' Card jumps in with a flicker of excitement. 'The runes around this circle are written in ancient Berian.'

'Nice to know,' Will drawls.

'Ancient Berian runes have a few different interpretations. The ones drawn here explain that a declaration of love and an expenditure of life can break a curse,' Card states. He takes a few steps round the edge and inspects the runes. His eyes narrow with that familiar fixation. 'But there doesn't have to be just *one* declaration. The sacrifice can be split. This word means like . . . "sharing a burden". Like carrying a proportional weight. Taking a village to raise a child, for example.'

Bastion clings to Card's every word. 'What are you saying?'

Card swallows. He rereads the runes once more. 'No one needs to die. I think the vitality of life that the spell requires can be shared among many to lessen the impact. Instead of it striking one person and killing them, it can be a softer divided blow, like . . . the difference between a focused explosion on one target and a candle burn on many. We can still use the spell.'

'Well, I don't care anymore about not being able to use magic. I made my peace with it when I met you,' Bash says. 'But . . .'

'We could break Fliss's curse. Together.'

Together? As in . . . Card wants to help too? After all I've done and said to him?

'How long can you keep that spell in suspension?' Bash asks.

Will blows out his cheeks and grips his wrist to keep his hand flat against the floor. The coils of magic around his arm are curling, searching, needy for a target. One spits sparks and his jaw clenches in concentration.

'Uh,' Will replies, 'a bit.'

Bash claps his hands together, calmer now that he can rely on his pragmatism.

'How convenient that our friends and family are all here,' he says, and raises his voice to explain the situation to the wedding guests.

I don't want to look away from Will. I don't want there to be a chance that he'll disappear. If I turn, if I blink, his heart might stop beating. The spread of murmurs and shuffles behind me are meaningless compared to Will staying alive and taking another breath.

A hand brushes my back, and the scent of carnations floats towards me.

'Fliss . . . darling,' Mum says. 'I'm so sorry. I'm sorry that you've lived so long with such an awful curse. I'm sorry for putting pressure on you and keeping things secret. I only wanted you to be happy, to live without fear. I gladly offer my love. I love you, my darling girl, my baby. You are the best thing to ever happen to me.'

'You're my best friend,' Card says nearby. 'I'm sorry. I know how much you've struggled and I could have done more to support you. After all these years, I think I forgot. I became complacent. You are more than your curse, Fliss. You always have been. I remember those early days, testing different sentences together and celebrating the loopholes. You deserve better. More. I love you so much and I'm sorry. There aren't enough languages in the world I could learn to tell you how much your friendship means to me and how stupid I was to jeopardise it. I love you, Fliss.'

A hot tear drips down my cheek.

Will grapples with the spell.

'Keep going,' he presses.

'Fliss,' Bastion says, 'I've always been blown away by your kindness and passion and, honestly, Card spends so much time talking about you, you quickly became family. It doesn't feel right unless you're here with us. Um . . . both of you. I love you.'

Ruth's voice comes from my right, from where Fern has been sobbing uncontrollably.

'I love you as well,' she says. 'I'm thrilled to have finally met you. I tried once before to heal your curse and will gladly try again. Thank you for making my son the happiest I've ever seen him. Thank you for being such a needed breath of fresh air. You are welcome home any time.'

Will's face crumples. He presses his mouth tight.

I lean my forehead on the barrier and let the tears flow freely. Too many. Too much. I never knew . . . I never considered . . .

From the bottom of the stairs, Pigeon pipes up.

'Fliss, I'm sorry I put you in a difficult position when I told you who I am. Thank you for keeping my secret. Thank you for giving me a chance. Thank you for seeing me, who I am, what I fight for, and accepting me. I love you.'

'Felicity, you're a wonderful friend,' Ava says. 'You are kind and supportive and always strive to see the good in everyone. I am grateful for all your generosity over the years. I love you.'

A beat. A scuffle like a nudge.

'Yeah, fine,' Nettle grumbles. 'I like you too, I guess. You're fine. You're nice. Whatever.'

'Fliss—' Lark starts.

The magic fluctuates. Will leans his whole weight behind his hand.

'*Not you*,' Will snaps. 'You don't get a turn.'

'I would also like to speak up,' an older voice says. It's Creon from the apothecary. 'Felicity is a delight. She always brightens my day. I never told her that chrysanthemums were my late wife's favourite, but she knew. She remembered. She notices details like that in people. And even recently, she was the reason for an old friend of mine making contact. Reed had nothing but compliments for Felicity. This kingdom needs more people like her. I adore her.'

'I agree with that. She created a bouquet that made a world of difference to my son. He *finally* stopped playing sad songs on his lute and confessed to Drew next door because of her services. They're so happy together, and *I'm* happy that my house is quiet again.'

'Back when I was captain, I took note of her mature and good-natured countenance. She's grown up to be an incredibly thoughtful and hardworking individual. Howell once said to me that if she weren't so clumsy, she'd make an excellent guard. He would be proud of you, Felicity. He would want your curse to be broken.'

'If I may add, she treats my daughter Marceline with so much care. Marcie finds it hard to fit in at school but seeing Felicity is the highlight of her week. I'm so relieved that my daughter has a great role model.'

'She . . .' The recognition of the voice forces a gasp out of me. 'Felicity was responsible for my son's mourning flowers. She went above and beyond, decorating the entire lower square in honour of Simon. I . . . I miss my son every day but thanks to her, I saw how loved he was. How much he meant to people. Your flowers made me feel understood. As I sat on that fountain day after day, lost in my grief, your flowers were there. I wasn't alone and I can never repay you for that.'

Mum's hand strokes soothing waves on my back as I cry and cry against the green barrier. My throat is a raw knot. People I'm not even close to, people I've barely spoken to . . . they're choosing to risk themselves for me. I made a *difference*. My flowers made a difference. I've helped people and made them feel understood, accepted, worthy of love, worthy of time and kindness.

I never realised it was mutual. I never realised that *I* was worthy of such things. That anyone would step in and save me, reach down and pull me out of the water. That I'm not alone.

Will chuckles, his own cheeks stained with tears. 'Well, they stole my thunder, didn't they? Do I even have anything to add?'

I wipe my face on my sleeve, overwhelmed by kindness and an outpouring of love that I never believed I deserved.

'Of course I do,' he says. 'You're my world, Fliss. You marched into my literal wards, at my most bored, my most useless, and changed my life. I want to tell you every day how you fascinate me. I want to listen to you talk about all the things you're passionate about and watch you fall asleep in my arms. I want to get you that bigger greenhouse, teach you more spells, and come up with more nicknames for Jemmy.'

I sniff a small laugh.

'I was willing to die for you, but instead, I'll live for you. I'll live every day thinking of ways to make you smile and pull that cute frowny face. It's an easy truth to tell, my love. I'm yours. I've wanted to tell you so many times. I love you. I'm so in love with you, Fliss, I can't believe I've been lucky enough to be with you. If this doesn't work and I end up taking the brunt of the spell, live. Be happy and live free. Fliss . . . I love you.'

Without allowing me a chance to reply, Will takes his hand off the floor.

A blast of green bursts from the runes. As sudden as chopping the head of a flower from its stem, there's an almighty snap in my throat.

A dire crack of pain worse than a thousand swords.

And the curse binding me splinters.

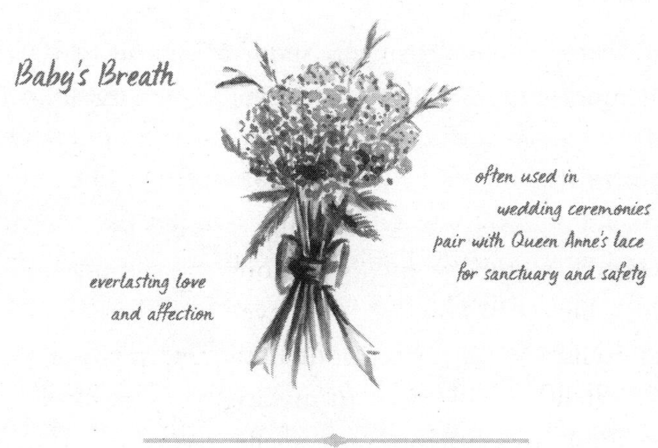

CHAPTER THIRTY

Once upon a time, there was a girl who loved flowers. She spent her days waltzing through fields under the light of the sun. '*You make the most beautiful bouquets*,' said the butterflies. '*Thank you for your generosity*,' said the bees. '*I want nothing else but this*,' lied the girl.

Once upon a time, there was a girl who was cursed. She spent her days trapped in a cage, suffocated by the shadows. '*No one trusts you*,' said the darkness. '*Tell us the truth*,' said the captors. '*It would be my pleasure*,' lied the girl.

Once upon a time, there was a girl who was loved. In the coldest of nights, a constellation of hands reached forth. '*Come*,' they said. '*We love you like the birds love the sky, like the rivers love the sea. We do not need the sum of you, we do not need your candour. We need only your honest smile*.'

The girl stood and followed the voices that willed her towards freedom. She left her chains behind and welcomed the dawn.

Mum has always smelled of carnations. A lifetime ago, when we first found out I could only tell the truth, I remember tracing their crinkled pastel petals as she explained how they represent a mother's love. I remember her scrawled notes and musty yellowed textbooks filled with inked floral illustrations. I remember how she'd tucked a dainty yellow cinquefoil behind my ear.

'And now the world knows you're my beloved daughter,' she'd said. 'Flowers are more than beauty, my dear. They are messages, stories, dreams, and memories. They can always provide people with hope, and one day, you'll see just how much they can change lives.'

'Can they change mine?' I had asked.

Mum had smiled, sadly, as she so often did.

'Maybe,' she had lied. 'But I will still love you, cursed or not.'

Now as I fight consciousness in the safety of her carnation perfume, I wonder if perhaps she hadn't been lying after all.

I can't open my eyes. My body is drained of energy and it's a feeling I'm sadly all too familiar with. When I was bleeding out, my muscles were a weak withered plant without sunlight or chance of survival. But this is different. I'm exhausted, worn to the brink, but there's no allure of death. I'm the morning after a broken fever – sweat-dappled and short of breath. I'm the first day of spring, when the buds break through the earth, optimistic that the weather will be warm enough to bloom, anticipating those light spring showers. I'm alive and my mother's arms are around me.

'Fliss, baby,' she says, her voice thick. 'Can you hear me? Please, wake up. Please. Ruth, help me. Please.'

A light touch on my forehead revives me further, soothes like a soft bed in a safe cottage. 'Give her time, Betty.'

The hand moves to my throat and magic dives under my skin. Ruth is silent. Mum gasps and starts to shake.

'R-Really? Are you sure?'

'Yes . . . It's gone.'

Mum's tears splatter on my shoulder as floating noises around us sharpen.

'Card, are you okay?'

'I'm good, babe. Help me up.'

'Borage, come here.'

'Yes, Your Majesty.'

'Take Morgana to the dungeons. I want the utmost security at all times. Inform me immediately when she regains consciousness.'

'Yes, sir.'

'Captain, send one of your guards for the physician. Tell him to bring something for my wife.'

'Of course, sir.'

'Will?' Bastion is panicked. 'Will? Will. Hey. Wake up. Will. *Will.*'

I groan.

I twitch a hand.

'Fliss?' Mum pushes back my hair. 'Come on, baby. I'm here. I've got you.'

I squint open my eyes and find the world a blur, a wash of colours. Mum and Ruth lean over me with identical concern.

'Will? Ruth! He's not waking up!' Bastion calls, and Ruth disappears from view.

Mum sits me up and wipes my cheeks. Her own are puffy and glistening with tears. There's something off about her expression, something lacking. She wobbles a smile. Guilt. That's what's missing. Replaced by insurmountable relief.

It worked.

'Will!' Bastion continues shouting.

My mind feels slow, fuzzy, like it's stuffed with cotton, a cloud stranded in the sky. I can't move. I can't open my mouth. I can't speak. What do I even say? What *can* I say?

'Will! Stop being an idiot and *wake up*. I swear if you die, I'll bring you back and kill you myself. Get up this instant!'

'Bastion, please. Give him some space.'

'Hey! *Will!*'

'Can you pipe down?' Will mumbles. 'I've got a killer headache.'

He's okay. He's alive. He loves me.

I blink until I can see more clearly, still resting against my mother's shoulder. Will is on his back in the centre of the burnt circle, the runes now a charcoal black. Ruth barely has time to finish healing the wounds on his temple and forearm before Bastion scoops him into a hug.

'Uh . . .' Will wavers, resting back on his elbows. Bastion refuses to let go. 'All right, all right. Get off me, you royal prick.'

'I'm sorry, I'm so sorry,' Bash repeats.

'One more time, please?'

Bash's shoulders tense. He pulls away and glares at Will. 'I'm *sorry*.'

'Ah, I think there are some people at the back there that didn't hear . . .'

'*Fine*. I screwed up! Everyone can know it. I was an awful friend. I should have stuck up for you and I didn't. Every time I saw you, I was reminded that I was at fault, so I lashed out and blamed you and shoved down the guilt and— Why are you smiling? Stop laughing.'

'I've waited a long time for you to grovel. Please keep going.'

The prince sighs and drops back on his heels.

'Are we really doing this now?' Bash asks.

'Do you have somewhere else to be? Or should I almost die another day?'

'Fine. *Fine* . . . I was jealous of you, Will. You had everything. A loving home, incredible magic, freedom to do what you wanted, and I had nothing compared to that. I had a bleak, lonely castle and increasing pressure to be the magic-wielding son my mother wanted. Before Card, you have no idea how isolating this place was – especially when Merit started going away to Dreah. Card lights up every room and keeps me sane and— Wait, no, I need to save all that for my vows. I just . . . I wanted to be like you, Will. I thought if the spell at the oak tree worked, I would be satisfied. When it failed, I was so ashamed, I couldn't face it. I'm sorry.'

There's a stunned silence.

'But!' Bastion scowls. 'You have to admit you didn't make it easy. You've been a complete nightmare. Do you know how many broken windows we've had to fix over the years because of you?' The prince sighs. 'I suppose I'm partly to blame for that too. I'm sorry I've put you through so much. I'm sorry for what I said about your dad. I'm sorry I let the situation get so out of control. You're my brother, Will. You always have been.'

'Oh.' Will's voice is small. I know without being close that he needs time to process that, needs time before he shares his response. 'Uh, while you're at it, I think there's someone else you need to apologise to.'

He pushes to his feet and Bastion steadies him. 'Pigeon!' Will calls.

Pigeon lifts a fallen chair among the wedding guests helping put the room back to rights. 'Hello?'

'You wanted an audience with the royals, right? Here's your chance. It seems the prince is in a particularly sentimental mood.'

Pigeon places the chair down and, for the first time since I've known her, shows a flash of nerves.

'Right,' she says, then adjusts her belt of pouches and fiddles with the bow slung over her shoulder. 'Yes. Um.'

Will pats Bastion's shoulder. 'I'll let you two take it from here. I have a florist I'd much rather be with,' he says.

Seconds later, Will drops to his knees beside me, waves of hair over his forehead, now healed and clean of blood. His eyes twinkle like the glint of his earrings. 'Hey, Princess. How are you doing?'

I hurl myself at him.

How dare you almost die? I pound a fist against his chest. *How dare you almost leave me?* And again. *Don't you ever scare me like that. Don't you dare. Don't you ever—*

I punch and hit and cry until my croaks turn feeble and he draws me into his arms, wrapping me in a calming chamomile refuge.

'I'm sorry,' Will whispers into my hair. 'I'm sorry, my love. I promise to never do that again. Unless you have any other curses that need breaking. Then I might have to.'

I clutch his jacket and butt my forehead against his collarbone. *Shut up.*

'Okay, okay. I promise,' he chuckles. 'Come here.'

He ropes a hand in my hair and with the other, rubs circles on my back. I fasten myself to him, anchor myself to the beat of his heart and the warmth of his touch. No more barriers or dungeons or magic separates us. I'm never letting him go. I'm never granting death a chance that close again.

Purposeful conversations sail on the sound of furniture being rearranged. Pigeon's determination as she solicits Bash. Family. Food. Simon. King Garland's serious tone. Card chiming in with ideas. The Library. Apologies far overdue and plans for the future. It doesn't mean a thing while I'm enveloped in Will. Each minute that ticks by in his embrace was earned, deserved. Each second is a new lease of life. A freedom everyone else has had that I've never experienced. The freedom to choose.

'Okay, anyone else?' Bastion announces, with a finality expected of a royal. 'Anything else so important that this wedding needs to be further put on hold? Because if not, then I am marrying this man, gods help me.'

Will adjusts to brush my jawline. He gazes into my eyes and smiles. My smile. 'Someone wants to talk to you, sweetheart,' he says.

Buttercups linger in the air and Card crouches down, his white suit ruffled.

'Fliss,' Card says, and averts his eyes. 'Um, I'd like you by my side . . . if you still want to be my maid of honour. If not, I understand. I get it. But, um . . .'

I grip the front of Will's shirt. I don't want to let him out of my sight.

'It's your choice, love,' Will says.

'I know there's more to talk about and apologise for. I know I've made too many demands of you already, but I want my best friend, Fliss. I want you with me.'

Cardamine offers his hand. *I want. I need.* How many times have I heard him say that to me? This is different. This time all he's asking for is me. Myself, as I am. I place my hand in my best friend's, and he helps me up, my legs thin, unsteady stems.

The wedding guests are seated once more, having organised the mess and ensured no one was badly injured. Finishing a handshake with Bash, Pigeon slinks down the stairs to the front row where Mum and Ruth sit beside a paralysed Fern. The king takes an empty tonic bottle from the queen's hand and thanks the court physician. Nearby, Godfrey has his broken leg propped up next to Nettle and Ava. Then there's the baker, the apothecary, parents, friends, neighbours. A room full of people who love me, who endured a painful blast of magic to liberate me from Morgana's chains.

Onstage, Merit sorts out Bastion's hair and brushes his suit. Card motions me towards the centre of the stage, to take my place opposite Merit on either side of the grooms.

'I'll be just over there,' Will says, the light brush of his fingers leaving my back. He gets halfway down the steps when he pauses. He clicks his tongue. 'Actually—'

Will spins and strides towards me with a single-minded smirk. My heart has time for one pounding beat before he grabs my jaw and kisses me. A whimper of delight ripples from my throat. I throw my arms around his neck, and he dips me back, locking our lips together – I'm certain that I hear a whoop from Pigeon. His hand trails down between my shoulder blades, to my waist, over my hip, and beyond the taste of him, over the fluttering in my chest, the fabric of my skirt changes, my blouse shifts to chiffon, and when Will breaks away, a cocky smile on his face, he eyes my transformed dress, and says, 'That's more like it.'

He plants me on my feet and twists his hand to conjure a bouquet of white wedding flowers. I'm dazed, trembling in the brand-new dress. It's a gorgeous pastel pink, with half sleeves that puff like a drooping petal and a sweetheart neckline above a corset with white boning and intricately laced satin ribbons. Pale chiffon flowers dot the bodice and decorate the dress, both on top and under a layered tulle skirt that floats in waterfall layers like the head of a bell flower. It's *beautiful*.

'Princess,' Will says, and holds out the bouquet.

The hall could disappear, could erupt with chaos once more, and I wouldn't notice. I take the flowers.

In the quietest voice, husky with nerves, I say my first uncursed words: 'Thank you. My *prince*.'

He grins, radiant.

'Even on my wedding day!' Bash snaps. 'Does he always have to one-up me?'

Card laughs and kisses Bash's knuckles.

'Shut up and marry me.'

The ceremony ends with no more interruptions and it's a sigh of ease when the guests can finally filter out towards the banquet hall just on the other side of the main entrance. Bash rests his forehead against Card's and intertwines their freshly ringed fingers around the bouquet I'd been holding. It's a solace, a sanctuary after a turmoil that ended lives and injured more. My own sanctuary waits by the front row. He hasn't taken his eyes off me once and it stains a blush across my cheeks as pink as the dress I'm in.

'Please help yourself to food and drink in the banquet hall,' Bastion says to the flow of guests. 'We'll be with you shortly. Celebrate and rest easy, friends.'

I hurry off the stage towards Will and hug my arms around his waist, under his jacket, so I'm shrouded in his warmth. He slings an arm over my shoulder, not a moment before Pigeon launches herself at the both of us. She squeezes us in a tight hug, then steps back, Lark hovering at her shoulder.

'Am I glad to see you two!' Pigeon beams.

'You survived!' I say. 'We tried looking but— What happened?'

'Of course I did. They threw me in a cell overnight, though. I really should talk to someone higher up about the human rights in this damn citadel. The food was worse than the scraps I steal,' she says, then gives Lark a teasing grin. 'Blondie here clearly missed me and broke me out just now. You should have seen his face when we bumped into his captain on our way here.'

Lark tuts and turns away.

'You broke her out?'

'She . . . saved my life,' he says, the muscle in his jaw standing out. 'It was only fair.'

'Oh, yeah, he was almost gone for good,' Pigeon chimes in. She digs her elbow into his arm and if I'm not wrong, the faintest of blushes appears on Lark's face. *Oh.* I see.

'I would have been fine,' he shoots back, still not looking at her.

She snorts. 'Hilarious. Anyway, we had to walk back to the citadel through the fields, so I used that long road wisely – meaning I told him all about the conditions in our villages. Apparently I can paint quite the picture.'

Beside me, Will barely restrains his laugh.

'She had some . . . good points,' Lark says, and rubs the back of his neck. 'I'm trying to do the right thing.'

There's a hint of Howell in his tone. A recognition of the lessons Howell drilled in him.

'Did you talk with Bash about what to do next?' I ask Pigeon.

'Yeah, the prince said he'd arrange a room for me here while we discuss things further. Apparently, he'd already drawn up a bunch of plans, but his parents had been keeping him on a leash. I was right about them being uptight, wasn't I? Add *way* overprotective to that list. Anyway, it sounds like they're ceding power to him from now on. Especially while they recover from whatever all that poisoning stuff was about . . .' She shakes her braid, baffled by recent events, but can't keep her attention away from the banquet for much longer. 'We have a lot to make up for, on both sides. The prince made it clear that he won't tolerate any more of my group's, uh, "accidents", and I heard Simon's mother back there . . . All apologies are best done on a full stomach, though. It would be a shame to let that food go cold.'

Will's laugh vibrates in his chest. 'Yes, you'd better get yourself a plate before they throw you back in the dungeon,' he says, and Pigeon sticks her tongue out.

She throws us a wild grin, her hair a mess, her face burned. Her spirit high. She flicks her hand in a wave and drags Lark away by his sleeve, past Mum, who has her hand tucked in Ruth's elbow, following the remaining guests out.

'I almost wish I could listen in on those meetings,' Will muses. 'Pigeon is going to tear this place apart.'

'Well,' Bash says, coming down the steps holding Card's hand, 'as long as it doesn't include explosives, I'm willing to hear her out so that no one else gets hurt. Or killed.'

They stop before us – our mirrors, our friends. We face each other, alone in the vast hall, with time enough to talk and space enough to see clearly. Will's arm around me tightens ever so slightly.

'I'm sure she'd agree it's about time,' Will says, and Bash fights his highly strung instincts. He forces his shoulders down.

'As do I. I was unaware how bad their conditions were, but my ignorance is my own fault. All I did was complain when my mother told me no. Instead, I should have found another solution.'

'I've suggested taking samples of the soil to the Library to have it undergo testing,' Card says. 'With their help, we can look for both magical and non-magical ways to encourage life back to the area.'

Bash nods. 'I've also asked Pigeon to take me around the affected villages and arrange meetings with the people. My parents have decided to take a long break from their duties while they heal. My mother says she no longer trusts herself to rule, so I'll be able to use the full extent of the kingdom's power to make amends.'

'Good,' Will says.

The silence that follows feels like a hard-won victory.

'Um,' Card starts, unusually uncomfortable for someone so social. 'We'd like you both to stay. For the party. Please.'

'Does this mean I'm not a wanted criminal anymore?' Will asks.

Bash glares. 'Of course you're not. I'll send out letters to the surrounding areas tomorrow.'

'Tomorrow? How kind of you.'

'What? You want me to do it right now?'

Card clears his throat and Bash takes a deep breath, in balance with each other like a bouquet of lisianthuses, their white petals dipped in violet and adoring admiration. Bash adjusts the cufflinks on his purple suit.

'I'm sorry for not listening to you earlier. I'd hate to blame my . . . *haste* on exposure to the poison in my mother's chambers, but either way, it was a lot to take in,' the prince says. 'To be honest, I'm still confused. How did you two even meet to begin with? And how did you figure out Morgana's plan?'

Will waits for me to answer first, and when I don't, he decides that a shrug is a decent enough response.

Card watches me, searching and sensitive. In a soft voice, he says, 'You don't have to tell us anything.'

We lock eyes and meet on a bridge of consideration, of courtesy and understanding. Of patience while I decide my next words.

'"Mr Wolf,"' I say quietly, quoting our school play, '"What could I possibly have to offer you, when you are strong and fast, and all in our forest know your name?"'

Card's face crumbles and he works hard to smooth out a smile, tears glistening on his eyelashes. '"Everything, my dear Rabbit, for you are all I am not. I have much to learn and this time I will not take what is not given freely."'

We break from our partners and Card crushes me in a hug.

'I'm so sorry,' he says, digging his fingers in my chiffon-cloaked shoulders, 'for everything. I missed you so much.'

Card leans back and there's a fragment of space between us, a lingering slice of the betrayals and anger and mistakes we both made. Something broke here that will take time to mend, but for now, there's a smile on his face, a future that takes him to the Library and a husband who stands by his side. Like a stream that splits in two, we've both changed, both gravitated in different directions, but it's okay. I want him to be happy. I want us both to grow so our friendship can be a healthy, sunlit blossom.

'I have a crown imperial flower in my garden,' I whisper. 'I never had a chance to give it to you.'

'I could come round? Soon? If that's okay with you, that is.'

I nod. Card smiles. He turns back to Bash.

'Come on, *husband*. They'll be waiting for us.'

Bastion's joy is as vibrant as the Lunarie's crackling petals. *Oh! The flowers.* I snap my head to the corner where the Lunarie should be and find it reduced to dust. Crumbled to grey soot. The other three vases share the same disappointing fate. The best flowers I've ever seen. Gone.

Will touches my back.

'They'll bloom again, as all things do,' he says.

'You coming?' Bash calls.

I take a last sad look at the flowers who died for me. The Feiyan, who gave me Will. The Odyssa, who gave me Pigeon. The Lunarie, who gave me a step towards the truth. I whisper a thank you, as I always do, and lead Will by the hand towards our friends.

CHAPTER THIRTY-ONE

The banquet hall is alive with chatter and gentle orchestra music arranged according to Card's precise plans. Similar to the Grand Hall, the spacious square room is decorated with white ribbons and flowers under sparkling crystal chandeliers. Circular tables dot the edges, their elegant tablecloths also meticulously chosen, and they overflow with a mountain of food that will surely please Pigeon.

As soon as Will and I enter, people swarm around us. They pat my elbow, offer anecdotes, ask how I am, and it's only when Will swerves us away from the crowds with the politest excuse he can muster that I find myself able to breathe. In a secluded corner, beside a large vase of perfumed white roses (grown in the castle greenhouses, not my own), Will exhales too.

'Don't think I've ever had so many people want to talk to me,' he says. 'Is it too late to go back to being unpopular?'

I give a short laugh and worm my hand around his waist again. Why is it so perfect if not for me to touch?

'No, you're not allowed. You're mine,' I say, enjoying how it feels to play with my words.

Will raises his eyebrows at me, even more so when I glance at the glisten left on his lips.

'Felicity Farrow . . .' He brings a finger under my chin and tilts my head up. There's a slice in his sleeve outlined in dried blood that I frown at.

'They ruined your favourite jacket.'

'I can take it off if you like,' Will suggests, delectably.

'You know, I would just *hate* that.'

Will's mouth drops open. A beat passes where he simply gapes at me, at my words, before he tugs up that sarcastic smirk and leans closer.

'Hmm. I'm sure we can agree on *some* kind of compromise.'

'Sorry to interrupt,' Lark says with a dash of reluctance. He stands a few steps away and greets us with his fist over his heart in a traditional guard salute.

Storms instantly summon to Will's eyes.

'I thought you both should know,' Lark says. 'Morgana is awake, and it seems she's lost her ability to use magic. The physicians agree it's a side effect of the spell being misused. She won't be able to cause any more harm. That's . . . That's all.'

'Huh. Interesting,' Will says. He angles his head, and I adore watching the fall of a stray wavy lock over his forehead. 'Guess that dark magic book had more secrets than it told.'

'Just like it didn't mention sharing the price of a life,' I add.

Lark's green eyes rest on me. We've said everything we need to say to each other. The bridge of us fell into a fast-flowing river and washed the pain away.

'Then . . . I'll see you around, Fliss.'

I nod, and Lark takes his leave. He refuses a drink from a passing servant and heads towards Pigeon, who has a face full of food at one of the tables. I don't see the weight of arrogance in him anymore. He's a sober stoic shield of a guard, with the ghost of Howell by his side. The thought reminds me of an idea I'd had.

'There's something I want to do,' I say, and tug Will over to where Godfrey is sitting with Nettle and Ava, a wine-flushed glow on their faces.

'Back to knock us out again?' Nettle asks, an arm slung over the back of Ava's chair.

'If that's what you're into,' Will says.

Ava downs her drink and shakes her head. 'I think I've aged ten years tonight. I'll be retiring from captaincy if you two decide to get up to any more mischief.'

'We've got no current plans.'

'Good. Because Prince Bastion tells me he's ordered a full pardon for you. I'd better not see you scrapping in the streets from now on.'

'Depends how annoying he is.'

Nettle's hackles rise.

'Gods, do you ever shut up?' she snaps, then throws a hand at me. 'First Lark, now this idiot. You have absolutely terrible taste, Felicity.'

'Yeah, he's the worst,' I casually let slip, and shine a smile at Will. There's a sparkle of a moment between us again where he notices what I'm doing, what I'm *saying*, and before his flush can redden too deeply, he clears his throat and turns to Godfrey.

'How's your leg, old man?'

'Old man?' Godfrey chuckles, laugh lines deep. 'I'm doing just fine, boy, don't you worry.'

'I'm sorry.'

'Don't be, Willoh. I heard the truth of it.'

'Still . . .'

'If possible,' I say, 'I'd like to be in charge of Howell's memorial flowers. It would mean a lot to take on that responsibility. I owe him my life.'

Godfrey and Ava smile, two captains of two ages, two people Howell entrusted Alrick to.

'That's a lovely idea, Felicity,' Godfrey says, and creativity stirs in the back of my mind. Flowers as grand as the man himself, colours and scents and expertly arranged bunches to represent Howell's lifetime of service. Just like with Simon, the lower square will be a flurry of petals once more. I'll see to it. We say our goodbyes and wander next to Mum and Ruth, who are sharing a plate of cake in the corner of the hall.

'Have you tried this yet?' Mum asks, tipping her head in greeting. 'It's delicious.'

'Blueberry,' Ruth adds.

'How did you know where to find us?' I ask.

'From the note Will sent this morning,' Ruth says, and readies another mouthful. 'We knew Morgana would be here, so we came as fast as we could.'

'Not by horseback,' Mum says pointedly, letting me know she hasn't forgotten our quick escape.

'We ran into a very kind guard by the castle stables on the way in. They assured us Jeremy is being safely looked after.'

'You can take him home,' Will says. 'I don't mind walking.'

Ruth holds her spoon out contemplatively. 'Hmm, I think I'll stay at Lilibeth's tonight. I've done too much rushing about today. Gill will be wanting some dinner, though . . .'

Will lightly brushes my lower back, and it sets my chest alight. I don't miss Ruth's implication that she's leaving the cottage empty for us. I could finally have Will to myself, away from all this attention.

Mum sighs into her spoonful of cake. 'We should probably talk to Fern at some point too. Garland sent her to bed with a sleeping draught, but she looked a wreck. Maybe in the morning she'll be up for visitors, but it could be months, years, before she fully recovers from the poison.'

'You're right,' Ruth says. 'Both she and Garland will be needing a lot of treatment. We chose isolation before. This time, we choose compassion.'

'Well, I mean, *after* I give her a talking-to about how she's treated my daughter. She's not getting off too lightly.'

'Have fun with that,' I say, and it feels weird to keep tossing out words so carelessly.

Mum waves her hand and turns her focus back on the cake. 'Go enjoy yourself, darling.'

'Keep my workshop tidy,' Ruth deadpans, and Will groans.

'Okay, bye,' he shoots back, and steers me away by my shoulders.

The rhythmic sounds of the orchestra fade, and as they reset their bows and breath, I take in the room. The king and Card are hugging in the centre of the dance floor, apologies on the king's mouth and a laugh on Card's. They appear to have just finished a few awkwardly stumbled dance steps together. The king leans on a cane that's been supplied by the court physician, but there's a joyful, and rare, pink flush on his face. Bastion gazes at them fondly from the high table, unaware that Merit is stealing a sip of his drink. Nearby, Pigeon squishes napkins of extra food in her satchel and grins at Lark's disapproval, Nettle drags Ava up for the next dance, and Mum's laughter floats in time with the first flute notes of a new song. I stamp the scene in my mind. My bouquet of loved ones, crowned in victorious laurels.

'How are you feeling?' Will asks.

'A little tired.'

'Too tired for a dance?'

I eye him curiously.

'A dance with Alrick's most infamous villain?' I tease. 'How could I refuse?'

A tendril of wind wraps around my waist and spins me into his arms.

'What *scathing* words you have, Felicity. A dance will certainly make up for it.'

Will guides us onto the dance floor, keeping us on the outskirts away from the other couples and groups. I lean into his chest and close my eyes, grateful for a moment of peace. The music is as gentle as he is, and we sway in silence, every slight brush of his fingers a shiver, every breath as warm as the notes in the air. It's a slow, stripped-down song that plays – a single flute backed by strings, poetic and ethereal, like the breeze itself is composing the music. The melody builds like ambition, hypnotically layering over each harmony, and in Will's arms, I feel full, like there's no room for my heart to beat. Like my greenhouse that's been struggling for space. I giggle and tilt my head up to look at Will.

'What is it?' he asks softly.

'So . . . when do I get this bigger greenhouse you promised?'

His surprised burst of laughter is enchanting. I don't think either of us care if it draws people's attention or not.

'Well, we do have a lot of space at the cottage,' he says. 'You can grow whatever you want and stay whenever you like. I mean, only because Gill would mope if you didn't. He got rather attached to you, I think.'

'Oh, I see,' I say. 'So it's *purely* for Gill's benefit, then.'

Will rattles with laughter. I doubt I'll ever get bored of hearing that sound. Of being the one to make it happen.

'I suppose there might be something in it for me too,' he says, and nudges our noses together.

I lift up on my toes and kiss him.

He almost died. He almost didn't make it back to me. We almost didn't have this, and I'll never take it for granted. I'm uncursed and free and choose this. I choose him.

From now on, I won't be able to speak and know the truth. I won't be able to calm arguments or solve misunderstandings as conveniently. And that's okay. Because no one else can either. In return, it means no more averted eyes or hushed whispers in my wake. I could actually make new friends. It means no more demands from the queen. No more agonising stress over who to tell what, and when to speak, and how to word it. I'm not cursed anymore. I'm simply, wonderfully, me.

'Will.'

'Mm?'

'Thank you.'

His chuckle tickles my nose. 'I told you. Anything for you, Princess.'

He needs to know I'm being serious.

My precious boy. My sunshine, my love.

'Will,' I say again, and fight the brimming tears. I've cried enough. 'Look at me.'

He does. He holds my waist and we forget the world exists.

I know my next words.

'I love you.'

There's a hitch in his chest.

'Fliss . . .'

'I love you.'

He's speechless like he's never been before. Willoh Vane without a sarcastic comment, swept away and stammering, eyes poring over me like I'm the moon herself, a sky away from the party and infinitely more resplendent. I hover my mouth closer.

'I love you,' I whisper once more.

I plant a quick kiss on his lips, then peck all over his cheeks, his forehead, his pierced ears, until he melts into a laughing, wriggling mess.

'Okay, okay! I surrender!' Will says, and catches my hands.

'You told me to live. This is me doing that!'

He snorts a laugh, and I smile at the sight of him. Those damned waves, his flushed skin, his glinting hazel eyes, admiring me the exact same way.

'I love you too,' he says.

My need for him is a trembling allure, a desperate desire to burn up in his atmosphere. I rally the sarcastic tone I've heard in so many other voices. The one I've never been able to use before now.

'Gods, how *terrible* it would be if someone were to whisk me away from this party . . .'

Will's eyebrow quirks. He leans towards my ear, and in a gravelly whisper that tugs at the bottom of my stomach, he gives me my orders.

'Keep talking.'

'A classic Fliss-and-Will move?'

'As you wish, Princess.'

He catches me the moment I jump into his arms. His hands take hold of my thighs under the layers of tulle, and I press myself against him, draped in layers of flowery fabric. It's not close enough. It's never close enough. With delicate fingers, I caress the pounding pulse of his throat, his breath a heavy quaver. Gods, I want him, unrestrained and relentless.

'This princess is wearing a dress with an *incredibly simple* corset,' I lie. 'I'm sure I'll need absolutely no help getting out of it.'

'Yes, it was becoming quite the distraction.'

'Perhaps I could use some assistance.'

He summons a breeze around us, ready to aid our escape as he has so many times before.

'Oh, darling,' Will breathes. 'You don't have to worry about a thing.'

I want to kiss him, so I do. I want those hands I've thought so much about all over me. So I place them there. I want flowers in my hair and him against my lips. I want the cottage garden and the aroma of wildflowers and the sound of birdsong. I want Gill in my lap and cosy afternoons with tea and cake and clear skies. I want the peace of that life with the people I love.

I want to make the most beautiful bouquets and find the rarest flora. I want my flowers to continue to make a difference. I want my flowers to change lives, as they changed mine.

I want to choose myself. Be myself. Find out who I am without my curse. And I will. I promise. That's the truth.

ACKNOWLEDGEMENTS

From writing this book alone in my apartment to being surrounded by such a dedicated and passionate team has been the most incredible experience of my life, and even though it's been some time now since my path to publication began, I don't think the shock has worn off yet.

To my fantastic agent Rachel Petty, who replied to my query faster than I could ever believe, and who has shown such enthusiasm and belief in my work, thank you for everything you do, it's truly magic to me.

To Kelly Smith, my darling editor at Zaffre, my book couldn't have found a better home than with you. Your support, understanding, and love for this story has meant the world, and I feel incredibly lucky to be on this journey with you at my side. Thank you for your hard work, impeccable feedback, and excitement; for being so amazing whenever I panic and email you a ton of questions; and for always sparing the time to nerd out about our great many shared interests.

A huge thank you to the other wonderful people at Bonnier Books UK and Zaffre involved in making this possible: the lovely Rianna Houghton; my genius marketing manager Tamara Douthwaite, whose talent and passion continues to blow me away; Stella Giatrakou, for such a warm welcome on my first trip to the office (and lunch!); Enisha Samra, Eleanor Stammeijer, Emily Langford, Chelsea Graham, Kelly Samler, Stacey Hamilton, Evie Kettlewell, and Alex May. I appreciate all of your hard work.

Completing our trinity of differing time zones, thank you to Anne Groell, my editor at Dey Rey, for immediately making me feel welcome and assured, for prompting me to consider those small details that really elevated this book to the next level, and for a great song recommendation to add to my *Wildflower* playlist. My work is in such good hands with you.

Thank you to all at Del Rey: the wonderful Madi Margolis, Gertie King, Tori Henson, Erica Brown, Julie Leung, Maya Fenter, Tricia Narwani, Shasta Clinch, Sara Bereta, Maggie Hart, Paul Gilbert, Annette Szlachta, David Moench, Marcelle Iten Busto, Alex Larned, Keith Clayton, and Scott Shannon. Your commitment and dedication mean the world.

Thank you to the incredible Olga Baumert for your gorgeous illustrations. I couldn't have wished for a more beautiful cover, it's beyond perfect! To Patrick Knowles for the amazing map (and for including the two tiny cat faces by the cottage! So cute!). And to the sensitivity readers and your feedback, my appreciation knows no bounds.

It's entirely factual that this book would not exist were it not for Lynsey White, who reignited my love for writing during those second-year university blues, and who became the first person I trusted to read my messiest first drafts. I will say it time and time again that I cannot thank you enough. I'll be forever grateful for all your feedback and encouragement over the years.

To Hazel, thank you for listening, for everything.

To my best friend, Oliver Flewitt, thank you thank you thank you. I don't think I can condense how important your friendship is to me (or the amount of inside jokes we have) into one single paragraph, or fully summarise how integral you have been to the creation of this book. I always have the most fun staying up late talking through story points with you, and my favourite thing is to wake up to notifications that you've added comments to the drafts I sent you. Thank you for being purposefully contrary at every turn and not budging on your undying love for Lark (sigh). #redemptionL-arc. You're the best.

To my biggest hype girl, my longest best friend, my absolute angel, Emma Naughton, thank you so much. It has meant the world to see how unabashedly proud you are of me, and you can instantly restore my self-confidence with a few words. Thank you for being so invested in this journey, your excitement is infectious, and I love you very much.

To Thomas Heslop, I'm so grateful to have you nearby. Thank you for sitting with me for hours in the park trying to come up with the perfect two-line pitch, and for helping me feel comfortable enough to take headshots on that lovely autumnal day. I hope they bring out a *Wildflower* LEGO set just for you.

Thank you to my NUA family, Chelsea, Katie, and Barnaby; to my gorgeous foundation girlies, Grace, Katie, and Mella; to my magical botanical cuties, Sarah and Mattie; to Emi; and to my home-away-from-home family, Sadie, Ryan, Deanna, and Amber. I couldn't have dreamed up better friends. To my co-workers, every day working with you is a delight, and to my wonderful students, who have taught me so much, your hard work continually impresses me and inspires me to do my best. ありがとうございます！ All your kindness, support and encouragement makes me cry actual tears on the regular.

Thank you to the podcasts and streams that have kept me company literally every day for over half a decade now: the McElroy family, the *Among Us* Morning Lobby, and koji. I'd be much lonelier without you. To Taylor Swift, for bringing the Eras Tour to Tokyo, and because I lie on the floor and listen to 'august' on repeat for hours every time I finish writing a book. To my favourite musical, *Hadestown*, and that one relatable lyric Orpheus sings in 'Promises' that goes, 'Now what do I do?' To *Genshin Impact, Kingdom Hearts,* and the many other video games I love and adore that have fed the creative cogs in my brain. And (obviously) to BBC's *Merlin*, a staple inspiration for everything I create.

To my brother, Mike, for being the logical half of my Gemini twin, my sister-in-law, Kana, and my niece, and my nephew. To my late Grandad, who I remember for cosy baking, gardening and puzzles, there is so much of what you taught me in this story.

To Mum and Dad, I cannot write this without crying, because I love you so much and am so lucky to have you as my parents. Thank you eternally for your generosity, your endless support, for supplying me with so many books when I was young, for the adventures to castles and lakes and islands, for giving me the freedom to choose my own path, even when it takes me to the other side of the world. And of course, for the frequent cat photos and video calls. I love you.

To child-me, who scribbled in notebooks late at night and spent so much time away with the fairies. You'll never be able to dream up what's coming.

Most importantly, thank you to the bestest boy in the world, the most handsomest meow meow, my cat, Curtis, who will remain unbothered and unimpressed by this acknowledgement. Kisses.

And to you, dear reader, for choosing this book. I had the most fun time with Fliss and Will, and hope you do too. It would be the greatest honour of my life to create a world where you feel safe and seen, no matter who you are.

With all my heart, thank you.

If you loved *Wildflower*, don't miss Becky Jenkinson's new cosy romantasy

WAYFINDER

Exhausted by the demands of her healing gift and eager for adventure, Peregrine Alcott bargains her way on an expedition to the mythical Island she's been obsessed with since childhood, where hidden relics and long-forgotten history await.

On the journey, Perrin finds friendship in a cartographer similarly keen to uncover the Island's secrets, a team that offer a reprieve from her overwhelmed magical senses and an unexpected reunion with an acquaintance from her past: Sloane Montrose, a calm and composed swordfighter whose presence unsettles Perrin more than the Island itself.

Following her own instincts – and curiosity – Perrin heads into ancient ruins, where she discovers cavernous tunnels, unusual animals and a darkness determined to cast a shadow over their camp. As the legends of the Island stir, Perrin finds what she never thought to seek: love that will last a lifetime.

COMING SOON

Do you want to lose yourself in a magical realm, journey beyond the known universe or fall for a charming rogue, all within the pages of a book?

Join

ZAFFRE DAWN

The home for all science fiction and fantasy readers

Be the first to hear about our new releases and access exclusive, subscriber-only fan content including author Q&As and interviews, competitions, events and so much more . . .

Scan to sign up to our newsletter:

Follow Zaffre Dawn on social media:

@zaffrebooks

@bonnierbooks_uk

@zaffrebooks

WE RISE AT DAWN . . .